- BOOK 1 -

DHARMAYODDHA

KA

AVATAR O

KEVIN MISSAL

FiNGERPRINT!

Published 2024

FiNGERPRINT!
An imprint of Prakash Books India Pvt. Ltd

113/A, Darya Ganj,
New Delhi-110 002
Email: info@prakashbooks.com/sales@prakashbooks.com

Fingerprint Publishing
@FingerprintP
@fingerprintpublishingbooks
www.fingerprintpublishing.com

New Edition published 2018

ISBN: 978 81 9350 330 0

To every writer who has inspired me…

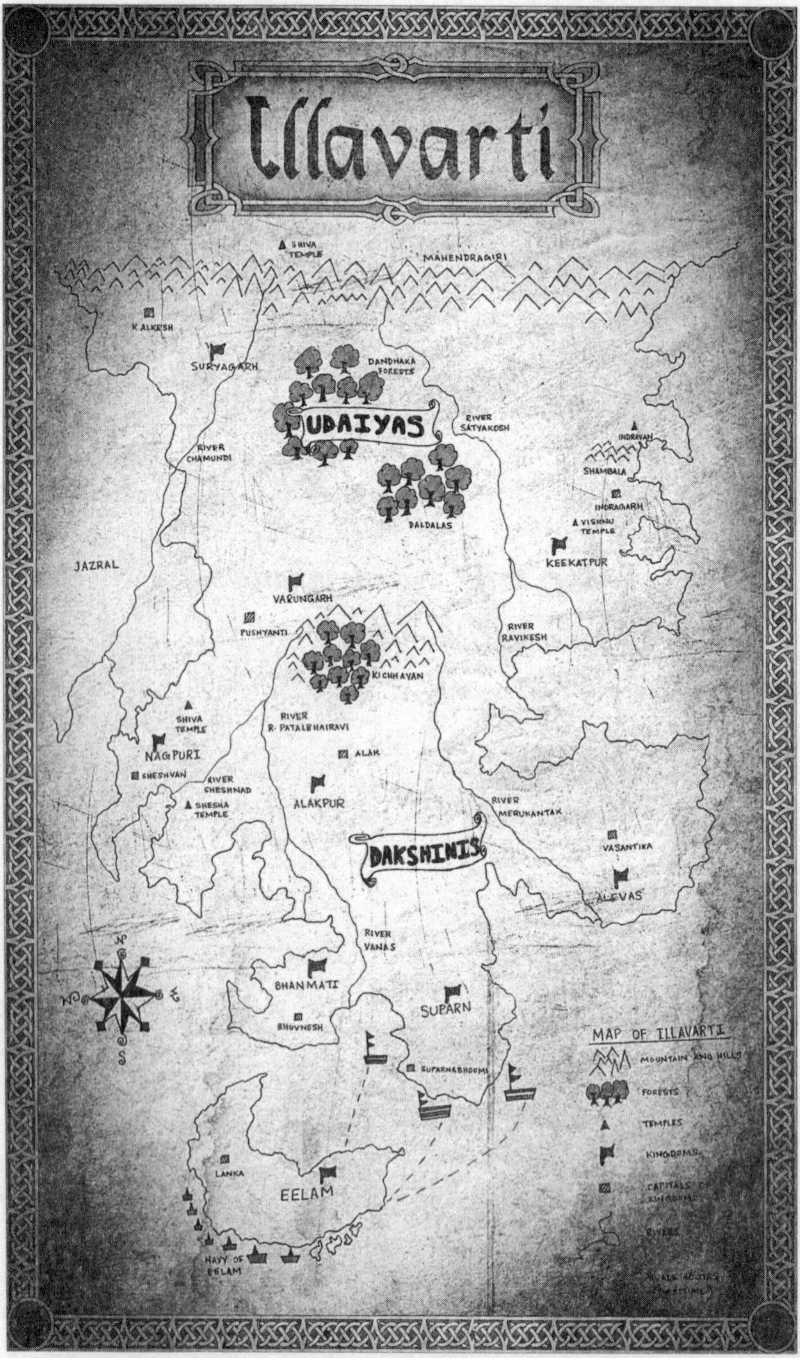
Illavarti
SHIVA TEMPLE
MAHENDRAGIRI
KALKESH
SURYAGARH
DANDHAKA FORESTS
UDAIYAS
RIVER SATYAKOSH
RIVER CHAMUNDI
INDRAVAN
SHAMBALA
INDRAGARH
VISHNU TEMPLE
DALDALAS
KEEKATPUR
JAZRAL
VARUNGARH
PUSHYANTI
RIVER RAVIKESH
KICHHAVAN
SHIVA TEMPLE
RIVER R. PATALBHAIRAVI
NAGPURI
ALAK
SHESHVAN
RIVER CHESHNAD
ALAKPUR
SHESHA TEMPLE
RIVER MERUKANTAK
VASANTIKA
DAKSHINIS
ALEVAS
RIVER VANAS
N
W
E
S
BHANMATI
SUPARN
BHUVNESH
MAP OF ILLAVARTI
MOUNTAIN AND HILLS
FORESTS
TEMPLES
KINGDOMS
CAPITALS OF
RIVERS
SUPARNABHOOMI
LANKA
EELAM
NAVY OF EELAM

NOTE TO THE READER

First and foremost, before you begin reading this book, I would urge you to read this note first. It'll take you less than five minutes and you will understand in what frame of mind this book was written.

This is not a historical or a modern re-adaptation of the Kalki Purana. This is a grounded fantasy book that takes inspiration from the life of Kalki, the idea of Kaliyug and other Mahabharata and Ramayan references. But it is an absolute work of fiction.

This is also a tribute to the stories and movies that I have read and seen like Star Wars, Lord of the Rings and Game of Thrones. They have inspired and made me realize it's not about how epic the book is, but how epic the characters in the story should be.

Thank you. You may turn the page now.

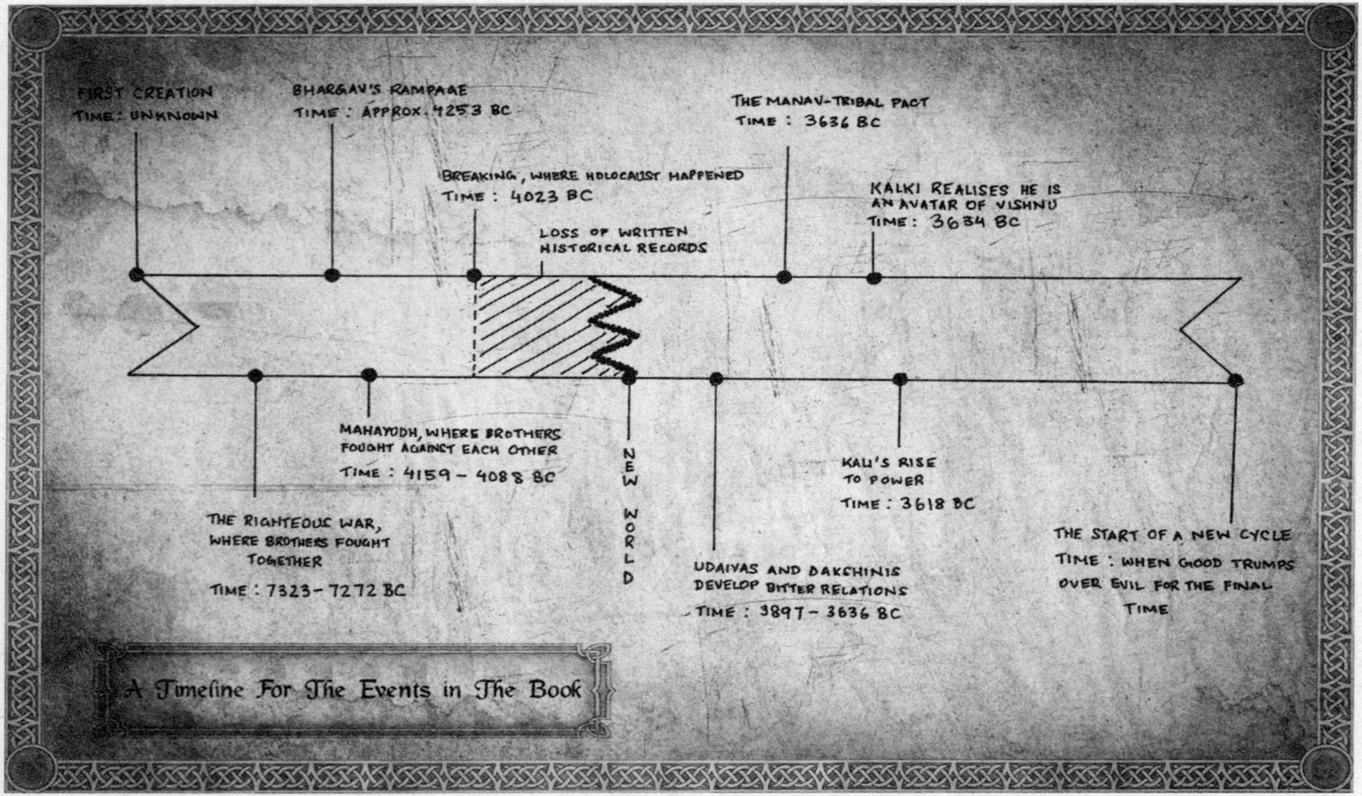

A Timeline For The Events in The Book
FIRST CREATION
TIME : UNKNOWN
BHARGAV'S RAMPAGE
TIME : APPROX. 4253 BC
BREAKING, WHERE HOLOCAUST HAPPENED
TIME : 4023 BC
LOSS OF WRITTEN HISTORICAL RECORDS
THE MANAV-TRIBAL PACT
TIME : 3636 BC
KALKI REALISES HE IS AN AVATAR OF VISHNU
TIME : 3634 BC
THE RIGHTEOUS WAR, WHERE BROTHERS FOUGHT TOGETHER
TIME : 7323 - 7272 BC
MAHAYUDH, WHERE BROTHERS FOUGHT AGAINST EACH OTHER
TIME : 4159 - 4088 BC
NEW WORLD
UDAIYAS AND DAKSHINIS DEVELOP BITTER RELATIONS
TIME : 3897 - 3636 BC
KALI'S RISE TO POWER
TIME : 3618 BC
THE START OF A NEW CYCLE
TIME : WHEN GOOD TRUMPS OVER EVIL FOR THE FINAL TIME

Prologue

Kalki Hari sat facing the impending cold winds of the north, legs crossed together, as he prayed to Lord Vishnu's idol. The wind blew harshly, whipping his wavy hair over his scarred face.

He looked up at the grandeur of the stone statue, the tall twenty feet marvel; it had four arms emanating from the muscular torso. One arm held a conch, while the others held a chakra, a mace and a lotus. The statue had a serene face; one you'd think had a determined look about it.

Kalki was dwarfed in front of it, but he didn't care. He would always be small in front of Lord Vishnu. He chanted, closing his eyes. Cold didn't seep into him; didn't set off tremors deep inside his marrow, like it would to another person. He had the patience and drive for it. He had the power of Lord Vishnu in him.

"Be with me."

And then he opened his eyes.

He stood up on his feet, brushing the snow from his feet, as a parrot casually landed on his bruised shoulder. He patted the bird, lightly scratching its neck. Then he reached out for the Ratna Maru sword, impaled in the frozen glacier. He pulled it out and studied the inscriptions over it. Aside from the obvious mysterious symbols on it, there was something enchanting about it. He sheathed the sword and then went for his horse, mounting it. Patting its head, he firmly grasped the reins and lightly nudged the creature's flanks. The horse was none other than Devadatta, named after a man he once knew.

The forelimbs of the horse rose up, momentarily blocking out the shape of the rising sun.

He was ready.

Fear now, for he was coming.

PART ONE

THE BATTLE OF SHAMBALA

1

In the midst of the raging desert heat, Kali could see the approaching army.

Their formation was large in size and circular, almost moving like a swarm of locusts. They were systematic, as if each step was calculated in terms of advanced military strategies. For now, his spyglass was affording only a very limited degree of vision. He could see the soldiers holding shields and spears at the outer flanks of the formation, wearing heavy helmets and metal pads over their entire bodies.

How will I do this?

Thousands of plans raced in his mind, to defeat his rival's retinue of soldiers, but he lowered his spyglass, handed it over to his general Koko, and made his way to the tent. He passed the dozens of bulls he had brought over from the north to aid in his battle, but he was yet to figure out how.

The mahogany table inside the tent was placed in the centre, with maps and figures crowding the top of it. The lamp overhead burnt brightly, giving him the much needed light. He was kneeling close and studying the map intently when he heard the voice of his general.

"They are here, my lord."

"Damn," Kali cursed under his breath.

"Has Vikoko returned?"

"Not yet," Koko answered placidly.

Kali wasn't astonished that despite sending over Koko's sister out in the dangerous fields to study the enemy's methods and plans, Koko didn't show any signs of hesitance. They were bound by blood oath to Kali and whatever he commanded would be executed by them even if it meant risking their lives.

The tent flaps opened and he saw Vasuki—the blue-eyed tribal prince—with Kuvera, an obese man with a hairy mongoose wrapped around his neck, and Raktapa, with ferocious physical proportions and a bad set of teeth.

"I'm quite surprised you all entered together in my humble abode; given you don't have a civilized history together."

Raktapa began, "Don't piss around with us, Kali. You promised us the government of Indragarh. We don't see that."

Kuvera, meanwhile, walked over to the wine glasses, near the fruit baskets, where he poured himself a drink. "I'm certain our dear ally doesn't want to disappoint us, since his promises have been fulfilled thus far. But I am also certain that if we lose this, there might come a time when I think, 'hmmm… why did my people and I aid you?'"

Kali grinned. "I don't lose."

Vasuki had a blue robe, matching his eyes. "Vedanta's army is reaching our base. And your people haven't even mounted their horses. I've told my men to depart instantly."

"So you have come here to bid me farewell? I'm sure you'll miss a pretty sight if you leave early."

"I'm not joking, man. They are coming. And we will all be dead."

"We have an hour till they reach," Kali assured him.

"An hour is not enough. We don't have enough men for Vedanta."

Kali nodded. "Yes, but…"

And that is when Vikoko entered, her golden hair surrounding her like a halo. She walked in with the heavy armour over her and whispered something in Kali's ears.

"Chakravyuh?"

Vikoko nodded.

Raktapa growled. "Tell us, man! What happened?"

Kali studied the Tribal Heads for a moment. They were all distinguished, hated each other and Kali was the one who had brought them together.

He knelt down and with a quill he drew a diagram over the map. "So according to my general Vikoko, Vedanta's army is in the chakravyuh formation."

"Chakravyuh?" Vasuki narrowed his eyes.

"A sort of concentric circle." Kali continued, "A warfare technique. So the chakravyuh is a method employed to confuse the opponent and then attack them."

"How effective is it?" Kuvera asked.

"We can lose."

"Oh dear lord," Vasuki cried. "How is it possible?"

"A chakravyuh," he began to draw multiple lines inside the big circle that he had drawn earlier, "has several layers. The first layer is the visible one, the people with shields and spears, basically the infantry. Those soldiers are basically sacrificial. No one really gives a damn about them. The second layer is the mounted swordsmen, the cavalry. The third layer consists of the archers and the fourth layer…" he made the last swirl on the page with his inked quill, "is where Vedanta is with his Senapati."

"So to get to him, we need to break three layers of trained, ruthless and bloodthirsty soldiers?" Kuvera's voice quivered at the end.

"Yes, but they are in a circle and they keep moving because if by chance, you try to attack one side of the circle…" he scribbled harshly on the page, "the circle manages to move and others, the less injured ones, will attack you."

"A circle of hell, indeed." Kuvera rolled his eyes.

"How did your general find that out, being a woman and all?" Raktapa asked.

Vikoko growled under her breath. Kali just laughed.

"She has a good eye and you just need to have a good eye for strategy to see the army."

"Is there a way to end this or do we just leave?" Vasuki blurted out.

"Leave and you'll be termed cowards of the war." Kali walked over to him, standing nose to nose.

"Better a coward than a stupid martyr," Vasuki said. The smell of betel leaves assaulted Kali's nostrils.

Kuvera sighed.

"How many men do you need from my side?" Raktapa came forward.

Kali smiled. "Men? Who said I need men?"

2

King Vedanta sat in his chariot, flanked by two soldiers who had long swords. Not that he needed them to protect him; but it was nice being in the protection of your own men.

Vedanta could see how the plans from the ancient scriptures worked. Legendary strategists used this method and now he was using it too. Vedanta promised himself he would return to his kingdom and write long passages about his bravery and fight against injustice.

"That Kali has been ravaging the land of Illavarti with his stupid and casteless outcasts! They think they can destroy the son of Indra," he proclaimed to his soldiers proudly.

"Son of Lord Indra?" One of the soldiers meekly asked. "Are we protecting a God's son, your highness?"

"Yes!" he frowned.

"Where is he?"

"Right in front of you!"

"You are a son of God?" The same soldier blurted out.

"Not literally! As in Lord Indra was spiritually my father, the one I worshipped."

"Oh all right." The soldier was disappointed.

"Shut your trap and worry about the battle," he murmured. "No use in talking to illiterates like you."

The soldier kept his silence.

Vedanta didn't notice anything until his chariot rocked and finally halted. He stuck his head out of the chariot to see what was wrong, cursing the driver.

"What is wrong?"

"The army has stopped, my lord."

"Stopped?" Vedanta jumped from the carriage and his soldiers hurriedly followed him.

He walked to his Senapati since he couldn't see through the layers properly. "What's with the hold up, eh?"

The Senapati leapt down from his horse to the ground and handed Vedanta the spyglass. He swallowed a huge lump as he spoke, before Vedanta could look. "Kali is not playing fair." He then instructed his army to make way and let Vedanta have a look at what was coming for them.

Vedanta moved forward, even as he adjusted the spyglass.

"Fair? Fair? He's a bloody mess, that Mleccha! He's no good. Why would you expect him to play fair? We are more in numbers. His men…" he continued until he paused to see through the spyglass, to look at the deranged sight of horror in front of him. "In the name of Lord Indra, what in seven heavens is that?" His feet were frozen to the dusty grounds.

"Those, your highness, are the bulls."

"I can see that." He looked away from the spyglass and to his general. "But why do th… they have fire on their heads?"

3

Kali, sitting astride his horse, leaned forward gleefully as he saw the huge number of bulls smash against the opponents' shields, almost cracking them. Most ran in fear while others tried to attack, but the bulls just flung them apart. They all staggered and ran for their lives.

It had worked, using oil-drenched cloth wrapped around the bulls' heads. When the cloth was lit on fire, the bulls saw red.

Kali whistled, and Koko and Vikoko appeared on either side of him. Behind them were the men given by Kuvera, all with rotten teeth and greasy hair.

"Take the Yakshas and position them to hit long and high, right in the middle. Since the first layer is broken, we have a limited, but a greater degree of visibility," he said.

They both nodded. They rode further up in the clear horizon with the dirty, swine-like Yakshas moving at the back. They were short in size and extremely fat, but were excellent archers. And that's what Kali needed right now.

Kuvera was watching from the tent with Vasuki and Raktapa. He walked over to Kali, his robe trailing in the sand.

"My men aren't the most proficient when it comes to battles, so you should know that those are Raktapa's men."

"Yes, but they have good eyes. And that's what I need right now. Rakshasas, on the other hand, are good for close combat, but

I promised you I wouldn't lose a lot of men in this war and that's what I plan to do right now."

"And what would that plan be exactly?"

Kali winked at Kuvera.

"Don't worry about that. Just get the horses dressed up, will you?"

"I don't know if that plan would even work."

"Trust me."

His general with the Yakshas was stationed well afar. Right now the bulls had distracted Vedanta's soldiers enough, making even the archers stop caring about what was about to hit them. Koko looked back when all the bows with their arrows were strung towards the sky. Koko gave a nod to Kali.

And Kali nodded back.

Koko yelled at that moment. Arrows flew like razors in the sky, pulsating in the air and then sharply bearing down upon and tearing into Vedanta's army.

4

Vedanta was running from the bulls as he jumped to hide in his chariot. The archers had killed a few of them, but the animals were in such a frenzy that they were difficult to target. Their hard skins were immune to swords as well as jabs from the lances.

And just when he saw the fiery bull attacks were beginning to lessen, there came another surprise. A volley of arrows rained down from the top. He was pulled inside instantaneously by the same illiterate soldier, as the arrows hit many of his men who were in the inner circle. He could see the Senapati's body gutted by the attack.

He shouted orders, but no one listened. The arrows didn't stop, so he closed his eyes, hiding inside the chariot, praying for himself whilst he could hear the decimation of his men as they cried out his name. Bodies were collapsing on the ground, the blood splashing around him. The scent of fire, smoke and brimstone engulfed him. The horrific tableau of violence around him reminded him of the wooden figurines of make-believe games from his childhood, when he would senselessly play God and wreak havoc all around. Today, he felt nauseous of the violence. And then the arrows were gone. Silence reigned where moments ago there were deafening sounds of destruction.

Vedanta moved from the chariot and made his way outside. He could see the bloodshed all around him, bodies piled over each other.

What kind of devil would do such a thing?

The commander from the inner circle appeared. "Your highness, what should we do? We have lost a huge number of men. We can't even move now since…"

"I know, I know. Just hold on for now. And wait for them to make a move."

"Yes, your highness."

As he proceeded to climb back into the chariot, Vedanta noticed that his horse was almost unscathed in the attack. It was clever of his Senapati to have suggested armour for the beast.

5

Kali saw that the army wasn't moving anymore. It had been static for a while. He knew it was the time to seize victory. He congratulated Koko and Vikoko, who stood with the Yakshas at the front.

Kuvera brought the horses, dressed confoundingly as elephants.

"Is this what you needed from my horses? We could have brought the big ones and sorted the trouble rather than dressing them this way."

"The fact that you think that way, mate, is why you are standing here under my command."

Kuvera's mouth was agape in. That was when Raktapa and Vasuki entered the scene, for they were already witnessing all of it from the confines of their tent.

"And what do you plan to do, man? They are weak now. Should I just send my men and finish the whole deal instantly?" Raktapa scoffed.

"Um, no need now really," Kali said. "I'm going to offer them a truce."

Vasuki growled, "Truce? What a joke!"

"I'm not humouring you, Prince Vasuki," Kali's voice hardened. "I'm going to offer them the truce."

Raktapa, Vasuki and Kuvera laughed at this declaration.

"And mind you, boy, how do you plan to move towards that direction and not get killed by Vedanta's soldiers?"

"Oh, he won't kill me." Kali sat on the elephant-trunked horse, with Koko and Vikoko on the side.

"So sure, are we?" Kuvera crooned.

"I'm not sending my men on this suicide mission," Raktapa announced.

"No need to," Kali said. "I am only going with my generals."

"With that ridiculous outfit for your horse and that absurd plan of yours, we should just find a new commander to aid us in the battles against the Manavs," Vasuki said. "Since you are clearly far from suitable for the job."

Kali just smiled. There was no use of explaining this. He manoeuvred the heavy horse and decided to ride towards Vedanta, when Kuvera's voice reached him.

"Since you are leaving for your death, would you mind telling us how you were able to cripple the Chakravyuh so that we can use it for our later battles?"

"You hit the heart." He signalled towards the drum beaters, who were sprawled on the ground, dead. "Their drummers were how the army was moving. Once the beats were dead, the army was confused. The beats made the synchronous structure and I just pulled away the structure when the bulls became their distraction. Now no matter how many people they have in the huddle over there, they are confused, scared and most of all broken. They don't have any heart to follow. And that's where we need to hit now."

And he rode on. But he could hear the sly whispers in the back, coming from Raktapa.

"Not so ridiculous after all," he said.

6

Vedanta could feel the major energy drop amongst his leftover army. They all stood still, with their weapons and shields intact, but they didn't have the same confidence anymore. A few of them were pulling across the injured men, close to the caravans for medical aid, while others were drinking from the water canisters placed on the mules.

He thought he would have won the war with no hassle since the outcasts were weak and scattered; mired in their own factional politics. Thus he had brought a relatively small army than what he had back in his kingdom. His arrogance was his downfall clearly, as here the outcasts were a cohesive unit. Vedanta cursed himself, for he wished that he had listened to the messages his allies had sent from Suryagarh and Varungarh, which had been taken hostage by the scoundrel outcasts. The remaining cities were already controlled by them and the last one was Indragarh, the capital of Illavarti. And here he was, facing the ultimate penalty for his vain belief in his own power.

And then in the midst of his thoughtful musing, he heard the cry of his commander.

"The envoys are coming from the rival camp!"

"Kill them from afar," Vedanta yelled back.

"All right your highness…" and then he paused. "Uh…"

Vedanta stepped forward to see three soldiers moving towards them, but riding atop baby elephants. They stopped ten paces away from them.

"I said kill them!"

"My lord, we can't."

"Why not?" Vedanta growled.

"They are...they are riding on baby elephants, the animal-vehicle of Lord Indra, the lord we worship."

Vedanta reluctantly saw the point. He moved forward, with his commander on the side cribbing about how they should send a bird for backup to Rajgirh, the royal palace of Indragarh. He knew they would take at least five to six hours to reach the battle zone.

Vedanta walked ahead of his defence, stopping and staring at the rival envoys, who were swathed in the light from the weak morning sun. "What do you want?" asked Vedanta, his voice roaring.

The envoy in the middle came off of his baby elephant and walked over. He was a tall man with jet-black hair, a fair cherubic face, a disarming smile and golden eyes. He was a handsome lad, no doubt, but he was devious; the way his eyes pierced Vedanta's soul.

"I am humbled to say my name is Kali."

"So you are the man who is leading the war against the Manavs, destroying my men and allying with the treacherous outcasts!"

"The Tribals, my friend, aren't outcasts. They have equal rights and that's what they and I have been fighting for." His voice grew louder for the soldiers to hear him now. "We don't want any more war since both of us have suffered tremendously. We come with peace."

"And what if we don't want peace? You see, what if I cut off your head and send it back? With no one to lead the outcasts, they'll suffer."

"You may try," he mocked.

Vedanta gritted his teeth as he pulled out his sword and

held it close to Kali's neck when his wrist was held back by his commander.

"No, your highness."

"How dare you stop me?"

"I wouldn't have, your highness, if it wasn't for that." The commander signalled over to the back, where the other two envoys with Kali had their swords held across the baby elephants' necks, ready to cut.

"You threaten me with my own beliefs. I never thought that my faith would hinder me in my progress."

Kali began to walk around Vedanta like a demanding, dark force.

"I just wish to have leverage. We protect your interests and you protect ours. Let's be fair. We have a bigger army than you." He stopped, nose to nose, inches away Vedanta. "We have the Rakshas, the Nagas, and the Yakshas while your men are depleting in numbers, dehydrated, starving, and in urgent need of medical supplies. You wouldn't stand a chance against us for one more night. Your fort is far from here. Travelling back will only cost you more; that is *if* we let you travel."

Vedanta looked at his men. They all looked convinced about what Kali was saying. He had a magnetic, soft voice, which made even Vedanta melt.

"Come with us to our tents. We will feed and give you water. I do not wish to hurt you or kill more of your men if you settle it with us. I want to find a middle ground for the city of Indragarh, where a truce can happen between the Tribals and the Manavs, nothing else. We can do that either by peace or..." he narrowed his eyes meaningfully. "We can take it from you. But I don't wish to do that. I don't want to kill you. I just want to work with you."

"You mean you want to take over like a dictator? To rob me of my city?"

"I promise you one thing. You will be the king. Always. We will just be your help," Kali explained.

"What about the outcasts? Will they agree to this?"

"They already have. We all just want peace. If you remember, you were the one charging at us here, at our safe post. We were just coming to your city for a compromise."

Vedanta mused. He was stubborn, almost mulish, but he agreed his entire army was next to nothing against the outcast forces. His death would unleash centrifugal forces in Illavarti. But to return without honour was also a serious matter; though honour would make sense only in the event of being alive.

"I want to know all the accords, the rules, the guidelines…"

"We can set up a council meeting for that."

"The people will be scared…"

Vedanta noticed Kali didn't have any weapon on him. He had worn flamboyant, multicoloured robes, with a cloak around the back. His boots were shiny but rugged and his skin, though perfectly sculpted, had seen the ravages of war. "Change is scary but good. Always good. It'll take time for them to settle, but they will, believe me."

Vedanta sighed.

"By the Vajra, I hope I don't regret this."

"It's not like a deal with the devil." Kali smiled.

Vedanta nodded. He would have to find a way some other time to get rid of Kali, perhaps ally with someone. But for now, it was Kali's triumph.

7

At the outskirts of Indragarh, the city was well-equipped with a number of villages, which aided the urban elites with agriculture, mining and husbandry. There were long tracts of green fields spread across the general landscape of lush forestry. They had no proper roads like in the city. They didn't have charioteers or horses, but bullock carts, and some of them even travelled on foot. Houses were made of clay. They had their own panchayats and followed the city instructions, but had their own laws passed by the sarpanch.

Out of these villages, one of the most sheltered ones was Shambala—a five hundred people strong tenement, where inhabitants knew each other by the first name. They were famous for cow grazing and the exportation of milk to the city and thus they had flourished the most. Shambala was even gifted with large terrains and caves that no one dared to enter for fear of bad luck. There were sculptures and trees more than twenty feet in height. The biggest one was where Sarpanch Devadatta would sit with his men and pass judgments.

Arjan Hari was the first to know about the ill-fated news—INDRAGARH HAD BEEN TAKEN OVER. This was the talk of the village when Sarpanch Devadatta instructed the villagers to welcome the change open-heartedly.

"They say King Vedanta was defeated by the outcasts..."

"The Tribals are scary people…will they come after us?"

Villagers murmured, and whispers and rumours flew fast.

Devadatta promised that no such thing would happen if the compromise was met. "We knew the day would come where we would have to look up to new leaders. I have got the news first-hand that they do not seek the destruction of Indragarh but want a settlement for everyone to live in peace and harmony." He pulled out a golden-coloured parchment and said, "We have been given the royal decree that even though there are changes in the city administration, the villages wouldn't be affected and the relationship between us will remain absolutely the same as before. And only, if only we rebel, only then we shall be punished. Now let's hope it doesn't come to that, eh people? Same as before, a little stricter, but yeah, same indeed."

Some said: "BAH! WHAT HORSESHIT!"

While others said: "It could be well for the development of Illavarti."

Arjan partially knew the truth though, from what he had heard about the other cities. Unlike the villagers, Arjan had heard rumours about what had happened with Suryagarh—the entire treasury had been looted away, the army was replaced and the king was just a mere puppet. But most of all, the villages were burnt and instead cities had been erected. They cared about development, but in the wrong sense. In the name of harmony, the Tribals spread anything but that.

He left the meeting and rushed to his hut, where he had some bread and vegetable soup with his mother, Sumati Amma.

"Where is your brother?"

"Absolutely no idea."

"Must be loitering around with that girl…"

"Lakshmi?"

"Yes."

"I suppose. You can't blame him for being with her today since she came from the city after many years," Arjan laughed. "Did you hear about King Vedanta?"

"Yes, and I hope it doesn't affect us."

Arjan assured it wouldn't, though he knew he was lying to her.

"I just hope we get to keep our jobs since we have worked so much on it. You can't really believe the Tribals. They are capable of just destruction and death."

"No one will steal from us."

She paused and composed her words. "Not when I have a brave warrior in our house."

"You mean Kalki?"

"Shush. No, you." She smiled.

Arjan chuckled.

"Thank you for the kind words." Arjan came to his feet with his wooden bowl, moving to the sink and pouring some water from the jug to clean it.

Kalki had always been the more jovial and casual son, while Arjan had been the dependable one. It was a surprise how maturity struck Arjan earlier than Kalki, since Arjan was eight years younger than him.

"Are you leaving for work?" Sumati Amma asked.

"Yes." And he placed the washed bowl on the side.

The setting sky bestowed the scenery with glimmering orange rays as Arjan walked to the pastureland, where his father, Vishnuyath, was working. He waved. His father glanced at him, sighing.

"You are late."

His father walked towards him after instructing his men to take the milk back to the warehouse. He stood, lanky, next to the bulky frame of Arjan. He wasn't the most handsome man, Arjan believed. But he was a kind person, with eyes that had warmth in it.

"Earlier than him."

"He hasn't been coming for work for the last two days," Vishnuyath cursed, walking over to Arjan.

The dairy farm had been part of Arjan's family for generations, passed from the forefathers of Vishnuyath to the point that Vishnuyath had learnt everything about breeding, milking and herding before he had hit his teenage years. There was no injustice on the poor animals unlike other places, where cows were beaten and milk was forcibly taken from them. Milch animals were treated with foremost respect; acknowledged for their milk and dairy products, which imbued Shambala with its prosperity.

Arjan was proud of this fact though he found all of this a tad exhausting and boring. It was not fun—cows and milking. Not the most interesting thing for a young lad like him.

He began to work for the day, wondering what his older, careless brother was be doing as of now. And then, across the farthest stretch of the field, he saw silhouettes of horsemen, with their swords and lances high in the air.

They were riding towards the farm.

8

Lakshmi had been washing her parents' clothes close to the river. She had hated returning from Indragarh; since there she had learnt much about mathematics, astronomy and was under her aunt's tutelage for education. But due to recent changes in the city, she was instructed to return here. The Tribals were changing the landscape and her aunt, being in the judicial and library departments of the city, had told Lakshmi to leave, as it was the only wise course of action.

As she had left, she had seen a little bit and it wasn't much of a surprise since nothing really had changed. It would take time, perhaps, but the inclusion of Tribals and the loss by Vedanta hadn't impacted the people. Sure, the scribes made a nuisance, rumours flew thick, but nothing drastic had happened. Not a sign of rebellion occurred, and everyone continued to do their own work. Some even migrated as she could see a lot of caravans and carts leaving. They did it perhaps out of fear that something would happen, but Lakshmi was certain the Tribals were good news. They should be given equal rights and responsibilities.

Now here she was, back in the sleepy and backward hamlet, feeling like a complete tool. She wanted to be fierce and not washing clothes in the clear waters. Though the river was deeper than the last time she had been here, and it didn't look still, it was in fact, stirring rapidly.

She narrowed her eyes, wondering whether she had come to the right river that her mother had instructed her about.

Or was it the one close to the hills?

The river's calm surface was shattered when a crocodile suddenly appeared and grabbed the clothes she had been washing. She pulled herself back, almost staggering.

Wrong one! Wrong one!

The crocodile viciously tore through her clothes and he was coming out of the river for her. She grabbed one end of her kurti while the crocodile grabbed the other end. They began to tug at it.

"Leave! You filthy creature!"

The crocodile was forceful, as he jerked Lakshmi forward. Her body was flung towards the creature and she felt the involuntary loss of her footing.

And then there were strong hands that grabbed her elbow and pulled her back. The shadowy figure lurched forward and literally kicked the crocodile in the stomach. It fell back with a splash. Then the figure rolled around with it until they both splashed under the surface of the water.

"Are you all right? Who is it? Are you all right?"

The water rippled and there were hands and a crocodile tail moving upwards. Lakshmi's heart came to her mouth as she hoped that her saviour wouldn't die trying to save her. She looked at the river for a while, but the water was now still. And then water splashed all over her clothes as the figure emerged from the water, turning out to be none other than her childhood friend Kalki.

He was older, bigger, and bulkier than before, with long, wavy hair, and the prayer beads of Lord Shiva tied around his biceps. His abs glistened with blood sustained from his fight with the crocodile, but his boyish smile gave nothing away.

Lakshmi came up to him, worried out of her mind, but Kalki just embraced her tightly. He pulled back and just smiled.

"You are always chasing danger, idiot." He smacked her on the head.

"And you are always chasing to save me," Lakshmi said. "And did you…just…did you just kill a crocodile?"

"Uh, not really killed, but scared him away," he paused, as he glanced at her lovingly. "Why didn't you inform me that you were coming?"

"Because it was sudden and before you ask me anything else, I just came to Shambala yesterday and mother gave me all of this stupid work," she frowned. "Already."

Kalki laughed as he grabbed hold of his kurta from the tree he had strung it on. He put on the kurta as he said, "What did you expect? Just because you live in the city doesn't mean you are one of them."

Lakshmi frowned. "I had been gone two years and look at you; you have changed so much."

"Two years is a long time, since my best friend only cared to send me a letter just once in two months. Sometimes, not even that."

"I was busy studying and you were clearly busy building your physique."

"More like finding odd jobs around the village to do, doing the heavy lifting and earning extra coins; so don't tell my father and mother," he flexed his biceps. "I know I look good, love. Now stop staring, it is creepy."

"Oh please, there are so many handsome men around in Indragarh…especially you should see…" she continued to talk. She had a large frown writ on her face by the attack and how it had led to her clothes being destroyed, "see the soldiers. They are so handsome."

"Oh, handsome, eh?"

She turned to go back when Kalki was standing right there, inches away from her. His hands went to her hips and grabbed it tightly, squeezing them, as her toes began to curl involuntarily.

"Handsome, are they?"

"Yes, handsome."

"What else did you learn or see in the city?" He came extremely close, his breath smelling of mint.

Even though she liked how Kalki held her, she pushed back playfully and said, "Also I've learnt you can't touch me without my permission."

"Permission?"

"Consent, yes." She blurted, walking back towards the village.

"I apologize. From next time, I will."

"Apology accepted since you saved my life and most of my clothes."

Kalki laughed, nervously scratching the back of his head.

"Now come to my home. I'll get you the medicine since you are bleeding," Lakshmi glanced at the bright, red spots that had appeared on his white kurta.

Kalki sighed and followed her.

9

"Brother…brother…"

Faint whispers could be heard as he opened his eyes, a white light blinding him and allowing him to see nothing for a while. And then slowly his sight began to recover. He saw Durukti towering over him, her face contorted into an expression of concern.

"Brother?"

"Uh, yes," Kali heaved. He couldn't stand. He was frozen to the spot. "Sorry, yeah…"

Durukti helped him up as Kali noticed there were two soldiers in the room, concerned for him. He waved and they immediately left, while he staggered over to the bed and sat.

"Why do you think you fainted?"

Kali shook his head. He had no idea how. He was relentlessly coughed till the point he had a blackout.

"Because of you, the council meeting has not begun."

Kali looked up at Durukti. How little she had been when he had saved her from their burning village. The sight of a young lad with an infant wrapped in his arms still haunted him to this day. He had seen horrors he was not ready to speak about. She had now grown into a woman of beauty and grace, topped with a noble heart. She had knee-length hair braided to perfection, while her eyes were the same as Kali. Golden. Only their tribe had these genetic traits.

"Thank you."

"You look sick."

"I am perhaps. I am seeing visions and…my lungs they don't feel all right."

Durukti sat beside him and held her palm against his chest. She felt his heartbeat.

"It's going too fast."

"Yes. I should be leaving."

Durukti nodded. "Take care, brother. I'll meet you in the chambers." She kissed his cheek and left.

He walked over to the polished brass plate, gazing at himself. And then he began to put on his clothes. He didn't have any sword with him for he hated weapons. Too violent for his own use, he would ponder.

Dressing up, he exited the room and made his way towards the council chamber. He had reached the central maze of the forest in Rajgirh. He passed the prefecture as the floor opened out to steps that led to a pedestal. The walls were made of glazed stones, strong and dark, tall enough to touch the skies. The stationed soldiers were like hawks, peering at everyone, standing formidably with their weapons. Unlike the other cities of Illavarti, Indragarh didn't have high ceilings or buildings, but were mostly open in plan, letting the skies play its magic.

He had entered the chamber, which was itself an open courtyard, in the midst of four trees, with a mammoth round table in between the bronze thrones.

Kali could see Vedanta sitting with his two guards, while Kuvera, Raktapa and Vasuki were waiting for Kali.

"I'm sorry for my delay, my friends."

"For an important day like this, you shouldn't have," Vasuki complained.

"I am having a few health issues." And his eyes darted towards Durukti, who slowly walked over to the throne, which belonged to Kali. She stood alongside Koko and Vikoko, who were wearing their bloody, dirty armour.

Kali sat on the chair and looked at everyone. "Shall we begin then?"

"You decide. After all, everything happens according to you," Vedanta rambled.

"Well someone is disrespectful," Kuvera playfully quipped.

"Of course I am. My people hate me. They call me a coward."

"And soon they will term you as a visionary," Kali said. "With the inclusion of Vasuki, you will have better ministers among your administrators, against Eastern and Western attacks. With Raktapa, you'll have a stronger army, and with Kuvera your mercantile business will grow tenfold. It looks like a curse right now, but it's only for the betterment of this kingdom."

Kuvera nodded. "Yes your highness, you will have my support."

Vedanta growled under his breath.

Kali looked at Koko as he brought the decree and placed it flat on the table. "The Treaty of Indragarh has been drafted by our legal advisors. Now it's time to sign it and make it real."

"The Dakshinis must be laughing at me," Vedanta said, gritting his teeth.

The Dakshinis were the Southern kings, like the Udaiyas who were the Northern Kings of Illavarti. The Udaiyas controlled cities like Indragarh and for now, Kali had conquered and created pacts in the north.

"The Dakshinis aren't my problem. They have their naval system, and they have their own relationship with Eelam," he spoke about the island of prosperity that was populated by the Rakshas, the dark-skinned and literate warriors. "They are not our problem."

"Exactly," Raktapa said.

"Let the people of this city and the rest be accustomed to the new life, a life where everyone is equal and looked up to as a respectful citizen, despite the caste and class they come from." Kali devotedly spoke. "Also, Lord Raktapa, I would need you at Agnigarh. There's a small rebellion that must be staved off. While you are there, stay and handle the situation with King Samrat."

"As you say, Lord Kali," Raktapa smiled, baring his small and sharp canines.

"Shall we move forward then?"

Everyone nodded except for Vedanta, who reluctantly growled. Kali walked casually over to the table, dipped his quill in the inkstand and signed off his name. The same was done by Kuvera, then Raktapa, followed by Vasuki and finally by the stern Vedanta. Once it was done, Kali handed the paper to Koko and told him to keep it in the safe.

"As of now, the plan is that we will have new forts built. So we would need King Vedanta's labourers at our disposal. Kuvera will handle the street bazaars." To which Kuvera humbly nodded. "The theatre, miscellaneous activities and the armouries will be handled by Vasuki's men. Tell Takshak look over the personal army of the state."

"What about my commanders?" the Manav king asked, astounded.

"To be fair, King Vedanta, we don't think they are capable enough."

Vedanta rolled his eyes.

"What about the villages? Are we calling off the taxes?"

"Since the treasury is almost extinguished, and Kuvera's promise to fill up the treasury has been delayed due to the problems in transportation, we should continue with taxation, at least temporarily."

"The farmers are the cornerstone of Indragarh. With any additional taxes, they'll be burdened unduly," Vedanta protested.

Kali looked at him with hard eyes. "Your highness, I don't really care. We need money to sustain this city, especially if we are building armed forts for ourselves."

"He's right," Kuvera began, "but who will be the lucky person to handle that?"

"Not you," Vasuki grinned.

Kuvera smothered a frown. Kali knew there was a bit of acrimony between these two tribes, but he toned it down with a timely and strategic announcement.

"My sister Durukti is capable of these affairs. She can enforce will when needed."

"What will *I* do then?" spat Vedanta.

Kali looked over through the pages that were scattered on the table. He pulled out one. "You have the most important job. You will travel around the city with your chariot and men and tell the tale about how good it was to make a pact with us and how well Indragarh will rise from the underdevelopment it was suffering from, for so long."

"You mean I should lie?"

"It's one way to look at it and the other way is you are instilling hope in people that you weren't defeated by us, which you clearly were, but you had worked with us because you saw them before yourself. You need to show you are still their king. You saw the future. You wanted me to make sure they don't hate you. With you out there promising them a good thing, that's exactly what I'm letting you have."

Vedanta was fuming with anger and his eyes had grown bloodshot, but he didn't say anything. He just clenched his fist and let go while Kali could only grin. *How can I be any more reasonable?*

Kali felt a burn in his chest that he ignored. He struggled with a smile as he ended the council meeting, "I'll be organizing a feast at Rajgirh as well as a feast outside for the city dwellers, at a meagre cost of one silver coin per person. It'll be good," he paused, as the chest burn began to increase, "for signifying the brighter future we have ahead of us."

"CHEERS!" Everyone said, except one.

10

Kalki had his bruises and wounds healed by the medicinal leaves from the Soma Caves of Shambala. They were up in the mountainous terrains, hidden from the village. Inside, Kalki had heard, there were the soma reservoirs, commonly referred to by the villagers as the "Gift from the Gods". According to the legends, Lord Indra, the God of thunder and king of all Gods, had situated himself in the land of Indragarh and he had told his celestial servants, the Gandharvas, to spread the medicine across Illavarti to aid the Manavs. So far this had been the only such repository discovered.

And the people who believed in science said the Soma Caves were nothing but shiny, blue stones that had developed due to intense heat and pressure, nothing else. They weren't magical per se.

People had tried extracting the juices from the stone, but many had been unsuccessful. Those who were successful, they had grown to be immortals or had gone mad, so the stories said. But for now, the caves had shut down as a quake had caused boulders to block the pathway. But the villagers still used the herbs found around the outskirts of the terrain. The Soma Caves, or popularly known as Indravan, were also the holiest place for worship, as it was considered the last place Lord Indra had stayed in, until his ascension to heaven. The caves had become almost too sacred, frightening and at the same time grandiose during the days of the festivals.

"I still don't believe you are able to fight all these animals with your bare hands," Lakshmi said to herself, as she slowly massaged the leaf paste over his wounds.

Kalki had learnt about his powers when he was nine years old and he was able to grab a poisonous snake and squeeze it hard till it choked to death. He had learnt he wasn't like other boys. He had powers unimaginably great. His skin wasn't impermeable to wounds, but his strength was. He had powers greater than the soldiers of the city; almost remarkable like the Rakshas, he imagined. But Kalki was humbled, especially when his father, Vishnuyath had made him sit down and narrated to him why he was like that.

"Some are born great and some embrace greatness. You are both. Use it wisely, but do not reveal it to anyone, for many won't understand your power and will be frightened of your potential."

"But why am I like this?"

He looked down, thoughtfully, perhaps searching for the right words. "If I knew the answer, I would have told you. But all you should worry about is to use it for the right cause, son, for power this great comes with a great price. One day you might have to pay for it, but for now, use it to help others."

Kalki hadn't got the answer then. He had hidden this fact from his brother and even his mother, but had been caught picking up a huge boulder effortlessly by Lakshmi. He told her this and she had said to him, "perhaps you are the son of a God."

Kalki had brushed it aside, a little bashfully. "I'm sure my father isn't any God. He's a dairy farmer. Perhaps he's the God of cows."

"The God of milk?"

And they had laughed, but both of them were puzzled. Kalki had known he found a friend in someone who didn't judge him for being who he was.

"You still have not got any answers for the powers I have, do you?" he asked.

"I know you told me to look up through the history books..."

"Or science textbooks."

"Yes, but I couldn't find anything substantial. Perhaps, there are some things that you don't need explanations for or perhaps it takes time to know for oneself. You'll know about whatever you have, soon in your life. You just need to wait." She paused. "Did you find anything here?"

"Bah! Here out of all the places? I'm devoid of any knowledge here. I seek to escape father. I feel I owe my parents a great deal and thus I'm stuck working on the farm for them."

"It's okay."

"I just want to know." He gritted his teeth.

"You will, I'm sure."

Kalki walked to the polished copper plate that was hung in the living room and saw a burnt mark over his right arm. "Yes, perhaps." He had got the burn when he was younger. "So many questions, and such few answers."

"Don't worry, we will find it. For now, worry about going back."

Kalki smiled, as he hugged her and made his way out. He saw Lakshmi's mother, to whom he waved as he passed her by.

He was going home late. He hadn't even gone to work today, though there was time till sunset to finish some leftover work on the farm. As he made his way to the field, he passed a tavern where an old hermit sat, drunkenly blabbering things to himself, before he lurched and fell on the floor.

As Kalki helped him get up, he saw the strange eyes of the hermit. They were wise beyond his visible age.

"I'm...I'm...so-sorry, mate."

"It's all right, man. Are you fine?"

"As always," he grinned foolishly, baring his rotten teeth.

"I should leave then…"

"Have I…have I seen you somewhere, mate?"

Kalki smiled. "I don't think so. In fact, by the looks of you, you are not from here. Came with the Tribals, perhaps?"

"Long lives the future, right?" he laughed and fell again.

This time, Kalki didn't pick him up. He strolled to the farm, which had a wooden entrance and high fences that didn't let the cows escape. The fields were pasture lands for the cows and there were sheds at the back, where the cows were tied. But as of now, the ground was soaked with blood and the cows had disappeared. He saw his father's men, sprawled on the floor, lifeless.

Then he saw Arjan who was at the side of the stable, whimpering and shaking, with a bloody nose and broken limbs.

"Where is Father?" he asked his little brother.

"They…they have taken him away."

"They… who?"

"The Mlecchas."

"The Tribals?"

"No, the bandits," Arjan looked at him.

11

Durukti laid her brother down on the bed, carefully placing his head on the lush pillows and laying a long blanket over him. It had been a while since the feast had occurred and many people had come outside the fort to partake in the celebrations.

"Are you fine now?"

"Better."

"The doctor has given me honey for your throat."

"It's not cold," he mourned, "it's worse. When I cough, it hurts my body and fire courses inside my veins,"

Durukti knew Kali was a lot of things—strategist, clever, and selfish. But he was never the one to complain. Even in the direst of times, he would be brave and strong, unlike now. She had tried all sorts of herbs, but none had worked.

"Doctors say it could be a western disease spread during the war."

"The sand affected me? Why didn't it get to Koko and Vikoko then?"

Durukti shared a glance with her handmaiden, Symrin, who was worriedly standing at the back. She followed Durukti everywhere, working with her not only on personal matters, but the overall arrangements for the fort. Symrin shook her head as she had no answer herself for Kali.

"Perhaps," Durukti began, "they have more immunity than you, brother."

"Oh please, I am equally strong."

"Just because you are strong doesn't mean you are fit."

He massaged his chest.

"You need to be in good health to run this state, otherwise the Tribals will take over and the peace you have been seeking for so long will die with you."

"Don't I know that?" he coughed and wheezed. He looked at Symrin, and then back at Durukti. "You have found a partner."

"Indeed," Durukti smiled. "More so, a friend."

"Yes," he glanced again at Symrin. "Do you know, my child, I saved your mistress from a burning town? We were stuck in a dilapidated hut and we escaped with great difficulty. She was almost three years old when we escaped."

"And saved yourself too," Durukti proudly added.

Symrin with her cherub voice began, "Yes, my lord. The tales of your bravery have travelled far. But if I may be allowed to ask, how did the fire start?"

The smile vanished from Kali's face. Durukti turned to Symrin. "It is not of importance. The past doesn't concern us, the future does."

"True words," Kali said, with a disarming smile.

Symrin just meekly nodded.

Durukti kissed her brother on the forehead and walked out. She didn't say anything to Symrin until they entered the room.

"Should I bring your nightgown, madam?"

"Not now," Durukti sighed as she sat next to the window, pulling off her earrings. "Never bring up the topic, Symrin. Never let Lord Kali talk about the fire."

"Why, my lady?"

"It might be vanity, but it has a history that no one should know," Durukti sighed. "Anyhow, do we have something on our worktable?"

Symrin walked over to the chestnut table which had a fire lamp. She then brought a register from there, on which the village names around Indragarh were written. Durukti began to skip through the names as none of them had any importance for her. "Almost fifty villages around Indragarh. We need to send a messenger to all of them with a royal decree that the new taxes have been implemented. Also a pocket of Vasuki's army to handle any rebellious efforts."

"Good idea, my lady," said the young handmaiden.

Durukti pinpointed the names of the villages they would start with, as Symrin noted down on a piece of paper. Symrin stopped at the mention of Shambala, when she looked up and said, "Did you say Shambala, my lady?"

"If I'm not mistaken, yes I did."

"I remember something about that village, although I don't know how true it is."

"What do you mean?"

"They say Shambala was a gifted village by the Gods and they had left a certain, celestial…"

Durukti snapped. "Out of all the people in this city, I am the last person to believe this."

"But it might help you, for Shambala is supposed to have rocks that have spiritual medicinal properties." She paused. "My father told me about it. He was a doctor and in the last days of his life, he had been met by a poor villager, an inhabitant of Shambala who told my father that his wife was ill, so ill by the pregnancy that she was close to death. My father couldn't give him anything for there was no cure for it. The villager mumbled about the magic rocks known as Soma and asked my father whether it would work. My father refused, saying they were all stories and legends. The villager went away disappointedly. A year later, my father had work in Shambala. He reached there and he met the same villager with a happy wife who wasn't ill at all. In fact, she even had a son. Father asked how she was cured and he had said, 'the legends were not legends, after all'." She stopped.

Durukti had digested all of this, but it sounded more of a childhood fable to her.

"It's supposed to cure everything," Symrin added.

"Could the villager be lying?"

"Perhaps and perhaps not."

"So you say no one has used these Soma rocks because they don't believe in them?"

"They've been closed off. At least that is what father said since he had gone up to check the caves himself and found them to be closed off. Someone clearly didn't want them to be used."

"How do we get in then, girl?"

"We have an army. We can use man power to push through. The villagers didn't have the education or the power. They were too superstitious also." She paused. "They say Soma would cure any disease or illness. I just wondered whether it would be good for Lord Kali."

"I suppose so as well," Durukti mused. "What if it's all unreal, just a story?"

"It's worth a try my lady, since Lord Kali's health is deteriorating by the hour and we have no other choice."

Durukti nodded. "Fine, Symrin. I'll think about it. He has been saving me my entire life," she stopped, as she let the moonlight shower over her translucent skin, the smell of freshly-cut flowers and the hooting of the owls adding to the pleasant aura, which gave her a sense of determination.

"I think it's my time to save his life."

12

Kalki was wearing a long cloak when he entered the forest.

The trickling of the rainwater, with the smell of tangerine, was enough for Kalki to feel he was in a very alien place. The sound was harsh and cold, and the wind swept against him harshly. He had wrapped himself in warm clothes as he sat in front of the fire, across from Lakshmi, Arjan and Bala.

Bala was a friend of Kalki's and he was one of the few who knew how to handle a mace. When Kalki had come to meet Bala for his help to defeat the Mlecchas, Bala was busy knocking off some drunkards who were disturbing in the taverns. He was six feet nine inches in height, with a frame that was heavier than both Arjan and Kalki combined. His face was covered with a thick, bushy beard and his eyes were beady black, with a strange coldness about them.

Kalki began, addressing Arjan, "Tell us about them."

Arjan nodded. "They arrived riding on horses and were wearing black clothes. They had masks on as they rampaged and killed the ones who interfered. I escaped at the right moment. More so, I was no threat to them. They had weapons, but not the ordinary swords we see around here. The hilt was the same as the ones we saw but the blade was curved from the top."

"A scimitar," Lakshmi answered.

"A scimi-what?" Bala scratched his head.

"It's a backhanded weapon used by the Dakshinis. One slice and it can go straight through your bones."

"Bones, you say? I shall knock sense into them, I tell you."

"We have to play smart," Lakshmi added. "And not dumb. They have Kalki and Arjan's father. We need to do it swiftly and carefully since we don't have weapons."

"Umph," Bala grunted. Playing swift and careful wasn't part of his dictionary, Kalki thought.

"They are most probably cow bandits, looking for food," Kalki said. "They have become more prominent since the Tribals' inclusion."

"Bloody outcasts! They must rot and die," Bala scoffed.

"But why did they want your father?" Lakshmi asked.

"They need someone to herd the cows, take responsibility while they feast on them." Arjan responded. "This is my reasoning. Because other than this, I don't see any other point of the kidnapping."

Kalki looked at Arjan, "How many cows were they able to take?"

"They managed to get three big ones as the others were hidden inside the stable."

Kalki nodded. "We don't have much time, days or hours. Mlecchas are unpredictable."

"We don't even know how to find them," Bala said.

"Division of labour," Kalki suggested. "Lakshmi and I will go to the city of Indragarh, which is a day's journey on horseback and get the weaponry we need. You and Arjan try to find the bandits, but if you do find them, don't go headlong against them or you'll not survive it."

Arjan nodded obediently. "I'll signal you if we do find them. Just know they would be somewhere around that signal."

Kalki patted his smart brother.

"How will we manage to get weapons from the city?" Lakshmi asked matter-of-factly.

"Um," Kalki cleared his throat, "you said you have your aunt there, right? And she works in the government. So she can help us with the weapons."

"You mean illegally giving you army weapons? Uh, no, not going to happen."

"More like borrowing, please," he pleaded, "for our father. I wouldn't have asked you otherwise."

"There must be some other way than to use weapons."

"Any other way than violence? There is no other way!" laughed off Bala.

"How did you get a big mace like that here?"

He hugged it closely as if it were his child and kissed the top of it. "Baba."

"His father and Bala are one of the few people who actually carry a weapon in this village, otherwise it's frowned upon here," Arjan said. "Lakshmi, I saw those people. The moment they see us, without weapons, they will kill us without even blinking. They had no remorse when they killed off our men. And while the Sarpanch is deciding what to do about it, it'll be too late. We have to act individually and fast."

Lakshmi sighed and reluctantly nodded.

13

General Takshak knocked on Lord Vasuki's door. He had been away for the entire day and at night, but had been summoned at this hour nonetheless. As he stood idly outside the door, he could hear the moans that came from inside. Vasuki, a father of three, didn't care about matrimonial fidelity. Pleasure, for him, came in a variety of ages and colours.

Since the pact had been made, Vasuki was considered a strong and influential figure of one of the mightiest Northern states. Initially, these cities run by Manavs were often the ones that would ridicule the Tribals, call them names, discriminate against them and speak ill. But now, they were all respected. Takshak had walked on the streets of the Mining Town, up till the Lotus Garden and everyone just watched him in awe. A Tribal being the head of security for a state? Manavs couldn't believe it was even possible in this lifetime.

Though most of them didn't know their history. Just after the Breaking, when the world had collapsed, and the plague had vanquished the remaining lands of the country and the tribes, the Tribals and Manavs had worked together. In fact, they were the same. The Tribal identity had been created due to pressure by the internal politics when both of them differed. Lord Shiva, Lord Vishnu and Lord Brahma were the spiritual leaders of the Manavs after the

Breaking. They supported the upper castes while the others didn't. They realized the Trimurti was worried about them and decided to distance them. They called themselves Tribals and they built settlements in different areas. Soon, the evils of war hindered them from forging any lasting attempts at peace, and continuous warfare led to tremendous losses for the Tribals. Egos were tarnished. They hid in the rough terrains, the cold mountains or the forests. Many continued fighting while others kept to themselves, pledging for internal penance such as the vanars, who were the worshippers of monkeys. There were others who began cannibalism, such as the pisaches.

And now after so many years, things had changed.

The door opened and it was a girl barely in her twenties, with a naked frame. Takshak didn't look at her and his eyes darted at the blanket wrapped Lord Vasuki.

"I apologize. I'll come later."

"Please enter, the girl was leaving."

The girl nodded. She put on her clothes and stormed out of the room.

"Such a fine ass." Vasuki laughed as he poured himself some wine from the side table, where a bottle and a goblet were placed. "In this town, there's something about Manav girls. They are wild."

"I'm sure, my lord." Takshak had a straight face. None of these trivial things mattered, since in the culture of the Nagas, the warriors were supposed to have no distraction, but knowledge and strength. Austerity and penance were foremost.

"Oh I wish you would unwind a little and watch them, but you can't, for to service me you paid a hefty price." He looked down to where Takshaka's privates were. "I wonder, do you ever regret it?"

"Never, my lord. Service for our Lord is my top priority."

"Great," he smiled.

Lord Vasuki had a very sharp nose, according to what Takshak had noticed of him.

"How's our fat friend doing?"

"Not being suspicious, my lord," he answered about Kuvera, the wretched man and the king of Yakshas; the rotten and dirty thieves and merchants. They were horrible in nature and Takshak hated them more than the Manavs.

"That's grand. I don't want him to shift alliances like the time he stole the mani from us." He laughed. "What a pretty sight it was when Kali made him surrender the stone and made us allies even though I hated him. But hey, we needed to do all of this for a change, didn't we?"

"Yes, my lord."

"Which makes me come to the main topic," Lord Vasuki began with a thoughtful pose, the same he was sculptured in back at the Naagpuri. "I want you to follow Vedanta and see if he's up to something. Leave our fat friend for the moment. He isn't the person we should be worried about since he's savouring in the glory of sweet victory right now. The Manav is being reluctant and frustrated, and frustration could lead to serious consequences. I want you to just spy on him. Take no more than two men with you and stay fifty yards away. He will be starting his useless journey around the city, promising everyone that everything is alright and helping them in their daily affairs. But I am certain he will be making arrangements with someone inside to topple us and I want you to poison them before he's able to do it. Once he gives us a reason to betray him, Kali will carry out his execution."

"But why wouldn't he do it now, my lord?"

"Because Kali knows Vedanta's useful now. He needs a face for the city to be calmed. After all, no one wants a people's revolution on our hands just after a battle, am I not right?"

"Yes, my lord."

"Good." Vasuki smiled. "Just don't die on me. You are the only person I trust, my friend."

Takshak smiled. He was just a soldier out of many for Vasuki's army, but when Takshak had single-handedly protected Vasuki's wife and children back in their lands; he was given a step up. Soon the post of a general turned into something warm and precious, for Lord Vasuki had become more than just a leader for him.

And with that Takshak bowed and departed from the room, with the new mission he had been assigned.

14

Sweat beads began to trickle down Kalki's chin as he made his way to the Sarpanch's house. At the stable outside, he was met with the sight of two muscled men, who were dozing late at night. Kalki confronted two horses, who instantly neighed at the look of the strangers. Kalki hushed at them and with the help of Lakshmi, he was able to pull the two horses aside. The sarpanch of the village was the only person wealthy enough to have horses at his disposal. Horses were quick compared to the bullocks; especially in the current circumstances.

Kalki got up on one horse while Lakshmi sat astride the other one. Unlike Lakshmi, he had little knowledge about horses and it took him time to bring it under his control.

"Use the rein and pull it towards yourself to control it, and then slowly push towards the direction you want to go," she whispered.

Kalki nodded. He didn't like the idea of stealing from the sarpanch, who was now busy at the meeting with a newsmonger, discussing the next plan of action against these unknown Mlecchas.

As he got out away from the muscle men, he told Lakshmi to ride close to the meeting, to hear what exactly was going on. From far off, he could see a huge group of people, mostly men, standing around the sarpanch, quarrelling and mumbling amongst themselves.

Kalki had camouflaged himself in the forest so he would be invisible to the eyes of the sarpanch, who would have otherwise known that his horse was being taken by a dairy farmer's son.

"We should leave." Lakshmi's voice came from behind.

"Shush." Kalki's finger swept across his lips.

Kalki heard the loud rants:

"We won't risk our lives. Let us send a letter to the closest town to get an army."

"No one will give us an army. I've heard that life in this village is going to get tough."

"We should investigate ourselves."

"No one cares about us."

Rants continued to pour in. One even had the audacity to say that perhaps it wasn't the Mlecchas, but Vishnu himself. "He must have run away from his life back here."

"No use of saving him, he is probably dead already."

No, he isn't, Kalki convinced himself. He had learnt all about the bandits. They would keep the person until the person was resourceful to them or at least that's what he had been taught at the Gurukul during the warfare classes. These classes were few in number in comparison to health studies, cooking and agriculture classes, but just the most interesting one of the lot. He was one of the few along with Arjan who had been to the Gurukul, an isolated temple that housed students from across the land, fed them and taught them. Kalki had been forced to go initially, but he understood why Vishnu wanted him to study. To survive adversity, one must be knowledgeable. Due to that knowledge, he now knew about his enemy.

Kalki manoeuvred the horse and went up the hill, his cloak brushing against the twigs on the forest floor. As he came out of the clearing, the sound of the hooves had grown monotonous. The trampling of the leaves didn't annoy him. The smell of flowers, of various kinds, had imparted a pleasant touch to the night.

"Why do you need weapons? You can beat them singlehandedly."

"You overestimate my strength. If there was one bandit, I would've done what you said, but there are many. Humans are worse than a crocodile when it comes to violence."

"Fine. How many do you plan to *borrow*?"

"Bala said he can muster up five more people from the tavern to aid us so we have more than we need. As for you..."

"Me? I'll go?"

"You don't want to?"

"No, it's just that I never presumed you thought girls are allowed to fight."

Kalki narrowed his eyes. "Why not? If boys fight, then why can't girls?" He paused when she took her time.

"So you plan to take a hefty bit of the loot back?"

"Perhaps," Kalki nodded. But Kalki was apprehensive about using weapons during the combat.

"Sometimes I regret that this village is not very well defended. In the event of a surprise battle, how will one survive?" She paused, answering her own question then. "They won't. They are too aloof to see the world outside, too naïve to know we live in unpredictable and difficult times."

Kalki had to agree.

As he moved forward, mired by the silence and monotony of their journey, his mind was quickly working through possibilities, even though his heart was sunk. He had blamed his father all the time for trapping him in this village, but now he was in danger's path and Kalki felt guilty. He wasn't afraid for he knew his father was clever, but he felt guilty for saying bad things about him all this time. It was this sinking feeling, trapping him into a void of pain. He had last felt like this when Arjan had eaten the wrong berries and fallen sick. Kalki did everything to take care of him, carrying Arjan every day to the shaman for therapeutic massages and potions.

He had been angry at his father for not knowing the answers behind his strength, he was angry when his brother Arjan was considered the serious, studious, and better one. He was the laughing stock. All of these things made him angry at Vishnu, but it also made him sad. He missed him more than anything now. And he wanted nothing more than his safe return.

"Are you okay?" Lakshmi softly asked.

He looked at the road ahead. It was empty, and far in the distance, the land met the skies, with the woods on either side seeming to converge at one point. "No. No, I'm not."

15

"Where are we going, man?" asked Bala.

Arjan ignored the question, as he finally stepped close to the hut he lived in. From the soot-stained windows, he saw his mother in the kitchen, sitting alone in her thoughts.

"We are supposed to find the kidnappers," Bala scowled.

"I have to meet my mother," he said. "You stay here."

Arjan walked inside, opening the tough door when he saw his mother instantly stand up in relief. She hugged him and asked, "Did they get to know anything about your father? Are they sending out a search party?"

Kalki had told him to lie to his mother that they would be assisting and convincing the villagers for a search party since Vishnu was an important member of the community.

"Yes, we tried. We still are."

"Is Kalki still there?"

"Yes." He lied again. Lying wasn't what he liked when it came to his innocent mother. But he knew she would be tremendously pained when she found out that Kalki has gone to the city; an entire day's journey. "I just want to tell you we will be out there, looking for him."

She clenched her teeth a little stubbornly.

"Don't stop us, Ma. Let us do what we have to do." His fingers were curling as he said this. He had been never afraid as much as he was right now.

"Wait," she said and went back in the room.

Arjan waited as he poured some water to drink. By the time he was done, he saw his mother enter again, but this time with a sickle in her hand.

"Use this."

"What? No!"

"You need something to defend yourself since you'll be out there."

Arjan nodded reluctantly, and as he grabbed the agricultural tool, he felt the heaviness of it, since it would be used for murdering someone rather than to harvest field produce.

"I got it when I worked on the farm. It's quite handy. I slashed a landowner's cheek when he tried to harass me," she mirthlessly chuckled, something Mother hardly did. But fear forces people to speak about their worst selves.

"I'm sure you were justified in your deeds, Ma."

She grabbed his cheek and came close, her eyes igniting with concern, but bravado as well. "I want you to find him, but do not be swayed. You are not a hero. You are a boy, a young boy added to that. You need to be smart rather than foolish enough to attack them."

"Yes, Ma."

She kissed him hard on the cheek. "I'll pray to the Gods, to Lord Indra, to bestow his Vajra on you."

Arjan didn't believe in the Gods, but he nodded. With Mother's blessings, he returned outside to Bala, who had been waiting with his weapon.

"What were you doing inside?"

"Nothing, let's go for the meeting."

"I thought we were looking for the bandits."

"First, we need to see where the village stands on this issue."

Bala nodded.

With this, they walked on foot to the biggest tree of the village, where the group would be assembling, but surprisingly no one was there. Moreover, the fire lamps were burnt off and it was completely isolated.

Arjan was surprised and frantically he made his way to the sarpanch's house, a multitude of huts built together in close proximity. The only way to enter was from the back, where the stables were located and from the front, there was the main door. He knocked on the door.

In a little while, the sarpanch opened the door, flanked by his musclemen.

"Arjan, my boy, what a pleasant surprise!" He was sweating, his eyes searching for something.

"Why isn't there a search party?" Arjan asked, without even continuing the charade of formality.

"I apologize if I seem hasseled my horses have been stolen…"

"Why aren't there any people?"

The sarpanch, Devadatta, had a wispy moustache, with a tired and dishevelled look. "We will start in the morning. At night, there is no use."

"No use? My father's life is at stake and you say there's no use?"

"There is…I never said…"

Arjan walked back without even listening. He could hear the entreaties of the sarpanch, but he didn't care.

"Should I smack his head?" asked Bala.

Arjan felt helpless. No one was there and by morning it would be too late. He looked at Bala as he recalled how Kalki had become friends with him in the first place. They had met during a drinking session. "You work at the local tavern, don't you?"

"As a guard, yes. I have taken days off so you don't worry…"

"No. Not that." Arjan stopped. "Taverns are occasionally filled with people who are well-informed. They make it their business to know other people's business."

"Range of people, yes. They come from all walks of life for fine sura and madira."

"And as a guard, you meet them often, don't you?" Arjan asked, his fingers twitching as he tapped over his lips. "All sorts of people."

"Yes."

"Know them by the first name, sometimes? Perhaps interact with them, even?"

"Many are too drowsy to interact, but yes, boy." He kept his mace comfortably resting on his shoulders. "What are you getting at?"

His head turned to see the wide range of woods that were beyond the village huts, where the bandits were supposed to be hiding.

"I want you to take me to the person who knows everything about those forests."

16

Arjan hadn't slept in the night. He had wandered till the edge of the forest, blankly watching the canopies, the winds sweeping the leaves as they fluttered. He even managed to go back to his home and watch his mother sleeping, with dried tear stains on her face. When he did eventually close his eyes, he was pushed by someone and he realized that dawn had broken, the skies were blue again and a new day had begun. Towering over him was the giant Bala with his favourite mace, this time casually concealed behind the long cloak he managed to arrange from somewhere.

Wryly, he said, "I found your man."

Arjan nodded. "Where is he?"

"He's at the Madira's Chalice."

Arjan nodded. Madira's Chalice was the only tavern-cum-inn in Shambala that housed visitors. However, it was frowned upon by the religious men of the village, especially the good-for-nothing sarpanch, who had begun this rebellion against the tavern. Personally, he hadn't been inside of it. It was never really something he was fond of, even though he was well above the statutory age of entry. It was all the drinking, the pipe smoking, and the retching that disgusted him. He would rather hold on to the books late at night and ponder about history and mathematics. But getting books in Shambala was itself a huge task, for it didn't house any library. The closest one could get to books were either in the Gurukul which is a quarter day's ride by a donkey cart or at the Wisdom's Tree, which was also an inn for the travellers to rest at. It didn't offer drinks of any sort, but it did offer different sorts of books, as the Wisdom Tree's owner was once a guru at the Gurukul, until he was stripped off of his post for reasons Arjan didn't care to remember.

Still deep in his thoughts, he realized he had reached the tavern and it seemed…quiet. There weren't any songs being played by the musicians or the usual humdrum of people. It still had drunkards snoring to glory with half-empty glasses in their hands. Arjan walked towards the back while Bala guided him to enter the dark room and make their way to the stairs, ascending until they reached the first floor. The place was littered with the paraphernalia typically found in cloistered inns and taverns.

"Where did you find a good guide in a place like this?"

"Where else would I, boy?" Bala meekly asked.

Arjan reached the balcony which was flanked by stone columns and had a wooden, almost burnished floor.

"I often wonder how one managed to have so much money for this."

"The owner was an upper caste noble," Bala responded. "The high borns that took money and bought this piece of land. The head of this damn village couldn't do bones about it, for he had political influence backing him."

"That's why the sarpanch just disowned the place."

"Of course."

Bala reached out to the drunkard who was still gleefully imbibing the spirits. Bala slapped him hard. "KRIPA! KRIPA!"

"Eh, eh." His eyes opened fully and he yawned and burped. "Wow, what a madness that was!"

"It's me."

"Oh hello, friend," he grinned. "What a disturbing sight to wake up to."

He had a black beard and wrinkles all over his face. He wore clothes that appeared scorched and torn in places, although there were no visible injuries on him. Arjan noticed all of it, with his fingers dancing on his lips thoughtfully.

"Bala, you didn't tell me our guide is a warrior."

"Warrior? This drunkard?" Bala slapped him on the head again.

"Hello!" snarled Kripa, but then retracted his outstretched hand. "How did you know?"

"Not many carry wounds around here."

"You caught me," Kripa grinned, with half of his teeth missing. "I might have added my valour in a few of the Northern wars."

"That doesn't concern us. What Bala says is you are quite adept in your knowledge about the woods of Shambala."

"What can I say? The village is like a home to me, mate." He laughed. "And when you don't know your home, you don't know yourself."

Bala just growled as he crisscrossed his arms across his torso.

"Would you by any chance help us to find the bandits?"

"The bandits? What bandits?" Kripa turned to Bala. "You said the boy just wanted to know about the woods. I said I knew about the woods and you said all right and that was about it. Nothing about the godforsaken bandits."

"Well, it is about bandits," said Arjan promptly. "The man who knows about the woods also knows what creatures lurk in there."

"I am sure about rabbits and rodents, nothing much else, mates."

"DO NOT LIE!" Bala slapped the large mace on the table, frightening not only Kripa, but also Arjan, who just backed off. The table broke into two pieces. "Uh, shat, sorry," he backed off. "That shouldn't have happened."

Arjan sighed. "It's all right. So, my man, are you ready to fight some bandits or get beaten to a pulp by this man?"

Kripa's sunken eyes glowered. "The bandits come from the

culture of Mlecchas. Now, mate, do you know who the Mlecchas are?"

"I've read about them."

"Oh, but reading and meeting them are two vastly different projects," he growled. "You see Mlecchas aren't just your average forest dwellers who prey on meat. They are vicious, with all sorts of weapons at their disposal…"

"My brother is bringing weapons for us to fight against them."

"Fight?" Kripa sniggered. "Let me tell you something. The Mlecchas are unorganized, disorderly, have no leader and prey on the villagers because they can't fight back. They range from nobles to soldiers of the city who have been wronged, disbanded and sometimes they are the convicts, the murderers, the rapists, kidnappers—all stuck together like a band with one common agenda: to survive and to spread violence. And from what I've garnered through my experience, the unorganized ones are the worst."

Arjan leaned forward. He could feel the tension building and he understood the consequences well, but he saw one goal in front of him—to save his father. Nothing else mattered. "The very fact that they hide in the forest shows that they are cowards." He paused as he pulled out two silver coins, tossing them over to the table. "I'm not hiring you to frighten me, but to work with me. Once you show me where they can be, you are set free, all right?"

"Fine, just the searching and that's it." Kripa looked at the silvers as he picked them up. "Your brother went to the city for weapons?"

"Yes," he leaned back; surprised that Kripa had hung on to that fact. "Why does it bother you?"

"It doesn't really, but it makes me wonder if he will survive to return from the city, as it isn't the same anymore." A toothless grin appeared again on Kripa's face.

17

Kalki opened his eyes to find himself staring at the bright sky. He felt his arms tangled into something and realized he was lying with someone. He swivelled his head to find Lakshmi, cuddling up to him, her face hidden in the crook of his arms.

How did we end up here?

He craned his neck a little, enough to not wake her up and enough to scan his surrounding, realizing the horses were tied to the trees and they still had a significant amount of path to go.

Must have been tired while riding and taken a break.

Kalki made short work of delicately awakening Lakshmi since they did not have too much time. She awoke at once, flustered. "I was supposed to guard, not sleep."

"Guard? What had happened?"

"You had begun dozing on your horse, which is when I tied your horse to my horse. Then I realized I was growing exhausted myself. I waited for the morning, but perhaps I must have gone to sleep too." She rubbed her head.

"I liked it."

Lakshmi didn't say anything, but just turned her face away from him. Kalki got up and went to the horse.

"I see the pine trees," she said, coughing. "We are close."

"That's great."

Kalki glanced at her once again before they began drawing the horse to the main roads and began travelling towards the city. Silence had crept in between them. Kalki could see carts and bullocks, as well as people travelling to the city from other villages. But he also saw the city gates were adjacent to a long stone bridge, where well-built soldiers were reading from pieces of paper before letting anyone enter.

"What are they doing?"

"Toll. The security has been increased. But why?"

"The Tribals," he said.

From afar, the city looked beautiful, larger than life, like a painting from a talented artist. It had variegated shades ranging from maroon to purple, with large buildings, forts and roads crisscrossing the tapestry of livelihoods. It was too big for him to even grasp where it ended, for Indragarh looked like it ended only where the horizon did.

Kalki had been to Indragarh when he was younger. But he subsequently declined to travel for he felt city life was not made for him. He was made for something far greater than the life in these lanes, crowded by the military and people from various ends of Illavarti. It was lethargy as well, for he felt a day's journey wasn't worth it. Unlike Arjan who always wanted to explore the ends of education for he knew education would be at its finest in the city, Kalki hindered himself with his lethargy.

"Oh God," she whimpered.

"What happened?"

"It just dawned on me that I have to ask my aunt for a favour. We are really doing this. We really bloody are." She took deep breaths. "I don't even know if she'll say yes."

"Don't worry, she will, once you make her understand the crisis."

"What if she doesn't?"

Kalki hadn't thought of that. What if? It was a big if which he struggled to not dwell over. "Let's just worry about how to enter the city."

As the horses slowed to merge with the foot traffic, they glanced at the people and creatures around them. It was weird for Kalki; he had heard about the Tribals, but never seen them. He had heard how they looked—dangerous, stout and dark, but they were anything but that. Some of them seemed civilized and nice, but most of all they looked *human.* Only a name separated them from Manavs. How rumours can ruin a person's reputation!

They reached the heavy gates, where chainmail-vest-clad Nagas stood with swords fastened to their belt. Kalki was coming up with all the believable excuses in his mind.

When his turn arrived, the Naga who had long, matted hair asked Kalki, "What is your business?"

"Ah well, we are supposed to drop off some gems for our uncle," lied Kalki in a very garbled accent.

The Naga glanced at the other soldiers. "Your accent seems off. Where are you from?"

"Two Shields, you must have heard of it, innit?"

"Uh, no." The Naga was embarrassed.

Ah well, how would he? Kalki had just made it up.

"I hope you let us get on with our business since we need to reach back by sunset."

The Naga soldier waved him off. "Not happening till you show me a signed letter given by your village headman." Kalki noticed how the Naga accent was almost raspy like a snake.

"A signed letter? My lady, do you have a signed letter?" Kalki looked at Lakshmi.

"Uh, no."

"I suppose we don't have it then."

"We had sent a letter to every village in the Indragarh province that to enter the city, one must have permission from the headman, stamped in order."

"I don't think we got that damn letter."

"Then I'm sorry you are not allowed to enter, now get off the bridge and let the others come."

Kalki clenched his fist. He could hear the rants and grumbles from the back for first cutting into the line and then taking so much time. He looked at Lakshmi gravely. "Just leave for your aunt as soon as I'm going to do what I'm going to do," he whispered.

"What are you going to do?"

"What's necessary—distract them."

He turned to the Naga. "Sorry for this." He began to use the cloth that was hanging at the back of his horse's straddle. He began to cover his face with it.

"What?" the Naga asked.

Kalki punched him in the face. It knocked him off. The crowd behind them gasped. The other Naga pulled out his sword as Kalki kicked at him, while seated atop the horse. The horse yelped and put its hooves in the air. Kalki realized that the Nagas from the gates were following him, by getting on their horses and making their way through the thronging crowd. Kalki, in that moment of desperation, yelled at Lakshmi, "GO!"

18

Kalki was now standing on the horse.

He had crossed streets and bazaars with the Nagas chasing him from all sides and he knew that being in the city on a horse would lead to his eventual capture and then beheading, which he clearly didn't want. He wanted to jump over to a first-storey building, hoping to escape from there.

But it wasn't easy.

As he was struggling to balance on the horse, a Naga appeared right next to his horse. He had a longsword aimed at Kalki. Kalki had been balancing on the back of the horse, which was moving really fast, but he noticed the fast thrusts being made with the longsword.

"You are so dead, village boy!"

Kalki felt his feet were about to leave the horse. He decided to jump from it when he saw the perfect opportunity. What lay in front was a small bridge with a road that led underneath it, to a short tunnel.

And so he jumped, hoping he had made the correct calculations.

With a sickening lurch, he threw himself on the ground and rolled over, the rough stones snagging at his cloak and ripping his clothes. Meanwhile, the Naga smacked his head against the side of the bridge, unable to control his momentum.

"Take that," Kalki grinned.

But he realized more horses were coming on his way. He sprinted away from the bazaar where most people were, as he made his way to the lanes where the clothes were being hung. The horses at the back stopped and the Nagas followed on foot.

Kalki grabbed hold of the walls, jumping across windows and doors, ascending with each jump. As he reached the top, he realized the Nagas were still behind him, though they had fallen significantly behind.

At the top of a three-storey building, he found himself cornered again, as Nagas from each end started towards him. He saw a rope that had washed clothes hung on it. He grabbed it and began to make a loop out of it as the Nagas struggled to reach him. He reached the far end of the parapet and tossed the loop across the building. He saw people were watching him from downstairs. The loop didn't catch anything concrete. He tried again, but by this time, the soldiers had appeared close to him with their swords drawn out.

He threw the loop once again and it didn't reach the other end, but fell down on the road.

"Damn!"

"You cannot get away now, imposter!"

That's when he realized the rope had tugged back hard, as if it had grabbed onto something. He saw there was a chariot below him.

"You wish," laughed Kalki as he leapt from the three-storey building, and on the top of the chariot, until he crashed inside.

In the midst of the broken wood and dust, he saw a woman with makeup and expensive clothes. She was probably a noblewoman.

"Hello there, sorry to disturb you."

"Who are you?"

"I'm not a robber, don't worry."

He heard the soldiers' cries from behind. "But I need to steal this, so if you don't mind…"

The lady was still stunned until she gathered her wits and began to yell. Kalki came forward, grabbing the lashes of the three horsed chariot. It wasn't really big, but it would be fast. He slapped the whip over the horse and it rushed forward.

"Yeah!" he smiled as the horses raced in the midst of the bazaars, destroying most of it, passing by the shops as well as the soldiers.

He saw there were Nagas on each end trying to catch up to him. They jumped from the horse and on to the chariot. With the whip he had for the horse, he used it on them. One soldier even managed to sit next to him, trying to take control over the reins, but Kalki didn't allow it. He punched him in his side, dodged the sword and then pushed him off the chariot as he rolled over the ground. Kalki held off the reins and then crashed the chariot to the building by the side. From there, he jumped down, rolling towards the river that ran inside the city. The chariot kept moving, and the Nagas kept following it without realizing he had dodged them.

Kalki triumphantly preened as he walked inside the gully when he realized he had no idea where to go now. He removed his face mask and tossed the cloak away.

He came on the main road now as he saw the chariot he was moving on had been stopped by the Naga soldiers, who were trying to find where he had disappeared. Kalki stood in the huddle of people who had crowded around this scene.

Naga soldiers were coming around, asking each member of the city that stood there, whether they have seen a masked man. One Naga came up to Kalki with a frantic look on his face, his blue eyes shimmering with intensity. "Have you seen a figure with a black cloak and a turban covered face?"

"Cloak?" Kalki shook his head innocently. "Sorry no, I have not."

19

Arjan was following the so-called guide across the woods, with Bala behind him to keep him in check. Kripa had a certain quality about him which Arjan felt was very unnecessary in this situation—and that was being pessimistic. He constantly cribbed about how they all were going to die.

Bala had shushed him on a couple of occasions, but that didn't work. As they went deeper into the woods, the canopies grew thicker and with that, it led to no sunlight illuminating the path ahead of them.

That was when Kripa stopped them. He carefully crouched down and that entire drunken swagger had disappeared from his body language. Now, he seemed calculative and urgent. He touched the grass, rubbed the mud between his fingers, smelled the surrounding air and with a flick of his wet finger, he tried to figure out the air movement.

"They are here, or at least close by, mate."

Arjan stood on alert, his legs and arm tight with tension. "How far?"

Kripa didn't answer. Rather he trudged forward and opened up a large bush with his bare hands, in between two mammoth size bamboo trees.

"Come here."

Bala and Arjan came forward. Arjan was the first one to gasp at the sight of the clearing, where the sun was brightest and the trees were less. The clearing had all sorts of flowers, with a burning fire that wasn't too bright to attract attention. There were stallions, thick and firm; not like the ones Arjan had seen close to Gurukul or even at the sarpanch's house. These horses were fed well. There were three purple tents, hammered to the ground. And he saw the Mlecchas in person, well and clear. They had initially been covered with silken cloaks and masks but here they looked just human. A few had scars and bruises with scorched clothes and were better in physique than the ordinary village folks. Bala could perhaps take two of them at most at one go.

He couldn't see his father and for a while, he thought that he had been killed and buried. But then he saw his father in chains, wearing the same clothes as yesterday, coming out of the tent with a man who had hair like thorns. Vishnu and the bandit talked to each other, the thorny haired one speaking for the most part before he took him to the side, where the remaining cows were.

"It's an evil practice," Arjan began, "if a Brahmin murders a cow with his own bare hands."

"That's just ancient history, mate," Kripa said. "Everyone eats cows now."

Arjan nodded distastefully as they backed off, hoping to not get caught.

"Well you saw it, now I should leave."

Kripa began to move, when Bala lay out his hand to stop him.

"Not so fast," Arjan said.

"What happened now?" Kripa asked irritably. "I did what you asked me to do and I brought you to the men who kidnapped your father. Now if you don't mind my suggestion, let him be like that. You can't save him, just so you know, mate."

"I didn't care about your opinion. Not then, and definitely not now," Arjan raised his brow. "I don't even know when Kalki will return," he mumbled to himself. "What should we do Bala?"

"Smash them?" Bala suggested.

Arjan had a fit of laughter. It was honestly relieving to see his father alive, but the cows were growing less in number and they didn't have a lot of time on their hands.

"You don't suggest we battle them all? That would be worse than death. That'll be torture, mate." He said. "Especially with the leader of this clique."

"Leader?"

"The thorny haired man? You didn't notice?"

"That's the one I noticed, yes," Arjan said. "What about him?"

"Oh, his name is Keshav Nand. When I was in the city, minding my own business and being the humble drunkard I am, I had seen this decree being pasted on the walls. I cared to look at it and learnt it was this man," Kripa signalled at the back, "he's a wanted man, just so you know, after he escaped the prison."

"What was he convicted of?"

Swallowing a lump of nervousness, Kripa answered, "Mostly killings, yes. But uh well killings of children and women, so that is the worst kind. He was a madman according to the decree. He has a dagger with many curved edges. I have heard it helped him to cut the human flesh nicely and tenderly."

He paused.

"Makes me wonder though why he has taken your father as a hostage," thoughtfully Kripa mused. "I am just saying, he isn't a man you should pick a fight with. Killers of this sort, they have neither remorse nor any understanding behind their actions. For them, it is mere fun."

Arjan saw the skies turning dusky. The evening was bound to descend at any moment and he had no time at his disposal.

"I have a plan," he said.

"A plan? Well, everyone has a plan, mate, until they are hit with a blade," he said, "and in your case you don't even have a shield or a blade to defend yourself; even if you know how to defend yourself which I'm sure you don't, so the best option you have is to be on your way." He looked at Bala. "But if there were three of them like him, there could have been a chance. There are ten bandits out there, all vicious and trained and you are just a pretty boy with a tough boy who loves his little toy dearly. Now let me put this plainly; who do you think will win?"

Arjan smiled after the long and arduous speech, which he filtered out of his ears. "Who said we need weapons to win?"

"No weapon? Eh, boring!" Bala exclaimed.

"Yes."

"And what do you propose we should kill them with then? Sticks and stones?"

Arjan looked at the trees. "Not really, but with ropes and branches." He smiled.

20

When Takshak learnt the masked figure had ruptured and destroyed the entire town, made fools out of his men, he came forth and slammed the map of Keekatpur, where Indragarh was the capital. He began to chalk out the places and magnify on the position of the east, south and west, as the north led up to the colder regions where the sustainability of villages wasn't a probability.

And when he did try to find Two Shields, nothing turned up.

Of course. He lied.

"Have we had any displeasure from any citizen?" Takshak asked his Lieutenant Ulupi. "Any robbing incidents?"

"None whatsoever, sir," said Ulupi.

Unlike Takshak who had his long hair winded into a top knot, Ulupi had short hair like grass blades. He had the same inherent sapphire eyes, but a meek exterior. Takshak didn't mind Ulupi for his exterior, for his mind played well; unlike others who were just brazen and brawny on the outside.

"Have the gates double checked and do not let anyone in, except for the chariots of the ones who work for the palace," Takshak said. "I want to find and execute this person."

"All right, sir."

That was when one of the guards entered the war room.

"Sir, the bird has exited the nest."

Takshak nodded.

Takshak left the room, saying he had personal work. He took two of his less armed guards, for he didn't want to attract any attention. The night had come forth and he was already seeing the stars now, and they were more in number than the previous night. Takshak had a thing for the stars.

Takshak had the intruder in his mind, but he also had to take care of the work Vasuki had given him. He was now on the road and had been on the east side of Indragarh close to the Peepal Street, while all of the humdrum was happening in the south, so he had no possibility of knowing it. But one thing the village intruder had done well was to disrupt the merchant practices of the Yakshas, in the very place where the bazaar was being held. Everything had been destroyed and Takshak had a plastic, wide grin when he heard about it.

He had seen Vedanta and how he travelled across the state talking to people, granting their wishes, giving out charity and promising a better future. This was the third day of following him. And then he had gone to an inn and hadn't come out…until now.

The bird was him and the nest was the Inn.

Takshak got off of his horse and concealed himself in the side lane, away from the multi-storied inn. Takshak then went across the road and inside the inn.

As he entered, everyone in the lobby just stood up, even the manager who was sitting behind the wooden counter.

Takshak slowly walked in the front with his two guards, his tunic flapping at the back, with his hand around the sheathed blade.

"How can I help you, General Takshak?" the moustached manager asked.

So he knew about him.

"I'm curious about your latest visitor."

"King Vedanta?"

"Yes." He tapped on the counter as he signalled his man.

The guard handed a few silvers on the counter which the manager just stared at.

"I'm sorry, sir, I am not allowed to…'

Takshak didn't smile. He held his gaze. "All right," he nodded, looking around, seeing some of the travellers seated in the lobby reading books and chatting. "I have been told by an informant that there is an involvement of soliciting at this inn."

The manager gasped. "No! No, sir! Those are outrageous lies!"

"All right," Takshak didn't care as he looked at his guards, "take all the keys."

The guards came behind the counter, pushing the weak manager against the wall as they grabbed the long, bronze keys.

"Wait here and make sure he doesn't escape since he's going to face a lockup today."

The manager pleaded with him, but Takshak turned a blind eye to him as he walked upstairs. At the first storey, he began to open doors. While some of the travellers were alone, others were with their lovers. Takshak didn't care about their privacy as he opened every door till he came to the final one on the top floor. It had two doors, one perhaps for the balcony, overlooking the entire city.

Takshak opened that and found a figure standing with his back towards Takshak.

"State your name and business in this town for a mandatory check up…" and then his voice trailed off when he saw a familiar mongoose wrapped around the figure's head.

No.

"Is that another name for spying now?" The sleek, slimy voice was too familiar.

"Kuvera," he sighed a little breathlessly.

Turning towards Takshak, the fat man, and the head of Yakshas grinned at him. He had thick, bushy brows making him ugly, but had no beard and was hairless on the rest of his body.

"How do you do, my good friend?"

"I am not your friend," Takshak came forward. "What was your business with the king?"

"Now, that's Vasuki speaking, not you." He smiled, "but if you are so eager to know the why then you might as well just ask him." He gave a slight nod.

Takshak turned to see Vedanta with his brusque, slightly obese figure, and belatedly noticed a hefty and bearded man entering the room and without a word stabbing a serrated dagger across his arm and then sliding it down, rupturing his arteries.

"Ugh, that's bloody," said Kuvera.

Takshak fell on the floor.

"W-w…"

"The snake shit is trying to speak," Vedanta said.

Kuvera walked casually and crouched a little. "Speak, darling."

"W-w-why?"

Kuvera grimaced. "Why, eh? Well, where should I start? But even if I do, I'm sure you'll not even live to hear it, so it's no use. All I can say is me and Vedanta, we have mutual interests."

21

Kalki had been leaning against a building wall as night had fallen. He had been waiting for Lakshmi outside the Government Residence, hoping she'd exit but it had been hours and he was unable to even enter the place. He began to take a stroll and then quickly decided to take a short nap. Suddenly there was a sound, the sound of broken wood.

He looked up and saw a figure. It was like a dream, as the figure was floating and soon Kalki realized, it wasn't so when it dropped in front of him.

Surely the Gods didn't send him for me.

Kalki felt guilty for feeling humorous at this juncture, but he made his way to the body and realized it was a Naga since there were the noticeable eyes and the inked design over his arm. But as he noticed the design, he saw it was more of a rattlesnake than an ordinary one.

Must be of the higher authority, but why was he here?

Kalki looked up again and there was no one.

He felt for his pulse, but he didn't find one. He had a long, fatal gash on his arm, the only place where he wasn't covered by the iron armour.

What's going on with this city, damn it?

"Hey, you!" he heard someone speak.

He looked up to find two Nagas standing in front of him.

"What are you…" one of them grew silent when they saw the corpse.

"I swear I found it here, it fell from…"

The one guard, in horror, swept his hand across his mouth as he said to another in nothing short of a frightened whisper, "It's the general."

"Fell?" The other pulled his blade out, instantly alerted. "Do not move, murderer. You shall be hanged for killing General Takshak of Indragarh."

"What? No, I didn't do…"

The blade was poked at him.

"Don't you dare speak again," the other one who was checking Takshaka's pulse now continued, "the boy even has blood on his cloth. He must be given away to the wolves, take him to Lord Vasuki."

"Lord Vasuki…no…"

"Hands at the back."

Reluctantly, Kalki did as he was ordered while he was tied with ropes behind his back.

"I will wait here while you call from the headquarters," the soldier said to the other. "And keep this suspect in the lockup until we are clear."

"You will regret this," Kalki added.

But he was still pushed around with the Government Residence in the background, drifting as he walked further. He was getting late and he had to reach by sunrise, otherwise it would cause him his father's life. He took a deep breath and tried to reason with the guard, but it was to no avail.

"I will give you money."

"Bribing a guard is a strict offence."

"I'll give you money to avoid that as well."

"All the money in the world can't save you. You were standing over a dead officer's body. You know what the punishment for that is? Death. As simple as that."

"That's a quick judgment to pass. I'm glad you aren't applying for the judiciary."

"Who says I haven't?"

"Oh you have, my my."

He saw a chariot exiting from the gates of the Government Residence just then, and it was none other than Lakshmi. Even from far, her eyes and her sculpted face was visible.

"I need to go…my friend…"

"Your friend, eh?

Kalki had had enough. He stopped and clenched his fist and with as much force as he could muster, he tore the ropes apart. The guard instantly got alarmed, but Kalki paid no attention to his shivering blade, held by weak hands. He grabbed him by the collar and pulled him up.

"I told you, you were committing a bad mistake. Sorry." And with a shove, he pushed the guard ten yards away.

Kalki rushed across the empty street to the chariot, whose reins were held by Lakshmi.

"You got a vehicle?"

"My aunt gave it to me."

"I suspect she gave you the weapons as well."

Lakshmi signalled at the back. Kalki pulled up the ornate curtains and there were all sorts of shields, swords, daggers, javelins and bows with arrows.

"How did you convince her?"

"Oh, that's my secret power, saddle up. She even told me a way out of the city that isn't guarded well till now, so we can sneak out from there."

Kalki sat up. "I'm ready."

"All right, also I want to know for sure if everything went all right as you sacrificed yourself…uh…hold on…is that blood?"

Kalki looked down. “Uh, yeah.”

“Don’t tell me you killed someone.”

“Oh no.”

“What happened then?”

“We have a pretty long journey,” Kalki wiped the sweat beads off of his forehead. “I think we can discuss that during the course of it.”

22

Vishnuyath had been exhausted. He didn't realize he would have to work at night as well, cutting off the fat, searing the loins and then chopping up the leftover meat. Vishnuyath had recommended leaving the cutaway tenders for two weeks, mostly covered with ice to bring out the softness, and eliminate the rawness, but Keshav didn't listen. He had a cleft lip with hair that resembled mini-sized daggers protruding from his skull. He spoke awkwardly, and if anyone would even by mistake chuckle or grin, he would suffer consequences.

Vishnuyath had trained himself to survive this turmoil when he told Keshav he knew how to take care of a cow, but Keshav had to spare his son, Arjan, in return.

"We only need one of them." Keshav had said glancing at the father and son.

Vishnuyath was perplexed by the statement and by the time he had been bound, Keshav's men reached for Arjan to kill him who dodged their attacks and escaped. The night had begun to fall and Keshav ordered his men to leave the premises, forgetting Arjan. Keshav made sure everyone who witnessed the invasion was cut apart just like the cows Vishnuyath was going through now.

And now, he had been forced to help them, being their chef for reasons only Keshav knew. He was so tired of doing this sinful act of cow slaughtering that he even tried to escape, but to no avail as Keshav's guards stood at every place. Vishnuyath had heard that Mlecchas don't take survivors and here they were doing the opposite

Vishnuyath didn't feel great about it. With each cut he made to the cow, he closed his eyes and prayed for forgiveness to Goddess Kamadhenu. But he had to do it for survival and for his son's survival. It was horrible, he knew. With each cut, Vishnuyath had to stop the blood that flowed all over his clothes. Luckily, Keshav was kind enough to give him a long piece of cloth to cover himself with.

"Why did you leave the tongue out?" Keshav asked.

Vishnuyath realized he was standing behind him. Keshav crouched and whispered in his ears, "cut the tongue for me."

With a disgusted frown, Vishnuyath pulled out the severed head of the cow, first slicing its tendons and then pulling out the tongue, slashing it with the thick knife he had been given.

"Give it to me."

The smell of the dead cattle disgusted Vishnuyath. The entire clearing of the woods had become dirty with all the littered carcass and entrails.

"Should I heat it up?"

Keshav didn't care to respond, but rather put the entire raw tongue in his mouth, chewing it fast. The sound from his mouth made Vishnuyath's stomach roil in disgust.

"You do a good job, villager." Keshav patted him on the shoulder. "We mean no harm to you. We are simply waiting."

But for what?

"Hey boss!" someone from his group called.

"What?" Keshav shouted back.

"How come a religious man like him is allowed to cut our meat? I mean, they have rules and all right? Don't they have their Gods and Goddesses of all kinds?"

"Yes, I wonder how."

"I don't mind," Vishnuyath quietly said.

"A propagator of atheism, my friends," Keshav clapped. "You believe in no God, am I right?"

Vishnuyath didn't answer. Keshav just looked at him eerily for a while before he slapped him on the back with appreciation. "He is fine."

Keshav went over to his tent. Just outside of it, there was a hanging cage which Vishnuyath had seen. The cage had a talking parrot and from what Vishnuyath had witnessed, the parrot was a genius. Keshav, to see any dangers lurking around, would let this parrot fly and come back. If the parrot would continue screeching, it was a sign that they had to be careful about the dangers lurking around. But Keshav didn't treat the parrot right, wouldn't give him enough food and had a chain locked around its ankles. Whenever he would send him out, he would tie stones to him so he couldn't travel too far. He would threaten the parrot as if it understood him, which Vishnuyath knew he did, for the parrot was indeed a genius placed in very wrong hands.

He tried squeezing the remaining life out of the parrot and it began to peck Keshav hard over his palms, but it didn't matter to him. He was just maniacally grinning at the blood from all the quick piercings.

"Yes, my love, do it, do it, I feel it." He squeezed harder and the parrot screeched loudly. And then Keshav dropped him inside. The parrot began creating an uncontrollable noise till Keshav just chuckled and closed the cage.

"Our eyes," he signalled at Vishnuyath, who had been continually staring at Keshav, which he had noticed. "Beautiful creatures."

By the Vajra, Lord Indra, save me from this horror.

"Who wants to gamble?" he shouted at his friends. Surely there was no hierarchy amongst them, since they all had respect and disrespect for each other on an equal measure. It was only Keshav who had been the craziest. He would lead the group, speak what he pleased even though he was least intimidating physically.

Vishnuyath walked over calmly to the cage, while the backs of the Mlecchas were to him. He knelt next to the cage and tried to pet the parrot, but it made an uncontrollable noise.

"Calm down, I'm one of the good men," he said, but the parrot didn't stop. "All right, fine, let me help you with a snack." He had a glimmer of happiness as he dug his hand into his dirty tunic pocket and brought out a piece of bread. "You want some, my friend? Here..." he prompted the parrot by feeding him from his hand. The parrot backed off. "Fine, I'll just leave it right here, so I hope you don't feel threatened then." He tossed the bread inside the cage as the parrot looked at it for a while. By just the look of it, the bird seemed to be scared, almost shocked that someone offered him sympathy. And then it bent down his neck like a crane and fetched the piece of bread.

"Hey, here you go, my friend." Vishnuyath clapped calmly. It was almost a moment of happiness for him. "You are friendly. What is your name?"

The parrot continued to eat the bread by keeping it next to him and pecking it. When it was over, the bird slowly walked with his tiny legs to the end of the cage and pushed his head out.

"What do you want? You want me to pat you?"

Quietly Vishnuyath chuckled to himself as he tapped on the parrot's head. Then he scratched the light feathers, feeling how something could be so soft and tender.

"What is your name, friend?"

The bird didn't say anything.

"These deviants must have not even have given you a name, eh? Well, you are quite friendly and beautiful. Why don't I call you...Shuko?"

The bird flapped in appreciation. "My name is Vishnuyath Hari. But you can call me Vishnu, my friend. I was named after the founding Gods of our creation. Lord Vishnu was the valiant warrior who brought order to our society, the seeker of dharma."

"Vishnu! Vishnu!" It began to cry out loud in happiness.

"What's going on there?" One of the Mlecchas shouted.

"Uh, nothing."

Vishnuyath came to his feet and stepped away from the cage. "Will give you a piece of bread later."

Everyone began to play their so-called in-house gambling game, where they had chalked out houses with pebbles and threw dice to see who one had the highest number, around a piece of cloth that had squares made on them. Vishnuyath was on the other side as he came towards the terrain, close to the uneven slab of rock, and leaned over it, the splash of cow blood on his hands and his feet as he felt a soothing relaxation finally coming over him.

I can't be here like this.

The last time he was in the land of heretics, was in an unknown village of a name he had forgotten and he was travelling with his cattle, travelling from the fire-ravaged city of Suryagarh. He had rushed, but he realized there was an infant, coiled in a white blanket in the midst of raging flames. Dust hadn't settled and Vishnu knew he had to choose between goodwill and business. And he did the initial thing, leaving the cows behind and saving the child he didn't know about. At the end of it, when half of the people had left the village and the other half had been the victims of the fire, he was with a child, smoke riling up around him and his face dark with all the ash and soot. He had retreated close to the remaining tree, hugging the weeping infant, when he looked at the wonderful eyes it had.

Who are you?

But it didn't matter for him. Vishnuyath knew what he had to do at that moment. He had to take it home, for leaving an infant in an infirmary or to another family would be a crime. Perhaps it was a gift from the Gods, and he was given this precious child as a chosen beneficiary. He hugged on to it and when he reached Shambala, he had already named the infant by the name of Arjan, after the warrior Lord Arjun.

But for now, his mind had returned again to reality for that fire in that village was nothing compared to the situation here. He watched the parrot again wondering how long the bird had been trapped here, amongst people like Keshav. He pitied the bird. He watched him for a while until he realized the bitter metaphor of his entrapment. Just like the bird, he was here as well. And for how long, he had no idea.

23

Arjan had grabbed all the twigs he could break from the trees as he moved to the centre where Bala had been scraping the land, digging what was left of the ground. He had a shovel he brought from his hut.

The morning had come by and all three hadn't slept one wink. Arjan wasn't tired, for his plan was in the process of materialising. Arjan dropped the twigs inside the dump.

"What do you plan to do with that, mate? Have a fire pit? That's a bad idea since Keshav's party will know about it. The smell of fire is more fragrant than the smell of…well anything," he stifled a laugh.

But Arjan didn't mind at all for his ears were immune to Kripa's insults and taunts. He took two stones and began to rub them together, for he hadn't brought the fire lamps with him. And going back to the village would only cause a delay in executing their plan. He began to rub it faster, the rocks creating a spark or two until dying down again. With the leaves, he tried to rub the rock on that, and create energy—he had learnt it at the Gurukul. He instantly saw sparks flying. He rubbed vigorously and eventually, a fire was created. With an utter exclamation of joy, he threw the burning leaves inside the pit. He began to give air to the fire to grow.

"You did it, shall we go back now?" Kripa asked.

Arjan turned back. "Time to have fun," He walked to the nine feet log while Bala followed him. The logs had been tied to the tree at one end, stuck to its trunk. The rope it was tied with was long and thick, and would go far if thrown in the right direction.

"Go to the opposite end and wait for my command."

Bala nodded and began to wander to the side with his bulky body avoiding the wet mud. The land in between the two trees was a little curved.

"What do you plan to do with those now?"

"Now it's your turn."

"Turn? What turn?"

"Go down, in the middle and call out Keshav."

"Are you kidding me, mate?"

"I'm not."

"Why me?"

"Because my hands are full if you can see."

"Bala has more chance of survival if you lose. I can push a log all by myself and I'm good at pushing logs, the very best I tell you. Please let me push the damn logs."

"Yeah about that, no," Arjan shook his head. He was having fun with all of this, finally getting back at him for so many pessimistic remarks. "You'll be safe. Just dodge the logs in time."

"Dodge the logs…" his voice quivered.

"Go now before it turns more dangerous than it already is."

"What do I have to do?"

Arjan thought for a while. "Do your thing," was what he could come up with in the most succinct manner possible.

Meekly Kripa walked over, sliding down the land. Arjan noticed it was visible from there. If Arjan could aim well, they would be able to hit a bunch of Mlecchas at one go.

"Hello there! Is anyone there? Anyone? I happen to realise I can find Keshav here. Is anyone there?" Kripa called with his usual drunken swagger.

Anticipation began to tighten Arjan's muscles as he pulled back the logs. He signalled Bala to do the same. They had stretched it far, hoping someone would come.

But no one did.

Kripa looked up at Arjan; he was almost glad no one appeared in front of him. He shrugged. Arjan gave a shush signal and told him to wait wordlessly.

That was when the forest shuddered. Kripa turned away from Arjan to his front. Out of the forest appeared Keshav with his three men. At the clearing, Arjan could notice how stocky Keshav was in comparison to the others, but he was deadly, with his sharp nose and cleft chin.

"What do you want?"

"Oh hello if it isn't the great Keshav Nand himself!"

Keshav looked at him for a while as if trying to understand the fool. "Kill him," he told his men.

The two men came forward with the curved blades.

"Now we can settle this like civilized people."

They still came forward.

Two was less, according to Arjan, but he had to do it. He looked up at Bala as the two of them began to come to the target zone. Casually Kripa moved back and he nodded at Arjan surreptitiously. Arjan nodded at Bala and when his fingers began to slip, he realized he was about to kill someone. The very idea of it haunted him, but he had to do it. *I have to, for my father.*

And that was when a sharp pain went through his arm. His eyes manoeuvred to the site of pain and he found an arrow seared in his arm as it began to bleed profusely. From the back, he saw two Mlecchas appearing. Arjan saw Bala had two arrows in his own back.

No.

They found us.

"PUSH!"

Arjan with his own mighty effort, pushed the log horizontally, the rope tightening in the process. The two guards looked at the side, where the log squeezed them in between, their bones cracking.

Arjan pulled out his arrow as he saw the Mlecchas smirking. The pain intensified when he had withdrawn the arrow, for it had sunken deep into his flesh and now he could see how his muscle was responding to it. His hand covered the gash.

He thought he had won by killing two outcasts, but he was wrong. Those were just baits to distract Arjan and Bala. *They are ready to make their own people baits. What monsters are they?*

One of them said, "It's time to meet your daddy, son." And he grinned brightly.

24

Kalki was about to reach Shambala when Lakshmi asked him quietly a question that had had her unsettled.

"Why is Bala helping us?"

"What makes you ask this?"

Kalki looked away to the clouds and the woods that they were leaving, as they were entering the village area. The city was darkened with smoke and industrial waste from the armoury, mines, dirt and bazaars that occupied the thinnest of lanes. He had seen the royal fort, but it was far off from the city.

"It just makes me wonder what a tavern's guardsman owes you. Why else would he offer to help you?"

"Owes me is not a neat thing to say," Kalki said. "I don't let people owe me. I help them without wanting any favours in return."

"I know. Which makes me wonder why he helps you," prompted Lakshmi.

"I help him occasionally at the tavern free of cost, the times when it is necessary."

Lakshmi looked at Kalki, studying his face. Her mouth had grown into a frown with her brows furrowed and her grey eyes staring at him unblinkingly. "You are lying," she said, finally concluding with a smile. "It's so evident. If you don't want to tell me, just say you don't want to tell me but it only makes me wonder what sort of crime you have committed, so as to hide a simple fact from me, since you tell me everything."

Kalki sighed, his chest feeling heavy. "We have reached." He diverted the topic as he saw a huge plume of smoke spiralling out of the woods, yards away from his dairy farm. "Something's burning, perhaps."

"Yeah."

"Where are the others?"

Kalki walked around, but found no one in the village. There were donkey and bullock carts. He bypassed the Mitra's household, crossing the Tripathi hut, finally reaching his house, where even mother Sumati wasn't present.

"Where did they all go?" he asked Lakshmi.

"Where did they all go together?"

Kalki instantly realized. *There's only one place.*

Kalki had reached the Soma Caves, passing the uneven trail of road that zigzagged across the ascending mountain. He had brought the chariot with him and he could see the people milling around Soma Caves, watching him in shock and delight. The kids began to get excited at the sight of the chariot while the adults just gasped. Sumati was in the front, carrying out prayers with a *thali* in front of the Soma Caves. That was what they did whenever they were in trouble—go and pray at Lord Indra's site, where he had performed penance and gifted Shambala the magic stones.

Sumati came forward, while the group behind her led by Devadatta stood still. He played with his moustache, curious about the exchange that was to emerge between mother and son.

"Where were you gone?" she asked.

"I was in the city."

Her expression didn't shift but she looked back at Lakshmi,

who was standing meekly. Kalki blocked her vision just then and Sumati just raised her eyebrows.

"It was my doing. Not her's," he said loudly for Lakshmi's furious parents to hear. "Why aren't we protecting my father? What are we doing here?"

"We are doing the same. I'm protecting my husband."

"With this?" he looked at the thali. "This is not saving him in any way."

"We are praying to God and we will make sure that Lord Indra and Lord Vishnu would bestow his safety over my family..."

Kalki ignored his mother.

"I believe in the greatness of this place, but it won't help us fight those outcasts."

Kalki's face remained impassive. He held Sumati for a moment almost in a state of tender love and then he made her stand beside him. Sumati was heaving with anger, but not after she laid her hands on him again, and Kalki knew why. Kalki had come forward and he had a certain leadership quality about him; his neck up, his eyes narrowed. Devadatta didn't even dare to speak as Kalki eyed him with calmness and clinical sterility.

"I had gone to the city of Indragarh, the nucleus of Illavarti, to bring back weapons to fight those Mlecchas. We can sit here and pray to the Gods or we can go up to those hills and fight our way through. Those Mlecchas didn't just kidnap my father, they kidnapped our peace, our love, our hopes and our desires. They made us think that we are weak and fragile, villagers, common folks. And we are proving them right by standing here in front of rocks, praying to a God who might never even come from the heavens. He might one day, but that day isn't today. Today is our day. Today is the day where we can prove to those outcasts and the Gods that we are not just villagers. We can be warriors as well; we just need to have bravery and valour on our side," he paused, as he took a deep breath.

Devadatta took a deep breath. "Let's just say, for argument's sake, if we agree to get the weapons, where should we scout?" he continued. "It's better to send a request to the city to send us a helping party than just scavenging the entire area."

Some of them nodded in the group while others just remained conflicted. Kalki knew there were a few, who, if convinced, would join his band to defeat the forest dwellers.

"The city won't send anyone, for they are already being corrupted by their political intrigue. It's horrible out there, with the infestation of the Tribals," Kalki said.

"Nevertheless we believe going up foolishly and wasting our time at that dark forest is just…well…" he continued, but Kalki chose to not listen.

At that point, a realization hit him. Kalki looked up at the woods again, the bright lush greenery that sprawled ahead of them. And there was the circle of smoke coming out.

I will signal you when we find them.

Signal? Of course.

"So your argument is we don't know where to look for, right?"

"Exactly," Devadatta nodded. "If we would know, I will personally take an axe and go there, I tell you. Sarpanch or not, I'll be the warrior. But unfortunately, we don't know where they are."

Kalki crossed his arms, trying to conceal his smirk. "Well, what if I say I know where they are?" Devadatta's mouth grew small as he tried to loosen the tight collar of his tunic. "I think you should get that axe you were talking about."

25

The evening had dawned and Vishnuyath saw his son Arjan wounded and tied around the peepal tree with his companions—a burly, mammoth man and another lanky individual whose face was entirely covered with hair. He had wrinkles and was quite old. That was when he realized who it was. The realisation came to him as the man watched him intently. There was a clear but wordless understanding between Vishnuyath and the old man.

Why is he with my son?

But Vishnuyath didn't ponder on that question for long since Keshav crossed him and came forward with his friends, circling around the tree. Keshav didn't speak, but one of his men did.

"You barge in as if it was your own land, you killed two of our men; and for that, your punishment is death."

Vishnuyath's feet weakened. He felt mortified at the very thought of his son's death. Kalki had been always the more adventurous and stronger one, unlike Arjan, who took steps only after thinking hard. What in his right mind made him lead two more lives here?

"Can I speak to him, please, my lord; please can I speak to him?"

Keshav grunted. "I had a father once; I wish he loved me this much. Go."

Vishnuyath staggered to his feet, and on reaching the tree, he hugged Arjan tightly.

Arjan whispered, "Are you all right? Are you hurt? You have blood on you."

"I'm fine son; you didn't have to do this."

"If I wouldn't have…I would have never forgiven myself."

Vishnuyath cupped his hands over Arjan's cheek. "You are a fool, you understand, you are a fool." And then he hugged him again.

"I always tried to be your real son, but I failed. I got caught."

Vishnuyath pulled him back, and locked eyes with him. "Don't say that. Don't you dare say that. You have no idea what I feel for you."

"It's always been there, even though you and Mother kept saying I was the more dependable son. But I could see that you were trying to please me, so I could forget I was adopted. I was nothing but a stranger to you; I was a weakling, found in a barn, an infant who had no parents."

Vishnuyath regretted telling him all of this. He hated Arjan for saying all of this, but he hated himself more for telling him the truth. He shouldn't have. He could have kept it inside, held it all together, but he had to spill it out—just for his damn penchant for honesty. Vishnuyath understood that it would have been far better to speak lies than to speak the truth.

He saw his broken son. His arm was bleeding, but he was hesitating. He was disappointed. And that was when Vishnuyath said to Arjan, "You are more a son to me than any father could ever have wished for."

Keshav's men grabbed him at that moment and pulled him behind. Vishnuyath turned to Keshav, his hands and legs feeling out of place, almost on the verge of collapse as if they had lost their bearing. He grabbed Keshav's feet tightly and began to beg, his eyes streaming with tears. Keshav looked at Vishnuyath for a while, with a sense of confusion in his eyes. Vishnu searched for some sign of forgiveness, but none was seen.

"Leave me." He kicked Vishnuyath in the face, as he rolled over on the other side. "I granted your wish. Now see your son suffer."

Arjan yelled, "You think you can escape! You have no idea."

One of Keshav's men asked, "What are you talking about? Who is coming?"

"Your death will…by my hands."

"Our death?" Keshav's accent was garbled. "Our death is in our hands," he spread out his palms.

"I don't believe it."

Keshav narrowed his eyes. He pulled out a dagger and went close to Arjan. Arjan just stood there with bloodshot eyes, watching Keshav.

Vishnuyath prayed. *Please don't. Please don't say anything. You have no idea what he's capable of.*

"Believe this."

Keshav used his dagger and began to slowly carve a scar. Arjan's skin tore, his mouth contorted into a silent shriek of pain as the blade slowly tore through his face. Just below his eyes, crossing his nose, to his other cheek, his face drenched in his own blood.

Vishnuyath yelled, his hands and his feet frozen on the floor.

"Something to remember me by," Keshav grinned. "Always mark the dead, to let others know who it was that did it."

"I challenge you. You say…you say…" Arjan began shivering. Vishnuyath could see he wanted to wish away the pain. "You say death is in our hands…why we…w-why don't don't we…" he gasped, "we play a game?"

"Game?"

"I saw you were playing pachisi." He signalled over to the gambling zone. "If you win, you kill us. If you lose, you leave us. You are a man who'll stick to your…eh…um…right? Eh? You don't want your friends..." his voice got loud, "to know you are not a man of your word. That would be a pity since they believe in your word so much."

Keshav looked at his men. For a moment, there was a flicker of uncertainty in their eyes.

"Oh right," Keshav nodded. "Those rules change...if I win, I'll kill your father first," he pointed at the frail Vishnuyath, "carve and torture him in front of you so you'll see what your loss has led to. Okay?"

Vishnuyath knew that Arjan now had his father's life in his hands.

"All right," Arjan nodded.

26

There was one problem. He didn't know how to play pachisi.

Arjan had confidently and clumsily agreed to a game he had seen from far off during his years in the Gurukul. The other students would sit around a cloth, which had multiple squares and cowries to move their *gitte* or pieces forward on. The pieces were of two colours. He had never been interested in that because he was mostly rummaging through ancient scriptures and books, learning about the ways after the Breaking and how life had evolved over a period of time. Arjan had curiously seen the same cloth and recognized there would be some gambling involved. Now he wished he had learnt it enough. He sat opposite the madman Keshav, while his father's life was at stake.

Where the heavens is Kalki? I gave him the signal.

He had to stall for time. Vishnuyath had been kept separate from Arjan. Bala and Kripa were still tied to the tree, their faces strongly marked by the restive atmosphere around them. Arjan had a cloth over his face to stop the bleeding. It had hurt worse than a fall he had experienced when he had been training to ride a horse at Gurukul. He had sprained his leg and had cried all the way back to the infirmary. Right now, it was worse and while tears were burning his eyes, he knew he had to bear the pain.

"Well?" Keshav's marble eyes glinted. "Shall we?"

Arjan nodded. The pieces were kept in the middle, and were of two colours. One was for Arjan, red; the other one, black, for Keshav. The middle had a round circular design. Keshav's entire gang had circled around the game now, except for the few who were standing to guard the prisoners.

"Beat him, boss! Beat him!" All of them goaded him.

Arjan was given brightly coloured cowries. "You go first." He had to see how he would play.

"Alright," Keshav took the cowries back and began to shuffle it in his hand. He tossed them softly on the ground, scratching his chin in the process. There were two cowries that faced up while the others were down. "Two steps." He took a piece and put it in front.

It depends on what is up and what is down.

Arjan began to shake it in his hands. He tossed it then. There were five cowries that faced up. Everyone gasped in shock.

"More than mine," Keshav chuckled.

Triumphantly Arjan forwarded the pieces. He had a hint of a smile, the little he could give with the amount of pain he was suffering from.

And thus the game continued. Arjan made sure that with each toss, he would rig the cowries by turning them inside his palm with his little finger, so that when he gently threw it, they would fall favourably. For a while, Keshav didn't notice anything amiss, until Arjan realized that Keshav had tossed a jackpot. No cowries were turned up.

Everyone clapped, almost to the point of annoyance. Arjan didn't know this part of the game. But then Keshav used his pieces and brought them forward by twenty-five squares. Arjan realized that with his cowries, he was supposed to reach the centre. From whence they had left, they had to return to the same point, without being overcome by the opponent player. That was the game. And it felt so much like Arjan's life right now.

Keshav was clearly winning. Arjan dropped three ups and he came forward with one of his pieces in the same square as that of Keshav's square. Keshav groaned, taking off his piece and putting it back in the circle. For a while Arjan was glad.

The game continued for an hour, where with each of Arjan's moves, the result was continuously being thrown off-kilter. Keshav's men kept abusing him and Arjan just shuffled and tossed while Keshav was able to bring the earlier piece from the centre back to the forefront, with all of his other pieces inside the circle except for one. Arjan had two pieces left, but he was almost twenty paces behind, while Keshav was just three. His heartbeat was pounding against his chest. He felt overwhelmed and shocked with what he had gambled. He was a fool.

No.

And that was when he heard it. It was a loud, screeching sound of a cough. He saw Kripa coughing continuously.

"I apologize."

Everyone frowned at the old drunkard.

Keshav began to shuffle in his hand again when Kripa coughed. "Shut up!" Keshav yelled. "I am trying to concentrate," he said with irritation. And that is when it hit Arjan. He looked back with his one eye while the other was folded by a cloth, tightly woven around his head. He saw Kripa and realized he wasn't such an old drunkard, after all.

He knew the game.

When you shuffle, that is when you try to distract. That is why whenever Arjan tried to shuffle, Keshav's men began to chant, talk and trouble him verbally so he wouldn't be able to concentrate on the cowries and throw them the right way.

Arjan gave a slight, acknowledging nod at Kripa.

Keshav was shuffling hard, his eyes maniacally watching the game as he was planning to throw and win the game of pachisi—and just as he was about to toss, Arjan sneezed. It was a matter of a split second, but it made all the difference. The result came with two cowries while the rest were down.

"*Dooga*," Arjan grinned, as Keshav angrily put his pieces two steps forward.

Arjan was given the cowries. He had to pull out twenty-five paces forward which meant all the cowries needed to be up. He prayed to Lord Vishnu as he began to loosen his grip and toss the cowries…

"What is that boss?" one of the Mlecchas spoke up.

Above the little view of the skyline the canopies offered, there was visible smoke, engulfing the blue skies.

"Fire?"

"Smoke," the other was horrified. "It's a trap!"

Keshav glanced at Arjan. Arjan felt a terrible void in his heart, mingled with extreme fear. His body had just turned cold, his toes curling, his skin growing white.

Where in the heavens are you, Kalki?

"Kill," said Keshav.

All of his men drew their swords out. The sound of clanging blade against the sheath mortified Arjan.

"And start with the father," he paused, "we leave after this, right now."

Everyone nodded. The guard close to the tree came to Vishnuyath, who had been cornered against the branch.

The blade came forward. Arjan yelled in agony.

And then there was the sounds of hooves—multiple hooves.

27

Startled, everyone looked up to the direction of the sound. The overgrowth and the bushes were torn, and the twigs were broken as a chariot appeared in the clearing, with Kalki on top of it, holding a bow and arrow, with Lakshmi wielding the reins beside him.

And with them, came an entire band of people, more than the awkward eight party band of Keshav. Keshav immediately stood up with his dagger, while Arjan leapt on to him before he could attack anyone. Kalki meanwhile had leapt from the chariot and was aiming arrows with deftness and precision.

But Arjan couldn't care less of what was happening around him as Arjan had grabbed hold of Keshav's arm and was not letting the dagger go in any direction. Keshav pushed and pummelled in the air but nothing worked until Arjan did the unthinkable. He bit his arm. Keshav yelled in pain as he left the blade, tossing it on the ground. Keshav pushed Arjan, and with his legs, locked him and pushed him down. Keshav continued to punch him hard till Arjan could feel his nose lose sensation. Arjan kicked him between the legs, leading Keshav to collapse back, groaning. Arjan wiped the blood from his nose. He went to grab Keshav, but he rolled over and began to get away.

Arjan saw Kalki was shooting arrows while Bala was using his mace. Lakshmi was using a spear and the others were pitching as and how they could, not used to any sort of warfare techniques. Many were injured, as they staggered, relentlessly in pursuit of a triumph, but clearly failing. He was unable to find Kripa and his father. His eyes scanned around as he called out to his father. Just then, he saw Kalki.

"You came early," Arjan grunted.

"You are no one to complain. I never thought you would be captured. You really are my brother." And his eyes narrowed. "Are you okay?"

Arjan couldn't help but smile. "We can talk about my miseries and injuries later."

"Take this." Kalki gave him a dagger. "Use it now," he panted, "and don't spare anyone. Fight like it's your last day."

"You don't even know how to fight and you are giving me life lessons?"

"Want to gamble on that?"

Arjan rolled his eyes. "I've gambled enough for today, brother."

And that was when Arjan's eyes met Vishnuyath's. Amidst the battle, he was the lonely old man, weak and fragile, unlike others. Arjan signalled Kalki to protect Vishnuyath as they moved forward.

Vishnuyath's face brightened on seeing both his sons, but just then, an arrow pierced his back. Arjan was the first to see as Kalki was shooting arrows at the enemies. At the sight of his father, Arjan yelled, even as he could feel numbness take hold of his body. Arjan knelt next to Vishnuyath. Kalki saw what had happened and shouted in agony.

Arjan grabbed Vishnuyath and put his head on his lap; Vishnuyath was giving him the same tolerant and patient look as the one he had given Arjan before he left for his educational tryst at the Gurukul. That look which asked him to bear difficult moments in life with positivity and equanimity.

Arjan held him tightly. Kalki came the other side as Arjan slowly massaged Vishnu's head. Kalki instantly pulled out the arrows.

"You two...are...the greatest...gifts to this world," he said. "Arjan, don't forget you are part of the Hari family, not anyone else's..."

Arjan beamed.

"And Kalki?"

"Yes, father?" Kalki lowered his head down.

Vishnuyath's arm went towards the other side and it signalled at Kripa, who was sitting away from the scene of violence.

"What about him?" Kalki asked.

"Kripa?" Arjan inquired.

Vishnuyath nodded. "Kripa...Kripa...cha..."

Arjan looked up, and at that moment, Kripa shared a distinct look of contact with him and Kalki. And that was when there was a sudden shift of weight and Vishnuyath's eyes glassed over.

Arjan dug his head against his dead father's chest while Kalki patted him on the shoulder. Arjan looked at him. "I can't believe...I can't...I can't...he wasn't supposed to...he wasn't supposed to die."

There was another arrow flung really close to Arjan when Kalki caught it. Arjan's eyes widened, shocked at what Kalki had just done. Kalki clenched the arrow and it broke in two.

Kalki stood up, as he began to walk further, heading straight towards the danger as the Mleccha shot another arrow. Arjan saw the arrow pierce Kalki's skin, but unlike Arjan, Kalki didn't yell. He withstood the pain. There was another arrow and another until there were five arrows sticking through Kalki's chest, tearing at his clothes. Kalki broke the arrows, pulling them out as he grabbed the Mleccha by the throat.

Arjan continued to watch spellbound, while Vishnuyath remained in his lap. Kalki grabbed the weak Mleccha by the throat and pulled him up with ease. Arjan could not believe his own eyes, seeing this virile display of strength in front of him. Kalki continued to squeeze the neck, holding it as tightly as possible until it snapped. Arjan turned away, though he could hear the body collapse.

The war was over. The village had won. But Kalki and he, they had lost.

Kalki stood over the dead Mleccha, before walking away as if none of it mattered to him. It was all maya, an illusion.

Arjan walked over to see the Mleccha. There was a gentle smile that played on his lips. It was of a mocking look of sadistic pleasure, for the corpse were none other than Keshav Nand.

28

The burning…the deaths…the horror…

A boy managed to rummage through the piles of burnt out books and charred remains as he saw the people succumbing to the flames. He managed to make his way out, hoping to be able to find—his sister. Seeking her, breaking barriers, entering the tents, he finally saw her just as he saw something horrible. The man who was responsible for it…the man who did all of it…it was just a glimpse, but he would remember his face forever. He was tall, taller than most of them…and he had a scar that ran over his forehead. It was so deep and so horrible that it was leaking pus and blood.

The boy managed to hold the infant in his hand while he heard the others. *The others…there were others…*

There were cries coming from his siblings.

Kali woke up. He could feel every inch of his frame burning and aching. He slowly touched his head and realized he was running a high temperature. And at that moment, the door opened. Perhaps it was his cry, but it had led Durukti to enter frantically. She knelt beside him in concern.

"I couldn't save them…I couldn't save our brothers…our sisters…"

"It's all right, it's all right." Durukti began to pat him, cleaning his clammy forehead and running her fingers through his hair to calm down.

"KOKO! VIKOKO!"

The two generals entered instantly.

"Get me cold water at this instant and get me the shaman as well!"

They nodded and stormed out.

"You'll be fine, brother." She kissed him on the head. "You'll be just fine. You just need some…"

"The sins of my failure…t-t-they are catching up to me…they are going to kill me," he mumbled, his pupils growing white, while his soul began to feel like it was ripping apart from his flesh.

"No, no one will kill you, no one will kill my brother, I promise you that." She hugged him as tightly as possible, his head against her chest. "You'll be just fine."

Kali was leaning against the bed now. A damp cloth, drenched with water, was placed around his head while Durukti held onto his hands. The sweat had dried and he felt better, but his chest hurt more than the last time. The shaman had left and Koko and Vikoko were standing aside, concerned. It was always a delight to see them together, for they both looked so similar and yet distant. Vikoko had her blond hair tied in a braid while Koko had short hair, but both of them had the same build, which complimented each other.

When he had met them for the first time, Kali was young, but they were younger.

We all have grown up together.

Durukti dismissed them.

"Are you all right?"

Kali nodded. He lied, because his chest felt heavy.

"Don't worry, I'll be fine."

"You said something in your hysteria."

"What?"

"About seeing a man with a scar," she said.

Kali narrowed his eyes. He didn't remember. "Did I?"

"You talked about leaving our siblings behind."

"I always do that when I feel afraid." Kali clenched his teeth. He was in a position of fear, over which he had no control. "You know that."

"What happened then wasn't your fault."

"But I should have known." Kali looked away from her.

"At least, you protected me."

"Yes."

Kali wasn't disappointed. He was glad he was able to do that. But it still haunted him, killed him from the inside, his stomach churning and his mind somersaulting, convulsing into morbid thoughts of the counterfactual.

"I HAVE TO SEE HIM!" There were yells from outside.

He could hear the protests and the way Koko and Vikoko tried to stop these protests.

"He's resting."

"Resting? He should be doing anything but resting. I have been betrayed and let down!"

Kali gave an acknowledging nod to Durukti, who went to the door and opened it.

"Let him in."

Koko and Vikoko stopped and Vasuki entered the chambers, clearly ticked off and agitated.

"How is your health, your highness? How do you feel? Should I bring you something else while bodies of my men continue to pile up?" Vasuki complained mockingly.

"Don't you dare speak to…"

Kali held her palm tightly and Durukti was silenced. He knew it was his fault, being in bed, but he had no idea what ramifications it had caused. "What happened, Lord Vasuki?"

"Takshak was apparently stabbed and thrown from a three-story inn," Vasuki added. "Imagine who would have the audacity to do that?"

Kali knew what Vasuki was implying.

"Do you have any proof?"

"I am searching for it, but just so you know, the slightest inkling, and it will mean war. I'll send an army to massacre that fat worm of a creature. Sitting on all that bloody wealth!

"I know Kuvera and he's a man of his words. He promised he wouldn't kill anyone to incite a war."

"Well, he's backing off from his word, for words don't matter anymore." Vasuki stopped pacing in the room. "Just so you know, Kali, we had a pact and I made sure to uphold my end of it. I gave you the responsibility for maintaining peace among us. But if you are not *fit* to do that, I will have to find alternatives and you won't like that at all."

"Is that a threat, Lord Vasuki?" Even in dire health, Kali's voice sent chilling tremors down Vasuki's spine.

Vasuki looked at him, stunned for a while. "I am investigating this myself. If I get time, I shall tell you what I find. Till then farewell, as my sister Princess Manasa is coming to visit and bid farewell to her best friend, General Takshak. I hope to see you there at his funeral as well."

And with that, he left.

Clasping his palms and placing them over his head, Kali began to frown and tried to think hard. *What should he do?*

"What happened?" Durukti asked.

"You know what happened," Kali shook his head. He called out to his generals, who were standing and guarding his room. They entered.

"I am sure you heard what the snake said," Kali began. "I want you two to find out who did this. And investigate faster than the snake. I don't want him to cause any break in the peace I have barely just negotiated and put into place."

The twins nodded and left, this time for the exit of the fort.

"It's almost sad when you lose something from your grip, something you achieved after so much effort."

"I understand, brother."

He gave a warm pat on her cheek before drifting back to sleep, hoping to recover from the fever and the body ache. But his mind wandered back to the village that burnt. There had been a reason why he wanted the so-called Tribal and Manav peace. For it was their bitter rivalry that had led to his family's demise and the burning of his village.

Who was the scarred man?

For it changed everything. The fight was never about peace, but about secrets. And those secrets rested in the ends of his mind, somewhere he was too frightened to unlock and look for them.

29

Kalki didn't leave for the *antyeshi* of his father. He was too weak for that, unlike Arjan, who carried out the funerary duties. He was changed; his face had a scar which instinctively made people recoil. The scar was a reminder that Arjan would lament every day of his life. That was worse than death. He had seen, from far, the *antyeshi*, away from his disappointed and grieving mother who knew no consolation. She deserved better than a bunch of Mlecchas taking away her husband. She deserved so much more for she had always been a noble woman.

He travelled to the place where the bloodshed had taken place. Kalki came here, not to recall the tragedy, but to see if his father had left anything behind. The tents of the Mlecchas had been torn down, and the horror of the fire pits was filled with Mleccha bodies.

The triumph of a battle often ends with innocent casualties.

And that was when he heard it. It was like a croak—a harsh noise that pricked his ears, as the words came glaringly clear—

"Vishnu! Vishnu!"

Kalki knelt down. In the midst of the broken down tent was a cage and in it there was a dishevelled but magnificent parrot, just looking up at Kalki.

"Hello!"

"Vishnu!"

"How do you know my father's name?"

"Shuko! Shuko!"

Kalki didn't understand. He pulled open the cage door and let the parrot fly away.

"Vishnu!"

The name was almost hurting him. The parrot must have known his father, some way or the other. Kalki didn't have anything to feed it, so he just patted it. The parrot climbed on his hand, slowly making his way up to his shoulder.

"Shuko!"

"Your name is Shuko then?"

The parrot pecked at his tunic in acknowledgement.

"I suppose we will call you Shuko then."

He walked up towards the village. "I hope you will tell me all about how you met my father."

He sat close to the river. The wounds were still hurting him, making it hard to even breathe properly. He picked up a pebble and tossed it across the water, making it skip across the surface. Shuko had flown away to get food, and he wasn't back yet. The funeral was over and Lakshmi had come looking for him.

She sat next to him and didn't say anything for the next half an hour. Kalki didn't mean to speak as well. They just remained silent and he liked that. Any other friend would have felt the need to speak up, say some comforting words and leave. Lakshmi wasn't like that. She understood Kalki more than anyone. And she understood that words don't cure grief. Kalki felt his fingers interlocking with hers as they watched the sky's bright blue meeting slowly with the orange tinged dusk, and the clouds looking like the handspun pieces of gauzy cloth.

"He did a mistake. And he wanted help. So I did," Kalki began.

"What do you mean?"

"Bala," he said, turning to her, "you asked me about him, right? What does he owe me? What does a guardsman of a tavern owe me? He allowed a young child inside. 'Allowed' is a strong word since the girl sneaked in without his permission. He couldn't stop her but it was his fault, for he didn't return for her, to pull her out, to make her understand that it was a bad place for kids like her. She was just thirteen."

Lakshmi's face was curious as Kalki kept watching her.

"She didn't understand that men don't see a kid as a kid when they are drunk. They see a woman, and they don't have limits, no rules that bind them."

"Who was she?"

"I don't know. We asked around."

"What happened exactly?" Her hand tightened around his palm.

Kalki began to narrate. It was a year back. The tavern wasn't just a place where you could get drinks. It had a lot of rooms and it had a lot of women offering sexual favours. Bala had forgotten about the girl who went inside. In the morning, he went through the rooms, with a bucket of water and a mop, coming to the last room that was locked. He called Arindam, the owner of the tavern, and he was surprised as well. No one dared to lock rooms there.

Bala smashed the door open, breaking it at the hinges to find the room was stinking of spilt wine and coitus. And in the corner, there was a girl. She had been hiding; her clothes were ripped, just like the blankets around her.

"Sometimes there are no resolutions to conundrums," Kalki continued, "We never got to know who the person was. Bala looked for me and asked for a favour, for me to help her find a home."

"Did you?"

"Yes, in another village," he paused. "He cried on my shoulder and it was awkward. He cried until he could no longer cry and he blamed himself for what had happened to the girl."

Lakshmi looked down.

"I didn't want to tell you, for you would judge Bala. He was forever in debt to me, even though I did it not for him but for her. He didn't care. He promised he would protect me and my little brother as long as he would be alive."

Lakshmi nodded. "I don't judge him. You are wrong about that, you know."

"Perhaps I am. We forgot who we were and we forget how we used to be around each other. It has been two years since we last saw each other."

Her fingers ran through his hair. "I missed you a lot. I have changed, yes, but don't forget me. I'm still the same, just with different ideas now."

Kalki smiled. The slight touch of her fingers gave him butterflies in his stomach. It was an eerie feeling for him. It made him feel happy, the touch of her. It made him feel glad and he wanted to just hold onto it.

"I also am a bearer of news."

"What happened?"

She took a deep breath, as if it was a way to apologize. "I know we have seen a lot, but the last time I went to meet my aunt, she asked me to return to the city, said things have settled down in Indragarh and it would be all right."

"Why didn't you tell me?"

"It wasn't the right place or time."

"For how long?" Kalki's voice quivered.

Not again. He would be left alone.

"I don't know for how long, but it'll be for a while, sure."

"I don't want you to go to the city again."

"I know."

"Will you then?"

She blinked, perhaps contemplating. "You know I will. I still will. I want to be like my aunt, authoritative and strong and educated. Shambala would make me anything but that."

Kalki wasn't disappointed. Rather, he expected that answer. "Well, that's something that's never changed about you." He paused. "I'll come to visit you this time, I promise."

"You better. My aunt promised me that she'll get me a job at a library. Imagine how cool would that be?"

Kalki nodded. "Books are interesting. Might I bring Arjan then as well?"

"Of course."

They both smiled each other. Kalki saw a glint of happiness in her eyes. Lakshmi made things better for him. Even little things, like the way she would keep complaining, or the way her brows would go up while nervous, it all made him see her in a different light. She was adorable.

She came forward and he did it too. His heart was pumping hard, his lips had gone cold, and his eyes were beginning to close, when…

Shuko appeared, croaking loudly.

"Kalki! Kalki!"

Kalki and Lakshmi pulled back instantly, realizing what they were about to do, especially on the day of the mourning. Lakshmi had gone red while Kalki felt his skin grow warm. His heart was beating hard and he had never felt so unsettled in his life.

"Who is this?"

"Shuko." The parrot sat idly on his shoulder. "Made a new friend today."

"Interesting." She laughed.

And they both saw the sun dip, their fingers still locked with each other.

Next morning, Kalki trudged on the path to the tavern with Bala. Arjan was left behind to take care of his mother.

"Are you sure, brother, it was him?" Bala asked.

"Oh I'm sure."

"He's no one but a…"

"No, he's someone, I bet you on that."

They reached the hill where the drunkard, Kripa, had been leaning against the rock, sleeping with a bunch of mugs around him. Kalki had even managed to bump into him once. He recalled how he had been walking from Lakshmi's home, the day she had returned from Indragarh and had met him.

That wasn't a coincidence.

"I followed him yesterday to this place. He was at your father's funeral, brother. Away from the crowd. Such a coward. On the day of the fighting, he had hidden himself."

"My father wanted me to talk to him, for he knows something," Kalki said to Bala. "I am sure my father didn't randomly pick him. He knew his name even. He said Kripa something."

"He said Kripa something." He paused.

"Let's see what he has to say in his defence."

30

Things were all hazy for him until his eyes opened and he found himself in a different atmosphere. It was cold; terribly, horrifically cold. Wrapping his lanky arms around his chest, Kripa came onto his feet. There was the sound of a crack underneath his feet and he realized he was standing on ice.

That's not nice.

The chilly breeze made it worse for him as it distracted him. Carefully, he tiptoed to the edge.

This is not what I expected.

"Well, you had your fun," he shouted to the skies, still precariously standing over the thin sheet of ice. "You can help and rescue me otherwise I'll die of cold, mate."

And then the ice broke at the edge, plunging into the freezing water below. Kripa pulled away and slowly made his way towards the solid layer of ice, where he saw a figure standing. Towering and bulky, the figure had a tiger skin wrapped around him, with an axe hanging from his back. His long hair was matted.

"You always have your fun, mate," Kripa remarked. "But stop calling me in these dreams, all right? It gets all heavy and hurts…"

The figure stayed there, silent, nostrils flaring.

"What do you want, Bhargav? I showed you the battle, right? We saw what he did. He's the one." Kripa's voice had changed. It had become stern and deeper.

"You *can* speak normally."

Kripa sighed.

"You have no idea how much energy it takes to get in your head and it isn't the most pleasant place to begin with." Bhargav Ram walked, while Kripa struggled to follow. In front of him, Kripa looked older and dirtier. There was something about Bhargav, a sense of grandeur and majesty.

"I never allowed that."

"Do you think I have a choice? Since your nephew has gone astray, away from his destiny, you are the only one I can count on."

Bhargav sat on the ice platform, which he had conjured up, harnessing the energy of Soma.

"In his defense, he was never supposed to follow a destiny, after that curse and all, the poor kid…"

Bhargav laid his palms flat. "No. He was. He was promised the heavens if he would agree to it and follow it. But he didn't. And he's hiding. He could be a far greater problem than Adharm right now. He was last seen in the Temple of Shiva…"

Kripa's blood ran cold. "I thought I had blocked that place well."

"Apparently you didn't. He found it." Bhargav stamped his feet, and a deep crack formed on the icy floor.

Kripa's heart skipped a beat.

"If he gets his hand on the Sword of Shiva, we are in great trouble. We are still stuck with the hero you think he is."

Kripa shook his head. "He is and I can feel it. You saw it for yourself. I was right there, showing you everything."

"I saw what he did, but he's weak." Bhargav listlessly remarked. "How will he defeat the prophetic evil? No one so emotional should be allowed to be Dharm in the first place. I don't know what the Gods planned for him to do."

Kripa shook his head. "No, I see the greater good in him. You call it emotional; mate, but I call it strength. For no good comes with cold calculations, mind you."

Lord Bhargav Ram turned. He walked towards Kripa. "Says the man who orchestrated all of this. Weren't you the one who paid the Mlecchas into kidnapping the boy's father so he would show what he's really capable of, and then backstabbed the Mlecchas, who didn't know what was coming for them? All the time consistently making use of your nom de plume and using middlemen to do your work?"

Kripa's heart sank. "I did it at your command. Don't blame me. I work for you. At least it worked. We didn't wait all this time for nothing, eh my friend?"

"I'm not your friend." Bhargav furrowed his brows. "I sense great awakening of the Adharm. Soon we will face an adversary. I wonder if the fates are playing games with us. We had tried so much for the prophecy to not start, but the fates bypassed us and made us their prey. I didn't want the Age of Adharm to start, but now I feel it is about to."

"I was one day late, I know," Kripa nodded. "Otherwise we wouldn't have a Dharm as of now," Kripa said, but he knew the fates would have improvised around that as well and done what was written according to the scriptures. The Words.

"The last Age had been horrible for us. We all were victims," Bhargav paused, as if he had let out too much of his emotions. "I want you to do the necessary arrangements, get him ready and bring him to me. He must have the sword before anything else, and must be trained; otherwise we will lose…again."

Kripa nodded. "You have my word."

And then his chest jerked and he was pulled from somewhere, everything going black around him. The sound of chirping birds and the smell of sura overpowered him, until he felt hard kicking against his thighs.

His eyes opened fast, watching two individuals standing in front of him. They were familiar. He was away from the ice and the coldness. It was something about snow, and the north, that horrified him, especially the mortifying lopsided and jagged hills.

Kalki had a parrot sitting on his shoulder which was odd but made sense. At least, it followed the Words—what it said. *He's the real deal. Thank God. No more searching for the hero anymore.*

He sighed with a grin on his face. This was the triumphant return of the secret manipulator, Kripacharya. He wanted to congratulate himself.

"What in the heavens are you smiling about, drunkard? Wake up and speak to my friend. You have had enough sleep for today."

Kalki knelt. He had a lot of scars, visible through his loose tunic. He had browner skin than most of the folks at Shambala.

"We need to talk," he said, pursing his lips.

I had figured so.

Kripa stretched his arms and then looked back at Kalki. "Would it be weird if I tell you that I was *just* dreaming about you?"

And both the visitors shared a look of puzzlement with each other.

31

"You should leave," Kalki told Bala, as they reached the Soma Caves. "Thank you for coming."

"Are you sure?" his thick, hoarse voice blurted.

"Yes, I am. I need to deal with this alone. Go back and see if my mother needs any help."

Bala nodded in understanding and then went off with his mace dangling from his shoulders. Kalki smiled as he realized he was one of the few friends around.

Kalki turned to face Kripa, who was standing gazing at the wonderful orchids that circled the Soma Caves whose exterior had been blocked by a huge boulder.

"Why did you bring me here?"

"You asked me how your father knew me. Well this is where we met for the first time." He laid his hands out. "He was a neat fellow, mate, and a worried man at the time I met him." He paused. "It was before you were born or at least, you were about to be born."

"How old are you?" Kalki asked.

"More than hundred, but I've lost count now."

"How is that possible? You drink like it's the end tomorrow."

Kripa smiled indulgently. "Because I have been gifted, though the correct term would be 'Endowed'."

"Endowed?"

"Yes." He said. "You believe this is the only Age we live in, full of peace and chaos. No. There were a lot of Yugs, or Ages to be precise, and I was in one of them, the last of it. I had saved plenty of lives and I had been endowed by the last Avatar. A chance at immortality."

Kalki couldn't believe his ears. He had read about immortals, the ones who would live on forever.

"The Endowed are also known as the Chiranjeevs."

"That's impossible."

"So is your strength, mate." Kripa grinned cheekily.. "Don't think I have not noticed that. Arjan, your brother, must be burning to ask the question—how can his brother withstand multiple arrows without dying?"

Kalki felt embarrassed. The look of suspicion had crossed Arjan's face and even the other villagers who had witnessed the miracle.

"We don't live in an ordinary world, mate. Not anymore, not since the Ancients have died down and the Breaking has happened." The words were just flying over his head.

"How do you know my father?"

"Let me start from the beginning." He sat cross-legged on the ground. "Every Yug has Dharm, the hero, and Adharm, the evil. The last Age, where I had played a prominent part, had had a vicious war. It had a hero named Lord Govind."

Kalki was mesmerized, for he recalled the name. It was during the history lesson that he had heard about the valour of Lord Govind, a strange advisor to the kings of Aryavarta, who had helped them in winning the Mahayudh. They were all history.

"He was the Avatar of Lord Narayan, or in simple words, Lord Vishnu, the God of all Gods." Kripa smiled. "Or at least he thought he was. I never believed the man. They are all bogus, you see. The scriptures say that Narayan, when he had departed from Illavarti, had promised to return in every Age, when evil would strike in a different form. He would become the Avatar. I don't know how true that is. I choose not to believe in this as I feel Govind chose his own path rather than following the path of Narayan. I'll come to the reasoning behind it." He paused. "Lord Govind had given me and my fr…not friend, but yes, an accomplice, a sacred duty of never letting this Age come again. He didn't believe in the prophecies, or the chosen ones. He felt it was stupid. He wanted to end the cause of all evil—Somas. He felt Somas were what made the heroes and madmen and he felt was best to end the line of madmen if it meant sacrificing a hero of this Age."

He signalled over to the caves.

"He wanted me to stop it with my nephew and my accomplice. My accomplice had to undergo severe penance for he had committed a great crime, and to seek redemption, he handed me the duty to travel alone around this country, and finding the Somas and destroying them."

"What about your nephew?"

Kripa's face turned grave. "He went on a different path. I don't know what he believed in, but he just left. I was all alone and I did it. Constant travel leads to fatigue and so I drink to carry on with my arduous mission. Lord Indra had spread the power of Somas across the country and they were all scattered so it was difficult, you know."

"I don't understand one thing. Why did Lord Govind believe the Somas were evil since they were the gifts of the Gods?"

"Not necessarily," he said. "Lord Indra had good intentions when he spread these stones, but what he didn't realise was—they weren't for Manavs. They were too weak to handle them for they were too sinful. They would go mad, they would make people crazy. That's why the last Yug had a Mahayudh. It was because many had inhaled the Soma fragrance. That's why Govind didn't want people to have it anymore."

"Did he have it?"

"Yes."

"How didn't he go mad?"

Kripa thoughtfully contemplated. "I am not sure about that. We aren't. The spiritual side says that there are the Dharm and Adharm, the only two entities in each Yug who can take the power of Somas and use it for good and evil practices, respectively. And science says some are just built better immunologically. They have better genes or better frames to withstand it, with better mental faculties. We don't have a definitive answer to this question."

"So the Adharm can also withstand the power of Soma?"

"Yes."

"Did you find him?"

"Not as of now. But my accomplice says he's close to getting him."

"What about the Dharm? Did you find…wait a minute…" Kalki narrowed his eyes as Kripa continued to smile at him. "You think I'm Dharm?"

Kripa nodded. "Now comes your father in the picture. I had travelled across the country to reach this godforsaken place. I reached and realized here were the Soma Caves. I knew I had to do something, so I decided to close them."

Kalki looked at the mounds of rock. "How did you do that?"

"I have my tricks," Kripa smiled. "There are some chemical mixtures that can lead to a blast. I'll teach you sometime." He paused. "I had done my job when I was attacked by a figure. He hit me and scolded me for doing this. And I stopped him, trapping him using his own strength against him. He wasn't a fighter, I could tell, but his arms were strong. He was your father."

Kalki never imagined Vishnu to be someone who would hit a fly let alone a man. But then, Kripa was someone who could get on your nerves.

"He said the Somas were God's gifts. I told him it was wrong, people go mad because of it. It's not the right way." He continued. "And he told me about you, about how your mother was so sick during her pregnancy and he had broken all rules, stolen the nectar out of the stones and given it to her, hoping the Gods would help her. And she became all right. Later on, when you grew up, Vishnu saw signs of your strength. He was shocked, but he also realized they could be given to others so we all could be strong like you. He was wrong and naïve."

Kalki recalled how his father would say he was special, he was chosen.

"And at that moment, I was curious. Never has it happened that the Somas could transfer its property like this. Your mother wasn't gifted anyway. It was you. You got the power. And you didn't go mad or die. You were fine; in fact, heroic. You were a spitting image of Lord Govind; the same nobility, valour, and morality, but also the arrogance. You made me believe in Dharm. I made Vishnu understand all of it and he got the idea, which was that it was right to let you grow into a good person."

"But I knew," he continued, "that you had to be looked over, that the amount of Soma you got was diluted. Maybe you were just lucky. But you proved me wrong in the battle with Mlecchas. You are the real deal, mate."

Kalki clenched his jaw. "I don't think…I don't know…"

"The Adharm is close; Kalki." He came forward. "And you need to decide. Are you going to stand by, watching it happen, or are you going to stop it? The Dark Age of the Adharm is where the world ends and we don't want innocent casualties again, not like the Mahayudh."

"What if it doesn't come, you know? You have closed all the Somas. I was lucky; it was just that," Kalki paused. "Why didn't you destroy it, rather than closing it?"

Kripa looked at the temple that was made out of the caves.

"Because one day, and there will be the day when the Dark Age ends, we will all have enriched minds, and on that day, when the sins will be exhausted, the drink of the Gods, this Soma will be opened to everyone and everyone will be able to use it. I have closed it off till then."

There was silence until Kripa spoke again.

"And for your initial question." Kripa laughed at himself. "My accomplice and I often laugh about this. Even though we tried stopping the Dark Age, to prevent the Rise of Adharm and even Dharm, the fates didn't allow us. It stopped us. Sometimes you can't cheat; karma always comes around and does what the destiny has planned. So if you think, the Somas are closed and anyone won't get it to become the next Adharm, there will always be a surprise planned for you, something you won't be expecting. This is how the world spits at and make jokes at you."

Kripa didn't sound like the drunkard he was. Rather, he looked like a man of wisdom and knowledge, someone Kalki really needed in his life.

"How?" he quietly asked.

"We need to leave Shambala as soon as possible, for the Mahendragiri Mountains, where my accomplice will teach you the ways of the Avatar to make you become worthy and fight evil when it rises."

Kalki nodded. "I have so many questions, and yet such few answers. My father knew all along and he never told me."

"Because he didn't want to believe it. He felt it was best for you to grow without having the burden of that knowledge on your shoulder. But now you are old, you are strong, and you are ready."

"Who are you?" Kalki turned. "I know about everyone except you and your mysterious nephew or accomplice. How do I know you are not Adharm?"

"Mate, I am far from that, though I cannot reveal my nephew's identity to you," he chuckled. "The point is, my name is Kripa Acharya."

"Acharya? That's given to the gurus who handle Gurukuls, isn't it?"

"Hence me."

Kalki walked to the cave. He touched the inner granite rocks and felt the strength of it. They were here for good.

"You won't open this again?"

"Not for now."

"What if I need more of this?"

"It's not good; it kills people's minds," Kripa said. "When you are ready and trained, you can do so. But right now, the amount your father ended up giving you still affects you. Soma is good when used once. For the Dharm perhaps, it is healthy, but more consumption can be tricky for we haven't tried it."

"But if I'm Dharm, I can sustain more ingestion of Soma, right?"

"We don't know and frankly, mate, we don't want to try." He shook his head. "We don't want to see how it would affect you, even if it means sacrificing for the good. We don't want to see what the flip side is. It's scary, mate. You need to be careful around it."

"What about Lord Govind?"

Kripa nodded. "He had more before the Mahayudh was about to begin, to get his powers charged. It didn't go very well. He did get the power, but um…it kind of gave him a side effect. His skin turned blue-black. It couldn't withstand the effects. It's scary, I told you. Don't consume more unless it's absolutely important—those were Lord Govind's words."

There was an absolute silence. Kalki recalled the paintings and the portraits of Lord Govind where he was shown blue or dark. His Guru said it's because he was the warrior who fought valiantly and blue is what represents valour, thus it ended up like that. The explanation was clearly all bogus now.

Kalki shook his head. "I have too much in my mind; I will talk to you tomorrow." And with that he moved, all the images in his mind coming in front of him.

32

Ratri had chosen the books from all over Illavarti, carrying each one of them personally, or by her allies, to be put in the library of Indragarh, the prestigious city in the kingdom of Keekatpur. Born in the villages of Indragarh, she had promised to uphold the culture of Indragarh. But much had gone astray as many hopped onto the violent bandwagon, something she had always detested.

Ratri had chosen and tried really hard to work her way through it, step by step. And that was what she had been gifted with—a library. She was exuberant about it. That was her ideal dream, to live and breathe among books. But it came with a price. King Vedanta had taken away her power over the hospitality and cultural programmes. No more theatre or flyers or free speech talks against any injustices done by Tribals. Truth be told, Ratri was never against the inclusion of Tribals. They were clearly the less developed race in front of the race of Manavs. But then it went against her when he took away from her the position that gave her power.

"Uh, we don't want any issues surrounding the recent events and I know you want to be the voice of the people, but the government can't handle this as of now." And he had left her alone. "It would be better if you concentrate on building our national library for now, till things begin to cool down and then you'll be reinstated again."

This had all happened before the moment Lakshmi had come for her help. She was proud to have a niece like her, who strived for knowledge. And she was beautiful, not just in terms of her physical exterior, but she was also beautiful by nature. She was a good person and they were hard to find nowadays. Not many remembered what it meant to be a good person.

Ratri had taken revenge on Vedanta by using her powers to find the leftover weapons from the armoury, which she had tried to pass off as theatre dummy props.

But now, given the library, she wanted Lakshmi more than ever. It was a temporary shift from her powers as the hospitality minister, but it was arduous. The entire library, though stocked with all genres, had no alphabetical listing or orderliness. Her compulsive disorder had kicked in and she was already working with an assigned Yaksha, Kumar. He would speak in a very strange dialect, half of it in his own native language.

Though as of now, things had grown quiet, without Kumar vocalizing anything. From the first floor of the library, amongst the leather-bound books, Ratri tucked a lock of hair behind her ears and looked down. "Where are you, Kumar?"

"Madam?" The voice quipped from far off.

The figure stumbled excitedly until he reached Ratri's vision.

"What happened, Kumar?"

"There's a visitor specially to see you."

"Tell him or her I'm busy! Don't you see I'm busy? I'm bloody, damn busy."

"But madam, it is… it is Lord Kali's sister, Princess Durukti."

"You mean Lady Durukti?"

"Yes, yes, that…" he chattered in his own language, "she wants to talk to you…" and his voice trailed when the booming voice of a woman came forth.

"I'll take it from here, Kumar."

"Oh your highness." Kumar propelled himself, bowed and

knelt down in respect. Durukti signalled for him to stand, as her guards took him aside.

Ratri looked at Durukti, wondering if it was about the weapons she had given away in a moment of hasty decision. *What has Lakshmi done with them?* All Ratri was told in terms of an explanation, was that she needed to trust Lakshmi.

And here Lady Durukti was, bearing down upon her at her library. She was a pretty woman, quite majestic for her age, but she had a sense of grandeur that went with her image. Ratri didn't find it strange, for she was all dressed up. Physical appearances, though, were just societal injunctions according to Ratri.

"Yes? How can I help you?" Ratri came to the point, without wasting time with niceties or polite small talk.

"I hear you are the most educated woman in this city." Her voice was gentle.

Ratri was impressed. Moreover, because Durukti had just complimented her and she had liked it.

"Yakshini is a complex language." Durukti was still on the ground floor. "It took me a while to learn it as well, but I promised myself to learn all the Tribal languages before I would bring them together with my brother."

"You did a good job out there, my lady, but how can I help you? I'm quite busy and it'll be great if you can get to the point…"

"Have you heard of Shambala?"

Ratri looked up from the books, peering through the iron rails that supported the first floor. "Shambala?"

"Yes."

I am from there, Ratri thought.

"I have heard about the Soma Caves there. Is it true that they hold the medicinal capacity to cure the weak and the dying?"

"The flowers, yes. You need a qualified botanist to extract the juices out of it. I had a cold and it cured it."

"I'm not talking about the flowers. I'm talking about the caves."

She furrowed her brows. "You have heard the bogus stories as well then eh? I'll just be very practical with you, my lady. I am a woman of science and books. The last thing I'll really believe in is a bunch of stones that give you flying powers and cure your diseases."

"Flying powers? I didn't know about that."

"Oh well, let's just say people who ingest Soma get superhuman strength, which has never been proven, so I hardly believe it."

"Has anyone ever taken it? If yes, what were the side effects?"

"Presently, no. The caves in the village have been shut down by the quakes. No one can enter. There was evidence of Soma consumption in the past, but they are all history book stories. They are all hearsay! Nothing true whatsoever, since nothing was definitively proven! Prove me wrong and I'll gladly agree to be hanged."

Durukti had a quiet, worried face. "I see. Just stories, then," she spoke disappointedly.

"Just stories indeed, my lady."

"Do you have a map to Shambala?"

Ratri nodded. "Check the G isle, and the map of Keekatpur would be in it. Many villages aren't listed, but you might find sufficient information on Shambala."

Durukti signalled her guardsman who checked the line. She studied the map intently as Ratri slyly peered over her shoulder while doing her work.

"You got it?"

"Yes," Durukti mused quietly. "Might I take this book for my reading?"

"Surely," Ratri struggled to pull up a grin. "We haven't started our memberships, but you are the first customer, so feel free to take it but don't forget to return it. I hate delayed returns."

"Don't worry," Durukti gently smiled. "I will."

Ratri waved her farewell as she left the library. Ratri rushed downstairs and ordered Kumar to close the doors. He did so and then returned as Ratri sat down next to her study table and pulled out a paper. With a quill and an ink, she began to write.

"What is wrong, madam?"

"Nothing." She began her letter to Lakshmi. "Do we still have the messenger eagle?"

"Yes we do."

She folded the letter and sealed it so that no one would open it. "Send it over to Shambala's message post."

Kumar looked at the letter. "What happened, madam?"

Pursing her lips, Ratri said, "My family is in danger."

33

Kalki had reached his hut. It was still the same. Regardless of whatever had happened, nothing changed about it. Bala stood like a guard outside. He looked sore from the wounds sustained on his back, as he stood crookedly, but he had a gentle smile on his face. He entered, moving past the living room and missing his father's presence. Kalki wished he could spend more time with him now. Regret burnt inside him, but he recalled those moments when he shared words of wisdom with him. He scanned the rooms, searching for his mother.

To his surprise, Kalki realized she was folding Vishnu's clothes and wrapping them into a mound.

"Where's Arjan?" Kalki asked. "I thought he was with you."

"He left a while back," she said without looking at him.

Kalki furrowed. Where could he go? Perhaps the farm, which he would check after he made sure his mother was all right.

"Mother, are you fine?"

She looked up. She did look tired and weary. She had large bags under her eyes.

"Are you?"

Kalki clenched his jaw. "Stupid question, I know."

"No it's fine, Kalki. Grief makes you lash out when you don't want to," she smiled wanly. "But you should never let it overcome you."

"Why?"

"Because it's transient."

"I'll miss him."

She nodded, but didn't say anything.

"Why are you packing his clothes?"

"I'll give it to the beggars. He would have wanted to share with the less fortunate."

That was his father. Kalki smiled to himself. "I'm sorry I couldn't save him. I could have if I was instinctive, but I was too…"

"I know he isn't alive. But that doesn't mean he isn't here."

Kalki couldn't help but think how right she was about this.

"Don't be apologetic. When you were given those powers by the Gods, they knew you couldn't save everyone."

Mother had said this in rhetoric terms, but she had no idea how true it was, for it had been the Gods who had given him the powers through the medium of Somas. She thought they were gifts when Kalki had exhibited them in front of her. It was Lakshmi and his parents who knew his secret which made Kalki feel guilty, for he should have told Arjan by now.

Why hadn't he? Did it scare him as to how he would react?

"Not even my father?" he paused. "He was the most important person, the one I should have saved."

Sumati nodded. "Perhaps. But everyone has their time." She came forward and grabbed his arms tightly. "You shouldn't let these things put you down for these things are what help you grow as a person and become someone extraordinary. We think tragedy is when something bad happens, but I see it differently. I feel tragedy is bad, but it makes you rise as a hero, because it gives you courage and a sense of reality. These are the true signs of a king."

Kalki sniggered. "I'll never be a king. I'll hate wearing the damn crown for one."

"A crown doesn't make someone a king,"

She put her face against his chest and Kalki could feel the hot tears on his chest. He couldn't help but tear up as well.

"What if I have to leave this place to become that king? What if I have to learn the ways for that?" Kalki recalled the conversation he had with Kripa and how he had to leave Shambala to become the Avatar.

She didn't say anything.

"Should I?"

"Why do you ask?"

"Do I need to have a reason?"

There was another pause.

"Vishnuyath told me something that I need to tell you."

"Yes?" His heart leapt with inquisitiveness.

"Strength in a person doesn't define a hero. But where he uses his strength is what matters the most. A hero isn't born. He's made. Through people, through journeys and most of all, through tragedy." She pulled back. "You can go wherever you have to, Kalki, but don't forget where you came from and what made you who you are. Because we often forget the people or place that made us when we become something. Make sure you always preach love and kindness, because there's less of that in this world,"

Kalki wiped her tears.

"How will I spread kindness?"

"By reciprocating," she said. "The Mlecchas had less of that, thus they lost their objectivity. Our world will be a lot greater if we stop spreading hate."

Kalki nodded. "I'll keep that in mind, Mother. Thank you."

And they embraced again.

Kalki reached the farm. Arjan had been standing close to the stable, watching the leftover cows. He had huge sacks of grain packed up and loaded on the bullock carts. The entire field seemed isolated, as the sun was going down and evening was about set in, with the twinkling stars that would brighten up the sky.

But Arjan stood alone, just watching. He didn't wander nor do something, to Kalki's surprise. Kalki watched from afar.

"I don't know what we should do with this, Kalki. I just don't know," Arjan said without looking back, his back facing Kalki. Arjan had his fingers, close to his lips in a thoughtful gesture. That was always what he did with them.

Kalki fed some grains to Shuko, who was sitting on his shoulder, as he walked to his brother. The sun died in the background as Kalki strolled along.

"With the place?"

"Yeah." Arjan's scar was starkly visible in the dusky light. It was horrendous what had happened to him, but he wore it like it was nothing. "I don't want to give it away."

"We shouldn't then."

"All of father's workers have died and so has he," Arjan said it flatly but Kalki knew there were emotions simmering beneath he surface. "Who will take care of it?"

"Perhaps we should."

Arjan scoffed, "I believe we can, but was it always your dream to be a dairy farmer?"

"Dreams are often not accomplished," Kalki said.

"For those, who don't dream big."

"And what do you dream to become?"

"Travel most probably, learn history, meet tribes and cultures of every kind and not just the ones who were allowed under the Treaty of Indragarh, but also those who are hidden from us." He paused. "I read in a western historical book that there's a tribe that suffers from a rare hair disease—they look like monkeys. It would be a wonder to see them. Just because of how they looked, they were outcasts and thrown in the jungles."

"Seeing monkey people?" sniggered Kalki. Kalki. "That sounds interesting." Arjan also smiled at the ridiculous idea he had formed in his head.

"What do you dream about?"

That was a question Kalki had to ask himself, for he had forgotten to think about himself at all. He had so much going on that he realized he had no passion, no drive, and no hopes at present. He had been lost, but this question prompted him to strain his brain and think hard.

What do I want to become?

"I know it sounds abysmal…" he chuckled at the mere thought of it, "but I just want to be happy and content."

"Do you not dream big? Do you not want to travel?"

Kalki rounded his arms around his little brother. "Perhaps I chose not to. Perhaps big doesn't always matter. It's also the little things, specks of happiness that we go through in a day that we should look out for. It's funny how grief makes you realize the good things you have overlooked in life."

"And what would that be?"

Kalki grabbed his neck and began pulling his hair. "Like my little, stupid brother."

Arjan pushed him with a grin. "You don't want to tackle me. After this scar, I have a power… hold on, why do you have a parrot on your shoulders?"

"He's my friend."

Arjan burst out laughing, to the point that he collapsed on the floor, his hand clutching his stomach. "You are… the… funniest… person ever."

"Shut up." Kalki was flustered in a good way. He couldn't help but smile as well about it.

Arjan stopped laughing and remained on the floor. Kalki began to explain the story behind acquiring him when he was interrupted by Lakshmi. She was in different clothes, panting and sweating hard as she had a note clutched tightly in her hand. Arjan's expression changed and so did Kalki's.

"What happened?"

"Your mother…uh…" she took deep breaths as she fought to catch her breath, "she told me…you…were…here." She wiped the sweat from her brow, her hair all tangled up.

"What happened?" Arjan pursued. "What's wrong?"

"What's wrong is that Lady Durukti…is coming to visit the village and she's not coming as a friend," and she showed the note to the two brothers.

34

The village council meeting had been held. All the elders were sitting under the peepal tree while the folks were sitting on the ground. Kalki noticed this was the biggest number of people at a meeting. To the heavens, he would never be a part of these boring meetings, but Sarpanch Devadatta had issued a mandatory attendance regarding it, for it was a matter of life and death.

It was a surprise for Kalki when he had reached Devadatta's hut and found he was rushing for the meeting.

"I need you for a moment. We have something important to tell you..." Kalki had begun, flanked by his two companions, Lakshmi and Arjan, who stood behind him, equally dumbfounded.

"All of it can wait, boy, we have pressing issues to address right now." Devadatta had shrugged.

Kalki now stood among the many in the crowd, while Arjan stood next to him. Sumati was on Kalki's side, clutching onto her saree. Kalki scanned the other folks of the village in the crowd.

There was Roshan Mitra and his parents. There was Lyla Sarvesh and her twin brothers, Agastya and Andhaka. There was Sagar and his sister Maya. Many of his age, many who Kalki had grown up with, stood like solid figures waiting for the momentous news to be revealed.

"I wonder what it could be," Arjan spoke quietly.

"Not more important than an army of Tribals ransacking our loving village."

Kalki shot Lakshmi a glance. "I thought you hated Shambala. What was it you had said? Godforsaken village?" He smiled.

Lakshmi frowned, her face contorting in disgust. "Well, clearly I didn't mean it. I love Shambala even though it gets on my nerves sometimes."

"If you both can stop quarrelling, the meeting is about to..."

"Shush, Arjan!" Sumati's tone furiously.

Arjan just looked at her in surprise. He wasn't even talking. Kalki chuckled during the serious situation and Lakshmi couldn't help her smile at the moment.

"What in the heavens are you laughing about? Where is your parrot?" Arjan's nostrils flared in indignation.

Devadatta, standing up on the pedestal, began his speech, while he held a scroll wrapped with a royal insignia. "Hello there, everyone. Namastey. Before I begin with what is written in this scroll, I would like to tell you that the last few days have been difficult for us and for this village as we lost an important member of our society—Vishnuyath Hari. It was with great admiration that we all joined hands to protect our own. And even though we were able to give them punishment for what they deserved, we were unable to save Vishnu. It was a great loss for us and we mourn with his family in this moment of grief." Everyone bowed with a sign of respect at Kalki and his mother.

Kalki hadn't expected this and it hurt to realise how many lives his father had touched. But it also startled him how Devadatta took all the appreciation of the rescue mission for Vishnu, when it was Kalki who had instigated them into action.

"We all had joined to save a brother and today I have called everyone to do the same. This scroll came from Indragarh, the office of Lord Kali, the Commander of Indragarh, who has sent a notice to welcome them in our village but at a grave cost. They want to excavate our temple—the resting place of Lord Indra, Indravan."

"Excavate?" Everyone gasped at the word.

Kalki knew that meant basically destroying the entire place to get the Soma stones for themselves. But how did the outsiders know about the significance behind it? Kalki looked over, searching for Kripa and found him, leaning with a mug of sura in his hand as he had a dire face as well.

"If we do not support it, we will be termed as 'rebellious' and will be attacked," he read the letter out. It gave people shivers down their spines the mere thought of Tribals ransacking their village. "Any support and love will be rewarded greatly."

Someone from the crowd said, "I don't understand. It is our temple. What are they coming to excavate?"

"Perhaps the Soma Stones."

"Are they even real?" someone else cried. "Has anyone seen them?"

"Yes, many have," Devadatta said. "But no one dared to touch them for they were sacred. They were supposed to be admired from far and worshipped, as they were the last remnants of Lord Indra." He paused. "The laws written by our ancestors were clear—those who touched the caves would be met by severe punishment." And yet Vishnuyath broke all those laws of the village and went inside the cave, for the love and safety of his wife, to save her from pain. "Unfortunately the earthquake led to our temple's destruction, even though its essence had not vanished. It was still there."

Everyone was silent.

"I am in great confusion. I do not know what to do. As an

elder, it's my duty to protect the traditions of our village, but at the cost of destroying it?"

No one knew the answer to it. The only place in the entire village which unified the entire community would be gone. Kalki knew this could mean the rise of Adharm, for if the Somas were out in public, perhaps in the hands of the evil Tribals, things would really go out of hand. If he could prevent it from happening, he wouldn't have to leave Shambala and it would be over. No more the Age of Adharm, no more Dark Age.

Kalki raised his voice. "I have something to say." The silence had been broken.

With the elders, Devadatta just watched Kalki, astonished. Kalki wondered what thoughts crowded in the old man's thick brain. But Devadatta simply nodded.

Kalki stepped up. Life had changed so much that he was the speaker now, no more the listener. "Sarpanch ji says it's our traditions that we need to protect and he's right. Shambala is a small village, but the most revered for the reason that our traditions are what makes us great. We are not warriors, but we are people who are ready to fight till we die for this place. I would never stand aside while what we pray to is getting destroyed just because we are afraid of a battle. I would rather fight. Now, many would be afraid of this, and they should be, but together, as a unified force, we can stop the band of armies. If we show our will, we can do wonders."

Some of them nodded, some didn't.

"How will we stop them without weapons?" Roshan Mitra was the one to ask. His parents were shocked at the question he asked, perhaps thinking of him as having fallen for the words of Kalki.

Kalki didn't have a good enough reason. He looked at Lakshmi, who just tilted her head down in embarrassment.

"We have a little bit."

"That would be all right for the Mlecchas," Lyla Sarvesh

interrupted. She was a strongly built female unlike her brothers. "But not for the army from the royal city."

"Might I add something?" a squeaky voice came from the crowd.

Kalki lowered his brows at the sight of Kripa. "Lass, we can make weapons if we have to. We are in the middle of a jungle with such varieties of trees."

"Who are you?" Agastya, brother of Lyla, asked.

"Yeah, who are you?" Andhaka repeated.

"Call me Kripa, okay?"

Kalki smiled. Kripa Acharya was getting defensive.

"But Shambalans aren't warriors, beta," another village elder prompted. Devadatta seemed to agree, but he didn't show it verbally. "We are peacemakers. Our ancestors were peacemakers and our progeny will be peacemakers too."

"Frankly, we don't live in a time of peace." Kalki's eyes blazed, as he spit venom with his words, targeting all those who backed away from the reality of this situation. "What our ancestors did shouldn't really matter, but what we do is what history will write about us." He looked at Kripa. "Say what you say, but at least he has an idea. We need heroes and innovators. Not cowards." He glanced at Devadatta.

And then Kalki took the stand without letting the elders speak again. "I don't know what the village elders plan to do, but I will be recruiting for this with the help of my friends. And we will be ready, so I plead with the elders, reject this scroll, tell them we are rebellious and let them come. All those who volunteer for my cause can meet me at my place at noon to discuss the arrangements. Let's prove we aren't just any village they can bully."

And with that he stepped down from the pedestal, hearing a thin round of applause from a few people.

35

Vasuki had been waiting for his sister at his fort. It was close to completion and his room had been set up, guarded by more than fifty Nagas who would operate in two shifts, morning and night. He had promised himself he would not let them leave at any cost and whoever felt exhausted would be exiled from their work as a guardsman. Ulupi had been promoted to the rank of the General, policing and parading around streets, finding who could have killed Takshak. The wound, when examined by the shaman, had revealed that Takshak was killed by a Naga blade, distinct for its thin and curved edges.

He knew it was Kuvera. He had some role in this. Kuvera had been always jealous of Vasuki, ever since he laid his eyes on the mani. The Nagas were popular among the Dakshinis; the only people who were respected for their cleanliness and their mid-level royal status.

All of it had changed later when Kuvera decided to steal the one precious mani that was the symbol of their power. It was called the Naagmani, used to worship Shesha, the snake that coiled around the neck of Lord Vishnu and was his protector. He was considered the highest God to Nagas. There was even a temple close to Vasuki's city, Naagpuri, where a large statue made of bronze and copper was housed. On its forehead was the fabled mani. And it had been stolen. They had seen it being taken by a Yaksha, for the footsteps were small just like the abhorrent Kuvera's.

Vasuki, along with Takshak, had attacked Alakpur, the domain of the Yakshas, a scarce wasteland amongst sand dunes. Vasuki had lost, but later when the Tribal agreement with Kali had come forth, Vasuki had stated that the only way he would provide the resources and his men, was if Kuvera would give him the mani back. Kuvera reluctantly agreed as Kali had made him see the bigger picture.

And that was the history behind it, fighting and quarreling with Kuvera, with no love, only hate. Even when Vasuki agreed to the pact, he had second doubts about working with Kuvera, but Kali had promised him equality and no hindrance, all of which now seemed like fables. Now he was so many miles away from Naagpuri and he wished to go, but he couldn't. He would be labelled a coward by his people. He was still a coward, in his own opinion, but in a hostile environment.

He had sent a good huge number of Nagas for Manasa to reach the city and close to the fortress without any hassle. He even made sure that it wouldn't look like a Naga was coming. The fort gates, made of iron, burst open as the ropes and the branch that bound it were let off. Entering with the cavalry and infantry, in a wagon that was drawn by three horses, he could see his sister from the top of the fort. He briskly walked, guards following him as he passed the laborers—who were Nagas from birth. He couldn't risk the menial workers to be Udaiyas in any way, for he had seen his father's assassination.

The very thought of his father's death slowed his pace and he meandered a bit before gaining pace and proceeding to the central chamber, where water spiraled from four directions. Guards wore breastplates with snake insignia over it and their swords' hilt had a symbol of Shesha's forehead.

Manasa exited the wagon, her one hand smaller than the other, something Vasuki had stopped noticing. She was born with a defect, a limp hand that people would ridicule and Vasuki would feel instantly irritated about. It was not something to joke about. It wasn't her fault. But now she didn't care, for her hand just dangled limply, gloved in a purple satin cloth. She was dressed in a high cut, flowy robe, and her hair, although long and loose, was tied into coiled knots at the end. Her eyes were the same blue colour as her brother. She embraced Vasuki and the warmth of his own blood made him exuberant. He liked that he had someone like her right now in the city.

"Thank you for coming."

"Always," Manasa said, having a hoarser voice than most Naga women. "Why don't you tell your men to dress up well? His straps are loose, his sheath is torn and his sandals are ripping. By the poor designs of it, they won't even last an hour if they fight in these."

Vasuki watched the strict Manasa, older than him, and taller than him, scolding him. "All right calm down, sister." Vasuki patted her, one arm grabbing her waist and dragging her away.

She was always a lover of designs, colours, fabrics and using odd plants and berries. And yet, regardless of all this vanity, she had the keenest knowledge of spies and how one could survive the longest on battlefields. The length of a tunic could determine a man's life expectancy during war as well as his knee pads and how his sword was designed.

They had reached his room which had pristine white walls, with bronze plates, cups and mugs stacked neatly on a long table. He served her wine while he drank as well. He needed it more than anyone. He then sat on his chair.

"What happened? You told me in the letter that you are in the midst of traitors."

"Yes, I am. I need someone I can trust by my side."

"Well, here I am, darling," she grinned. "Your big sister is always here whenever you need her."

Vasuki sighed, sipping his drink, touching the edges of the

goblet to his lips. He began telling her about Takshak and how he had sent him to spy on Vedanta.

"My dear, never let a thick-headed fellow like Takshak go and spy on someone. He knows nothing of spying. He thinks beating up individuals and demanding answers is spying while spying is an art itself. The way you speak, the way you dress, the way you carry yourself; all that matters."

"I know. I was stupid."

"All's fair now," she said her three favourite words that Vasuki had the misery of hearing multiple times all through his life. "We need a new plan to take down your enemies, but for that we need to identify the enemies."

"I know two of them."

"Great and what about that handsome but sickly fellow, Kali?"

"Oh yes, he's sort of out of commission, unable to do his chores properly," mocked Vasuki, almost spitting the leftover wine in his mouth.

"Eh?" she sounded alarmed. "He and his sister, they seemed a strong fit with each other. Almost a surprise, darling, that they aren't capable enough."

"He's weak and delusional." Vasuki thumped the goblet on the mahogany side table. "It was just yesterday, I remember, how we were able to escape the clutches of our own men betraying their masters."

"And how we had triumphed over them, darling. I know," smiled Manasa. "Civil wars are a common thing in tribes. You needn't be surprised. After all, we are all uncivilized in our personal lives."

"We will triumph this as well." Vasuki stood, his draped robes slowly brushing the ground, as he walked forward. He was a neat fellow for a king. While others had battle scars, he looked flawless because he never fought in the frontline, except the time they were attacked outside Indragarh and Kali had surprisingly stopped them.

He was a genius back then, but a poor man's pig now. "Do you have any spies as of now?"

"Patience, darling." She came forward, touching his robe and slowly turning it on the other side so the golden, laced fabric could be seen properly. "A king must wear his clothes carefully."

Vasuki nodded, pursing his lips. "I know. I apologize. You have taught me enough to not make this mistake continuously."

"An assassin, if we think of having any, must be very quick and unnoticeable, someone who can just get under the skin of our enemies and be able to dethrone them without even letting them know." She smiled her lopsided smile. "And we will get this kind of a spy through patience and through destiny. Let Lord Shesha guide us."

Vasuki nodded. "As you say. But what about Kali?"

She didn't say anything, but continued to watch Vasuki. "He was of use to us when he promised he would provide peace amongst all the tribes. If there's no peace, darling," a devious smirk lifted her lips up, "what use is he to us then?"

36

They waited.

Kalki sat outside his home for a while, drifting into an uneasy sleep. He was tired. Arjan was leaning against the tree whose canopy shadowed their hut. He was playing with a coin, flipping and twisting it in the air, out of mundane curiosity. Lakshmi was reading a book and Arjan kept trying to peek into it. Bala was busy cleaning his mace.

Sumati had scolded Kalki to be more respectful towards adults and not barge into a council meeting just because he was able to convince them once. He was enamored by the idea that the Avatar of this Age was doing all of it. Did Lord Govind allow himself to do all this? But then he was a man who loved curd and stole it. He had his own likings and flaws, just like Kalki, whose greatest flaw was his verbose nature, which often made him forget about his surroundings.

Shuko appeared on his shoulder and he let him have a piece of bread. After a while, when Shuko had occupied himself with his dietary fastidiousness, Kalki realized Kripa hadn't come. He was the one who had suggested making weapons out of natural forest resources, and yet he hadn't come. He was an Acharya, yet such lack of punctuality hardly suited him.

There was a tale about a Mleccha, who was a noble one from the times in Mahayudh. He wanted to be a great archer and he had the talent for it. The respectable Acharya realized that he was a threat to the hero of the Age and he made the Mleccha give his thumb in return. Without the thumb, the Mleccha was no more a good archer and it was this tragedy that cost him his love for archery. Kalki knew that the Acharyas weren't the noblest of men, even though they pursued noble practices. There was never really good or evil in this world. There were just people and their choices that lead to devastating consequences. The story was apt, and it was the only one Kalki remembered from his Gurukul days. It made him wonder now whether Kripa was a good man after all, for his intentions were often belied by his actions.

Kalki was a bit surprised as to why Kripa had not divulged the names of either his nephew or the accomplice. He thought to himself that perhaps the time was not right, and eventually he would receive answers once he had definitively chosen the path of righteousness.

"I don't think anyone is coming, brother," Arjan began with a hint of humor. "I suppose your speech wasn't really that impactful. Were you impacted?" he probed Bala.

Bala had been wiping the mace when he got sidelined. "Uh, what? Uh…yeah…"

Kalki shook his head in dismay. "I am not surprised my own people don't trust my judgment." He coughed for Lakshmi to look up from her book and answer, but she remained still, merely flipping through the pages. "Great, thanks for the encouragement."

She still didn't say anything.

"I don't think she's listening."

Lakshmi snapped without even glancing up, "I am. I just choose not to answer."

"Makes me feel good, everyone, thank you." Kalki sarcastically shook his head and swivelled to face the direction of the forest.

Then he saw a person walking towards him. He wasn't exactly tall, more average in height and build. Roshan Mitra was walking alongside, sluggishly moving forward with him. While often dismissed by most people as weak, Kalki had seen him loading and unloading sacks in his father's farm during periods of harvest. The chit of a man had a surprising amount of strength.

"Is this where I…where I volunteer?"

"Uh, sure, yes." Kalki stood up. "How can you help us?"

"I can help you with making weapons."

"Do you know how to make weapons?"

Roshan shook his head. "Someone needs to teach me, but well, I'm a quick learner."

"That's uh…that's great." Kalki turned to his friends, who were struggling not to laugh. "And you won't fight?"

"No, Mother said I shouldn't do something to kill myself."

"Oh, I see." Kalki smiled. "Well, thank you for coming, Roshan…"

"HOLD ON!" A voice shouted.

Kalki turned, and he could feel the all the heads turning as well. It was Lyla with her two brothers, along with Sagar, Maya and ten more friends. But they weren't just ten; they were in hundreds if Kalki was correct. They were coming in large groups, excitedly chattering about this opportunity to go against the panchayati dictum and fight against the Tribal audacity of demanding to excavate their temple.

Lakshmi had closed her book. Bala straightened himself. Arjan wasn't playing with the coin anymore.

"I hope this is enough, Kalki," Lyla said with a smirk. She had onyx black hair, with curled eyelashes and a thin mouth. Her brothers didn't look anything like her, but they were tall and strong and Kalki needed that.

"This is more than enough and uh thank you for coming." Kalki lowered his brows as he acknowledged all of their presence. "But how did you manage to convince everyone?" he asked Lyla.

"Me? I didn't manage to do anything. I was bringing my brothers along when I saw this group. They were all coming this way."

"So who grouped them?"

"Well…" Lyla signalled with her thumb at the back, towards a familiar face that appeared from amidst the crowd. Clad in plain white clothes, Devadatta looked at Kalki with a generous smile. He gave an acknowledging nod.

"Sarpanch ji?" He gasped. He had never believed that the old man, whom he had called a coward indirectly, would step up and bring so many people for Kalki. "I thought you didn't believe in me."

Devadatta sighed. "I don't know what to believe in anymore. But I do know one thing. I'll regret my entire life if I let those Tribals invade our temple. I don't have a lot to regret so I hope to make the most of it."

Kalki laughed, along with Arjan, who patted Kalki's shoulder in respect. Lakshmi held his hand, their palms brushing against each other and Kalki felt the same current zapping inside him, as on the day of his father's last rites, when Lakshmi and he had almost kissed. Kalki even managed to see Sumati, who had come out due to the commotion, and was greeted by so many people. She was silent, but was grinning with delight and awe.

Devadatta pulled out the scroll, lifted it up in front of Kalki and tore it apart, flinging it in the air; definitively letting the congregation know that a choice had been made. And now Kalki had to steer them towards fortunate consequences.

37

Arjan had spoken the truth when he had said that it'd be difficult to handle so many people, as Kalki didn't know anything about warfare. They had sat in Kalki's house as Sumati brought for them some curd and milk to feast upon, while the hundred or so volunteers had returned after announcing their partnership.

"I can teach them to hold a mace." Bala rushed though the curd as he said so, devouring mouthfuls of it. "They will be warriors."

"A mace is too heavy for an average man," Kalki said. "Not all of them will be taught one thing."

"We need to divide them up skill-wise," Lakshmi said. "See what each person can offer and give them the desired role to play in this battle."

"They are all Shambalans, most of them will choose the road of non-violence." Kalki stood up, angsty and exhausted. Morning had arrived and none had had any sleep, for time was of absolute importance. "We were able to attack the Mlecchas for they were small in number in comparison to the volunteers we had that time. Even a hundred of us won't be enough for a Tribal army. Worse, we don't even know how the Tribal army operates. Our folks need thorough training and we need to make short work of it."

Arjan nodded, his fingers dancing on his lips as the sheathed sickle dangled from his waist. He had said he received the weapon from their mother, which had only made Kalki jealous about not receiving anything from her. He shouldn't have felt that way, but envy was a childish emotion. More so because without the aid of soma-induced strengths, Arjan was in greater need of the weapons than Kalki. It was all getting over his head, the fact that so many people had posited their faith in him, had believed in what he would be able to achieve for them. It was hard for a boy of his age. He wasn't an older person, ready to take the responsibilities of his life, let alone the lives of the entire village. In the field of boundless courage, he had mustered up words that had instilled hope in the average villager's eyes, but that didn't mean he'd necessarily win.

Would he? How?

The thought of pessimism had crossed his mind and that was the one of the major reasons why he wouldn't sleep until he proved everyone right and became the hero Shambala deserved right now. Right after finishing his cup of milk though.

"We need a guru," Arjan said. "An Acharya. I can contact Guru Vashishta for his help, but he'll probably reject us, for he has opened his doors to a lot of wanderers out there. And even if he accepts, coming from there to here would be just as problematic and time-consuming. And time is exactly what we lack right now."

Guru?

Lakshmi had her brows pulled down, the way she usually did whenever she was deep in thoughts. "I agree. The raven will drop the message to Kali's office and according to my estimates, as they prepare an army and all, it'll take him a maximum of ten days to gather and travel here."

"Why so much, little girl?" Bala huskily asked.

Lakshmi glanced at him, wide-eyed. Kalki knew why. She wasn't really fond of being called a 'little girl' since she was quite old. Lakshmi was the one person he knew who hated being a child, unlike Kalki who missed how everything was innocent back then. "Um, yeah, because well… Kalki and I travelled in a day and a half as we were less in number, but for an army, which will necessarily need rests and stops, it would require more time. Three days of journey would be the minimum amount of time required."

Arjan added an inquiry. "How will we know when they appear?"

"Parrots can fly high and see incoming intruders!" Bala exclaimed. "Parrots are intelligent if used rightly."

Everyone except Kalki watched Shuko, who had curd smeared over his beak. It flapped its wings and noisily squawked.

Kalki's body stiffened. "I know someone who can help us. But he's not really the most trustworthy man around. In fact, you two might know him." He signalled over to Bala and Arjan.

"The only person, we know," Arjan began, narrowing his eyes and then broadening them in horror, "oh no, please don't say it's him."

"Unfortunately, yeah," Kalki nervously laughed.

Arjan struck his hand against his forehead, while Bala was still musing thoughtfully about it.

He looked like a sadhu. Sadhus were usually the wandering priests, having no prescribed religion that they believed in. They didn't have a temple like the priests nor were they looking for materialism. They had eschewed worldly affairs. They would remain dirty and forgotten, persisting with their nomadic existence. Strongly resembling a sadhu, Kripa was leaning against the rock. There was a peaceful smile dancing on his lips and his hands were wrapped around his torso.

Kalki and his friends walked onto the scene just then. They were met by the image of a haggard drunkard, his head lolling against the ground, who was surrounded by innumerable empty cups of sura. Kalki knew his friends wouldn't trust his judgment in this matter, but Kripa was the only hope he had since he was much more than an ordinary Acharya. He was a Chiranjeev, who had played a pivotal role in the Mahayudh and must have innate knowledge about weaponry. All of this wasn't known to his friends and he wished the Gods didn't know it either.

"Must say, Kalki, you really believe anyone who says he's a Guru, right?" Arjan said. "I'm sure Kripa could be a good enough guide in knowing what's out there in the woods, but I'm not sure if he can help us fight an army of Tribals."

Lakshmi grunted. "Yeah, just look at him. Look at this egregious man who just…"

"Bah! I can train our people better, Kalki. Give me a chance!" Bala busted forth with such energy that he shook even Kripa, who noisily awoke from his slumber.

"Am I having a nightmare?" Kripa looked around, his eyes pale, with dark bags under them, his mouth grim and foul, and his hair all twisted and greasy. "Why do I see so many imbeciles in one place?"

Kalki shook his head. He shouldn't say anything deplorable and let the situation worsen.

"Are you an Acharya, old man?" Bala grabbed Kripa and pulled him up, shaking him furiously. "Are you? Can you teach us, old man?"

Kalki came forward and forced Bala to release the Chiranjeev, as he tripped and struggled on the floor, reeling.

"Yeah, I'll just tell what I know. He was once a Guru, but… uh…he got addicted to suras until he forgot what was right and what was wrong. Now he's just a wanderer, a hermit."

"A drunken one at that," Lakshmi grimaced.

Kripa looked, sheepishly at Kalki and then at everyone. "What are you all prattling about, mates? Why in God's name are you disturbing my morning slumber? Have I not had enough of you?"

"We need your help." Kalki came forward, eyeing him hard. "You told me in the meeting we could make weapons out of the forest. We need your help in training and crafting armoury for the battle that is about to begin in ten days."

"Is he for real?" Kripa squeaked, asking Kalki's friend. "In ten days, you'll only get half a warrior and not a good half, if I am honest with you."

"I don't care. That'll be all right for me."

Kripa watched him in confusion. "You really are serious about it, mate? That's good, aye. We should all be merry about heroes and hope it will make us win a battle. But then why should I do what you want me to do?"

"Because it's the right thing to do," Lakshmi responded grimly.

"Right thing? Yes, well how should I respond to this in a genteel fashion? Lass, the right thing is for those who have morality. And unfortunately, I lost mine a while back."

"You supported me in the meeting. I thought you supported that decision."

"I don't even know what I dreamt about right now let alone what I said in that meeting. I say a lot of things, but I mean little. Does that make any sense or should I try some different words for you?"

Kalki came forward, avoiding his friends. He grabbed hold of the stupid, old man and lifted him slightly. "We are in need of an Acharya. If you do this, I promise I will come with you to meet your mysterious accomplice to whatever mountains you wanted me to go to." Kalki stared at him steadfastly.

"Mahendragiri," his voice chortled.

"What?"

"The whatever mountains you had mentioned, you know."

Kalki left him, sighing in relief. "Yes, whatever."

"Fine," Kripa brushed off his tunic. "I'll help you."

Kalki's friends weren't relieved, but they were glad. Help was on its way even though the help was deadly drunk all the time.

"First, we need to go to the woods, and gather supplies, as many as he can. We need milk too."

"Milk? For war?" Arjan asked.

"Energy, mate. Strength. Milk is health as they say, you know."

Lakshmi interrupted, "No one says that."

"Someone definitely said it."

"No one, not one person."

"I'm pretty sure someone had said that, lass," he chuckled. "I'm pretty sure, all right."

Kalki snapped in between. "Whoever has said whatever should not matter right now. We will do as you say; you must meet our volunteers and select each of them for a specific kind of duty."

"All right, as you command." Kripa mock-saluted him.

Kalki began to walk with him, while his friends followed them, when Kripa whispered a gentle statement: "You and your brother have vastly different ways of persuasion, mate. I need to be careful around with you both. That's nice. Even your friends seem gleeful around you, but you see, to become an Avatar, you might have to make sacrifices, so enjoy this while it lasts." And he walked off, Kalki trailing behind him, with a dazed expression on his face.

38

Placidly lying down on his bed, Kali had never felt so useless in his life. He had promised himself he would rest when death would be near. Not before that; for resting meant sparing time for innocuous pleasures. Kali was suffocating and not because of all the dirt that had accumulated his lungs, but because he was stuck in a room, just as his sister was worried about his well-being. Where was she anyway, he asked himself, as he worried about not having seen her for an entire day.

Though, that could be a blessing in disguise.

Kali lifted himself up, brushing his legs against the floor, stretching his back. He knew he would die if he remained in the bed for long. He walked to the door to find his two generals standing, on opposite sides, wearing their plated suit of armour. They instantly stiffened at the sight of Kali.

"At ease," Kali said, sighing, even speaking feeling like a huge tax on his throat.

Koko timidly said, "My lord, you should be resting."

"I know I should be, but I choose not to."

"Lady Durukti has commanded us…"

Kali shot Vikoko a look of pure poison. She didn't meet her master's eyes. Kali realized how small he was in comparison to the twins. They were both more than six feet tall, broad and agile, while he was decidedly diffident next to them.

"I want to travel outside. I want to see how the city is working."

"All right, my lord."

Kali was guided by the twins, outside the fort, as he saw the simmering rays of the sun, washing over him after the longest time. The twins opened the chariot door for him, which was attached to two white stallions. At the sight of his ride, Kali shook his head.

"I want a horse, and a personal one."

The guards around the fort stood shocked. The twins walked forward, incredulously. Koko began, "My lord, this is better for your back."

"I don't want to be protected anymore." Kali patted his general with a warm smile, hoping to make him understand his plight. "I want to breathe in the fresh air as I ride through the streets of the city."

The twins didn't quarrel much. They brought him a horse, while he waited, watching all the guards. It was only his fort where the Manavs, Rakshas, Yakshas and Naga soldiers were together, for he allowed every capable warrior to be appointed. He didn't let prejudices dictate the professions they were engaged in. There was a small garden in between, with a statue of Kali and Durukti in the centre, flanked by trees on both sides. The officials of his government were walking casually, going about their duties. When they saw Kali, they bowed down to him and he waved with a grin.

The horse appeared in front of him. Kali sat on it, feeling powerful like before. He was clad in black, wearing his metal armour over it. He had a small cloth, wrapped around his neck, red in colour. He pulled it up to his mouth, partially hiding his face. It was for security purposes as well as to protect his lungs. The horse galloped forward, leaving the iron gates behind and making way to the city. The twins were in the front, and two guards were leading the rear.

Moving after a prolonged period of inactivity, he was assaulted by the various sights and smells. The bazaars were operating in full force, while the merchants and the customers noisily haggled. Everywhere, people parted and quietened in deference to Lord Kali. They were all whispering and quivering, some in fear, while others had a look of delight. The bazaar was his brainchild, conceived as an open wholesale market, where traders and vendors from the entire northern province could congregate with their wares. They would be taxed at forty percent of what they'd earn, but it was worth it. He could see books, food and utensils being sold in different lanes. The shops were constructed in narrow spaces, covered with brightly-coloured canopies overhead.

Kali came off his horse with his guards in tow. Kali signaled them not to follow, except for Koko and Vikoko, who went wherever he went. He entered the bazaar and made his way. Some were so busy negotiating prices, they didn't notice the new Commander of the city walking past them, but Kali showed no haste in portraying himself as someone like that. He chose to show he was an ordinary man. His arms were sprawled wide, as his eyes fell upon an old lady sitting behind a table. She had a lot of cards on the table, with multiple gemstones over each pair of cards.

Kali was interested. He had always believed in destiny and the fates. He was innately superstitious. Fortune-telling, Kali had learnt, was the extension of astrology. Kali went there and sat opposite the woman. She had blue eyes, hence she was probably a Naga. But her eyes weren't exactly the colour of sapphire, but cloudy and pale… until it hit Kali. She was blind, of course. "Kaliyan Seth," Kali said. The last name, though unknown to many, was his surname. In fact, it had been so long since he had uttered it, he had forgotten it himself.

"Designation?" The woman began shuffling her cards now.

"Middle-class caste," Kali said.

"Hmph." She laid the cards in front of him. "Pick one."

"But I didn't ask you a question." He knew about cards a little. They were already around when he was small as well. There were some who read faces, while others who would look at hands and some even just touched the person, interpreted the energy and understood. They were all bogus in his eyes, until once he met a fortune teller, before his expedition of uniting the Manavs and the Tribals. The teller had said it would happen easily, but with a price. Perhaps his deteriorating health was that price, or perhaps it was something else.

"Pick a card," the woman coldly continued. She had no wrinkles and yet she looked old. That was odd, for her eyes had wisdom and her voice sounded quite young. She had duskier skin than any Naga and had hands that were too small for her body.

Kali did so. The woman touched the card softly, as if feeling it, and then smashed it on the white sheet on which all of her stuff was placed.

"You are lying," she said. "About your name and your designation."

Kali smiled. He couldn't believe the woman had caught on to his lies. Was there a slight uncertainty in his lies or was it really magic?

"All right. I choose not to share either."

"That won't be an issue. Touch the card for that."

Kali did so. "Your energies have been passed into it." She shuffled the deck and then spread it again. "How many cards do you want me to pick up?"

Kali didn't have any particular number in mind. "Three," he entreated his lips to speak for themselves. "Am I not asking any questions?"

"For those who ask questions, they look for a certain answer in every answer and that is how a fraudulent tantric is able to work around that answer until she hits the heart. It's called reading an individual; the earnestness, the resoluteness, and the body language helps in determining that answer. As such, other astrologers make a lot of money doing this." She paused, explaining the structure of astrological shams, impressing Kali in the process. "I had the powers of interpreting the future." She wasn't even trying to be modest. "To prove I am not like others, I burnt my eyes for I couldn't see an individual then. I could only feel their energies."

Kali pursed his lips. He was excited, as he now began to pull three cards out of the scattered bunch. He could feel his stomach lurch and his fingertips growing cold with nervous enthusiasm. She lifted the three cards, brushing her palms across them, to feel the energy of the cards. Kali had never felt so nervous about something. He shouldn't believe in all of it, like Durukti, but all of this magic and wonder had really interested him.

"Hmmm," she said, "I see partnership, and a strong one."

Kali nodded. "Yes, I already have…"

"No, not now. I don't speak of now. I speak of then. I see partnership between you and an unlikely individual or a group you thought would never be right for a partnership. It'll change the course of time and help you build a bigger empire if you use them correctly." The woman kept speaking and Kali peered over the card. It was of two individuals holding each other's hands as a pact. "And amongst trusted people."

"What if I don't?"

"It'll be one of the reasons for your downfall."

Kali felt strained. Downfall? He had fought his way till here. He couldn't believe he would die because of some partnership he failed to live up to. She pulled out a second card, turning it over to reveal a man coming on a white horse, with a blazing sword and long hair. She did the same movements with her hands.

"You will have an adversary with equal brains and strength as you. He will combat you and he will try to destroy you."

"That's all right." Kali shrugged. He was in such an influential position that his life would obviously be at risk.

"He'll be your greatest foe, but he won't be the cause of your downfall."

And the words pierced his chest, even though it was already burning up inside.

"He?"

"Yes, a male." She paused, sniffing. "Ah, but there is a problem. He's not ready yet. He's exploring."

Kali shook his head. She turned the third card over.

"You will face betrayal from the ones you trust," she said with a crooked smile.

Kali couldn't take this anymore. He came onto his feet, the chair rocking from the sudden movement. "This is stupid. Is there no good written for me?"

"I see great power coming your way, Lord Kali," her voice had turned into a snarl, as she giggled.

How did she know my name?

"Use it wisely otherwise it'll corrupt you," she said craftily.

And just then he felt a sharp lunge from the back, and the plunging dagger twisted deep within him. His hand swept at the back, holding the serrated dagger that had been stabbed into him. He pulled out the dagger, turning around to see a man, dressed in a cloak. Kali called out to the twins, who were busy watching a performer. When they heard him, they rushed over. The assassin decided to run in the ensuing confusion.

Kali collapsed, but he tried his best to hold onto the assassin's leg. He tripped. Kali pulled away the cloak. By the time the twins came, they were quick enough to plunge their blades inside his neck, ripping his throat and spraying blood on the unsuspecting bystanders. The entire bustling bazaar had come to a standstill. Koko and Vikoko made way for Kali now, as they lifted him up. A sharp, crackling pain was careening down his spine, as he slowly swiveled his head and saw the old woman had disappeared.

"We should leave, my lord."

"Sho…show me the body."

Kali was pulled forward by his generals, and by this time, the guards who waited outside the bazaar had come in and pushed the crowd from coming too close. Kali knelt down, his hand going for the man's hood that concealed his chest. He tore it open, with the leftover strength he had in him.

And there it was—the breastplate of the blue-eyed assassin, with a snake on it.

39

The reality was worse than the method.

Arjan hadn't realized it would be so difficult working with Kripa. He looked like an incapable lout. But Arjan was so wrong, for the first thing he said when he saw the volunteers, was:

"We need a bigger place."

Bala was the first to recommend Madira's Chalice. Many had objected for its sinful connotations. "We won't practice for this sacred mission under a roof owned by an unreligious man," Devadatta spoke out agitatedly.

Arindam, the owner of Madira's Chalice, was standing away from the group. He was a volunteer as well, for his own reasons. Arjan had learnt he was part of it because he wanted to save his tavern from being destructed. He knew that if the Commander's army would race inside the village, things would go downhill as they would massively tax a successful commercial spot like the tavern. But perhaps, there was an ulterior motive, something Arindam hid about himself. Or it could be the fact that he just cared about Shambala like the others. It was hard to believe how people changed and evolved when danger lurked around.

"The Madira's Chalice is the only place which is big enough to host so many people," Kalki said, in support. "I don't go to the place, but it's good for what we are doing."

"Add to that, wine and suras for us," cheered Kripa, who was instantly chastened by Kalki's frosty glare. It was decided then. The Madira's Chalice would be their practice ground. But that wasn't the problem for Arjan, as that was one of the problems solved quickly. What happened after that was the toughest. Arjan never believed himself to be a physically agile person. Regardless of the misadventures with the Mlecchas and the harsh scar he had got out of that, it was his only daring mission. He wanted to protect himself and his people. To him, it made no sense that they were potentially laying down their lives merely to protect some Godly cave. Indravan could go to the dogs, for all he cared! In fact, Kalki was the same like Arjan, about saving humans rather than idols, but somehow something had changed in him.

Arjan couldn't forget what he had seen. Those weren't mere human capabilities. No one could survive such an attack. Even a slice against his face hurt till he used herbal creams over it, to rein in the pain. It had died down into this mark that wasn't going anywhere for now. And it hurt, for people looked at him differently. He wasn't the same cherub boy anymore.

And yet Kalki's chest had wounds, but they were healing, faster than an average person's. Arjan hadn't read about this kind of regenerative physiology and he had asked Lakshmi, about quick healing, hoping that perhaps she had read something in the city.

"Why would you ask?" she had asked.

Arjan didn't respond.

"Yes, there have been cases like that, but mostly superstitious," Lakshmi had said. The answer wasn't satisfactory.

He would have asked Kalki, in person, for that was the kind of relationship they had with each other. But he was afraid, perhaps of knowing the truth or perhaps of learning something much beyond his own understanding. Arjan's mind had drifted from all of this. Kripa had shut himself from the liquor, and had gone to the woods, bringing people with him. Arjan was there as well, but Kalki wasn't.

When they had come to the forest, Kripa had said they needed to make a weapon out of these.

Arjan learnt the important tactics of weapon craftsmanship through natural means. The metal and iron weapons that were given by Lakshmi's aunt would be used by the fit warriors, who knew how to pick up and use the heavy objects. The natural weapons would be more lightweight. Arjan chose something he could shoot from far, as he didn't want to get into the middle of the battle, but still be productive. Arjan could have chosen to fight in a duel with Keshav Nand, but he didn't. He chose tactics over brute strength every time.

He chose a bow, and with the use of a kitchen knife, he cut open the bamboo, pulling the two ends back to form a curved back. For the arrow, he carved and sharpened long twigs, making the ends razor sharp.

Lyla had made herself a nice long spear with a blade on each other, wrapped by the thin slices of bark from a tree. Arindam and Agastya had made themselves sling clubs, with a rope on each end attached by a huge rock. They tried spinning it, but they ended up hurting themselves. Roshan Mitra was good at craftsmanship, and through the use of his knife, he crafted each log for people to use as their weapon.

Kripa had said that not everyone should have a weapon, but everyone should have a plan in order to go into battle. "Weapons are incentives, only to be used when absolute necessity. We have to win this war without the weapons."

Sagar and Maya, brother and sister, got themselves doubled-sided swords. Kripa didn't have a weapon, per se, but he was burning utensils, and with the mixture of tree sap, zinc and charcoal, he was creating small circular balls. Arjan had walked to him with his bow and a quiver made of jute that held a lot of arrows in it. He had worked hard; his skin felt burnt, his eyes weak and his energy drained.

"What is this?" Arjan asked.

Kripa had been kneeling down. He looked up. "These, mate, are the explosives. One fiery touch and they blow up at least ten of their men or at least, startle them."

"When are we going to train?"

"In two days, let them first make their weapons. I need to talk to Kalki as well, to see where we can trap the army as we know what side they will be coming from. We need to find a way that'll choke them, and they would have no other way but to return back."

The entrance to Shambala had been one way, but it was divided into many uneven paths across the dense forest.

"Where is Kalki?"

"I've told him to do his own practice. He needs his alone time."

"I see." Suspiciously, Arjan moved from the so-called guru and as he turned back, Kripa was watching him the same way Arjan had regarded Kripa: with doubt.

It was nightfall and he stood at the entrance of the village. It was guarded by a bamboo entrance, but there was no gate. He was standing next to his big brother and his mother, who was carefully positioned on the horse.

"Don't fall while you leave," Kalki said with a smile, as he handed her a pot and wrapped up her clothes into a bundle. Sumati carefully draped her cloth. "I don't want to leave this village at this time, beta. Please, don't force me."

Arjan knew she had to go. Kalki knew that as well. They had both lost a parent and they weren't ready to lose another if they faced turmoil or things went down. Even if they ended up dying due to the war, and the very thought made Arjan shiver, they wanted to die with the thought that they were able to secure the safety of their mother.

"When will you both come see me?" Sumati asked.

"When all of this is over."

"How long? Tell me the number of days."

Kalki and Arjan shared a look. "We will let you know soon, and send you a pigeon."

Sumati watched them in dismay and yet embraced them tightly. "Take care, and fight hard. Make me proud."

Kalki had teared up, but Arjan remained frozen. "The journey to Badrinath Ashram will be almost four days. Take care."

"Don't worry. Just remember, a doubtful mind means you are on the right path. May the Vajra of Indra be with you, children." Sumati smiled, as she grabbed the reins and moved.

Kalki and Arjan stood together as the horse began to gallop forward. And soon, it had been covered in the shadows. Fear had engulfed their hearts.

"Will we win?" Kalki asked.

Arjan was surprised. He had forced everyone to stand up on that day and claim their land. Arjan didn't want it and now here he was, afraid of being a hero.

"We don't have a choice." Arjan responded, slowly comforting his brother, by wrapping his arms around his bulky back.

40

Durukti was standing next to the floral-trellised window, watching the sunset. She could barely remember the time when Kali was just a boy, light-skinned and golden-eyed. Always her savior, he would go hungry on days when he felt she was lying about feeling full, just so that he could peacefully eat his bread.

"Yes, I have eaten."

But Durukti knew he lied for his ribs were protruding, his skin was dull and his face looked absolutely exhausted. He had been travelling from one place to another, hoping to find jobs. He would get to be a miner or a helper at a local tavern, but things wouldn't be smooth for him and they would kick him out, without even paying him his dues. Things were going against him and Durukti; the world was cruel and innocence had been lost.

And that was when he had begun the life of crime.

Her thoughts were disrupted before she could remember how everything had turned in Kali's favour. The door opened, with Symrin walking inside, looking apprehensive. She had a letter rolled up as a scroll.

Durukti didn't have to read. Her face told everything.

"They didn't respond to our plea," Durukti said.

"In their defense, my lady, it wasn't exactly a plea, but more of an order," Symrin responded.

For such an insensitive and obtuse statement, Durukti would have banished her, but Symrin was right. It wasn't a plea. It was a horribly conceived, ill-written letter to the chief of Shambala, one of the most prosperous villages in the Keekatpur province. She had wanted to sound like she owned Shambala, she had wanted to enforce her will, but the last thing she wanted was to wage an ill-advised battle against a group of ragtag bumpkins, for their audacity to repudiate against a royal order.

"I wanted this to be a smooth run for us. I didn't want bloodshed. The very fact that they have rejected this means they are looking for a war." Durukti came to Symrin's side. "What do we know about Shambala?"

"Does not include a warrior community and has no armoury. In fact, I'm quite surprised they have rejected it. They are quite cowardly when it comes to the sight of blood and blades or as the stories say. We can go there and frighten them."

"We need a big army for that." Durukti pursed her lips. Big army meant a big distraction, which also meant Kali would know and stop it immediately. The last thing he wanted was a civil war and a lot of casualties just for the sake of his health. What he didn't realise was that Durukti would be more than ready to destroy the world if it meant saving her brother. "I'll speak to Lord…"

A shadow fell over the floor and Durukti turned to see Vikoko, sweat trickling down her head. She had blood across her breastplate.

"My lady!"

No.

Vikoko added. "I have some bad news."

Durukti rushed to the infirmary that was inside the fort itself. Durukti made her way inside, while Symrin rushed after her. Koko stood outside, frail and frightened.

"Your duty was to protect my brother. What have you done? If he dies, I will exile you." Durukti spat out the words, anger creating a blinding maelstrom of emotions, hurt and fear within her.

"I apologize for our transgression, my lady..."

Durukti swept her palm up. "Words wouldn't cure my brother's wound."

Right in the centre of a circle of candles, over a mat, was her brother, Kali, laid flat with his back on top and his chest against the floor. The wound was visible, a deep gash that bared his very bones.

"How is he?"

"Fortunate," the shaman said, circling around Kali and then kneeling next to him as he began to use a colourless gel on his wound, "that the cut was close to his spine, but not in his spine."

She could feel her choking sense of fear alleviate. She wasn't frightened, but was still worried.

"How long will he stay like this?"

"Give me few days, my lady," the shaman paused and looked up. "Let his wounds heal naturally rather than expediting the healing process artificially."

"I want to ask you something." Durukti walked around the circle of candles that acted as a barrier between her and her naked brother. "Have you heard of Soma?"

"Yes," the old man nodded. "Extinct medicinal nectar, extrapolated from somalata, used to be found in the cold hills up north."

"Why is it extinct?"

"The world moves on and leaves behind many of its wonders." The old man could only muster up these words in a show of helplessness.

"I heard it was inside the stone."

"Like every medicine, it has different forms, some in stones and some in plants. Either way, you need to suck the nectar out of it."

Durukti stopped circling, her sandal irritating her sole.

"How difficult is it extracting out of the stone?"

The shaman stopped. "Well, you need to first break it, dissolve it inside…"

"*How difficult*?" she rasped.

The shaman's eyes widened in fear, as his lips quivered. "Not much, if I have the right tools, but it is impossible to get Somas anymore, since they are extinct."

"How many days?" Her voice had calmed down. "How many days will it take to make the solution?"

"Perhaps three or less." The shaman nodded meekly.

"I want you to know," Durukti stood over the shaman, her shadow crossing his face as he watched her in discomfort, shifting uneasy next to Kali's body. The light danced on her face, the smell of incense engulfed her nostrils. "That you would be free from your duties when you perform this process and you shall not speak to anyone of this. If you do, by mistake or intentionally, I shall cut your head off with my own bare hands." Her teeth clenched as she threatened the man. Perhaps, it was the anticipation of the very thought of what she would do, that made her feel that way.

The shaman nodded.

"Keep me updated about his Lordship's health."

Durukti left the room and heaved a sigh of relief against the door. Koko and Vikoko were watching her, sweaty and unstable at the moment. She realized she couldn't show her weak demeanor in front of them, and struggling to her feet, she stood up, chin high and her hands clasped together.

"Redemption comes to those who work for it," Durukti began, glancing at the twins. Symrin shied away from uttering a single word at the moment, concealing herself in the shadows of the corridor, as Durukti continued, "I want you two to not just guard my brother's life as if it's your life, just like you had given a blood oath when he had saved your life, but you will also make sure to do one thing for him."

The twins waited.

"Lie to him," Durukti said. "Lie that his sister is inside, in her chambers and wishes to see no one since she's unhappy and filled with grief that she's unable to save her brother from the circumstances. Lie for me and I shall forgive you."

The twins blinked. They served Kali but they felt guilty for disappointing Durukti, and they would do everything to return back in her favours.

"Because I won't be here for a few days, and I will be taking Raktapa's band of army that he has left stationed here."

The twins nodded in unison.

"Do you want us to investigate Lord Vasuki, since it was a Naga who had killed our Lord?" Koko asked, since Vikoko was drenched in sweat and mute fear. Durukti shook her head. "That is a political matter which only Kali can work out. For us, we need to make sure he's in absolute good health."

And she began to walk away from the twins, Symrin trying to closely walk behind her. "My lady, what happened inside?"

"Realisations." Durukti had a straight face, eyes trained at the dark corridor.

"What are we going to do now? You are taking Lord Raktapa's army; is it perhaps the case that you are thinking of going to Shambala after all?"

"I always had," Durukti said matter-of-factly. But she knew why Symrin had asked her that. Durukti had been failing to take a decision; she looked afraid, upset and doubtful for the simple reason that she would go to Shambala and create disruptions, disruptions that Kali usually smoothed through his political acumen and bargaining diplomacy. "Mark my words, Symrin; nothing can stop me from entering those caves anymore."

41

It had been three days of exhaustive practicing. Kripa had taught him the ways of Channelling and learning from the predecessors, the ones who had ingested Soma. Kripa had told Kalki that the souls of the Avatars were connected, even though they were no longer manifest physically on the planet. By concentrating and channelling his faculties, he would be able to tap into the resources of common experiences that had been passed down through the ages.

Kalki sat in penance and it was worse. He'd get bored and he'd open his eyes, lie down and watch the skies. And sometimes, when things wouldn't turn out the way it was supposed to, he'd feel it was a waste of time. But this is not how it was supposed to be. He should have been practicing like the others, learning different combat techniques rather than sitting cross-legged with closed eyes.

And he sat again today, waiting. It had been an hour when things around him began to feel like they were dissolving. His eyes were closed, but he felt he was no longer on land. He opened his eyes and there it was. Darkness. All over the place. It had engulfed him, and tossed him from his familiar terrain into this dark oblivion. His heart raced as he wanted to escape this place, when suddenly, he was instantly plunged forward.

Things were blurry. There was a hut. There was a huge flying bird on top and that was when Kalki realized it wasn't a bird, but a machine from way behind its time. A mustached man exited from the mechanical bird.

He was again plunged somewhere else, in the forest, perhaps the same one where he saw a man with matted hair, shooting an arrow.

"Well done, Raghav." A man walked alongside the man named Raghav, and patted him on the shoulder.

Kalki collapsed to find himself in a wasteland now. A peacock-feathered man, rushing and sprinting against the field, with a volley of arrows bearing down over him, as he dodged. In retaliation, he pulled out a chakra, and threw it across. It went straight towards Kalki and he closed his eyes in fear. When he opened it, he found himself again in a different setting, this time in a colder region, perhaps somewhere in the mountains.

"I am surprised to see you here, honestly."

Kalki turned at the voice. Sitting, cross-legged, on a slab of ice was a man with a long beard and matted hair, with a huge axe mounted at his back. He was wearing a tiger skin around his lower body. Kalki felt cold, but the man seemed impervious to the elements.

"How are you surviving in such w-w-weather?" Kalki shivered.

"You are not feeling cold. You are thinking you are feeling cold," the figure said. "This is a dream state. This is unreal, all of it. At a snap of a second, you can wake up. You are in meditational yoga."

Kalki still felt cold. What was this man honestly trying to say?

"Who are you?"

"You," he said, standing up on his feet. "Years back, I was you. I was the sixth one."

Kalki automatically let his mouth run, "Lord Bhargav Ram," and then he knelt down in respect.

"Impressive. Your Channelling powers are indeed working."

"How am I able to communicate with you and not the others?"

"Those are snapshots," Lord Bhargav said, "of history, of what happened. Those are your previous selves as well, but you can also connect with them if you really try. But I am real, alive, and waiting for you in the flesh."

"You are Kripa's accomplice, are you not?"

Lord Bhargav nodded. "I do not surround myself with the best company, but I do not have many on my side. Maruti has left me to protect his own..."

"Maruti?"

"You might know him as Lord Bajrang."

Of course! Kalki had read about him in the Gurukul, how he had helped Lord Raghav in defending against a Rakshas, who was still a Tribal back then. They were all Gods now, in his time.

"You are saying I'm all of them?"

"Yes, you are part of a bigger picture, and we are all part of Lord Narayan, who has given us the power that we needed."

Kalki shook his head. "Kripacharya said that the fact that we got Soma was our choice and Lord Govind had said to stop the Soma so that others couldn't be turned mad. He said all of it as if it was scientific, but you say it as if it was meant to be, as if it were all premeditated."

"Kripacharya is a non-believer when it comes to destiny. Yes. Practically speaking, we aren't same. We were all mistakenly or intentionally exposed to Soma, in some way or the other. But I believe we were exposed for a greater cause, for our time. Just because one person doesn't believe it, he has no right to impose any restrictions on the other person as well," Bhargav smiled. "So tell me, what do you believe in?"

Kalki was quiet, contemplating, choosing his words carefully for he was dealing with a strange man who could meet him in his dreams. He was tall, brusque and hard, with veins protruding in his arms, his eyes bulging and his chest flexing. He was old evidently, but he was strong as a rock.

"I haven't figured it out."

"It is because you have not seen the world. You live in your nest, but once you come out, you'll get the answers of who we are—whether we were bestowed or whether we were just mistakes."

Kalki narrowed his eyes. "All the other Avatars like us have died. How come you didn't?"

Bhargav went silent. "I would prefer to tell you when you come and meet me. These answers can be understood when you have learnt and lost enough..." and his words trailed off, as he turned to face a visceral image of a woman watching over him.

And with a mighty slap across his cheek, Kalki came into his senses and realized he wasn't seeing any image, but was back to where he had been—amongst shrubs and twigs, concealed by the canopy. The sun was bright and there was no trace of the bone-chilling cold. Everything had felt so unreal and real at the same time. He could feel his fingertips were cold as ice. There was another smack and Kalki woke up from the delirious dream, watching his hands.

"What in the heavens are you doing in a field?" Lakshmi asked with a concerned look.

"What was I doing?"

"You were comatose. Eyes opened, but not speaking anything. I was worried." Lakshmi knelt down, to his level. "I was sickly worried for a fool like you. What were you doing?"

Kalki sighed. He wanted to tell her everything, but it would just make things complicated. "I told Shuko to wake me up when someone would be around. Where is that..." he began to scan the environment, when Lakshmi turned his face, inches away from her.

"He said he wouldn't interfere again like he did last time."

"Uh." Kalki felt still delirious. "I see," he coughed to mask his disorientedness. "Well, uh, I'm sure he didn't say *that*."

"Yeah, well, not in the literal sense, but I got it and you should too."

Kalki watched her. And he smiled. He couldn't help but smile. She would bring stability in his life, more than ever. He was stuck in a hole and she had pulled him out. How would he survive without her in this world?

"I'm afraid," Lakshmi said, her arms wrapping around his neck. "I want you to know I'm afraid. I don't want to die."

"You won't. I promise." Kalki wrapped his arms around her waist. They were close, so close that he could hear her heartbeat and smell her breath. "I'm afraid too. I want to admit to the world that I'm afraid."

"I know. I can see it."

"I know you can. You always do."

"It's okay, you know," she nodded vigorously. "It's all right if we are afraid. It's not the end of the world. It's absolutely all right."

"I know it is. I know. I wish I could feel it. That it's okay. But I don't feel it."

"What if I die?" Lakshmi asked.

Kalki hadn't managed to think it through. It was like a pain he wouldn't be able to face. "I don't want to think of that kind of a scenario. In my eyes, you live every time, with each blink and each sigh."

They looked at each other for a while, holding each other tightly. Kalki's heart skipped a beat when he came forward, hoping to meet her lips, brushing against hers, but then there were multiple sounds, before he could even do something. The horns were blown, the temple bells were rung, and the matter at hand had to be postponed. They looked at each other, both flustered and frightened as they knew what the horns and the bells meant.

The war had begun.

42

Sending out Shuko to see how much of the army was out there at the entrance, Kalki had left for Madira's Chalice where everyone had gathered. There were other elders as well. The entire tavern was filled with the village folks, some worried, while some were ranting about giving up the battle. When they all saw Kalki and Lakshmi coming together, their voices grew silent.

Kalki walked forward, his arms by his side, while his impassive face swivelled to see everyone from the village. They were all frightened, worried, almost on the verge of hopeless fear.

Kalki said, "I don't want to impose my will, but if you care about this village, detest those monsters that stand outside and then go to Indravan, stand outside the caves, and don't let them destroy it."

"What if they kill us?" one of them asked.

"They won't." Kalki licked his dry lips, his hands shaking even as he sought to continue, "If you all stand together."

Another one shouted from the crowd, "Will you win?"

Kalki sighed. That was a scary question. He wanted to be honest and tell them it was difficult, but his hands were clasped by another pair of hands, warm and soft. They were of Lakshmi's, who gave him an acknowledging nod.

"Yes." Kalki had a surge of energy inside him. "The very fact that we don't believe we will win is exactly why we will lose. We must begin to believe, in the most optimistic way, that we will rise from this darkness and beat the monsters who decided to take away our tradition."

No one uttered another word. Silence begin to creep in. Kalki didn't like it. It meant they had begun to believe in him. That's what he wanted, right? Why did he immediately fear this hope towards him? Why was he so afraid of taking a responsibility? The lives of many people now rested on him, many families and their children looked up to him. They believed he could do it. The pressure was intense. There was a little part of him that felt he should go back in time and not stand on the pedestal, proclaiming his adversarial attitude towards the city royals. He was just a village boy from a small place. Perhaps he had dreamt too big.

NO!

He couldn't have these thoughts. He tightly cupped his hands with Lakshmi's and gave a nod at the village folks before moving inside. Time changed people, but our choices dictated whether it was for the better or for the worse.

The inside of the tavern was haphazard. Half were climbing the stairs carrying boulders, rocks and weapons, while others were mapping out, standing close to the fire lamps and candles. The smell of sweat and the palpable adrenaline was overpowering. Each volunteer gave a nod at Kalki; it was a sign of respect and admiration. He had gained a lot of that over these period of days, but they were all so young, so naïve. Would they be able to fight?

He reached the main room where Arindam sat silently in the corner. Kripa was leaning forward and tracing the map that was placed on the centre table. Devadatta was there with Arjan and Bala as well. Arjan had a new weapon: a bow and arrow, a fit choice for a lad like him. Bala had a mace now, heavier than him, but he carried it effortlessly. Devadatta didn't carry anything, just like Kripa.

He had said to Kalki, Shambala was a village where weapons were an extraordinary overture. There was no armoury in Shambala as it was an agricultural village. Things had changed now, of course.

"Where were you, mate?" Kripa said.

Kalki left Lakshmi's hand and made his way around the table. "All right, what do we see?"

"What does your parrot see?"

He hadn't returned till now. Was he hit by an arrow? He hoped not.

"We checked from the top of this inn," Arjan spoke aloud, silencing the others. "The entrance of the village is blocked completely. There are tents erected in the forest. The army, well they are quite different from what we had expected."

"Do they have snakes on their breastplates?" Kalki recalled how there were Nagas, policing the streets in Indragarh. Perhaps they would have come all the way.

"No. In fact, there was no symbol at all. Just armour, and some of them, if I recall, didn't have any armour at all."

Lakshmi sat on the ground instantly, as if she had heard some terrible news. Kalki came to her rescue as he held her arm. "What happened?"

"No symbols, which means, they don't follow a God of their own," Lakshmi said. "That means…"

"Rakshas," ended Kripa, with his voice grave and hoarse.

"No," gasped Devadatta, as he cowered against the wall.

Kalki knew why everyone was worried. The most fascinating part about Gurukul was the fact that he had learnt about the Tribals, the once homogenous race that coexisted with Manavs, but who had long since been disbanded. One of the foremost men who had begun the rebellion for his fight for survival was King Dashanan of Eelam, down in the south. He was the same man Kalki had seen when he had Channeled and gone back in time. He was the man who was exiting a flying machine.

Rakshas, in the most realistic term, were ravagers. They didn't care. They didn't mind. They would eat their own after killing them. They had no remorse. They were creatures of the dark. And they were Tribals. But unlike Pisaches, the ones who had lost their mind, Rakshas were supremely intelligent. They weren't pawns. They were all dark-skinned, one of their major features, and many of their names were related to their earlier chiefs. They didn't have a God, because they believed in themselves; positing faith in war and its consequences. They didn't have armour because they didn't need it.

"Sarpanch ji." Kalki turned towards Devadatta. "There are a number of people waiting outside," he said, as he looked at the old, weak man who wouldn't be of any use to them here. "You must guide them to Indravan, where you have to make them shield the entrance of the cave. They'll be protected, under the wing of Lord Indra."

Devadatta nodded. "May the thunder of Vajra be with you, son." He nodded at everyone and briskly exited from the room.

As he did, a parrot entered from the half-opened door, gliding inside. But before he could even say anything, Arjan stormed in anger. "You made so many people go there to the one place where the enemies want to go. Don't you understand? Has your mind been thickened with all this religious nonsense?"

An unbeliever he was, Kalki knew, but the anger was so real that Kalki had to tell him the rationale behind his action. "I sent them there, not to be in any God's wing, but to be standing outside in large numbers, because no matter how big the army is, they will not kill anyone on a holy land."

"They are Rakshas, they don't believe in what is holy." Arjan carefully settled back now, perhaps a pang of embarrassment finally breaking through his angry obstinacy.

"But the person who is leading them would believe in it," Kalki retorted.

Bala coughed to interfere between the brothers' quarrel. "And who would that be? Parrot, seize the moment and regale us with your unlimited vision of knowledge!"

The parrot squawked after watching everyone. "LADY! LADY! TALL LADY!" Kalki got the answer.

"Well, we know who is leading them now." Kalki made Shuko sit over his shoulder. Arjan was still angry, while Kripa was just watching the drama around him, silently.

"Mates, today is not the day to fight amongst ourselves. We have to fight against them."

Kalki nodded as he came to the map and began to study the in-depth cartography of Shambala.

"The entrance is here," he pointed at the north-east end of the village, "the pillars cover the two ends. Have we blocked the entrance?"

"No," Bala said. "But the archers are ready to hit them from far."

"They are Rakshas," Kripa said. "Their skins are tougher than the average. An arrow made of bamboo would do little harm to them. We need to harm them repeatedly to drive them back."

Bala's mouth went grim. He hadn't expected that.

"Look at this," Kalki's finger danced over the long conical hillsides. The two terrains, on either side, were slanting and gave way downwards. "What if we bring two boulders on either side, and push them down? That'll take them by surprise."

Kripa studied the terrain carefully and gave a grudging smile. "Not bad, just like how your brother had planned, but it won't kill many."

"We can block their way, perhaps," Kalki said. "And harm the others."

"Sounds fair," Kripa said. "What about the others who make past the boulder? You see, a war doesn't end in a day, it goes on for quite a few days, and so they can push and break through."

"We have people ready to throw your explosives," added Arjan quietly.

Lakshmi had come forward, watching all the planning. "Yes, they could throw it at them from the trees that we have here and there," she pointed at the forest that densely surrounded the place. "Rakshas are afraid of heights, right?"

"Those were the old times," Kripa shrugged. "Many have overcome that handicap and chosen to conquer their fear."

Lakshmi pursed her lips.

"Catapults can be used from either end," Arjan said, pointing to the opposite side of the area where the Rakshas would enter from, and come in the main circle. "We can throw fire boulders at them."

Kalki listened to all of those ideas. "There will be no close combat, all right?"

"Even if we wanted to, we can't. There are too many of them and we are quite less in number."

Kalki turned to Shuko. "How many?"

"LOT!"

"That's helpful, bird!" exclaimed Bala irritatedly.

"How reliable are the catapults?"

"We haven't tried them enough," Arjan admitted. "They have come earlier than they were supposed to."

Lakshmi said, "The amount of resources we have would just last us for a day or perhaps two in the battle."

Kalki shook his head. He couldn't understand how to solve the issue. "Arjan, I want you to put most of the archers here on the east, and a few over the terrains on the west. The south will be empty as there are only huts and they don't care about them. I would like you to send the infantry in groups of ten to each house and scout if everyone has left for Indravan. If a Rakshas finds anyone alone in one of our homes…I want fifty men, bearing axes and swords, with Lyla and Sagar leading them," Kalki concluded. "That'll give us a systematic way of working rather than just ramming them forward."

"The question is why haven't they entered till now?" Roshan

Mitra, biting his nails, asked. Kalki turned to see him. *Need to get into my headspace again.* "Don't you all think it's kind of odd to not attack an unguarded entrance? I mean, they should be all over it."

The entire room was silent.

"They can be getting their supplies, woodcutter," Lyla spat. "Like us, they must be planning."

"Or…" Lakshmi gasped. "I read it in a book that the war doesn't start until…"

There was a huge bang on the door before she could complete her sentence. Kalki nodded his head, signalling to hold the thought while he went for the door.

Kalki opened the door to find a tall man, with uneven teeth, perhaps half-broken, standing outside with three more men. They were dark as coal, with hair that was unbelievably matted.

Kalki had been in Indragarh, but he hadn't laid his eyes on the Rakshas properly, for there were next to none in the main city area. The few that were still present were in Lord Kali's employment. By the look of the Rakshas, they were exactly what he had imagined them to be—ugly and grotesque, though not imbeciles like the Mlecchas. And they were tall; perhaps their average size was of Bala's height, somewhat more perhaps.

"A message for you from Lady Durukti," the messenger said, his voice having a thick Dakshini ring to it, as their origins were in Eelam, which was south of Illavarti.

Kalki opened the scroll and began to read it while Kripa just glanced at it and backed off. Bala, Lyla, Sagar and the others had lined to see the scroll each, reading it again and again to comprehend what the so-called Lady Durukti had written.

The messenger returned to his horse and looked at the tavern. He scoffed, and with his people, they mockingly laughed, speaking in their own dialect. It was said that the unrelentingly hot Dakshini sun made their skin so dark. Others gave it a spiritual spin, by ascribing it to their sinful way of living.

But even faced with the horror of their façade, Kalki knew all these tales about them being supernatural were bogus, because they were built and armed differently but were similar to Manavs, representing an entire different culture. That also means they were killable. Kalki found hope in that thought. A ghost is only scary till you see it. Then it just becomes an image.

"We do not wish to harm queer folks like you. We hope you choose the right decision," they all scoffed in unison. And then they rode off, their retreating horses' hooves setting into motion dust from the ground.

The scroll said: "Either surrender now, or have a close combat duel between the two best fighters from each side. Whoever wins, will seize the result without any protest."

"If they win," Lakshmi read it seriously, "they will raid the village. If we win, they will return home."

And Kalki knew who would have to go for this duel.

43

Durukti had travelled from Indragarh to Shambala and it had not been an easy ride. The chariot she had travelled in had been tough. The tents were erected for rest, but it was uneven and rocky, with the sound of wild animals keeping her awake for the better part of the night.

And all this while, she had talked to Chief Martanja, the paramilitary leader of the Rakshas. Unlike other Rakshas, he wasn't so tall and daunting. He had calm and a soft-spoken exterior. Durukti had all these kinds of notions about Rakshas. They were unclean, dirty and mortifying. But many of her notions had been cleared when she met them in real life.

She could still recall how she was old enough to see Lord Raktapa and Kali's deal. Unlike others who didn't know how that had happened, Kali had taken help from the Dakshinis, who had even given the gift of a ship to travel to Eelam and have a rich discussion with Raktapa. It had taken him a month and a lot of promises by Kali to finally let the Rakshas come on the plains of Illavarti.

Raktapa was a calm person, which was surprising for Durukti, who always imagined the Rakshas to be violent. They were, in fact great believers of Lord Shiva and had a protected Temple, deep in the cold regions to the north of Eelam, where they would undertake a pilgrimage every year. Unlike some theories, Eelam wasn't the hottest place to live. Sun killed the skin, sure, but at night the winds from the sea would soothe too. And during winters, which she had experienced while staying in Eelam, there was even snow. Raktapa had said that their bodies weren't dark because of the heat, but because of their heritage. They had been born like this, since time immemorial.

Chief Martanja reminded her of Raktapa a lot. He had a carefree smile and a noble, broad face, with a Trishul-shaped pendant hanging around his neck. But the most noticeable feature about him was his left eye. It was stitched shut and had healed now, the skin over it having peeled back. It showed Martanja had faced death from close.

When they were in the tent, examining the map of Shambala, it was then that Durukti had asked him: "I thought your men don't wear a symbol and yet you wear something to worship to Lord Shiva."

"We don't tell we love Lord Shiva. All this ink on your arms, the golden plate in the name of lords, it's all just flimsy to us, my lady. We aren't like that. We are true believers and this..." he signalled at his chest, thumping it then with a grin. "This is our symbol. Not even this pendant, for this is just a token given by my mother. Lord Shiva is in our hearts, our soul. Not in any materialistic sense."

Durukti was impressed by the Brahmarakshas. The Brahmarakshas were the chiefs, mostly who were Brahmins by birth and were of the Rakshas tribe, the most learnt and the most affluent, the most skilled of them all. When killed, the Brahmarakshas' title would be passed on to other chiefs like Martanja.

When they had reached close to Shambala, Martanja could figure out the state of the.

"My lady, it is surprising no one is there, it's empty."

"They must be hiding," she said, but her voice was drowned by the breeze blowing against the ferns, and the other Rakshas continuously training, clanging their iron spears, tossing and swinging their javelins. Durukti scanned the many red tents and horses. Symrin was right behind her, afraid, almost clutching to her robe.

They were so close to Soma and yet so far. They couldn't attack just like that. With no army to face, they couldn't enter. That would be a shame and tarnish to the image of the Rakshas, who fought in valiance and in self-defense only.

Martanja sent two men around to scout. They waited by the fire, as the poached bear roasted. They ate that till the scouts came back on their horses.

"Chief, half of them are close to the caves and half of them are preparing for archery. They have some kind of explosives too. They also happen to be hiding, some of them, in a local tavern," the scout said.

Martanja, eating the roast bear, just nodded.

Durukti shot Symrin a look, who was feeding on beans. "You told me they didn't have an armoury?"

Symrin looked down in disappointment. Already exhausted, she didn't have her usual smart quips.

"We don't need iron for swords. Back in the South, we practiced with only bamboo, stronger than the bloody iron if you ask me, my lady," Martanja quipped thoughtfully. "The estimate says there are almost five hundred members and we can't attack them at once. It'll be a foolish move and something that'll attract attention of your brother and the other Tribal Lords, my lady. We both don't want that as we need to do this discreetly."

Durukti nodded. "I don't want a bloodbath here. Shambala is an important village for Indragarh and Lord Vedanta would despise my brother and me if I choose to tarnish the image. But we also need to win."

"We can do so by honor, my lady. The best fighter from each side could come forth and battle. Whoever wins will have free access to execute their plan."

Durukti thought for a while. That did made sense.

"I don't expect a lot from them, but they are preparing. Surely, we will be attacked preemptively if we don't send out a message. I don't want to lose my men." He sounded like a hired mercenary. Durukti had paid him a lot in gold and silver to secure his loyalty and discreteness for this expedition.

"So the duel sounds good?"

"Surely, and on many levels, for they might have some tricks up their sleeves," he said, "like a vidhyadhar." He mentioned the magic practitioners of the land. "They used to have a tribe but are now dispersed and are limited to theatre shows or road shows where they awe people with their tricks. "But they wouldn't be having a strong warrior like we do."

Durukti scanned the Rakshas—they were all so tall and broad, it made Durukti feel small. Manavs had ordinary height as well, while the Nagas and Rakshas were all just tree-sized.

"Who would you send for the duel?"

"I have Kumbh," he said. "Named after Lord Dashanan's brother, my lady."

"I hope he won't sleep a lot like your Lord's brother." Durukti had read about Dashanan. While many considered him an eccentric man, he was a seeker of peace or that's what Raktapa had portrayed him as. It was a long time back, back when Dashanan had come, but he had given them Eelam, carving a nice island for them to stay and prosper on.

Martanja laughed. "Anything, but that. He's quite handy."

Durukti nodded, standing on her feet, for she had finished her food. At that instant, Symrin also stood up. "All right. But just remember one thing." The image of her weak and wounded brother who was suffering from a debilating disease and injury, began to choke her voice a little. "We *have* to win."

44

Arjan shook his head. "They are mocking us."

Kripa nodded. "True." He moved forward looking at everyone, his hands dangling beside his body. "It's like the old times, as they used to do. Best way to not end up with a lot of casualties. Whoever this lady Durukti is…"

"Lord Kali's blood sister," Lakshmi said, while everyone turned to see how she knew this piece of information. "My aunt. She works in the government, remember?"

"Anyway," Kripa continued, "she doesn't want a bloodbath, so she's choosing the less cumbersome way. In this manner, she will win because she knows we have no fighter on our side who is strong enough, while she has the strongest Tribal on her side. She can freely enter with our defeat. It's good either ways, though. If we by happenchance win, then they will leave."

Arjan had crossed his arms. "Okay, but what is the guarantee?"

"Mate, this is a battle," Kripa smiled cheekily. "There aren't guarantees. There are only exchanged words and promises that they ought to keep with each other."

"Better than scavenging for bodies if we reject this offer," Kalki said.

Lyla interrupted, "We should reject it and fight with all our might."

Kripa shook his head. "Not the smartest move to make by the way, lass. We are untrained, weak and dispersed. Right now our only hope is this combat."

"Can I ask how will we find someone who's as strong as that big, dark and tough man we saw right now?" Roshan Mitra cleared his throat in inquiry.

Everyone turned to face Bala, who arrogantly lifted up his mace and grinned. But Kalki saw Lakshmi and Kripa watching him intently. And then his eyes met Arjan's, who didn't look at Bala, but at Kalki. They had a silent exchange of approval with each other, but Kalki knew he couldn't expose himself in front of Lord Kali's sister. If she knew how strong he was, what he held inside him, things would take a wholly bitter turn.

They were standing opposite the Rakshas army. Kalki had agreed to the duel, but he came with his own preparations. There were people standing on the top of the terrains, invisible to the Rakshas and Lady Durukti, ready to trample them under stones, given a chance. All the archers and the swordsmen were in place, while folks with bolas were standing, ready to hurt them with the explosives. Kalki had seen the effects of it. It wouldn't kill the Rakshas, but easily wound their face or at most blind them.

Lakshmi had sent a number of men to scout and see if the village was empty. Lyla and Samrat were fifty yards away, on the same path that led to Indravan. Arjan and Kripa were on the eastern front while Roshan was on the west, waiting for a volley of arrows to be shot if anything went wrong. There were a few dispersed soldiers who were standing at guard, away from the Rakshas camp. Some were on trees with their bows, while others were on bullock carts, hiding. Any disturbance and they would pounce with their weapons. Most of the elders and non-volunteers were at Indravan, perhaps praying for the ones who were risking their lives to save them. Kalki and Bala were standing with two more volunteers at the back, holding axes. They didn't come prepared, but Durukti had. She brought a pack of Rakshas at the back, while she was on the horse with another woman.

How did he know who Durukti was out of the two? It was because of the way she entered. She had an air about her, the way her chin was lifted up. But most of all, Kalki was surprised that she was…his age, or perhaps even younger. And exceptionally pretty. The mere thought of acknowledging the enemy's beauty flustered him. He concentrated on the moment at hand. Durukti had a flamboyant golden and maroon laced robe. Tightly clutching the horse's reins, she looked over the entire terrain, studying Kalki. He was in torn and dull clothes, unlike them. The lady next to her was perhaps Arjan's age, but not as pretty as Durukti. She was pretending to be an aristocratic woman but something about her made him feel like she was a native, perhaps from a village. The only distinguishing feature about the girl was her seven fingers. They said it meant she was lucky, though Kalki doubted it. What was so lucky being with a woman who wanted to destroy an innocent village?

"I am grateful you have accepted our combat idea. We were worried you wanted a battle. Hopefully, we have both come to a decent resolution." Durukti smiled, her voice gentle.

What was she doing? Why was she being so sweet? Questions plagued him and pierced his conscience. He was worried, since the sweetest ones were also the most dangerous.

"This is Bala." Kalki thumped his friend's back as he came forward with his mace, frowning and huffing.

Durukti nodded. "Chief Martanja," she said, pointing to the one-eyed Rakshas, who was the only one wearing a breastplate amongst the other ones, "call your fighter."

Martanja signalled towards his men. Kalki waited for a mammoth-sized enemy from their end. Passing through the

Rakshas band of men, appeared a lanky, short man with a javelin in his hand, wearing nothing but a dhoti. He had scars lined across his dark skin and he had little hair on his head and his body. But his face was heavily bearded.

Bala looked at Kalki. And they both knew they weren't expecting this.

"His name is Kumbh," Durukti said with a straight face.

Kalki began to breathe a sigh of relief. Bala was a trained guardsman and Kumbh was half his size. Bala's one slap would send him sprawling on the ground, never to get up again. Kalki heaved a sigh of relief when Bala went forward, his mace ready to wreak damage.

The battle spot wasn't anything to write home about. It was a gently undulating clearing near the forest, with heavily flowering shrubs on one side, and weak sunlight filtering from the tree canopies above them. The whole area smelled of dried, burning leaves and oil. Perhaps these Rakshas anointed themselves with a lot of oil as they stank of it. Kalki could see all of them glistening with oil and wearing their armours and carrying their weapons. They looked far more ready as compared to his own ragtag side.

"Let it begin," Durukti signalled.

This was it

The circular area, where the patch of land was, became their ground for the combat. They circled each other. Kalki studied each move Kumbh made. He was walking casually, while Bala was crouched forward, legs bent, ready to lurch.

That was when Bala rushed towards Kumbh ready to attack, but not with the mace. He was hoping to use brute strength against Kumbh. Kumbh rolled over, dodging the attack and coming out of the clearing. He did it in a snap of a second. Bala couldn't realise where he went. He turned around. Kumbh was there behind him. He was smirking.

Kalki saw Bala now begin to use his mace, twisting the handle and circling it around the top, his mouth contorting into an almighty yell as he was about to strike Kumbh. Except he struck only air. Kumbh had again escaped. He was standing behind Bala again. He could have easily climbed on top of Bala and pierced him with his weapon, but he didn't. He was savouring each such futile attack that Bala made.

Kumbh's each calculated movement was a marvel of its own. He moved like a snake, slithered and rattled, dodged and swept, and unlike other Rakshas, he wasn't built well either. Rather, his arms were slim and his stomach was concave. But his face was full of vitality and energy. He was a strange enigma.

Bala again went forward, but he missed each strike. And that only led to his frustration. Kalki could see Bala was growing impatient. He was furious, his throat convulsing with anger. He yelled loudly in anger and charged once again at the quick Kumbh.

And yet again he dodged.

Kalki looked at Durukti and then at Martanja. They were enjoying this.

No. He's tiring him out.

And before he could spill the secret to Bala, the six feet nine inch guardsman rushed to hit Kumbh, who just slyly sidestepped the attack, gave a somersault in the air and came over Bala's shoulder. With one of his hands, he grabbed his neck and the other grabbed the weapon. He didn't kill Bala instantly. Rather, he pushed himself down, letting Bala collapse as well, due to the combined weight. Bala tripped and as he did, Kumbh pushed himself away from the big man and rolled back. Kumbh came forward, while Bala was trying to regain his footing, somersaulting again and letting his javelin pierce Bala's chest.

Except he couldn't.

The astonished eyes of Kumbh looked up at what stopped his javelin so fast.

Holding his javelin was none other than Kalki, his fist clenching around the iron rod, almost twisting the spear at the end with brute force. A trickle of blood dripped over Bala, who was in shock of what had happened. Kumbh had a dumbfounded expression; he was weak, almost shuddering.

Kalki began to clench the javelin tighter and the blade just broke in one piece. He grabbed the end of the javelin and with tremendous force, he plunged the javelin's weak end against Kumbh's chest. He fell back just like how Bala had collapsed a while back. Kalki came forward, tossing the javelin on the side and grabbing hold of Kumbh, as he began to drag him against the muddy ground, choking him. Kalki rained a few punches over his gut. Bleeding from his nose and mouth, Kumbh had lost his earlier frenzied look of vitality. He was weak and timid. Kalki looked at Martanja and Durukti, who were watching him intently, mortified, but also awed by the grand sight of what Kalki was able to do to their best warrior. And then Kalki let go off his throat. Kumbh's body just fell on the ground. The very fact that he was able to surprise Kumbh was what gave him leverage on the quick warrior.

Kumbh was on the ground and Kalki watched him with narrowed eyes. He had a bloody nose, that Rakshas. Kalki looked up, wiping the blood from his palm, tearing a piece of his tunic and wrapping it around his palm as he looked up at the disappointed Durukti.

Bala came on to his feet, grabbing Kalki's face. He was shivering and for someone who knew Bala, it was a surprise. Perhaps the fact that he was so close to death made him realise the finiteness of life.

"We have won," Kalki calmly said. Martanja just watched Kumbh as if he couldn't believe his best warrior had been knocked down by a village simpleton. But he didn't know Kalki was more than just that. "You have to leave…now," he ordered and he began to move away when he heard the same gentle voice.

"You were never part of the fight!"

"Well what do you know? I was the surprise element in the fight."

A flash of anger swept across Durukti's face. "You want to play it like this?"

Kalki turned to face the sister of Kali and nodded.

"All right then." Durukti looked at Martanja. "Grab the boy and raid the village."

Kalki's body stiffened, before he realized that ten Rakshas came to his side. He looked at Bala and signalled at him to rush off with the guards he had brought. Bala did so, while Kalki tried to get rid of as many Rakshas as possible. Some of them even chased Bala, but he was quick enough to escape deep in the woods.

They didn't kill Kalki so he punched a few, before his arms were trapped and his legs were tightly bound together. Kalki was forced into a strap, as he looked up in the sky. He could see his father's image in it for a while, as he was bound and taken forward, his back being flayed by the continuous lashes from their whips. He was forcibly made to kneel before Durukti. He couldn't hear or see Bala anywhere and he only wished they would fight valiantly.

"You betrayed the agreement."

"I played the way you played." Durukti smiled, the ingeniousness and deviousness clearly visible in her. "Don't kill him," she told the Rakshas who were holding Kalki.

Martanja was surprised. "Why, my lady?"

"A peasant who needs ten of your men to be tamed," Durukti narrowed her eyes, piercingly glaring at Kalki, who was held against his will by many arms, "cannot be just a mere peasant."

Kalki looked up, straining his arms against the back. He could see the village folks had brought the boulders on the opposite side, above the battle site.

"NOW!" Kalki yelled.

Durukti and Martanja yelled at the incoming surprise as the villagers pushed the rock and escaped from there. The boulders rolled down against the terrain, smacking each other as well as the Rakshas and their tents, destroying their food and shields. While it did not cause any significant casualty, but it did raise the temper of Martanja, who by now was seething in rage.

"Take this imbecile to the cage! And attack each and every house, raid it and find the caves!"

Kalki while being dragged away, could only think about one thing: *has Lakshmi returned to the secure place?*

45

Arjan had seen little as to what had happened. The archers had strung their bows, and they were waiting for his command. Even now, he could see from far the western end where Roshan Mitra was waiting with his own set of archers. Kripa was on that side too, hiding behind a rock. Nothing had happened.

And then in the midst of the green, hot plain, he was able to see someone running. His eyes terrified, his mouth agape. It was someone big, large…Bala. The thought crossed his mind, but it was idiotic to think that a person like Bala would be running from the war.

No. It was indeed Bala.

He was coming towards them.

"Hold your fire," Kripa said what Arjan wanted to say.

As he came forward, away from the bushes that concealed him, he saw two guards running behind Bala. And just yards away from them were Rakshas. They weren't sprinting like ordinary beings, but were fighting the breeze, as if trying to tackle it. They lurched on the guards, with their axes, and chopped their heads off. They reached for Bala, but before that Kripa ordered the volley of arrows.

The two Rakshas were hit by the arrows. Bala staggered past the line of archers that were meters from Arjan and Kripa. He grabbed for the leaves and the grass, panting restlessly, demanding water that Arjan rushed to get. There were five pots filled with fresh water from the lake that they had planned to use when the archers would get tired. Arjan helped Bala as he began to quench his thirst. Once done, he said, "They are coming. It's over. They got…uh… they got…" he was having a hard time breathing, "they got Kalki."

Kripa exchanged a worried glance with Arjan.

"We need to get him, mate," Kripa urgently bade Arjan.

"Who won the combat?"

Bala looked down. He had lost.

"We did. Kalki saved me from getting killed." He was on the verge of tears. But Arjan saw more than just the sadness. He saw disappointment. "The fighter, he was so…he was so small. I should have been able to…"

Kripa knelt down and grabbed him by the tunic. "Now listen, fat man. Get this in your thick head." He had a rather blunt way of speaking now, which one would not very easily reconcile with his usual drunken swagger. "We are about to die, so I don't need your weeping. I need your brawns."

"But he was so…so…small."

Kripa sighed. "Never underestimate your enemy. Size, big or small, doesn't matter if the other knows what the pressure points are."

And that was when they heard the roars. Kripa came forward, while Arjan saw what he couldn't believe. Like bees swarming around a hive, it was Rakshas all over the place. They had entered with axes, swords, spears and javelins. Arjan ran for cover as he grabbed a bow from his quiver and shot an arrow, hitting a rakshas who was sprinting towards him.

And just like that, Arjan saw they had even taken control of the huts, along Roshan Mitra's side. Some were even moving towards Lyla's group, where most of the guards had been stationed. Perhaps, she would be able to stop them. Perhaps.

That was when the Rakshas entered his territory. A group

of people at the back of the archers began to use the bolas. They tossed it towards the Rakshas. Initially caught unawares, soon they paid no heed to the small explosions. The archers shot the arrows, but most of them just dodged them. The ones who got hit were hit on their necks or in their foreheads, just knocking them down on the spot.

The surviving Rakshas just lurched from their positions, grabbing the bows, and stabbed the archers. They even managed to cut them deep, ripping their torsos apart. Seeing all the people he had lived his entire life with being killed like this, Arjan couldn't believe his eyes at what was happening. The volunteers fought hard, some even managed to kill, but most of the time they were beaten and became victims of the wrath that was the Rakshas.

Arjan saw Bala, who was hiding behind the tree. Finding his foothold on the path, he raced to him and grabbed him by the waist, "What are you doing? Help us! Fight!" He shot another arrow that instantly pierced a Rakshas' head.

"I am…I don't know…I don't know if I'll be able to. I'm not…not strong…I lost." Bala's pupils were dilated in mute fear.

"Strength doesn't mean you win every time. It also means to stand up again when you fall down once."

And at that time, the Rakshas had come forward. Arjan pulled back the string after fitting the bow, when he was grabbed by the Rakshas and thrown to the side. It went on to attack Bala, who could have easily attacked him back, but he just let him kick and choke him. Arjan saw no hope in Bala anymore. But he did see something fascinating in Kripa, who had a sword in his hand, just plunging it deep inside the Rakshas who had attacked Bala.

"Fat man; get us where we can get to Kalki."

"We will all die," said the wimpy Bala.

The Rakshas had managed to ravage most of the archers, but there were three of them still alive, ready to pounce at Arjan now. He was out of bows. Kripa held out the swords in front of him.

The three Rakshas grinned in unison, as if linked. One of them went for Arjan, and that was when he felt helpless as the Rakshas jumped on him and began to attack him. With each plunge of the axe that was directed towards his head, Arjan tried to dodge as best as he could. He used his knee and hit the Rakshas between his knees. Scavenging for his fallen bow, he staggered over the grass and smacked the bow across the Rakshas, which did not really yield the effect he desired. He lunged, his blade glimmering in the sunlight, when a big figure rammed against it.

Arjan realized it was none other than Bala, who was over the Rakshas and had his mace pummeling the hapless and bewildered Rakshas. Bala then casually, with blood sprayed all over his chest and face, walked to the Rakshas who was leering at Kripa. Arjan realized the third Rakshas who had attacked Bala was already ripped in half, as if Bala had broken a piece from a loaf of bread. When the Rakshas who was attacking Kripa saw what happened to his friends, he backed off, leaning against the tree in fear. Bala came forward, thumping his mace over his palm as if waiting to smack the man instantly.

And he was about to do that, Kripa stopped him.

"We need to know more about the camp."

The Rakshas just blinked. "Honestly, I have no idea about the camp." His accent was thick.

"You can kill him." Kripa shrugged, wiping the blood from his face.

Bala began the massive pounding session once again, when Arjan stopped him.

"Can you stop scaring me?" the Rakshas pleaded, almost falling over the ground and begging. It was funny since he was trying to be dominating earlier. "Just kill me if you have to, don't put me on the verge of..." his voice trailed off and he began speaking rapidly in his native tongue.

Kripa pulled him back up. Frightened, the Rakshas asked, "What do you want, you all?"

"How many men are in the camp?"

"One too many."

"That's not a number. Don't run your smart mouth. Not now especially." Bala thumped the tree and it shook.

Surprising as it was, Arjan was happy that Bala had returned. For a moment there, he had forgotten who he was and what he was like. He had been different, so uniquely distinguished that Arjan realized how real death encounters really make the strongest person falter. Bala was a great personality, someone who everyone would look at and fear, but here he had been, just crying to himself. Battles do so many things to an individual, one of them being crushing their soul. Though, he was back, perhaps from a sense of duty to save his friends or perhaps Arjan's words might have just worked.

"Around a-a-a hundred."

"All right," Kripa said. "What are the exact points of the camp?"

Kripa began to make a rough sketch with a twig over the little sandy area on the ground. He made a rectangle and inside it, he made circles that represented tents and stars that represented the Rakshas. "Now tell me clearly, mate, who are there and how are they placed?"

"I…I…I will die," he coughed, "if they find out I revealed it…"

"And what do you think we will do to you if you don't tell us?" Kripa signalled at the back where dead Rakshas lay.

By the Gods, Arjan couldn't believe he was in the midst of an adventure he was not ready for. He couldn't feel anything except dreadful fear and surging adrenaline, in equal measures. Rather, he didn't want to feel. He was hoping to get out of this entire duel, with his calm rationality and practicality. If they went about the whole scheme of things systematically, then it would not be long until they could roast these outcasts.

"All right, all right." The Rakshas nodded glumly, as he knelt down and began to explain the entire camp to Kripa. "Your friend could be uh, could be placed here, in the cage where we have kept the mules and the horses. This is our employer's tent…"

"Durukti?"

"Yes, that damn woman," the Rakshas cursed. "Because of her, I'm stuck here."

"It's close to the cage, the employer's tent." Kripa nodded. "That means heightened security. How many are left behind in the camp?"

"Perhaps twenty, most probably, just to make sure nothing goes wrong."

Kripa didn't like the idea. "You can do what you want to with him now, mate." He tapped Bala's shoulder.

The Rakshas began to plead again, like the way he was doing earlier, with his palms flat, his mouth contorted into a helpless plea, before Bala used his mace and just hit him hard on the head, knocking him out.

"What should we do?" Arjan stepped forward, addressing the old guru.

"We need to escape." Kripa looked at Bala and Arjan at the same time, "Get your brother out of here and just leave."

"What about Shambala?"

Kripa squared in front of Arjan, tightening his clutches over his shoulder. "Shambala is just one part of the world and to save the world, we need to sacrifice a small part of it. See the bigger picture."

"What do you mean?"

"Your brother is more than who he thinks he is," Kripa revealed, "And I will explain to you both how important it is for us to save him, more than many people out here. He can't die because if he does, oh…well…it'll not just be Shambala that'll be devoured by the destruction. Entire Illavarti will be up in flames."

Arjan could understand the gravity of the situation, but he also couldn't believe his brother was someone who would save the world. He was a simpleton after all.

"All right, lead us on," Arjan nodded.

Kripa began to enter the forest, followed by the silent Bala and Arjan, when Arjan revealed something going on in his mind. "Hold on, we are going inside the enemy lines and we don't even know if we will escape. What if *we* die?"

Studying the scenery, Kripa scratched his head. "Uh well, I haven't figured that part in this entire rescuing mission." And he sniggered.

God, I hate that laugh, Arjan thought, but he continued to follow him.

46

It was horrible, sitting in the stench of horseshit, seeing the Rakshas swinging from one place to another. He had been trapped in a cage that could easily include a dozen more. He had enough space, and yet he could not breathe. It wasn't like Kalki didn't try to open the cage. With all his might, he tried to push it apart, punch it, and even pull the bars apart, but nothing happened. Perhaps, it was the way the metal had been made or perhaps he had weakened.

With his tongue out to quench his dry mouth, he let the wind touch him. Kalki saw the camp from inside and it was more organized that had been perceivable earlier. There were a lot of weapons in one tent, from where each Rakshas would go and get one. There were some bigger tents, perhaps to house Durukti and Martanja. There were pots filled with water and suras, while fire pits were made for logs to be stacked up on. He couldn't hear anything but wails and yells from either side. But he couldn't distinguish which were from his people and which were from the Rakshas. *Who must one sympathize with, when you can't even hear the truth?*

Kalki felt restless as he walked back and began to punch the cage. It rattled, but it didn't break. He continued to punch until his knuckles bled and he felt the hurt stinging his arms, almost temporarily leaving them numb. He had nothing on him to cover his wound and that would only make it septic.

"Anger is good," a voice came from the back, "but never use it against yourself." Kalki turned to see Durukti, with her lady companion on her side. In the midst of the ultimate humdrum and the loud clangs of the weapons, Durukti remained calm as if she knew she would win this battle.

"I'm sure this didn't go as you thought it would."

Durukti simply nodded. "I would agree with you on that." She paused. "It was a brave little attempt from a village like Shambala, but you must all realise that you are facing trained men."

"They are Tribals." Kalki wiped the blood over his dhoti. "They are as trained as us."

"Just because they are called Tribals doesn't make them uncivilized. You have not seen the world as much as I have. I have travelled all around and I can say one thing. Manavs are the most ruthless and idiosyncratic when it comes to constructing narratives about and justifying their existence."

"What tribe are you from?" Kalki spat, surging anger just boiling inside him.

Durukti pushed her tongue against one side of her mouth. She had a playful habit about her, something that disturbed Kalki for they were in the midst of a war.

"Do I look like a Tribal?" Durukti asked, while her companion remained silent. "Do I look fat like a Yaksha, or do I have blue eyes like Nagas, or do I have dark skin like the Rakshas? Please, tell me."

She had none. In fact, she was of fair complexion, with straight face and an angular frame.

"You might be of some other tribe, one we don't know about."

Durukti continued to hold her tongue inside her mouth, thoughtfully musing to herself. "They said me and my brother, we were Asuras."

The name sent shivers down his spine. *Weren't they extinct?*

"Kali," he muttered to himself

"What is your name?"

"Kalki."

"Ah, destroyer of filth," she spoke. "Quite ironic for someone who is standing amidst filth?" She paused. "And it is Lord Kali for you."

"I don't worship those who make themselves lord in this world," Kalki sat, cross-legged, just massaging his bloody hand. He had an impassive face, his soul urging him to jump from this cage and escape to Shambala, and help the ones he was supposed to help.

"Every God was once a man." Durukti smiled. "Let's take from the Trimurti—Vishnu, Brahma, Shiva. They were all Prajapatis; the seers, the beginners, the first men. In fact, they were even present when the Ancients were living among us. They had different names; in fact, all Gods we worship now; they had different names then."

The Ancients…they were the civilization that lived before the Breaking, the plague that caught on to people like Lord Govind. Some of them were worshipped as Gods now.

"We think they were born after the Breaking, but we are living in a different reality altogether." Durukti surprised Kalki, for he couldn't believe how such a young girl could hold so much wisdom. "They were all there since the dawn. And you don't know all of this because you live in a small world of your own making."

Kalki shrugged. "I don't want to entertain you with a conversation anymore. I will only speak to King Vedanta."

Durukti clenched her jaw at that name. "The king has given me the right to do whatever I wish to do with the villages that surround his city."

"What if he finds out what you have done is against the basic rules?"

"I'll just say you rebelled. What proof would he have to castigate me?" Durukti laughed cheekily at the end, almost to the point of mocking him.

Kalki remained stiff. "What do you plan to do with me?"

"Study you, most probably. A fine tough man like you

shouldn't be wasted as a casualty of war, but put on as an exhibit of entertainment perhaps," she chuckled.

Kalki shook his head. "Just kill me and get on with it. It'll be over for you and me. I can't stand mute while my people die by the hands of your men," he said, reaching for the rails, his eyes slowly tearing up. "All these lives, they depended on me and I can't even die by their side, like a real friend. I couldn't fulfill my duties. It was me who defied your plea to break down the caves."

She looked at him for a while. All the mocking hatred had just left from her face. She was standing there, confused perhaps, and a little sad. She came forward, inches away from the railing. "You shouldn't have."

"I'm trying to protect the city and you. What's inside the caves, they shouldn't be touched. They are cursed. That wouldn't be...that wouldn't be right." He couldn't just say that the Soma, if exposed, could mistakenly get into the hands of the next Adharm, who could evidently be a Tribal, since they are absolute evil. He wanted to stop it, as long as he could, for the Dark Age would descend when the Adharm would rise.

"I apologize." Her voice was genuine, her gaze lowering with embarrassment. "I didn't want to hurt you people. I just...I just have to do this, get to the rocks. If I don't, there will be grave consequences." She was helpless, just like Kalki. "And nothing can come in between us. I had promised myself that."

Kalki sighed. "Please don't kill them, please."

That was when their talk was interrupted by Martanja, who entered after watching the scene unfold from afar. He stood there, awkwardly, until Durukti signalled him to come forward and speak.

"I hope this little urchin is not disrespecting you, my lady," Martanja said, while he stayed firm and square in front of Durukti.

Durukti glanced at Kalki as if she had known him for a while. "No, he isn't. He's being docile as of now." She paused, as Kalki noticed she was contemplating something. "Is there any other news?"

"Yes, my lady. We have located the caves and the path is free."

No! That meant Lyla and Sagar were dead or injured, or at any rate beaten, while the other volunteers had clearly failed to obstruct the path leading to the caves.

"My men are still searching for anyone in the homes of the villagers, hoping to make a brief check before we make way there since we don't want to be attacked from the back again." He eyed Kalki balefully.

Kalki didn't look down, but stared straight. He gritted his teeth. He had to escape, anyhow.

"How many of the villagers have been killed?"

"Plenty, my lady." Kalki could see Martanja was almost grinning, but struggling really hard not to.

"I want you to tell your men not to hurt anyone, anymore. You understand me?"

Martanja was puzzled, brows furrowing down, his unseeing eye rapidly blinking. "My lady, but…"

"No! No more. Not even an armed one. They will be subdued, but not killed," Durukti sternly ordered.

Kalki turned over to the girl who had become such an important person in the city that she was now being respectfully followed by the paramilitary chief of the Rakshas. But he couldn't believe she had agreed with him. He had pleaded and she had listened. She had a conscience after all, behind the exterior that she concealed herself with.

"All right, my lady, as you please." Martanja gave a slight bow.

"Let's go." Durukti signalled her companion and with that she left, following Martanja.

Kalki saw them leaving, when instantly Durukti's companion returned. She had eyes as big as a fish, her seven fingers grabbing onto the rail, and a feverish smile dancing on her lips. "He told me all about you. Oh, you are a grand sight, after all, White Horse!"

Her eyes were manic. At one moment, she was a docile maidservant to Durukti, and here she was acting all different.

"Who?"

"He will come, don't worry. Oh, he will. You'll meet him soon." Her smile widened.

Kalki grabbed on to her knuckles, his blood tainting her hands. She gasped and pulled back. "I want to know who it is. How do you know me? Who is this person?"

The girl giggled and her yellow teeth were visible now. "He's the bearer of truth. He will tell you everything, unlike me. He thinks I'm not ready, but he also thinks you are not ready. I can see he's right. You are too immature," she giggled again, hiccupping slightly. It was a whirlwind of emotions that were smacking Kalki from the inside.

"SYMRIN!" the voice from the other side came.

"I should leave," the girl called Symrin said, "his pawn is calling me."

His pawn?

And with that, she raced away. Kalki hated his cage even more now, for he could only see one part of the scenery, as the back was blocked by multiple shields that acted like a cover.

Kalki saw there were two Rakshas standing in front of him, a few yards away, talking to each other. They had been there before as well, and he had been eyeing them, for one of them held a key dangling from their arms.

I need to get those damn keys. But how?

And that was when his eyes fell on the gliding bird that circled on the top, squawking. It was a parrot. Kalki's lips spread in a smile at the thought of him, about how much he had missed him and how he had just vanished earlier. But he had returned. "Shuko," he breathed, relieved at last.

47

Lakshmi had heard the wails first. Swivelling her head, she saw the prowling Rakshas breaking through the tall grass, their mouths curled in a grotesque snarl. Lakshmi had managed to drive most of the villagers to Indravan, but there were still a few houses that had not been vacated yet. Struggling for safety, she watched the incoming army colliding with the volley of arrows that stung half of them, but they still managed to lurch into the houses, damaging the property. The swordsmen with Lakshmi who were carrying lighter weapons tried to fend them off, but to no avail as the Rakshas were quick on their feet, almost killing and ripping half of them.

She dragged herself to the hut, hiding behind the stone walls, peering from the broken window. That was when she saw none other than the volunteers who were up on trees. They began to throw explosives at the Rakshas. Some of them burst in their faces, while most missed their target. Lakshmi could see the Rakshas were just grinning at the sight. They pounced and made their way up to the trees. The volunteers jumped and the Rakshas caught them by their clothes and pinned them against the tree, with a spear ramming through their chests.

They are the devil incarnates.

In all of this, Lakshmi saw no remorse of any kind on their faces. It was the end of Shambala and she knew it. How much she despised Kalki now, for bringing up the decision to fight. How foolish he was! But he did it for a reason that was noble. *And dying nobly is far greater an achievement than being a coward survivor.*

Grabbing a splinter from a damaged tree, Lakshmi came out, her feet and fingers becoming numb with cold. She knew it would kill her, but she had to do it. They would find her eventually, killing her in her hideout. The surviving Rakshas looked at her, gleefully grinning at the fresh target she offered to them.

They began to walk towards her, some of them wiping the blood of her friends from their putrid faces and hands, against the rest of their body.

Lakshmi clasped the splintered weapon tightly, feeling its uneven edges dig into her palms.

"Come you, you all," Lakshmi breathed. It was a stupid decision, and she knew it, but there was no other choice.

The other Rakshas remained at the back, seeing the opportunity to see how this played out, while the one came forward with his blade.

"A beautiful girl like you shouldn't be in a place like this," the voice was thick with lust, coarsely accented. "Come with us and drink and rejoice, huh? We won't do anything to you that you won't enjoy."

He came forward to grab her. Lakshmi turned a little bit and with a quick stroke, smashed the splinter against the Rakshas' chest, creating a massive gash. Blood gushed out as he fell forward, shocked by the attack. The other Rakshas just watched her in confusion. Aunt Ratri hadn't just taught her about the books, but also about the weaknesses in the human body, teaching her where the thinnest veins were, and how much impact was required to injure in a specific degree.

Two more Rakshas came forward, this time charging, with absolute no leniency in their eyes. Instead of a splinter, she used a bola in one hand this time. As the two came forward, she leapt, rolling in the air almost. While they looked on in confusion, she threw the bola at them and jammed the splintered makeshift spear into one's foot. The other Rakshas brought out a blade, but Lakshmi did a backward somersault to dodge it. The other one stormed at her and as she was about to move, when four hands grabbed her from the back. She began to struggle and realized more had come from behind her.

"Little girl wants to play. Let's give it to her then," they grinned.

She pushed and pulled her legs and arms, wailing as she was lifted above their heads. The Rakshas came forward and began to look at her with wide and appreciative eyes. "Interesting." His thick, greasy hands began to run slowly over her exposed waist.

That was when a sharp arrow went through the Rakshas' head. His eyes were confused at what had happened until he fell back. The other Rakshas looked away, and so did Lakshmi, when she saw Roshan Mitra on the same chariot that Lakshmi and Kalki had brought from Indragarh. He had two archers in the front, shooting in quick succession.

The Rakshas left Lakshmi as she fell on the surface, her back cracking, and a surging pain running up her spine. She couldn't feel or hear anything for a while, her eyes staring at the skies as she took deep breaths to calm her pain. She diverted her attention to her left side, where Roshan Mitra was standing with his arrows. He must have come down from the woods of Shambala, ready to attack the savage Tribals. She saw the Rakshas, who had tossed her on the floor, jumping on the chariot as Roshan was trying to fend him off. He fell back; the wheels of the chariot broke and rolled over to Lakshmi.

Grabbing the wheel and pulling out the spoke from it, Lakshmi mustered the spirit to stand up straight and use it to her advantage. The chariot had gone to pieces now. Three Rakshas lay on the ground, arrows sticking out of their faces. One of them had killed an archer and was now targeting Roshan, who had fallen over on the ground.

Lakshmi made way, her legs rushing towards the Rakshas as she pounced in the air, everything going hazy in front of her, as her hands felt a strong recoiling pressure. She opened her eyes and realized the rod was inside the Rakshas' head. Lakshmi fell on the ground, panting, as the Rakshas lay dead.

Roshan scampered over to her and decided to calm her down as Lakshmi dry-heaved at the sight in front of them. Lakshmi came on her feet, struggling, but she couldn't hear anything. They had been defeated, but she could see the directed army of Rakshas was moving towards the Soma caves.

The shattered chariot, the dead Rakshas and bodies of innumerable villagers crowded the once pious grounds of Shambala. Everything truly seemed over now.

Roshan limped as Lakshmi said, "We should go and check more homes."

"What about the Soma Caves?" he asked.

"We can't go there unless we check the homes."

"They are coming." Roshan patted Lakshmi's head with a sense of finality.

Lakshmi saw at the back. There was a surging number of Rakshas making way for the huts. Lakshmi walked with her friend, as they made their way downwards, where the ground sloped and where there were more huts.

Lakshmi couldn't believe there was so much darkness around them. Roshan went for the nearest hut so he could rest his leg. Hidden in the home of another Shambala family, they stayed and rested. Lakshmi resisted the urge for water as she began to unwrap Roshan's leg that had a huge, swelling wound.

"Oh no, oh dear no." Roshan had a peek and immediately tilted his head back. "This was suicide, I knew it. This was suicide. My mother told me it was…"

Lakshmi slapped him hard on the face. "Just shut up!" She couldn't believe she had it in her to just smack another boy, but she did it with ease. She was just furious, sad and reeling from the effects of adrenaline coursing through her system. She tore a piece of her dupatta and wrapped the wound. "We can't let the blood…"

And then she heard the wails. They came from inside the hut. Peering from the window again like last time, she saw the Rakshas were making their way in. They were just three in number. Three Rakshas were equivalent to ten villagers and Lakshmi and Roshan were clearly in no state to tackle them, injured as they both were. She had no weapon anymore, nor did Roshan.

"Wait here."

Lakshmi went scavenging in the unknown house, hoping to find something inside. She looked in the living room, checked for the pots and was able to find a still simmering hearth, and a knife from the kitchen.

That was when she heard a thud.

No.

Lakshmi went for the room where Roshan was when she heard the thud again, perhaps coming from the direction of the kitchen. She bent down and pushed the rug away. She saw some grills over a big hole that went deep underground. She peered, removing the grills and saw in the darkness, two individuals.

They were hiding.

She couldn't figure out who it was down there so she decided to interact with them. "My name is Lakshmi. I'm from Shambala. Please respond."

No one did.

"You do not need to be frightened. We need to stick together and leave. If you stay down there, you might pay a heavy price."

She heard a voice just then. It was a meek little tone. "Hello?"

"Shut up!" was what followed it.

There were two of them, Lakshmi already knew.

"You don't need to worry, come up here." She laid her hand out. "It'll be all right, I promise."

She waited for a while, and just as she gave up, another hand clung on to her. Tightly grasping it, she pulled them out one after the other. It was a mother and a daughter, drenched in muddy water. Such holes were common in most houses, for purposes of indoor sanitation.

"What is your name?" Lakshmi asked the frightened woman.

"Aarti," the woman said, "and this is Pia."

"Hello, Pia," Lakshmi struggled to smile at the little girl who was no more than four years old, with gently curling hair over her forehead. "Why have you been hiding out here?"

Aarti looked at her in disbelief, unable to perhaps comprehend that there was another villager from Shambala, alive.

"Speak up, woman."

"I-I…I was afraid."

"Didn't you go with all of them to Indravan?"

"I was uh…I was told by my husband to not leave the house."

"Where is he now?" Lakshmi shook her head. He must have been dead as well, and she felt absolutely ridiculous when she asked this question. Her mind, despite being quick usually, wasn't thinking straight. She had to stop, think a little and then act. The way she always did with every aspect of her life.

"I-I don't know. He never returned."

Seems just as well.

Lakshmi felt horrible for the lady. She had gone through so much, stuck in a hole for so long with her baby daughter.

"I want you to tell me if you have any medicinal herbs in the hut."

The woman looked confused, her brows furrowed.

"For my friend, he's outside."

"How many are there?" Aarti asked, bewildered. "How many survivors?"

By just the looks of it, Lakshmi couldn't give a proper answer to it. There were less on this side, perhaps more towards the path that led to Indravan.

"Don't worry about it. Just stay positive. We will survive, I'm sure."

"Are they out there? I can hear them sometimes. They had heavy voices…" she trailed off, mumbling, while Pia began to cry. Lakshmi patted the kid and sternly told the mother, "You need to stop talking like this. It scares the girl."

"You have no idea how it feels to be stuck there."

And she didn't. She agreed. And she felt horrible.

Aarti showed her the medicinal leaves that she had been collecting and they were plenty in number, placed close to the hearth she had seen earlier. She took the leaf and smelled it. It was the same fragrance that Lakshmi had smelt when she was cleaning off Kalki's wound. Lakshmi naturally trusted her own instincts about first aid, rarely taking help of the shaman.

"Are there any weapons out here?" Lakshmi asked.

"Weapons? Dear no, we are just mere fisherpeople…"

There was a huge commotion at the entrance of the house. Swivelling her head, Lakshmi realized something was amiss. She began to slowly make way to the path that led to the front when she saw two Rakshas inside, checking and scanning the hut. Her eyes slowly reached Roshan Mitra who had a small axe plunged into his head, as he lifelessly looked back at Lakshmi.

Lakshmi gasped in horror as she exchanged a glance with Aarti. *I am sorry.* Lakshmi's eyes started tearing up.

"Go down again," Lakshmi mouthed silently.

Aarti and Pia reached down again and Lakshmi found it ridiculous and stupid on her part that she had called them up in the first place. She thought she could escape the Rakshas, but she was an utter fool. As they began to move down, Lakshmi hid the hole with the carpet, but perhaps the sound of their movement had alerted the Rakshas, for they charged inside the room.

Lakshmi closed her eyes and prayed to the Goddess, and after opening her eyes and turning around, she saw the Rakshas held twin-sided blades. They were just watching her, emotionless. Huffing and breathing heavily, they began to come forward. Lakshmi purposely stood over the carpet so they wouldn't notice. But that only ended up making a grating noise.

No.

"What was that?" the gruff voice of one of the Rakshas asked.

Lakshmi didn't respond.

"We are told not to kill anyone," said one Rakshas to another.

"Wasn't she the one who spliced our friend's head off?" the other said. "The very beauty of death is that no knows *when* someone is killed."

Lakshmi used the knife she had got from the kitchen. Swinging in the air, the Rakshas dodged in the nick of time, grabbing her wrist and tossed her against the wall. Dust swept over her as she fell on the floor, retching against the ground. The Rakshas began to move the carpet and then slowly lifted the rails that guarded Aarti and Pia. They looked down.

"Interesting," the Rakshas coughed. "Protecting some of your friends, perhaps, eh?"

Lakshmi didn't say anything. The other Rakshas grabbed her and smacked her against the wall, this time his thick arms restraining Lakshmi. She tried really hard to push against him. The Rakshas, close to the hole, pulled a small circular rock from his belt. "Courtesy of your friends."

It was the explosive Kripa had been making.

The Rakshas tossed the explosive down. Lakshmi screamed so hard that her chest burnt, her mind reeling at his blatant show of heartless monstrosity. It exploded inside the hole and the worst part was that she didn't even hear anything. Not even a cry or a protest.

Please no.

Lakshmi had never felt so terrible in her life. She could feel her very bones weakening with guilt.

"Now, what should we do with you?"

"Have some fun perhaps," the other said.

"Hmph," the first one grinned, "take her outside."

Lakshmi felt her feet being dragged, unable to understand what was going to happen next.

48

Kalki had been waiting for Shuko to do something, but nevertheless, he was just fluttering and hovering over the Rakshas guards. But he was quick enough to miss their gaze and Kalki couldn't help but smile.

Do something. Come on.

That was when he saw Shuko reach the railing and squawking at the cell. The guards saw that and instantly tried to catch him by the leg. Successful in doing so, Shuko tried to get away, but he couldn't. Kalki, out of breath with fear, ranted and retaliated, yelling abuses to distract the guard.

"You filthy, dirty animal! A cow dung cake smells better than you!"

The Rakshas who held Shuko by the legs looked at the other one in disbelief. In fact, Kalki couldn't believe he had said it himself. At that moment, the Rakshas jerked his hand involuntarily after Shuko excreted on him, letting Shuko fly away.

"Why did you leave him?" snarled the other Rakshas.

"He shat on my hand." The Rakshas wiped it against his lower body. "God, a parrot's shit. Already my day is bad and it just got..."

"Worse?" Kalki suggested.

"Yeah, yeah," the Rakshas said.

The first one thumped him again. "You don't agree with the prisoner. The Chief said, no talking."

"I'm not talking. I'm just agreeing."

"That's still vocal. I have to report it to the chief."

Kalki cleared his throat, interrupting them. "You don't have to be such a tattletale, you know."

"Exactly," the second one said. "He's always like that. I can't even do one simple, straight thing, without the threat of being reported."

Kalki found it humorous to distract them, his eyes wandering close the keys that dangled from the Rakshas' belt. He had to let Shuko get them. He whistled softly, letting Shuko hear the sound of his whistle, giving him directions.

"What are you doing?"

Kalki stopped. "What?"

"What was that sound?" the second one, the stricter one asked.

The first one shrugged. "Can you stop being like this?"

"Yes, can you?" Kalki joined forces against the strict guard.

"He was signalling someone," the second one snarled.

"Who is signalling?" the first one looked around, "no one is here. We are packed with our own men. So stop worrying, you!" He slapped the second one's chest.

"You know it hurts." The second one began to massage his chest.

"And to be fair you were talking to the prisoner as well, I'll report you too."

"You can't report me just because I inquired."

"But isn't inquiry talking?"

"It's uh…" the second one contemplated the situation, frantically, he looked up at the prisoner. "You tell us? Was my inquiry in relation to talking to you?"

Kalki shrugged. "Since your inquiry had a vocal element, sure. You were talking to me."

"Hah!" the first one gleamed with pride. "Got you, you tattletale!"

The second one frowned.

All of this seemed inconsequential, and as of now his eyes were still directed towards the key. A little closer and Kalki could get the key himself. As he tried to not interject between the two Rakshas, Shuko glided down, and with his small claws, scratched the first Rakshas. The Rakshas swung at the bird, but missed it.

"What is wrong with the birds here?" he said, groaning, wiping the blood off of him.

"They hate you," the second one grinned, finally able to ridicule his partner.

The first one just managed to frown and wiped his face.

Kalki whistled softly again. Shuko came forward and scratched the second one's face, before flying back up.

"I'll shoot the parrot!" the second one moaned. "Let me get my bow."

Kalki could see Shuko slowly pull at the keys now. That was when, out of nowhere, a huge man appeared with a mace in his hand. Bala! Then from the other side, Kripa and Arjan came. The two Rakshas looked at them, astonished.

"INTRUDERS!" The first one yelled.

Before he could yell again though, Bala grabbed him and twisted his neck while Arjan shot an arrow right against the second one's chest, who tripped and fell close to the cage.

"Thank the heavens you are here." Kalki breathed a sigh of relief, when instantly he saw Rakshas were beginning to crowd them. There were almost five of them with long spears.

Bala and Arjan can't die.

He saw them prepare as Kripa used his sword, dodging and fencing against attacks. Kripa had a sense of Machiavellian within him, even though he mostly tried to portray himself as drunk. He was quite handy with the sword, just rolling and moving it with ease and then somersaulting over the ground and cutting off the Rakshas' limbs.

Bala was, on the other hand, more rugged. While he was unable to defeat Kumbh, here he fought against the other Rakshas as if they were figures made of wood. In quick succession, he choked one while smashing his mace against the other one. When a javelin stabbed him in the back, he yelled in agony, pulled out the javelin and thrust it against the Rakshas' eyes.

Arjan was least prepared, probably just trying to stop the attacks. Even in trying to deflect the attack, he was repeatedly facing the brunt of the Rakshas' wrath.

The number of the Rakshas attacking them increased and Kalki knew he had to save his friends. He began to inch his hands towards the body of the Rakshas, trying to grab the belt of the Rakshas and propelling him over to the cage. But the keys were just out of his reach. That was when a pair of feet trampled over the keys. Kalki looked up and saw it was another Rakshas. He stepped on Kalki's hand, but Kalki grabbed him by the ankle, his fingers sinking into the skin until the Rakshas began to cry in pain. Blood flowed over his fingers and the Rakshas shook in agony. Shuko began to peck the Rakshas until he collapsed, which was when Kripa plunged the sword into his head.

Kripa winked at Kalki and, for a man his age, he was quite adroit with his reflexes. Shuko reached down, squawking, as he began to reach the keys and give them to Kalki. Kalki quickly patted him and made his way towards the lock, which he unlocked.

He let himself out, the bird slowly rising and sitting over his shoulder as he left the cage behind. He was out there finally. It seemed that nature too was congratulating him for making an escape, with the sun peeking out from the cloud cover and the winds that had slowly picked up pace. Kalki went for Arjan, who was dodging the blade attacks. As another blade was plunged by the Rakshas, but it stopped, for Kalki jumped on the Rakshas' back.

The Rakshas looked back, confused. Kalki forced the Rakshas to let go of his blade and with a quick punch, he knocked him out.

He picked up his brother and they embraced, Arjan's short hands rounding around him. "I missed you."

"I am sorry." Kalki nodded.

It was impossible to kill so many Rakshas, but they had to at least try. Kalki used his blade, swinging it inefficiently, a little lopsided, until it fell off from his hand and hit a Rakshas, cutting off his toe. Growling with hurt, he raced towards Kalki, who just dodged. He was now charging towards Arjan, who shot an arrow at him. A Rakshas grabbed Kalki from the back, throwing him to the ground. Kalki came to his senses, his stomach lurching with pain, as his spine began to unbearably hurt. Two big hands grabbed him again, but Kalki kicked him in the stomach. The Rakshas moved back and Kalki scampered for a weapon until he found a javelin on the ground. He grabbed for it and swung it against the charging Rakshas, letting it go deep inside his neck.

Bala was able to muster his spirit and with his one hand holding the Rakshas and the other holding his mace, he began to repeatedly bash it against the Rakshas' skull until it was broken. Arjan was out of arrows, but he had found an axe which he clumsily tried to wield, before being grabbed by a Rakshas.

Kalki went, seeking to protect his brother, and grabbed the Rakshas from the waist. With all of his energy, he picked up the tribal and flipped him at the back, the impact killing the Rakshas instantly. Kripa was able to fight two Rakshas at a time when both of them attacked him, though with Kripa's skilful manipulation, they ended up stabbing each other.

Kalki stood up, knees hurting. He felt he was pushing himself too much, panting while he tried to take some rest. But he didn't have to worry about them since Kripa made sure the Rakshas met their deaths. He stabbed them straight inside their skulls, unerring every time.

Arjan was wounded. Kalki couldn't believe that a boy like Arjan was in the midst of a deadly war like this, but regardless of his initial misgivings, he had done a fine job. He was able to do what other warriors strive to do the most.

Survive.

Kalki reached out to Bala and embraced his friend as tightly as possible. As they pulled apart, Bala, who had wounds deeper than any one of them and was yet acting as if nothing had gone wrong with him, said, "I'm sorry. I was overconfident, brother."

"No, it's all right. We were both wrong."

"How did you do it?" Bala asked.

Kalki pursed his lips. It was a story to tell for another time. He was glad when Kripa came in between them, with a sword in his hand, "I haven't picked this one up for a while, mate. Feels odd now. I knew a family who had all these swords. I belonged to that family, partially, you can say."

"What should we do now?" Arjan came forward, and they had formed a close circle.

"We can't stay here for long as they'll return. Perhaps they all went to see the caves," Kripa explained.

"I have to leave." Kalki instantly realized he had a duty he had to perform. Protect the villagers at any cost.

Lakshmi. I hope she's alive.

Kalki made his way towards the nearest horse with Shuko on his shoulders. He grabbed on to the reins and started to make the animal wear a saddle when Kripa cleared his throat.

"Well we all are happy you want to go and protect this village, but we need to leave."

Kalki turned, confused. "Leave where?" He looked at Bala and Arjan, who were now staring down in embarrassment.

"You know where."

"I can't go *now*," Kalki clenched his teeth.

"So you mean we came here for nothing?" Kripa grunted. "You have to leave. You don't understand…"

Kalki swept his hand up. "I don't care. I don't care what I understand and what I don't understand." He went over and grabbed for the saddle, and sat down, tightly clutching onto the reins of the horse. "But I know you don't understand one thing. Those are real, human lives out there and you said I am the saviour of this age. Well, if I can't even save my village, how will I save my entire country?" He looked at the sheepish figures of Arjan and Bala. "I'll return. You leave and hide in the woods."

"We can't just hide," Arjan blurted.

Kalki turned the horse. He knew they were right. "All right, go for Indravan. Stop them from acting on their plan."

"Where are you going?"

"I'm going to scout the village and meet you there." And check if Lakshmi is still there or not.

Kripa came forward and calmed the horse. He looked closely at Kalki and his voice had grown bleakly quiet, "You can't stop the Adharm from rising. I had tried that when I closed the caves and look where it got me. You still managed to be born. And he will also be…"

Kalki didn't listen. He couldn't care less what Kripa had to say. He pulled the reins and the horse started to move, with the wing whipping against his face. His body crouched forward, his eyes closing in on his destination.

He was coming.

49

Durukti was on her horse, slowly striding behind an army of Rakshas, some were on foot while others were on their horses. Chief Martanja rode next to her, on a black stallion. Symrin, on the other hand, had a weak horse for herself, but it was all right for her size. She was acting different, happier than usual.

"Is Shambala a sight to be glad about?" Durukti inquired in a leading way.

Symrin instantly wiped the foolish grin she had on herself. "No, my lady. Not particularly."

"No?" Durukti was surprised. She must have been lying, for Shambala was the most beautiful sight one could see. Durukti had travelled a lot, but she hadn't seen anything like this place. The lakes were pure, and crystal-clear, while the flowers were blooming; a sight to behold even though they were sprayed by blood. The forest's greenery was so pure and lush, that it felt unreal. In contrast to all the beauty was the reality of what had happened on the ground, for it was scattered with bodies. Some had already begun to rot, while others were still twitching. All this destruction and loss of lives, despite Durukti's strict instructions to the contrary.

She had reached close to the Soma Caves, also known as Indravan. Durukti had read about the "God" Indra. Many titles suggested he wasn't a God to be feared or adored, but a madman who took revenge on Illavarti for being chosen by the Danavs, his counterparts. They were two warring brother clans, as she had read. One was the Danavs, the literal giants. They were extinct, or at any rate in hiding, since they hadn't been seen in recent times. They were rumoured to be nine feet in height and having hands bigger than an average door. And their counterpart cousins were the Suras, such as the likes of Indra. The Suras realized the Danavs were worthless, ugly hybrids, causing them ill-reputation. Indra and his brothers had killed most of their cousins, while others were put to eternal sleep through various herbs. But eternal sleep, Durukti knew, meant being 'poisoned'.

Those were stories. Mythology was funny. Many quarreled over it, of what was right or wrong, even though they knew there was no correct answer. Who has seen history play out after all, without also seeing it being twisted to suit the needs of the victors?

The orchids lay flat, stretching across the horizon where the setting sun cast its glow. Nature was her passion; it had always been. Perhaps it had been cultivated and slowly grown over a period of time, as she had seen the entire Illavarti and known what this country was capable of, even though the Breaking had caused most of this capability to now become dormant. The acrid smell of fire and blood was replaced by the fresh breeze, fragranced by the citrusy smell of the fruits and flowers. It made her smile and brightened her mood a little. She could hear the whistling and chirping of the birds which was then followed by the wails and yells. She didn't realise she had closed her eyes and when she opened them, she was unable to comprehend the scene around her. A huge group of people were standing in front of the Soma Caves.

At best, the caves were the most unimpressive part of this village's topography. And like any village which believed in the myths of these Gods, they had built a temple around it, with little inscriptions and idols, designed to worship the Vajra of Lord Indra. The mass of people were cornered, near the rocky, uneven path that led to the caves. They had occupied that space, almost hugging it out of fear.

She got off her horse and so did Martanja, as she made her way towards the entrance of the path. She calmly saw all of them. They were blocking it. It would be the peasant's plan after all, since he was their so-called leader. The peasant had a different look about him. He wasn't a usual boy. He had a different aura which she wasn't able to explain. It was perhaps that he was extremely handsome, with exotic eyes, long wavy hair, and an angular jaw. He had an uneven nose, though. But all of it didn't matter since he exhibited a radiance she had seen in only one other person—Kali. While Durukti had seen Kali make that radiance come to life, this boy had been born with the radiance. Also, it was perhaps the way he talked, as if he really cared. Durukti had seen a lot of men and women who showed as if the world mattered to them, but behind the curtains, they would twist and manipulate every situation to their benefit. This boy wasn't like that. He had a genuine heart, pouring love out in his statements. He was nice. And in a world like this, it was difficult to find someone like him. Thus, she had agreed to not hurt anyone. It wasn't just her guilt, but also his passion that had guided her decision. All of it flustered her, reddening her cheeks for she never believed she would be thinking and musing about a boy. She shook her head, as she watched the villagers standing in front of her.

All the panicky, afflicted faces of the villagers created a hole inside her chest. She couldn't believe she had hurt them all. She had even trampled over the huge mass of the so-called army, who were coming in the way, led by a headstrong boy. She wasn't there to clearly witness the win from her side, but it was bloody. But she didn't want more of it. She was exhausted and a lot of deaths were on her head. She wanted to let go and just get what she wanted. Durukti walked in front, with her palms clasping each other. Symrin was behind her, with Martanja.

From the audience, appeared an old man, with little hair, a wrinkly face and eyes that held great wisdom.

"Have they all died?" He had a straight face, but even Durukti could see he was concealing his anguish.

Durukti contorted her face in apology. "I apologize."

"Are you here to kill us as well?" the man asked.

"What is your name?"

"Devadatta," he breathed out quietly.

"God-given," she responded with a gentle smile.

"I'm anything but that. I brought misery to this village."

Durukti looked at the sad, old man, but she just nodded. "You should have agreed. Standing by your religious traditions is important, but not at the cost of innocent lives."

"You haven't answered me. Will you kill us all?" He had knelt down now, his weak legs folded in genuflection.

"No, I won't," she said straightforwardly, "I don't want to make more enemies. Also, I have promised someone I wouldn't hurt any more of his friends."

Perhaps, it was the glint in the old man's eyes, but he nodded as if he knew who Durukti was talking about. "It's funny how you say someone stopped you." The old man had his face down and Durukti was unable to see him properly. "Because if it's the same person I think you mean, then he was the one who told me to shove a dagger inside your navel."

And then he pounced. For an old man, he was swift, almost pulling out the blade out of nowhere. Everyone was alarmed, but Durukti, anticipating it, quickly dodged. She grabbed the dagger's hilt, her hands cupping the old man's hands and with a sudden jerk, she twisted it back inside the old man. He had stabbed himself, as he staggered back in horror.

Durukti had learnt enough self-defense tricks. Surprise attacks weren't really her combat style, as she liked slow agonising deaths, but Durukti was still skilled enough to know how to twist the attack into the offense. Devadatta collapsed on the floor, hands clutched over the dagger, his kurta pooling with his own blood.

Durukti had promised she wouldn't kill anyone else. But it was self-defense, so she didn't go back on her word technically. She came forward, this time, with merciless, blazing eyes, arched brows and a thin mouth, grim with anger. She placed her feet over the dagger which instantly sunk deeper inside Devadatta's flesh. With one foot up and another on the dusty ground, she looked at everyone.

"I would request you to not tempt me anymore. I would request you all," it came off as a strict order, her sleek, luscious voice booming with authority, "to leave this place. The chief will show you where to stay together until we are done. But we are going to open those caves today. And no one, I dare you, no one should try to stop me *again*."

50

Kalki had checked everywhere. The village was shattered, the huts were destroyed, and most were ransacked. Even though Durukti wanted no more destruction, the Rakshas had sought for it. They showed they listened, but did they really? It was almost sad as Kalki saw his friends, his mother's friends, sprawled across the field where once greenery used to blossom. He watched the dilapidated chariot which he had brought from the city. It was in partial ruins, the wheels missing. In the west, he saw Lyla's dead body, surrounded by a retinue of other bodies. And it was over. All the grand plans he had made had come to nothing but futility. He had lost so much and it had deepened his senses and caused him to go into a void of guilt.

Kalki began to trudge downwards with the horse. He wasn't a trained horseman so it took him time to even go down the slope, where there were more huts. With a deep sigh, he went down, staggering, until he saw the isolated huts, where a few more bodies were lying sprawled. The sound of the birds was now replaced by the angry audible grunts.

He knew where the sounds were coming from, but who were they?

He stopped his horse and got off. With a battle axe on his side, he began to move, crouching slightly until he saw that in the midst of the huts, there was Roshan Mitra. His eyes lifelessly watching Kalki now, as he had been pulled out to the hut's entrance, with a message written in blood, in the Rakshasi language.

What kind of creatures would do such a thing to anyone?

"LAKSHMI!" he yelled, hoping to hear her reply. He wasn't afraid anymore, since it was no use being afraid. Even if he would die, it'd not matter. He felt dead from inside. He yelled again. There was a feeling in his chest that made him realise she must have left for the caves. But did it make any sense? He wondered. She was supposed to be here and for all he knew, she would stay, even if it meant sacrificing her own life.

No.

Kalki yelled Lakshmi's name again.

But this time, he heard something.

"KALK…" and her voice trailed off.

Kalki began to instantly run towards the direction of the sound, his fingers sweating around the axe. No matter what peril she was in, he'd make sure she was safe. Kalki came forward and finally witnessed the sight. There were three Rakshas around her and she was being dragged on the ground by them. She was being pulled by her long hair. One had forcibly held her legs together.

The Rakshas saw each other and then looked at Kalki, dumbfounded.

Blazing with wrath, Kalki came forward, his steps trampling the ground, mud spilling around him, and his mouth tasting dry. His feet picked up speed. The Rakshas armed themselves, afraid, for they never thought they would witness someone like this. In the shadows of the sun, Kalki's skin was glimmering darkly. His eyes were of different colours. The Rakshas came forward, one of them with a spear. He threw the javelin across at Kalki.

But Kalki's hand came before it, deflecting it. He turned towards the Rakshas and plunged it inside the Rakshas. With the Rakshas on the other end, he pulled him up, impaling him. He pushed the spear into the ground. The other two Rakshas just watched the sight.

But Kalki didn't have to do anything because Lakshmi immediately came to her feet, and knocked the Rakshas with a rock. Kalki flung an axe to her, which she caught by the handle. With the axe in her hands, Lakshmi ripped apart a Rakshas' throat and it was a filthy sight for him, as the blood began to spill over the Rakshas' dark chest. He fell down, lifeless.

Kalki watched Lakshmi. They shared a moment of quietness. At least, he could save someone. He reached out to her, bidding his feet to move faster so that he could finally embrace her.

But he was too slow.

His eyes darted over to the shadow that crossed Lakshmi. It was the Rakshas she had hit with the rock. He had a spear in his hand and he plunged it deep inside Lakshmi's chest. With a wavering smile, she sank on the ground, her head falling flat on the grounds of the village she had a love-hate relationship with.

He couldn't even breathe for a moment witnessing what just happened. Everything spiralled around him, but he knew he still had to save her. He didn't use any weapon, instead, he pounced at the murderous Rakshas, tossing him over, making him fall and beating him until the Rakshas spilled its filthy blood out. The Rakshas didn't go out without a struggle. With strong arms, he pushed him back. Kalki felt an impact, but he tried his best to stand up. He stormed at the Rakshas and knocked him at the back. The Rakshas fell again, but he used his strength to turn him over.

"You can't get me," the Rakshas snarled.

Kalki tried to break the lock as much as he could, but the Rakshas, twice his size, was stronger. He grabbed for the mud that surrounded them and tossed it over at the Rakshas' face. That led to the Rakshas yelling in agony, for the dirt had entered his eyes. Kalki used force and kicked him hard, continuously. He plunged the axe that had fallen away from Lakshmi's hand inside the Rakshas' skull.

Blood sprayed it over his face and he wiped it. He had killed it, but no…

He began to scamper over Lakshmi. The first thing he did was pull out the spear. All the moments that he had spent with her, right from the childhood to the times when he had saved her so many times, he started seeing in flashes. He was extremely happy the day she had come back, the time he protected her from the crocodile, the times he went to Indragarh and got himself into trouble and the time he was about to kiss her but was interrupted by Shuko. And yet at this moment, there was no one to disturb them, when they most needed the medical supplies.

There was no one.

Lakshmi was still in her senses. Her eyes were getting glassy, but were still conscious. Kalki grabbed her by the chest, his arms curving over her back. She was hurt and wounded and she was coughing up blood.

No. This can't be happening.

"It's all right, all right, fine, we have gone through worse, and we will do it, all right?" He was repeating words frantically. "All right, no please, don't die on me." He hugged her, kissed her on the head and tried to hold her tight.

"I'm s-sorry…" she breathed. "I've let people down," her voice was coming weakly. "I should have made more effort in trying to find why you are the w-w-way you are."

"I know about it now. I was meaning to tell you, Lakshmi." He was tearing up, hot burning rivulets coursing down his cheeks. "I am supposed to be some kind of a saviour."

"Saviour?" A soft smile dancing on her lips. "You?"

He chuckled. "I know, right?"

"I don't think they got that right."

"I know." Kalki clenched his jaw, his smile disappearing. "Let's go."

"No, please." She stopped him, her pale hands lightly touching his chest, "Don't do it to yourself. I am…uh…" she moaned, "I'm a little beyond the saving stage."

Kalki contorted his face, his eyes struggling hard not to tear up.

"But don't let this make you think that you aren't fit to be the people's saviour," she said, "because I've read somewhere."

"From all the stupid books?" he struggled with a smile.

"Yes, from all the stupid books," she smiled, "and I had read that heroes are born out of tragedies."

"I don't want to be a hero if I have to go through this tragedy. I just want to be a boy who loves a girl," he clutched her hard, "a boy from Shambala with no care in the world. I just wanted to grow up like that."

Slowly her hand reached his cheek. "Kalki, we both know that isn't going to happen anymore."

Kalki nodded. But he couldn't believe he had lost everything with his one decision. At this moment, he regretted everything about his life. In fact, he was angry at himself for being the Avatar.

"Kiss me," she said, "with no disturbance this time." She smiled.

Kalki nodded. And he did. He kissed her as softly as he could, their tears slowly mingling with each other. That was when he realized her lips had gone still and cold. And as he looked down, she saw her eyes were closed.

She was gone.

Kalki's chest heaved. And he yelled, letting all the jackals and the sheep hear him. He yelled so loud that even the birds left their nests. And he yelled loud enough to let his enemies know that he was coming for them.

51

Durukti had shifted all the villagers to one side and after the Devadatta incident, no one even dared to come in between her and her objective. They were all made to sit down, with Rakshas walking around them, poking them with spears if anyone even fidgeted.

She was so close to her cure, or whatever there was beyond the boulders. She saw Martanja had dug hooks inside the rocks. Five horses had harnesses wrapped around them, on which Rakshas sat. They began to pull in the opposite direction. With each pull, the boulder moved a little, but it was still stuck around the edges of the cave.

Martanja sprinted over to Durukti, who stood at the pathway that led to the caves. He went past the guards and panted for a while before he began, "My lady, the boulder seems to be stuck; I think we need to use more labour."

"Use your men."

"More, my lady."

Durukti clenched her teeth. "Is it possible to arrange for more men?"

"If we try, we can see it's possible."

Quite a clever answer!

Durukti grinned at that as she moved away from her guards and watched the villagers, whimpering in the fields, holding onto each other. For them, she would be the epitome of evil, but she had reasons that they wouldn't understand. All the Gods they loved and pleaded to, and yet they didn't know that the Manavs had been alienated after the Breaking.

"Use the natives," answered Durukti. "Tell them to work."

"All right, my lady," Martanja blinked.

He left and ordered his men around the villagers, while Durukti thought for a moment. She hadn't disclosed to Martanja what was in there and she had given him extra money just for not asking questions. But he was a man, that too from the Rakshasi tribe. He was intelligent; he knew there was something valuable inside it.

It wasn't just the gold and copper that drove him to pull the boulder out, but it was also inquisitiveness. Martanja was a clever chief, who showed he respected Durukti but he surely had ulterior motives. But as of now, she had to stop second guessing and start worrying if the caves really held what it said they did. She was afraid, of course. She had made people lose their sons and daughters, their husbands and wives, for her goal. And if her goal was just a waste of time, she would hate herself forever. But more so, she would never forgive Symrin who had started all of this. If it wasn't for her, she wouldn't have ever thought about Soma.

The villagers began to work and they started using sickles and knives to cut the overgrowth around the edges. The ones that resisted, the Rakshas subdued them with ropes. Little by little, the boulder started to move from its position. The villagers kept digging at the crevices.

It was a painful sight for her, but she was so close to what she had wanted.

"DURUKTI!" A voice came, startling her, freezing her to the bones.

Swivelling her head frantically, she looked where the voice had come from. And she saw it. Standing across her guards was Kalki, with a blood drenched dhoti, an axe in his hand, his chest caked in dust and blood.

He began to run. The harness stopped. Martanja instantly yelled to his guards to chase and stop him. The guards that surrounded Durukti went forth, almost twenty in number, as they grabbed onto him. Kalki was able to stave off most of them, blindly kicking out and punching them, hitting some of them grievously with his axe. His presence here meant that all the guards near the clearing had surely been decimated.

How did he escape?

"YOU KILLED EVERYONE!" He yelled, his body held back by the Rakshas.

"I WILL KILL YOU NOW," he said through gritted teeth.

"Men," Martanja announced. "Kill the peasant!"

A Rakshas came forward with a blade in his hand, ready to slice off Kalki's head.

Durukti knew the end of her misery was near. Symrin whispered in her ears before the attack could happen. "My lady, you shouldn't hurt an already hurt person. If you must remember, he is special, right? Don't you think when his anger lessens, he can be used to your advantage against the Tribals who are secretly plotting against Lord Kali and you?"

Durukti arched her brows.

"Stop!" Durukti yelled. But not just because of what Symrin said, but also because she didn't want to upset the villagers any further. Though Symrin was right. Kalki had powers like that of the fabled heroes she had read about when she was small.

Martanja strolled towards her, interjecting her. "I apologize, my lady, but that man is wreaking havoc on our men. We should make an example out of him. He even managed to escape; I wonder what he did back at the camp."

"He deserves punishment in the city, not here," she looked at him, "he killed your men, right? According to the bylaws, he has to be judged in front of the Tribal Lords and Lord Kali, before being punished by death."

If Kalki wouldn't turn on her side later after deliberate persuasion, she would simply hand him off to her brother to deal with. She didn't want a headache.

"I thought," coughed Martanja, coming forward slyly, "you wanted all of this to be discreet."

Durukti nodded. "It'll be. For all they will know, this was a compulsory act to subdue the rebellion that was brewing against the Tribals."

Martanja looked at her for a while, hardly believing that a person could be so cold and calculative yet warm and desirable at the same time, at such a young age. Durukti pursed her lips, amused by her improvised plan. "I suppose you should continue working, chief. You don't want to be late. If that boy stays there for long, he's going to crumple your army."

Kalki was tied up with a rope, his mouth strapped, with five spears close to his neck. Even if he would try to struggle, he would be stabbed.

"For your sake, just stop moving. I'm trying to save you. Don't force me to kill," Durukti calmly said, trying as much as she could to hold her emotions back, to sound cold.

Kalki's eyes spoke a thousand words. He looked as if he didn't care that she was doing him a favour and he would rather die than take her up on it. But it was all his anger and hatred towards her that spoke through his eyes. *A sentimental person is a dangerous entity.*

Durukti focused her attention back at the harness. She came forward, her robe slowly tracing the ground. She saw it was near, her goal. Her eyes flashed with brilliance. The boulder shifted and manoeuvred away from the opening. The horses tried moving faster, as the villagers continued to chip away at the rock. And then the rock was pushed apart. They all began to rush away, with some getting trampled under it.

Durukti said to Martanja, "Go and tend to them, I'll see the inside." She wanted to get rid of the Rakshas, so that he did not see the so-called Somas. Martanja gave a reluctant nod and moved to the fields with his men. Half of them stayed with the yelling Kalki, as they tried to stop him. He wasn't able to properly shout, for his mouth was closed. Durukti looked at him unapologetically, before moving towards the caves, her heart thumping furiously.

"You should very well hope I'm going to see something wonderful inside. Otherwise..." she eyed Symrin, who barely managed to swallow a lump of nervousness.

Three Rakshas followed her. At the entrance, the Rakshas lit the fire lamps and she could hear how the lamps made a sound when they were lit. It smelled of putrid dampness. When she trained the lamp light against the wall...

She didn't see anything.

She shot a glance at Symrin, who was looking back at her.

As she went deeper, Durukti crossed the walls that were tainted a bright sapphire blue, she saw there were inscriptions carved on it, comprising of various symbols and glyphs. She touched it; the symbol was of an infinity that was wrapped inside a zigzag structure.

"I'm sorry, my lady, I was told...I was told..."

"You know what this is?" Durukti had a pallid face when she asked her foolish handmaiden. "This is the symbol of Vishnu the Preserver." She moved towards the other glyph which had a strange design. "This is a shape of a horse, a white horse," and she came to the last one, "and this is victory.'

"My lady, I thought they were..." her voice had been echoing, Durukti just noticed.

Durukti shot a finger up, against her lips, to silence Symrin. She walked forward as the cave turned out to be leaking some kind of liquid. She touched it; it was blue in colour, perhaps tainted with the colour that had leached from the walls.

"Speak again now," she instructed the girl.

"Yes?" meekly Symrin said.

"Loudly, girl!" rasped Durukti. But she couldn't really hear Symrin's voice for her own voice echoed so much that Durukti knew what it was.

Durukti grabbed the fire lamp from one of the Rakshas and tossed it across to the front.

"My lady!" exclaimed Symrin.

But what the lamp did was extraordinary, as it broke forth, and the fire caught on. The light was emitted, and lo and behold, the wall in front of them morphed with blue stones protruding out jaggedly. The funny part was; it had been the fire that led her to the Somas.

"This is it," she said.

Symrin's face brightened. "Yes, madam, I was right."

Durukti came forward with a smile dancing on her lips, touching the blue fossil, and with a snap of her finger, she broke it. It had seemed crystalline from afar, but was in fact quite malleable and soft. And as she chipped away at the ends, a strange blue liquid poured out over her skin.

She smelled it, but it smelled of …nothing.

She dipped her finger and even tasted it, it was just some liquid.

"Are you sure this is it?"

Symrin beamed. "Yes ma'm, we have just found the cure for your brother." And despite the smile she gave, there was something unsettling about it that Durukti couldn't understand. But perhaps it was her unwarranted suspicion that probed her into thinking this. Perhaps, she should be happy. And she struggled with a smile, even though she knew to save one, plenty of lives had been lost.

52

Arjan had been seeing it all. It was a day after the entire pack of Rakshas with Durukti had left, that they had emerged. Till then, they had subsisted on fruits scavenged from the ground. Exhausted, Arjan walked on the path of Shambala again, trudging away from people who eyed at him, Kripa and Bala, for they were all accessories to what had happened here.

But he paid no heed. The corpses were being picked, the pyres were being lit. As they reached his home, which had been untouched by all the violence, Arjan spoke up. "You should have let me go."

"And get yourself killed?" Kripa said, glancing at Bala. "You talk crazier than your brother sometimes, mate."

Arjan had been dragged by Bala when he saw what happened to Kalki. Arjan, Kripa and Bala were making their way towards the caves after gathering enough weapons and supplies when they saw Kalki had already reached and he was being trapped by so many Rakshas, unable to move, forced by them to kneel so he could be subdued. He was bounded and gagged by them. Arjan wanted to move, and attack, but Kripa stopped him.

"You will meet your brother's fate. The lady of the court likes your brother, but not you, so beware," Kripa warned.

Arjan didn't listen to the old man, for he always talked idiotically, but it was Bala who knew it was the end. They couldn't do anything that would save Kalki. They had to be smart.

"Where is Lakshmi?" Arjan asked, standing beside his hut in the present.

Kripa and Bala exchanged glances.

"All right, this is not going according to the plan." Arjan clenched his fist.

"To be fair, mate, we didn't have a plan in the first place," Kripa said, "but at least we were able to survive and so did Kalki. That was grand, in its own way."

Arjan nodded. He glanced at the village once again. More than half the residents had been killed. "I can't stay here."

"And I hope you don't, because now…" Kripa beamed.

"Now, nothing," Arjan stopped, as he began to walk inside the hut, rummaging through the things, picking up his clothes. For some reason, the very thought of him entering and being greeted by his mother was something he was looking forward to. But there was no family. And Arjan was glad he had sent his mother away, for he knew it would have only resulted in her going down the road like the others. The thought created a powerful knot in his chest.

"Where do you plan to go?" The old man fidgeted. He bored him to death. He was a guru and he couldn't even teach a bunch of villagers to fight. It was also his fault.

"I don't know. Not decided it yet."

Bala kept his palm on Arjan's shoulder to stop him. It was heavy, he could feel, but also sticky with blood. Arjan just realized he hadn't bathed after the war. He had to take a dip in the lake perhaps, but then the lake would be filled with the ashes of the men and women who died for a lost cause.

"We need to help your brother."

"He's gone." Arjan wrapped a long dupatta across his chest and he used another to wrap a bundle of clothes for him to carry. "And he's dead."

"We can't give up like that, mate. I know you feel disheartened..."

"Disheartened?" snapped Arjan. "That's an understatement. I feel horrible. I feel like I was supposed to die in his place. There are people out there who hate us, hate my family. I can't even bring my mother back here. Shambala is no more the place it used to be. It's all over. The saviour of mankind, well he's rotting in some jail perhaps."

Kripa shrugged. "Kind words for your blood."

"He's not my blood. I am not anyone's blood."

Kripa arched his brows. "I don't know what that was about, but the fact that you want to leave for somewhere is stupid. You can't do this to the people. You owe it to your brother, to protect him."

Owe? He didn't owe anything. Not to anyone.

He walked to his room to pick up his things. With a heavy heart, he looked through the important books he could use for the journey to...somewhere. The thought scared him, but perhaps he could go to Mother. But then, she would ask so many questions, and he'd be afraid to answer them, especially that Kalki was not returning back anytime soon.

But what really put him off? Was it the people or was it the inevitability of their defeat? Was it failure that scared him? Ever since the time in Gurukul, he had been winning. Even with the Mlecchas, he had won with Kalki. All of those times, failure was just a word for him; but now it had become his reality.

And that was when his eyes darted and he noticed a sickle. It was the same weapon his mother had given him when he was going out there to find the Mlecchas. He had barely used it during the fight against the Mlecchas, as it was taken by them. He had later retrieved it from their tent, but never once he cared about it.

Looking back now, he felt instead of bows and arrows, he should have just stuck to using the sickle.

Cowards give up after a defeat. But those who get up after the defeat are the real winners.

Why was he giving up on finding Kalki? His mother had told him to stay together, to never separate. So why was he giving up at all? What had happened? He stood there in silence, viewing his culpability in the entire turn of events.

Something had taken over me. Perhaps it was guilt, sadness and failure; he said to himself, shaking his head.

"Well, it'll be dishonest if I say it isn't entertaining to see you mutter to yourself," Kripa grinned cheekily, "but can I ask what you are thinking about, with that thing in your hand?"

Arjan turned. The voices were back, and the momentary but deafening silence had vanished. He sighed, as he began. "What will happen to Shambala if we leave?"

"Let me tell you a story." Kripa stretched his arms as he calmly sat on the mat where Arjan slept at night. "Years back, a war had happened, more or less close to the Breaking. The war was pathetic in its outcome. Many lost their lives, and many forgot about it. It was the worst war…"

"Like the Mahayudh?" Arjan asked, recalling the time of Lord Arjun, from whom he had received his name. Arjun played a pivotal role in that, being an archer of unprecedented fame.

Kripa gulped nervously. "Well, more or less, the Mahayudh was something that stretched for years. Yes. And many towns, villages and cities were burnt. The biggest war of all time, it had affected millions of lives. After that, the Breaking caused a worse impact. It was in the aftermath of the Mahayudh." Kripa shook his head. "Regardless of whatever had happened, my point is that this country has seen so much worse, but it always stands up on its feet and moves on. It takes time, but it heals. Everything heals if you have patience."

Arjan nodded.

"And sometimes, you or I can't do anything about it. We cannot hasten the process. We can just watch it happen." Arjan felt Kripa was now talking to himself more than to him, but then he snapped back with his grin. "All said and done, I suppose I made my point and if I didn't then you must believe I'm extremely tired since I haven't slept or drank. Dear me, I haven't drunk at all. I need to visit Madira's Chalice…"

Bala heaved aloud.

"Or not," Kripa nervously chuckled, "whatever our great, big friend says we should do."

Arjan always believed the books, whatever they taught, but things were always contradictory. At one moment, someone wrote something and at another, it meant something else. They were unreal. Rakshas were often considered beastly, paranormal, and straight from hell. But when seen upfront, they were wise. Dangerous sure, but they had an air about them. They weren't so beastly after all. The world he lived in, it was full of relative contradictions and subjectivities. What was true or false, it depended on a person's normativity.

"What do you plan to do then?" Arjan asked.

"Oh finally!" clapped Kripa childishly. "I'm glad you are on track, mate, because I have a very innovative plan."

Bala nodded. "Speak, foulmouth."

"We are going to Indragarh, where he's being taken. And we need to free Kalki and take him to the north, to my frie…well not friend, but yeah, someone I know because the Somas is out."

"We didn't see them taking anything…" Arjan still didn't believe in the myth of the Somas, but seeing Kalki in his glory, had basically turned around his judgments.

Kripa interjected, "Oh they did, because there was a whole lot of it. They must have taken in bulk. And just be sure, if that little blue liquid is out there, we are in great, great trouble because there's going to be a lot of bad things we shall need to reckon with. And we need your brother to fight it. For that, he needs to be prepared and not be a fool and confront a court aristocrat out in the open, in front of her fifty or so guards. That boy lacks wisdom, but he makes up for it with his brawns."

Arjan glanced at Bala. "All right, so what's the plan?"

"I just told you."

"You explained to us what would happen if we don't help Kalki," Arjan said. "But what is the plan to release him from the prison or from his execution?"

Kripa thought for a moment. There was a brief silence. "We'll go to Indragarh."

"All right," Arjan nodded, so did Bala. "Then?

"And then," Kripa smiled like a wizened man, "we *improvise*."

And Arjan reluctantly nodded, thinking one thing.

Here we go again.

PART TWO

THE RISE OF KALI

53

He was supposed to be here.

Amidst the thick, misty night where the chilliness froze Vedanta's bones, he waited. Indragarh, in the aftermath of the torrential downpour, often became climatically hostile for its residents.

He hated the meetings outside of his fort, in the middle of the night, right where the main membrane of the city was. It was dangerous out there, for Vedanta. His lungs felt polluted. But it wasn't just the olfactory senses that were the mediums of his ill-health; it was also his enemies that lurked in the shadows. Walls bled with their names. He was still revered as the king, but his adversaries were many; especially since the outrageous pact he had signed at the behest of Kali.

Assassinations had been fairly common earlier, but now Kuvera had promised him, no one would harm him if he worked with Kuvera. He'd make sure that his entry in the middle of *his* city would be safe. Just to make sure though, he had been asked not to bring many men and to disguise any guards as civilians.

But tonight the lanes were isolated. The guards stood some distance away, making sure no one attacked Vedanta. There were archers over the buildings, aiming at any possible threat.

One had to be careful, Vedanta thought.

Tonight, Vedanta was supposed to meet the Yaksha king close to the tailor's shop. And only one was there to the north of Indragarh. It was a cleaner side of the city, where only the rich and noble walked. The peasants who had migrated from their villages would work in either west or east, though preferably west, where most of the fishing, exporting and mercantile activities were based.

Vedanta couldn't believe he would partner with Kuvera. Seemingly odd as a team, but that was exactly what Kuvera wanted—an odd pair that'd be above suspicion. No one would look at them and believe that a Tribal and a Manav could ever work together.

And that is exactly what Vedanta had thought initially. He didn't like the prospect of working with Kuvera, but the Yaksha king had allowed himself in one day, in his fort, demanding his presence.

"I know you are suffocated, my lord." There was a thinness to his voice, unlike the others, who roared as they spoke. He had a rhythm with his words, his bald-egg-like head, with the weird mongoose curled up around him. Whenever Vedanta would even come close, the mongoose would snarl and then Kuvera would have to pet it. "You don't like the rules and believe it or not, I don't either. You see, I'm just a mere investor in Kali's expeditions. These aren't mine. In fact, I was very prejudicial about attacking you, but Kali forced me into it."

Vedanta had listened calmly, not believing a word, but he had to congratulate the man for his ingenious way of telling lies. Spiteful lies, indeed. But he didn't care for he had known why Kuvera had come to him in the first place.

Support.

"I thought to be an investor had its benefits," Vedanta spat.

Kuvera had a pallid and drawn face. "Indeed, and I am admitting that. But you must realise a man has needs. A place where I come from, Alak, the city of gold…" he trailed off.

Vedanta nodded. He had heard about the central city. For some, it had been mythical, where the Gods had tossed their riches before departing from Illavarti. But Vedanta largely regarded these stories as mythical.

"It was a treasury for the Gods," Kuvera had smiled, "just something our city is proud of. But let us be honest. Gods were humans with a large following of fanatics around them, who made them kings of religion. We had a lot of people vouching for our treasury, the biggest one there is, mind you. We have worked very hard to conjure all the money in there; it's considered the bank of Illavarti if I'm not being too bombastic in my own estimates."

Not bombastic at all, Vedanta gritted his teeth.

"But that is just the background of my story. My reality is I was given the name of Kuvera after the God of Treasure—Kuber, or in our native language, Kuver. My father thought it would suit me best, for I was born in riches and rightfully would die in it as well."

Vedanta had waited for the truth to be laid out, but the man didn't speak properly. He kept circling around the main topic.

"Kali had come to me for monetary help. More so, it was about buying mercenary armies comprising of the Rakshas, the Nagas and the Yakshas. Moreover he insisted on my personal presence. He had a proposal and I thought that it would be best to help him in the plan, and come here, to tell my plan to you."

"And what would that be?" Vedanta had been growing restless. "I demand an answer."

"And the answer shall be given," Kuvera slyly chided. "I don't just like to be an investor in a man's quest for world domination. In fact, I don't even believe in it. Getting kingdoms together that had been dispersed after the Mahayudh was a tough job that Kali had embarked on, but it is time to be lead by someone else now."

Vedanta had known the answer to that. "And let me foretell, that someone will be you."

"Oh no, my lord," Kuvera had smiled benignly. "It's you."

"Me?"

"Yes." he smiled. "But at a cost, of course."

Here it came. Kuvera might be able to butter him with praises and false platitudes, but he had an ulterior motive. Vedanta could see right through it but he spoke no word. He waited, for patience is a virtue.

"It would be just the two of us."

"And what benefit will you provide me if I do this?" Vedanta narrowed his eyes.

"Riches and trade. Alak is prosperous, mind you and once I take over the Rakshas territory and the Naga lands, I'll extend more of it towards you."

"Hold on, you want to take over? How would you do that?" Alak might be the richest city in Illavarti, but it was ridden with an outmoded armoury.

"And that's where you come in. You give me the people. I give you the money."

"How do you plan to take over the territories?"

Kuvera had scanned the room until he found a potted plant in Vedanta's study. He was a plant enthusiast, having varieties of it back in Alak.

Kuvera pulled out the flower.

"HOW DARE YOU?" roared Vedanta.

"Just like this," he grinned. "Cut them from their roots. The territories belong to the leaders and if there are no leaders, there is no territory to be ruled over."

Vedanta had thought for a moment. The idea wasn't bad at all.

"What about Kali?"

"He's just a clay figure that needs to be shaped according to our needs and if he begins to create problems, we will squash him to the ground," he grinned.

Vedanta had understood the plan. He would give the army in

exchange for money. They would kill all the other Tribal Lords, even Kali if it came down to it.

"You get so many territories, what about me?"

"I thought you didn't want to mingle with the Tribal affairs. What sort of reputation would that be? After all, the plan I dictated, would lead you to get back all the kingdoms that Kali controls. Indragarh will be yours again and not puppet-ruled by you."

The very image of him getting all of that back was tempting.

Vedanta had stood up. "No. What guarantee is there that you'll not backstab me, if we even succeed in this outrageous plan?"

"Am I not trustworthy?" he had smiled.

Vedanta's thought process came to the present. He wasn't trustworthy sure, but he was useful. Once he was back on track, he would kill Kuvera as well. It wasn't much of a problem for him. It was horrible though, on the other hand, working with the Tribal, going against his own morals and judgments, but he had to make a friend out of an enemy to dissipate the other bitter enemies. Thus, they were first going for Vasuki. Vedanta had used his influence over the commoners to trap Vasuki's right-hand man.

At present, the shadows appeared in front of him. They were the Yakshas, short in size, but quite efficient, with long bows and daggers dangling from their belt. Kuvera entered shortly. He had been feeding his mongoose, Vedanta realised, eyes.

"Took care of a few men today." He tossed the eye to the mongoose.

"For what?"

Kuvera scanned his environment. "Remind me again to never call you here, henceforth."

"Who were you *taking care of*?" Vedanta asked.

"Uh, just some fellow Nagas."

"Naga? What if Vasuki…"

"Ah, don't worry," he shook his head, "they are not my

problem. I got rid of them, and Vasuki wouldn't even know he lost two of his men."

"Why did you do it?"

"I called you here for that only, my lord. We are in jeopardy, for Kali has another enemy."

"Enemy?" Vedanta mused.

"Oh yes, he left his fort and had an assassination attempted on him by none other than a Naga. Hence I had to torture their ilk to figure out who could be behind the attack."

"Couldn't it be Vasuki?"

"It was too stupid for Vasuki to send his own man. He would hire someone on a mercenary basis, from another tribe. Oh, this person is clever, whoever it is. He wanted the blame to be on the Naga Tribe. You think it could be his own supporters trying to go against him?"

Vedanta nodded. "Where is Kali now?"

"Probably on his deathbed," he said. "But fear not, his sister has brought some medicine from one of your villages."

Vedanta's feet stilled. "What village?"

"Shambala."

Vedanta shook his head. "How dare she go behind my back?"

Kuvera patted Vedanta on his shoulder. "Calm down, my lord. The last thing you want is to enrage Kali. He'll be fine soon enough and he'll take control. After all, the power over the villages was given to his sister and you signed on it, remember? Poor you, but we might use it as an advantage in this case."

"Advantage?" he paused. "How do you plan to do that?"

Kuvera had that simple smile dancing over his lips. "Don't worry, my lord. Leave that on me."

54

She just knew how to attract an audience.

Standing in the middle of the bustling road, Padma had a drum and sticks, and she repeatedly beat on it to direct everyone's attention to her. Aakash, her friend and partner, began yelling for everyone to hear.

"Listen! Listen! People, my dear folks, this is the time of the reckoning. We have been seduced by the evils of our king to accept the Tribals and go along with the fateful plan that everything will be all right. But nah, nothing will be all right."

He had a burly voice, so Padma had let him to say these things. You needed to have a strong voice, but Padma lacked that or so she thought.

"They steal our jobs, the opportunities, they build up a market and remove us, the Manavs, from the map." The crowd began to be attracted and Padma was glad. This was the second time that month but people always gathered to listen to them. "Listen, my dear friends! Forget the lies they have fed us. Nothing has progressed in this city. Nothing!"

The crowd began to increase in number; they all nodded at what Aakash said. After all, he was handsome and charismatic. He had a way with words and reminded her of her second brother. She closed her eyes at the thought of her sibling and tried to draw herself away from the meandering thoughts of love and loss. She had to concentrate on the event. She wouldn't consider this propaganda. This was just bashing the empire and forcing the people to *think*, because it was important. An idea must be fed to the people, so that when it translated into action, it would create a revolution.

"Come, everyone! Come! Hear more truths about our king. Apparently, he works for an…" his voice turned into a whisper, "an idiot." He went back and grabbed a portrait. It was handmade and poorly drawn, but it was clear, it was Kali with his long hair and slit-like eyes, but a nose that was caricaturishly long.

"What do they say about men with long noses?" he raised his brows mischievously. Everyone grinned and laughed. No one would have believed, but they were saying all of this in the middle of the street. Ratri, their leader of street propaganda, had told them to choose a suitable place and time. Early in the morning, patrolling by the Nagas was less.

Last time too, they had tried to pull a stunt like this. They had put hand-drawn posters across the city, ridiculing in different languages and saying: YOU ARE A FAILURE, KINGSHIP! It was all over the place and while it didn't harm the Tribals, it did get the attention of the Nagas, and they had chased Aakash and Padma to the ends of the city, where they had to dive into the river and float along the other side of the bank, where they reached the western part.

Ratri had said that it was all right to be supportive of the Tribals, but on an equal measure. If it would lead to disruption of the Manav life, then such an empowerment and equality was sham.

An owl flapped in the air until it placed its small body over Padma's shoulder, close to her bright silver hair. Everyone wondered how one could get silver hair at this age, but it wasn't genetics. She had used chemicals to cover her head. And she had reasons for it. She had been part of a great tragedy in her life and her face if recognized by the king, would mean execution. It wasn't what she had done but what her brothers had done to the king. They weren't his greatest supporters of him, even before the Tribal inclusion. They had looked for democracy over dictatorship; and in all fairness, it hadn't gone too well. Things began to swing against her fates and Padma had to face the dire consequences.

She kissed the corners of her owl's ears, who blinked at her and narrowed her eyes adorably. That was when Padma noticed a scroll had been tied around her small feet. With one hand now beating the drums, she picked up the scroll. She unrolled it, struggling to do it with one hand, but she managed it and realized what had happened.

They are coming your way. She's new.

– Ratri

Her eyes darted up. She stopped the beating. Aakash looked at her, eyeing her to continue, but Padma shook her head.

"We need to leave."

He gave a charming grin to the awaiting public and reached out to her, whispering, "Stop getting worried, all right? It'll be fine."

"We can get caught," Padma said. "Ratri sent a message…"

He cut her off. "Ratri is paranoid ever since she has been shifted to a stupid library. Stop worrying and beat the damn drums…"

And that was when she heard it. The galloping horses appeared and the crowd began to instantly disperse, afraid of being seen next to enemies of the state.

No.

There were four Nagas in front of her on horses, and in the middle there was a woman with onyx black hair, so long, it had to be braided.

"Now what is this going on? Seditions perhaps, darling?" asked the woman.

It was supposed to be some kind of threat, but it came off as a seductive comment. Perhaps this woman was working for the Nagas, but the way she positioned herself clearly showed she was more authoritative than just a usual commander. She had an air about her, with her chin up, her angular nose and eyebrows lifted up.

"Don't kill them. I love the pseudo-revolutionaries!" She clapped with delight.

What the…

And that was when the first Naga appeared with a blade, reaching out for Aakash, who whimpered and fell back. Padma had to do something. She also saw another Naga coming, while the rest of the crowd around them simply melted away. As they came close, Padma and Aakash were cornered against the brick building. She tossed the drum on the side and…

Padma whistled. Instantly, the owl on her shoulder launched itself, smashing one of the Nagas on the face. It fell back. The Naga was a tall person, not too muscular like the Rakshas, but with snake-shaped tattoos on their bodies. And for all the toughness they showed, one of them was knocked down by a bird. As the other Nagas got puzzled by the bird attack, Padma took the advantage of the wall, leaping against it, in the process pulling out two long daggers. To the one who had reached out to the frightened Aakash, she flung her dagger.

Akash yelled.

Padma rolled her eyes. He was not even helping and he was creating such noise. It was irritating on a whole lot of fronts. The other Nagas came towards her, seemingly as she was more confrontational and dangerous. The fact that she had killed the officers of the court meant she was getting the noose or the axe. And she out of all the people knew how horrifying it was to even watch it, let alone be a victim of the draconian ritual.

She couldn't kill the Nagas, she knew. She didn't use her dagger, but she pulled out copper coins—panas, out of her pocket. They were reddish and rounder than usual, with the strange carvings of Indragarh's motto inscribed over it. She tossed them across towards the Nagas' feet, which made them trip when they clumsily stepped over the coins.

Padma chuckled. They stood up and by the time they did, Padma kneed one of them. He fell back. While the other managed to stand up, launching towards her with a blade. She dodged it, her body rolling on the ground and falling at the back. She tapped on the confused Naga's shoulder, who looked behind himself and was punched for his efforts.

The other man had no weapon, but he was bigger than the rest. He began to shake his fist.

"I'm going to kill you."

Ugh.

"I'm done being nice." Padma flung another of her daggers right across the Naga's upper chest, where the breastplate didn't cover the skin. He looked down at it and pulled it out, only to realise Padma had just hit him at the veins. Blood sprayed and he collapsed on the ground.

She grabbed for the body that covered Aakash. She tossed him to the side, pulling the dagger from him.

"Let's go."

Aakash stood up, gulping and shivering. They turned and as they did, Padma realized she was standing in front of ten more Nagas. They all had spears in their hands; shields covered them. They were ready to war with a commoner like her. And they stood there, with their weapons, drawn inches away from their neck.

How did they even manage to come so fast?

"Oh God, we are dead, I told you we should have gone," Aakash whimpered, "Please! Please don't hurt us! Please! I don't want to die."

You must be joking?

Padma rolled her eyes, but squared her shoulders and came in front of Aakash. She was not afraid, for she had seen and felt something worse than death.

And that was grief.

"You really thought you would escape, darling?" asked the lady as she rounded off with a black stallion, with several more men stationed behind her.

"You mustn't underestimate those you oppose."

Padma didn't utter a word.

"Take the boy," she ordered. "You know where to send him."

"Sorry, sorry," Aakash pleaded before Padma was pushed to the ground and Aakash was taken by the Nagas.

Another one was gone.

To be fair, she didn't feel bad. Sure, he was helpful, but he was indeed just derailing her mission. The woman on the black horse came on to her feet and the moment her legs met the floor there was a *clink* sound. Padma noticed a small anklet wrapped around her ankle. Padma noticed how the woman had one limp hand while the other was functional.

"Take the injured and send them over to the infirmary. If they aren't all right by tomorrow, tell them they are exiled." The woman said, before her eyes caught the attention of Padma. She had light blue irises that seemed to reflect the colour of the skies.

"My name is Princess Manasa, sister of Lord Vasuki." The Naga royal studied Padma intently. "I hope you don't feel bad for your friend. He wasn't really helping your cause and those who don't help in your cause should just be debarred from existing."

Manasa walked over the panas, which Padma had tossed on the ground. "These are coins which were used during the Mahayudh. How did you find them?"

How did she know what coins were used during the Mahayudh?

"I am a collector," Padma said. Collecting coins had been her hobby. It was something she loved doing since she was seven years old. Manasa handed her back the coin. Padma took it, surprised by the generosity of the Naga princess. She stuffed it in her dangling pouch.

"I like your hair," she played with it, lacing her thin long fingernails painted, painted a dark ruby red, through her hair. "Is it natural?"

Padma shook her head. She felt like she had a mother at that moment, in the midst of the humdrum market, flanked by Naga guards.

"You are special, my dear," Manasa continued playing with the silver hair, rolling it in her fist as if it to feel it, and Padma could feel a slight, soft jerk, "quite special. A girl so young who is able to fend off trained men—now that's a sight I have been dying for, in this godforsaken city. Unlike the Manavs, the Nagas take pride in giving the best of education and warfare technique. Spying is a crucial art they perform, in which the women are more important than their male counterparts. Men are taught about philosophy, but they end up with suras and wines at their disposal while women are the harbingers of knowledge and peace. You remind me of a Naga."

"Why do you do what you were doing?"

Padma remained quiet. Anything spoken against the state would be sedition.

"Do you hate the ruler?"

Padma looked up at her.

"Ah, indeed, this is where we both align, because I hate him too," she softly smiled, "My dear, we both, if we worked together, could achieve something wonderful. If you do decide to take my offer, drop into my office sometime," she said.

So why was she going around the city stopping propagandists? Was it that she was trying to build an army of people who hated the state rulers? But why? What did she have against the king?

"To me, all of this seems like an endlessly tedious affair, with little fruit to savour in the end." She grabbed her by the arms and began to walk with her, the Nagas trailing around. "And I love fruits. You deserve a good ending after waiting for so long, am I not right?"

Padma nodded. She didn't know where the Naga was going with this, but wherever it was, she knew she was going to be a part of it. Also, she had never felt what power really looked like until today.

"You work too hard at the wrong end. The real fruit you shall receive, if you do what I say, and we can both get rid of the man you detest."

"Are there others like me?"

"Everyone failed to impress me except you, darling," Princess Manasa said. "For your favours, you will be given everything you desire."

Padma realized that they had reached a building which was none other than the entry gates of the Naga fort. After the inclusion of the Tribals, forts were built that suited them, and Manavs had to work for them to be built. Many detested the idea, but the look of the entire fort was beautiful. She didn't know what to feel or what not to feel, but she knew aligning with Manasa could be good in the long run. She could either get killed or be revered and rewarded. But she didn't mind the initial, if it somehow led her to achieve her vendetta against Vedanta.

As they walked along the corridors of the fort, they were closing on the path that led to a short door. The guards departed and Padma's heartbeat increased. She was in enemy land and this was one of the places she had been fighting against and yet here she was, in the midst of it. The thought of Aakash being dragged to the jail cell did cross her mind, but a parole would be granted by Ratri and he would be free. These thoughts shouldn't crowd her mind now.

She sat in the magnificent room that had been robbed of its glory by all the books that were kept on the racks. She hated books.

She had tried reading a few of them, but none appealed to her varied interests.

"What do you want me to do?"

"Oh, yes, I will tell you, but first..." she took out another pouch from the drawers and tossed it over at the table.

Padma looked at it, confused, before opening it up to find gold and silver panas, karshapanas, surashtras and cowries. Grinning, she held them out in the open. They were no longer valid currency forms, and were only useful as collectible treasure.

"I am sort of a collector as well. I'm glad we have same interests, darling," Manasa said.

Padma looked up.

"You can have all of it."

Padma left the pouch. It was blood money. It came with a price. The point was, was she ready to pay the price?

"Don't worry."

"What do I have to do for you?" Padma asked again, this time sternly.

"Oh, it'll be fun," Manasa had a glint in her eyes. "You get to play with weapons for sure."

"I can't...I can't do this," it was hard refusing all of it. "I can't work for..."

"Me? I am an innocent woman, my dear. You should realise we are aligned more towards peace and non-violence than you know." She laid her hand in the front, over the table. A voice boomed from the back. Padma turned to see a handsome, black-haired man standing, with crystal blue eyes and a grin that was lazily playing on his face. He had long robes of dark blue wrapped around his frame. He came forward with the same snide, royal attitude, rounding close to Manasa.

"She is right," he hissed.

By the very virtues, it was clear who the man was—Vasuki, the prince of Nagas or the king. More or less, the Nagas didn't have a lot of titles to go with in the first place, so they chose whatever suited their names best. That was what the talk of the town was.

Manasa's voice had automatically turned far more sinister, rasping, as she said, "Because in the end, it comes down to this-either you do what I say and get these beautiful coins as a token of my gratitude for being a valuable servant of the court or you'll be executed tomorrow for attacking a state official." Her fist clenched and the smile was not friendly anymore.

"Now it is your choice, love."

55

Kali had been running. He had forgotten for how long.

When he did manage to open his eyes, they darted over to the front. He walked to the white marble pedestal of sorts, resting againt the cool balustrade. His hands began to trace the droplets of water inside the shallow pool, as he saw the reflection of the man he had become. He had changed. The illness had eaten into his skin, exposing his emaciated frame, bony limbs and sparse hair. He was growing bald and that was the last thing he wanted. He had been revered as a handsome man always, but now he felt he was changing.

If it wasn't for his loving sister, Kali would have died perhaps. The illness and the stab had caused him tremendous pain. He couldn't believe he had clawed his way out with the help of Durukti. She had given him some sort of a tasteless, odourless liquid, blue as the Nagas' irises. He had swallowed it in one gulp. He took one more shot a few days later and felt instantly better.

That was three days back.

Now, he had slowly started gaining in strength. He didn't feel sick. No matter what that liquid was, he had come out of the illness because of it.

There were guards and his officials that operated insides of the fort, working on their daily chores. He didn't care for that. He had forgotten about the politics he had been going through. He stood up, stretching his body a little, when his eyes were drawn to his reflection. It had changed. Slowly, he crept forward and he realized, he hadn't changed, but the water had—it had turned red. Bloody.

But it wasn't dark or opaque. It was light where his reflection was visible, and he looked horrible. His skin had deteriorated in the reflection and he had gone bald and hairless. He was wearing a strange scarf around his neck to hide his leprosy. And at that moment, he saw the juxtaposition of various images that swiftly began to come forth in front of him. He couldn't understand it. A sharp, splitting headache shot across his head and he felt he had gone through something worse than death. His body felt frail and he fell on his knees, his eyes trained at the bloody water, until he saw a few more individuals coming in beside his reflection, standing right next to him. And the worst part was, they were all burnt.

"You couldn't protect us, brother. You couldn't protect us," the burnt reflection of a child said, but his voice echoed as if he spoke from an alternate world. "You left us there. You left your brothers," they all were speaking in unison. The water began to furiously froth and bubble.

What is happening?

"How should I redeem myself?" he cried out. "How should I? You keep coming to me and I don't know what I should do."

"Honor us," they said in unison, their voice growing in frequency now.

"Honor you how? What do you want me to do?"

The hands lifted out of the water, and the burnt fingers of the ghosts pulled and grabbed him by the neck. He choked until he was pulled inside the bloody water, his eyes wide as he saw the burnt siblings of his, who had no face, no eyes, but were a mere façade. They were indescribably grotesque, just like a burnt victim would be.

"Honor your roots. Seek your heritage," and the hands pushed him back. Right out of the bloody water, he was tossed over the ground.

And recovering from a deadly bout of choking cough, he realized he was still sitting at the same spot. He wasn't wet. The water was…blue and everything was stable. It was a delusion, he told himself. Why? A message from the dead to find his heritage—it wasn't the illness. This was a sign, Kali knew, some sort of an odd sign.

His heritage was dark, but he knew it already. Half the reason he thought the village had burnt was because the ones who burnt it got to know who Kali was and what sort of a family he had been hiding. His kind was a plague. The Asuras. The worst of the kind, the lepers of existence, called the so-called demons, even though they were simple-minded people. All Asuras were supposed to grow into the Dark Age, the so-called prophesized future where murder and chaos ruled the world. He hadn't told anyone except Durukti who they were. Not because it was dangerous, but because he wouldn't like the way they would look at him after that. Let him be a mystery, he thought, that would be for the best.

Kali thought of not running anywhere and decided to trudge off to his office, when he ran into Kuvera, who was entering the fort in his typically portly manner, accompanied by a beautiful consort and a few Yakshas.

For a man who was supposed to be controlling the city finances, Kuvera seemed rather modest at first glance.

"I see you are doing well."

"Yes, I'll be returning for the Council meeting," Kali said.

What was he doing here? He didn't ask too many questions though, for that would come off as blunt. He didn't want Kuvera to be on his bad side since he was the first one who volunteered to take down Keekatpur, and the rest of the northern kingdoms in Illavarti.

"Are we having that now?"

"We have to."

"I apologize for being too forward," Kuvera smiled. "But how is your back?" he asked, looking not the least bit apologetic about his intrusive question.

And Kali would have had joy in breaking his fat face, but he chose not to. He was being grumpy for some reason. He would always be calm and quiet, and yet now he wanted to shake off the restlessness from his fingers and his chest, that had a certain heaviness to it. He felt jittery and aggressive for some reason.

"You know too much for your sake, Lord Kuvera," he said, in a simultaneously placating and menacing voice.

"I'm being polite and inquisitive merely," Kuvera began, "but I've heard it was a Naga that had tried a ploy against you, but then the Gods were kind and had gifted you another life."

Kali shook his head as he began to move towards his office, passing guards who bowed at him and Kali just nodded in return. "You out of all people know I don't believe in the bloody Gods. There are no Gods or Goddesses. There are just men."

"I know. I understand your religious scepticism."

Kali had been tired of all the opposition by the temple priests, who wanted the Manavs, the progenitors and the first born, to be at the forefront of the ruling kingdoms. The Tribals were the backwards, the less developed in front of them. Now Kali hadn't practised any sort of measure on the temples, for they were places of worship and one shouldn't touch the Gods if one wanted to avoid a violent reaction or revolution. They had reached the office when Kuvera continued, "You must not forget that an attack on you means an attack on me. Let me find out why the Naga rebelled."

Kali sat on his seat and contemplated.

"Or you don't think he rebelled?" Kuvera came forward, sitting in the opposite armed chair. "Oh no, you don't think it was Vasuki, after all, do you?"

Kali had a certain distasteful feeling about how Kuvera was

leading up to this, but he couldn't help it and admitted flat out. "Koko and Vikoko investigated, and they said the Naga was not from here, at least not a part of any enlisted regiment."

"Then it just couldn't be Vasuki." Kuvera leaned back with a straight face. "I mean, I'm sure he wouldn't risk it all by bringing an outsider to do this work so you won't get suspicions about him. That just sounds very unlike him."

Kali clenched his teeth. Where was the fat man going with this?

"I'm sure it isn't Vasuki. He just likes you a lot. He believed in you the most. I'm sure it was my money too, but it was his persistence…"

Kali laid his hand in the front and banged it over the table to cut the king of the Yakshas off. "After Takshak died, he blamed it on me and said he would take care of it himself and I wouldn't like it the way he would do it."

Kuvera lifted his eyebrows innocently. "Dear Gods, you are being targeted by him after all. I thought he would keep the differences aside and be a good man. I've never told you why I stole the mani from him, which he loves so much. Not because I like shiny things, but because I wanted his ego to be brought down. The mani made him beg to me, and I liked that. It brought him to the level where snakes are supposed to be, you know."

The mongoose wrapped around Kuvera's neck tighter. He had even named it, which Kali failed to contemplate. He didn't care much about Kuvera's mongoose, but it was funny how his animal and Vasuki's reptile had one thing in common—they were both arch enemies in reality and in nature.

"We don't know yet," Kali said, sighing. "These are just assumptions."

"I know. I hope you do the right thing, Kali. I don't want you to be hurt. You have returned and you are strong and I want that you get all the riches possible."

Kali stamped his feet and went for a pair of dice he had kept in a small, wooden box. He began to rub them together as if he was about to throw them, but he didn't. He continued to rub them, in order to alleviate the growing sense of unease building inside him.

"Do you think if it comes to be proven, we should plan something against Vasuki?" Slowly, Kuvera brought up the issue after a brief silence that Kali was enjoying. And before Kali could even say no, there was a knock at the door and Koko entered with his thickly covered armour.

"My lord, we have a street offender that Lady Manasa, sister of Lord Vasuki, caught," Koko said.

Kali and Kuvera shared a brief glance. What were the odds that the person they talked about was mentioned a second later by another person who didn't even know about their conversation?

"What had he done?" Kali asked. Offenders were hundreds in number and they would be brought here to meet a higher-order official to decide the fate of the offender.

Koko came inside and placed a folded paper. "He was promoting seditious comments about the state and had been influencing the public."

Casually lifted the paper and unfolding it, Kali asked, "Were they influenced?"

"I wasn't there, my lord, but to my knowledge, I'm sure they weren't."

Kali saw the paper. It was a diagram of his face with abuses written over it.

"Should I send him for laborious exile or for a fifty day imprisonment, my lord?"

Kali scratched his head, as he burnt the paper in the fire lamp. He looked at Kuvera, who was surprised by his act. Kali was glad there was a flicker of nervousness crossing Kuvera's face.

"Where is he?"

"Outside, my lord," Koko said.

Kali opened the door, with Kuvera and Koko following and saw

Vikoko standing with two Manav guards, holding the offender. He was young, just a boy, perhaps in his twenties. He had a handsome, cherubic face. For someone like him, Kali was surprised that he was promoting propaganda against Kali and his people. It were kinds of people that angered him, who had absolutely no idea how much hard work Kali had put in to reach this stage in his life.

Kali came forward, watching the boy who was looking down. He was surely embarrassed, perhaps seeking forgiveness genuinely. But Kali had other plans prodding him. Kali didn't utter a word and he didn't let the boy say anything as well. He grabbed the javelin that the Rakshas had, plunging it inside the boy's chest. Kali lifted the javelin to accommodate the boy's body weight with ease, as he began to walk with it, leading it away from the corridors until he was out in the sun. With a sharp twist of his wrist, he dug one end of the javelin on the ground while the other one was up high, almost blocking the sun. The body of the boy writhed over the javelin, as he got impaled deeper, his flesh slowly sliding down the pole.

All the nobles and the women in the fort watched this scene, horrified, whispering to each other. He turned to face Koko, Vikoko and Kuvera, who remained stunned by the act he had just performed. He was surprised himself, but he was glad too.

"Listen," he calmly said to Koko, "call an artist and make a sketch of this and spread it across the entire city. Anyone who goes against the state will face this consequence. I'm tired of this community's irritating wretchedness." Kali yawned. Turning to Kuvera, "I suppose I should get to bed.'

Kuvera watched him for a while, incredulously. "Uh…" he coughed gently, "yes, I suppose you should. You must be, um, tired, yes."

Kali nodded with a smirk. He moved away from Kuvera, and the impaled body behind him, which was drawing in a crowd; but his smile didn't wear off. He had begun planning things for all the

Tribal Heads now. He had plans for Vasuki as well, but it would take time, for he knew the visit by Kuvera meant one thing—he couldn't trust anyone anymore from the council. He had to depend on himself and the ones he could trust.

In all these musings, a funny thought popped in his head. His restlessness had vanished, and he knew exactly why.

56

Lord Raghav breathed calmly in Kalki's ears. "Don't grip the bow with your fingers. Let it rest in your hand." Raghav walked around it, his fair-skinned body, his face with striking eyes, watching Kalki, as he made him put his leg at the back and one in the front. "Always remember, forty-five degrees angled grip, with your fingers over the bow."

Kalki nodded. He had a bead of sweat trickling down his cheek as he clutched on to the bow, as tight as possible with an arrow strung up, facing the sky.

"Now, when you strike," Raghav had a tough voice, effortlessly brusque and deep. "you push forward your bow arm towards the target."

"What should I hit?" Kalki whispered to himself. "Could it be the elk in front of me?" He looked at the elk which was grazing over the grass, unaware of the two men who stood behind the bushes.

Raghav shook his head. "Animals have as much soul as we do. Never forget that." He tilted the bow towards the bark of a tree, "hit here and if you can, make a twig fall."

Kalki nodded, feeling a pang of guilt for wanting to have hit an animal, but the way Raghav explained it to him, made Kalki respect him more than he already did. He never believed he would be in this lush scenery, in the midst of the croaking frogs and the hooting owls, and the bristling wind that made a whistling sound. Everything was so beautiful here, unreal to a point. Because it was, in the end, his image formed through Channelling. He wasn't able to meet Bhargav Ram, but he was able to learn a little bit about Channelling and how to interact with his previous Avatars. They were reflections through time, residing in our subconscious, so that they could teach us the ways to hone a particular craft in warfare.

Kalki left the arrow. It created a slithering sound as it went past in the air, attacking the twig, but failing to have an impact. The arrow fell down.

Kalki cursed under his breath, stamping his feet.

Raghav walked to the arrow and picked it up. "Never despair." He walked back to Kalki and handed him the arrow again. "For what falls down can always be picked up."

Kalki nodded. He took the arrow again, but then his target began to distort. He felt this reality was crumbling around him and a soft sound began to plague his ears…

"MAN! MAN!" The sound echoed in the corridors of his conscience.

And he was snapped back, his body jerking, and he realized he had returned to the prison. It was dingy, smelling of dead rodents and had a guttery feel to it, with the walls leaking black water. He was sitting in a position of penance, before he uncurled his legs and moved to the side, from where the voice had originated. It came from his cell inmate, another one in the hole like him.

"What are ya in for?"

"Murder," replied Kalki.

"You seem like simple folk from a small village, ya?"

Kalki nodded.

"Which one would that be, ya?"

"Shambala."

He couldn't see the face of the inmate right now, but he had seen it earlier when they were all locked in cages and put at the trial in the centre of the city. They were supposed to be witnesses for no reason, but Kalki knew why. It was to set the fear in the other prisoners that if they revolted, they died.

The inmate had no name and even if he had, he had forgotten about it. He had a grainy beard that covered his face, with a bald head. Even though the characteristics were same, he didn't remind him even a bit of Kripa. While Kripa had a cunning glint running in his eyes, this man was just sad and tired.

"Why are you here?" Kalki asked.

"Because I'm innocent."

"Aren't we all?"

"Not sure about ya, but I was blamed for the mistakes I didn't commit," the old man sniggered. "Ya as well?"

"Hmmm."

"You are a quiet man."

"I've become one."

"There's a special kind of hell for those who remain silent," he laughed, clapping his hands and Kalki couldn't help but smile. "In the time of the conflict."

"There is no conflict here."

"A conflict doesn't need to be always spatial," he paused, his breathing sounding more like wheezing. "Ya have a family out there, ya?"

"I don't know. Perhaps, yes." Kalki wondered if Arjan and Bala were safe.

"Do ya know anyone here in the city?"

Not know directly, but yes, he knew of Ratri, Lakshmi's aunt.

"I have this one little trick. If ya want anything out there for someone to know, let me know, all right? I'll help ya in that. I often do that for a price, but for ya, I'll do it for free."

Kalki smiled. "What makes me so special?"

"You seem like a nice boy, a sight for the sore eyes ya can say," he laughed.

That was when their conversation had to stop, as the tinkling of sandals was heard. The guards moved, who were guarding Kalki's cage, and they opened it. They made sure to tie Kalki to shackles, and he was forced to bend down.

It turned out to be none other than Durukti. She stood there, majestic as always. Just like Arjan, she had a way of pursing her mouth or playing with her fingers whenever she was musing. Kalki had seen enough of Durukti to stop looking at her with contempt but. She was a respected woman here and yet she had a shadow of sadness masking her eyes, wherever she went. She wasn't supposed to be hated, but to be pitied.

"Have you thought about it?"

Every day she would come with the same offer: work with her. And Kalki would shake his head and say, "I would rather die than work with the woman who destroyed my home." It was a legitimate answer to an absurd question. Why would she think that he would work for her? Out of all the reasons, even if he got a chance to be out due to her, he would hate himself. He wanted to get out on his own.

"No, thank you."

Durukti turned to see the inmate who had his eyes trained next to the railing. Durukti stamped her feet and the Nagas came in the inmate's cell and pulled him on the other side, with their blades against his neck.

"Don't hurt him!" Kalki exclaimed. "He has already suffered enough."

Durukti told her guards to release the inmate.

Durukti knelt down, and it was the first time her eyes pleaded to him. "Please, I don't want to beg to you, but if that is what it takes, I'm ready to do it." Her voice had grown so quiet that the Nagas couldn't hear her. "If my brother finds out I hold you here, he will make sure you get executed. I don't want that."

Kalki narrowed his eyes. "Why?

She remained impassive for a moment, but shook her head as if trying to banish the thought. "You can be useful to me."

"And what do I get?"

"Freedom from death."

"I have already suffered enough because of you." Flashes of Lakshmi's image came in front of him. The very thought of her poked him hard in his chest. He didn't like to think about her, but he couldn't help it.

"There is no freedom from death, only freedom from life."

"I did what I did to save my brother. He means the world to me. You have no idea how much he means to me," she paused, fighting back tears. "I wanted him to be well…"

Kalki narrowed his eyes. "You gave it to him? The Soma?"

"Yes," her brows arched, "why?"

"Did it have an adverse affect on him?"

"What do you mean?"

That meant no. Soma could be consumed easily by only two people—Dharm and Adharm. Tension filled his muscles.

"No, it can't be." Kalki clenched his fist. "Have you given it to anyone else?"

Durukti shook her head. "No."

"Please, if you want me to work for you, make sure you don't let anyone else touch that. And also make sure, to not give your brother any more, no matter what," Kalki's eyes met Durukti's eyes urgently.

Durukti looked at him, and then nodded. "What if his health fails again?"

"You don't realise the effect Soma has on people."

"What effect does it have?"

"It is said, it'll take men on the brink of madness, for the power is too great for an ordinary individual." But is Kali an ordinary individual? If Durukti was an Asura, so was Kali. That would make the prophecies…true. Asuras were born to bring chaos in this world. It all fitted perfectly, into a clear puzzle.

Durukti stood up. "Your words make no sense. My brother is strong-willed. And all these things you hear, they are village talk! Nothing else. What I had given him was tested by shamans and not hazardous for anyone. I keep reserves for him, for the future, and nothing can stop him from taking it. So stop being so…"

And Kalki lifted his chains, his body feeling the effect of it, his muscles stretching more than it should as he looked at the royal princess. "You are a fool. You don't see the truth. Science has corrupted your brain!"

That was it. The fiery blazing in Durukti's eyes signalled that she didn't wish to entertain this conversation any further. Kalki saw her leave the cage and close it behind her.

"Put him in confinement and don't let him out until he apologizes and wishes to see me, in order to work for me. I want him out of here."

Kalki knew what the confinement meant—being in a dark room, tied inside a bucket of water, with only the head out; until you felt your bones chilling. Kalki knew he wouldn't like any of that at all.

"What if he doesn't speak, my lady?" the hesitant Naga asked.

She looked at him briefly once again. The softness in her face was spoiled by her anger. "Let him suffer. I don't care." But she did care; there was a slight hint of it on her face, before she left for the main doors. At that instant, Kalki rushed to the rails that were joined with his fellow inmate. His voice was desperate.

"Get a message to the government official, Ratri."

The Nagas came forward and grabbed him by his leash and tugged him hard. He fell back.

"What should I tell her?" begged the inmate.

"Tell her," he was being pulled outside of the cell now and he raised his voice as the two Nagas pulled him towards confinement, "tell her to know that perhaps—perhaps Kali, the commander of Indragarh is the Adharm and if it is so…that the DARK AGE HAS BEGUN!"

Kalki was engulfed in complete darkness after that, with the last remnants of the light and the parting image of the horrified inmate playing in his mind repeatedly.

57

Arjan had never been to Indragarh, unlike Kalki who had had his chance of going there. Arjan was never allowed in the first place, but most importantly, he also didn't want to go. He was too lazy to eschew the comforts of his home, although this often contradicted with his inner desire to explore and see the world. While Kalki felt suffocated in Shambala, it was Arjan who loved it. But that didn't mean he wanted to stay there forever. He intended on seeing other civilizations that lay beyond Keekatpur.

And when he came forth to the city, it was difficult as the guards didn't allow villagers who had no cause to be inside. Kripa had to use his persuasion powers that was basically putting some copper in the Naga's pockets and saying, "Mate, we are harmless villagers who want to see the city grandeur." He had joined his hands. "Please let us go through."

The Naga had agreed. Arjan felt it was a waste of money. The resources on them were already of a frugal amount; they had to find help from Guru Vashishta while travelling to Indragarh. They had stopped at the Gurukul and to Arjan's surprise, Vashishta didn't recall Kripa from any of the other Gurukuls. Every Acharya was interrelated from somewhere, yet Vashishta, who was named after a popular Guru from Lord Raghav's time, didn't have prior knowledge.

Arjan didn't pay heed to this development, his hand running over the ground and touching pebbles, when he saw Kripa sitting beside him. Arjan didn't say anything, though he was puzzled about Bala's whereabouts—perhaps he had been getting supplies.

"I had a sister once," Kripa said, "with an almost same name like me. Kripi. She was everything to me." He had continued. "We were both quite, uh, playful and as we grew up, we chose our loves and we fought our battles."

"What battle?"

He hadn't said anything, choosing to remain silent.

"I'm telling you all of this because I know you miss Kalki, mate." His gray eyes shone under the glint of sun. "He might not be your blood brother…"

"I didn't mean that," Arjan cut him off.

"I know, I know. Anger forces us to spew venom, but one must never forget that the wounds from venom never heal," he said, almost looking heartbroken by some memory.

Arjan had nodded. "Where is your sister?"

He looked down, as if embarrassed. "She passed away. Quite the curse for people like me," he grinned cheekily, but there was profound sadness behind it.

Like you? Arjan arched his brows in puzzlement. But before he could even ask a question, Kripa continued. "I know you are sorry, mate. I've heard enough sorry in my time and let me tell you, there's no one logic or effect behind it. No one cares about it. That's the world we live in."

He stood up, stretching his arms. "When one's family dies, they show regret, but they don't mean it. When one gets hurt, they show worry, but they don't mean it. Indeed, it's a sad thought."

"Then why do we continue to hope and fight for such people?"

Kripa had stopped. "Because I think regardless of all the darkness in people, there's still a part of them that's good. And I've lived long enough to see every bit of it. So yes, we fight for the little goodness in the world; but I think as long as there is a fight, the goodness will live on. I might seem like a callous man, but I believe in all this. It makes me glad, mate, for I live in this world and sometimes it's good to be just glad. Cherish your existence, once in a while. There's no harm in it."

Arjan had grinned. "Positivity is very uncommon as a personality trait of yours; I presume something has gone amiss. What is it that troubles you?"

"I've been a victim of an emotion, honestly speaking. I was angry once; a long time back and I did something I shouldn't have." He had swallowed. "I let the anger overcome me and I let it influence my actions."

"What did you do?"

Arjan noticed a few tears forming in Kripa's eyes. This was unbelievable!

"I know you were angry," he had drifted from the question that Arjan had thrown towards him, "you were angry for losing, for letting people down. You were angry at Kalki for standing up in that meeting. But when you see it from his side, you'll know he meant goodness. Perhaps sometimes the best way to end the anger in this world is to just look at things from the other person's perspective."

Goodness, indeed. Arjan had learnt in the journey towards Guru Vashishta's ashram, who Kalki really was and what he had been capable of performing—feats of greatness. He hadn't believed all of this was even possible in this day and age. It seemed like a supernatural impossibility to him.

Presently, Arjan was travelling in the bustling city life of Indragarh, pushing through and being shoved by individuals. Bala had no problem in this regard. At the very sight of him, most of the civilians just turned around or dodged past him. Arjan almost wondered if Bala was even a Manav. Perhaps, he came from the Danav Tribe—the very large folks, who were now extinct. They said there were descendants of them, still roaming around, but there was no incontrovertible proof, for they were two names that scared everyone—Danavs and Asuras. They were the Tribals from the Ancient times when Lord Indra was on Illavarti.

Arjan had trudged over to the main street. There was a lot of talking from each side, with Nagas in the corner, eyeing them closely. Long bright flags fluttered on each of the buildings, the air pungent with spices and an odour Arjan was not familiar with. There were fire lamps spread across the entire section.

"This should be the house of Lakshmi's aunt, most probably," Kripa was looking through the city map that he had stolen from the Naga's back pocket. Arjan knew Kripa was a lot of things, but had never considered him to be a thief.

They walked to the building and knocked on the door. The door was opened, but they couldn't immediately see who had opened it, until they looked down at the sound of coughing. And his eyes were drawn down to a small man. It was funny seeing a Yaksha upfront. He hadn't seen one in quite a while. Nagas were exotic looking, most of them sculpted with brilliant angular faces and handsome bodies. But Yakshas, on the other hand, were small and dirty. The one at the door wasn't however.

"Who are you?" he spat. He had a weasel-like voice. "And why are you here with a giant?" he signalled over at Bala.

Arjan smiled. "We are looking for Lady Ratri." He tried to peer in, but the Yaksha just closed the door.

Arjan knocked again.

"Should I just break it?" Bala asked from behind. "It'll be easier. We can throw the little man outside and enter."

"Yeah, uh, and then we can forget about asking her for the favour."

The door whipped open. "Yes? Who are you?" asked the Yaksha again.

"My name is Arjan Hari, this is Kripacharya and this Bala Chandra."

"All right," the Yaksha nodded, "and why should I care about who you all are?"

"You just asked us who we are."

"That meant how are you related to Lady Ratri," he sighed. "I did not know your names. I don't care what your names are. You are nobodies to me. In fact, you are worse than nobodies to me. You don't exist for me. So can you please…"

"I'm breaking the door!" Bala announced, stepping up to him.

The Yaksha got scared and that was when a smooth voice came from the back. "KUMAR!"

"Yes, madam?"

"Who is it?"

"Someone called Arjan Hari."

"Hari?" the voice was piqued with interest. There was a sound of fallen books, until a lady appeared at the door, shoving the little man behind. "By any chance, are you related to Kalki Hari?"

"Yes, my lady, he is my brother," Arjan smiled.

Ratri came forward and grabbed Arjan by the throat. She had delicate bangles dangling from her wrists, kohl around her eyes and curly hair wrapped with a scarf over her head. Her entire body was covered with a golden robe and a shawl wrapped and secured using a silver brooch. But Arjan didn't care about all the materialistic things she was wearing since her fist was close to his face. And he didn't understand why.

"Your brother tricked my niece into bringing weapons. Where is he? And where is she?"

Arjan remained still until she removed her hands from his throat.

"I have some bad news, my lady." Arjan nodded, feeling awkward about being the messenger of bad news.

Sitting inside, Arjan sipped on to the drink she had given to them. It was not sura, so Kripa wasn't really fond of it. He had told Arjan that he had been sober for quite some time now and he didn't like how it felt.

Ratri's house was filled with books; clearly one could mistake it for a library too. Arjan loved every bit of it and in the time Ratri did brought for them something to eat, Arjan went through as many as he could, selecting a few of them and hoping to borrow them. But as of now, Ratri didn't feel like saying or doing anything. She didn't cry either.

"She wanted to be like me," Ratri said, finally breaking the silence. "She wanted to work in the library."

Arjan nodded.

"Did you see her? Was she given a funeral at least?"

"We couldn't. We had to leave out of compulsion," Kripa lied. "The villagers were gathering the bodies and they sent us to the city to know more about the administrative machinations and how one could seek redress from the Council for this one-sided slaughter."

Ratri nodded. "Indeed. I can't help you in that if you think I'll be of any guidance. I have been shifted to library duty from hospitality, so I apologize."

"Uh, that's all right, we just wanted to bear the news to you." Arjan leaned forward. "With the inclusion of the Tri…" he looked at Kumar, who hadn't noticed his slip up, "the royals, things have changed. More dictators mean more terror."

"Yes. Even Vedanta has forgotten his duties as the ruler of Indragarh," gritting her teeth, Ratri said. "How did you all survive the battle?"

"We, uh, improvised, my lady," grinned Kripa.

"You are a dirty, ridiculous looking man. Are you really an Acharya?" asked Ratri.

"Guilty as a murderer," Kripa stood up and bowed. "Though I think the comparison wasn't really correct."

Ratri placed her drink back. She stood up and announced, "You are capable of surviving then. I'm sure the reason you are here is to free your brother, and spite the ones who destroyed your village. Work with me and you shall achieve both, but with patience and time."

"Uh, I don't think you should say all of this in front of…"

"Kumar?" Ratri slapped him on the back good-naturedly. "He's a sweetheart. He's loyal to me and not to Kuvera."

"Why is that?" Kripa asked.

"Because, old man," Kumar said, leaving Ratri's hold, and walking up to Kripa and looking at him with an angry, contorted face, "not all Tribals are fanatics about their kings. Some of them have their individuality as well."

Ratri clapped her hands. "All right then! That is great. We have a team now."

"And what are we supposed to do? Should we bash the skulls of the Nagas?" Bala asked, scratching his head.

"Violence is not the answer," Ratri said, "even Lord Govind managed to outsmart everyone in the Mahayudh when he killed his enemies through wit than his brawns."

Arjan smiled. "I didn't take you for a religious woman."

"And I am not. But that doesn't mean you can't take inspiration from a myth." Ratri smiled at him back.

"My dear sweet lady, that is all right, but what do you plan to do? The entire city is against us and they are big in number while we are…" Kripa trailed off. "How would we stop them?"

"I have a girl working for us. She can help. I don't know where she is though. She has been getting tardy nowadays," Ratri mused. "But do not worry; I suppose we can work through it. We have to spread hate against the state and once we put the seed of doubt in everyone's mind, we will have a revolution on our hands."

Propaganda. Arjan had read about it; fighting against the state by spreading the truth, letting people know they were following the wrong leader. But these were barbaric times and one did not know whether that would even work. But he had a roof over his head, a cup of hot drink in his hand and like-minded people around him. For now, he had to settle for this plan, while he thought of another plan to release Kalki and leave for the mountains.

Arjan took Kripa to the side while Bala sat uncomfortably on the small cushion. "This is all right, but if the Somas you say are out, that means we have a situation of Adharm walking among us, right?"

"Yeah, I mean, it won't be so fast, but..."

The door was knocked upon at the moment. Arjan paid scant heed as Kumar scurried towards the entrance.

"We can use the woman's help while we think of a better plan out there. With her, we can walk the roads freely, find what we need to know to escape and get to Kalki."

"You don't have any plans as of now?" Arjan clenched his teeth.

Kripa nodded his head. "I have a plan. But that demands the location of the prison and the location of the Somas."

"You want to use the Somas?"

"Yeah, well sort of," shrugged Kripa.

"They were the very things we were trying to run away from," he paused, "why would we go towards it?"

"Because the improvised plan dictates it."

"It's not improvised if you have planned it," Arjan corrected him.

"Well, then just the plan," he grinned.

Arjan shook his head. Whatever, Kripa had in his mind was obviously a bad idea. But as of now, Arjan didn't have a good one to counter him.

Ratri came back into the room with a rolled out parchment in her hand. "I have a message from your brother, Arjan."

Arjan came forward, his heart thumping. "Who gave this to you?"

"An urchin."

Can they be trusted?

"What is Adharm and what is the Dark Age? I've read it somewhere…" she began to contemplate, as she paraphrased the message.

Arjan looked at Kripa and whispered, "All right, whatever your plan is, we need to work it out fast. This is already not going well for us."

58

When not working and scheming against the ones he held the province of Keekatpur with, Vedanta would sit down close to the bed of his daughter Urvashi and tell her stories of heroes and villains. But today though, she had been asleep when he had entered with a fire lamp in one hand. Occasionally it would be a guard who would come along, holding the light for him, wherever he went at night. But not when it came to Urvashi. She was schooled at home and was by far the only one protected by the walls of this fort. Ten guards would stand outside and none would dare to hurt her.

Half the reason he had given up to Kali was because of Urvashi. She was his little princess, with a beautiful face and a golden heart, rightly like her mother. And he didn't want his ego to wreck her life. It would be more understandable to work with Kali than to fight him and to lose. You can have your city again, but once you lose your daughter, there isn't going back.

Today, she was already asleep. He came inside and stood there, smiling. Perhaps, she didn't want a story to be told or perhaps she was tired. Not only was he educating her through books, but also about warfare; about how to ride a horse and handle a sword. It was important to survive in this world and royalty is a fickle disease. The title and associated privilege came and went. What if tomorrow it was robbed from Vedanta? Urvashi should know how to go out there and fight like a warrior.

"Father?" a soft voice squeaked.

"I apologize for troubling you; I thought you weren't asleep so I came…"

She interjected. "I'm your daughter. You don't need to apologize to me." She shifted on the bed, turning to Vedanta. She was just thirteen years of age. In the light of the candles, her face had ignited and resembled someone whom Vedanta loved dearly.

"You remind me so much of your mother."

She stretched a grin. "Tell me about her."

Vedanta shook his head. "Another time, sweetheart."

"It's always like that with you," she frowned, "you always escape from something that has happened in the past, father. Never let your failures overcome your present or even future." She came up and leaned against the headboard.

"Where have you learnt that from?"

"From the same stories that you preach."

Vedanta chuckled. He was caught in the snare of his own words. He swivelled his head, the smell of a plant coming to his nose, and he knew what it was. He stood up and walked to the plant that was close to the window, with its leaves unfurling into a lotus. It was light green in colour. He began to touch it tenderly. "I'm glad you have not *mistakenly* lost this one." Urvashi would clumsily lose the plants he would give her. He was not an idiot. He knew she didn't like the gifts, but she didn't realise their value, so he didn't blame her entirely.

"Yeah, it doesn't smell as bad as the last one."

"It's supposed to get rid of the evil spirits." Vedanta patted the plant gently.

"Your love for these little things is kind of scary." Urvashi grinned.

"As if you don't have your own strange hobbies." Vedanta signalled over at the wooden figurines she loved carving with her pocket knife. "We all have our passions, for they establish our character, the way we are in reality."

He walked back to the chair. "Don't you lose the plant, child. I have brought it for a specific reason. We are not living in luxury now. In fact, we are in times of turbulence. We need to be careful. Each step should be well thought out."

Urvashi nodded. "Don't worry, it will be. I am being careful. When do you plan to get rid of the Tribals?"

"Soon." Vedanta had expressed his doubts earlier to Urvashi, about how he was annoyed by the Tribal inclusion. But he didn't tell her that he was working with one of them now. "You question me like your mother."

"Well since she has passed, there needs to be someone to take care of the man of the fort."

Vedanta smiled. He hugged her tightly while she wrapped her arms around his frame. They remained like that for a while, until there was a knock on the door.

"Whoever it is, not now!" Vedanta roared.

"My lord," it came as a whisper, as if afraid.

Vedanta sighed. He looked at Urvashi, mouthed "I love you" and with a bitter frown masking his face, he made his way outside. Once outside, he saw the man was panting and sweating, clearly flustered by something. But worst of all, his silver breastplate was sprayed with blood.

"What happened?"

"My lord," the guardsman's eyes widened, "it's a bloodbath."

Vedanta stood over the blood that had splashed over the floor. He was standing inside a brothel that would be active at night, but in the morning, it would be just another inn. Vedanta walked around, seeing all of the known faces with their throats slit.

The manager whimpered behind Vedanta, following him wherever he went. Vedanta entered every room, where it was the same disturbing image of men with their throats slit. All the pillows were now drenched in blood. The floor was stained by the bloody footsteps of the prostitutes. And the smell, by the Gods, was terrible. Vedanta had a shawl wrapped around his nose as he watched all of it.

They weren't just any men. They were his ministers, and his Senapati. He had no one any more, or at least that was the first thought that crossed his mind. He chose not to dwell on it. He closed the door behind him and put the shawl down, breathing heavily.

"Why were they in a bloody brothel?" he asked his guardsman. The manager was at the side, not saying anything except rocking back and forth on the balls of his feet, clearly still in shock. "What in the world were they celebrating?"

The guardsman didn't utter a word, but the manager did.

"Kingship, they come often in groups to party and enjoy with my girls."

Vedanta couldn't believe his ministers were partaking in an illegal activity. It was against the morals of the society he had upheld for so long. Why had he built temples to Lord Vishnu and Lord Shiva and Lord Indra if he had to have escorts on the other end, dallying with immorality? The thought disgusted him to the core. He felt crippled by not just their deaths, but by their dishonesty towards his rule. The very fact they did it meant they didn't respect Vedanta as a ruler in the first place.

"Girls? They didn't see anyone who did it?"

"Kingship, I have not asked. They are quite traumatized about what they have seen."

Five ministers dead and he was worried his bloody prostitutes were traumatized. Grabbing him by the collarbone, Vedanta pulled him towards him. "Now bring them and line them in front of me. I want to see each one of them, right now."

The manager nodded instantly, scampering off. Waiting diligently, Vedanta came forward with his five guards. The prostitutes were lined up. They were all wearing skimpy clothes, with a white cloth around their body that barely concealed their chest. He had never seen so much skin on a woman except his wife. She was the only woman he really loved, in and out.

He walked forward, slowly, watching each of them intently. He was trying to study the flickering emotions that crossed their faces. And he stopped at one.

"What did you see?" he asked her.

"I…uh…" the woman had a shifty mien, as if trying at all costs to avoid the questions. There was something off about her.

Vedanta shook his head as he grabbed the woman's hair. The manager gasped. It was a fake. He tossed it on the ground. Standing in front of him, was a man in disguise. "Sell yourself the way you want to, it's your choice. But don't be ashamed of it by hiding behind a woman's image."

He had seen in other cities when he had travelled, rulers of his kind complaining how they had ordered for a woman at a brothel but found a man. And for these men who sold themselves, it was their own preference. It was surely against the rules of the Gods, but those rules were written a long time back. Things were different then, and Vedanta didn't mind all of it now. But prostitution was still illegal in Keekatpur.

"You all stood there while my ministers were murdered, one by one, and you are saying, you didn't see anything." His voice had an impassive quality, almost shrivelling others with the sheer menace it held. "Either you speak now or this brothel shuts down and you all go to prison for soliciting sex." He would do that even if they would tell him the truth. But that was a good leverage he could play around with right now.

The manager was crying. He was a wimp. But then, there was hesitance. Vedanta walked to the woman and stood there. "Yes? You want to say something?"

"All of it happened while we were sleeping alongside them." The woman had a way with her words. She was afraid to look at him, but her words showed no fear. "It had seemed like the person was waiting for us to fall asleep."

"All of you were sleeping?"

"Sleeping, yes," they said in unison.

Vedanta narrowed his eyes. His ministers were calculatedly murdered, perhaps given a drug-laced wine to make the job easier. "Has anyone seen, by any chance?"

A hand went up. Vedanta walked to it.

"Yes?"

The woman had blue eyes, and was perhaps a Naga. "I woke up earlier than I was supposed to and I saw the figure."

This is something.

"Yes, please tell me." He waited, curiosity burning his mind.

"The person saw me…Erm…and it ran, right through the window."

"What was it wearing?"

"A shawl wrapped around the face; it was all covered."

"Anything in particular that stood out?" Vedanta waited while the woman concentrated really hard, her mouth pursing and her eyes squeezing tight in contemplation.

"Yes," she sighed, her eyes widening with a sense of realisation. Vedanta's heart thumped. This could be a little clue to find the culprit. "The person, whoever it was, was in a hurry. When it leapt from the window, I was able to glance at the hair due to the wind."

"Yes?"

"It was the hair I could see."

"What's so special about that?"

"My kingship," she said, "it was silver in colour and we all know, not many silver-haired people walk in this city."

59

Lord Kali didn't really worry about finding Chief Martanja. Like every other Rakshas, he would be sitting in his building, or perhaps working his way through the street, marching his soldiers. But most likely, he would be in a tavern, drinking sura and enjoying the little things in life. Koko and Vikoko found him wasted in such an establishment.

Kali entered, seeing the man reeking of liquor. For a Rakshas, this was a surprising sight. Rakshas were disciplined men from the South, working their way up to the top. They were quite extraordinary and yet the paramilitary chief of Rakshas was here, in this state. Surely, if Raktapa found out, Martanja would have a hard time explaining his lackadaisical attitude to him. Unlike Martanja, Raktapa didn't have a bad day. His bad days were the good days and his good days were his better days. It was perhaps the one eye that troubled Martanja.

A man who is wounded sees more folly in himself than a man who has no wounds.

At the sound of Kali's boots, Martanja fidgeted, but he continued to remain half asleep. Kali looked at his guards, who weren't drinking, but rather kneeling behind him. Kali always liked this kind of respect, for it gave him a boost of confidence and made him feel good about himself.

Kali sat on the opposite chair, one leg on top of another. He didn't do anything, but sat there watching the man. Drinking made pathetic losers out of the strongest of men. That was one reason why despite all his other vices, he kept drinks at an abeyance.

Koko came forward and shook Martanja. He was dumbfounded for a moment, before he realized it was Kali's personal guard who had the temerity to wake him up. He frantically came to his feet, spilling the wine in the process when he saw Kali.

"Sorry," he blinked hard, "I was uh..."

"It's all right," Kali waved at him with a friendly grin. "Cheer, don't worry. We all deserve a rest, right?"

Martanja watched him for a moment, as if Lord Kali, the Usurper of Indragarh, had really said what he thought he had just said.

"I was ill, a while back and I rested, and I'm fine now."

"What's wrong with your hair?"

Kali felt anger surging inside him. No one should talk about his hair, not even a mild chief of a stupid tribe. He had a few sparse tufts growing unevenly over his scalp, while his face was getting duller by the day. "It's my uh...it's my illness, nothing else. I'll be fine."

Martanja must have sensed his insecurity, for he leaned forward.

"You know, I heard what happened to you."

"Rumors are poison, surely you know that?"

"But if it's true, the rumours, my lord, then I am positive you were poisoned," Martanja smiled foolishly, looking at Kali. "Now I'm not pointing anything out, my lord." He had a way of speaking, his words slipping and half-eaten, not the most coherent words Kali had ever heard someone speak. "But you must really watch your back. There's a saying in Eelam. It goes like: the winners often have arrows in their backs from the very ones they love."

Kali nodded. "I've heard that. That's why I have them." He signalled at Koko and Vikoko, who straightened at being mentioned by their Lord.

"Loyalists," Martanja nodded back. "And why have I been honoured with your company, my lord? What kind of deed have I done, good or bad?"

Kali pulled out a small vial from the pocket of his tunic, which he sipped. "What is this, really?" he signalled at the vial.

Martanja took the vial of blue liquid. "And why do you ask a humble Rakshas, my lord?"

"Because," Kali leaned forward, his fingers clasping together, his face half hidden in the shadows of the room, "I got to know what you two did. And it was not nice. Durukti is an impulsive child. She sees terror and she seeks a solution. She saw her brother probably dying and she tried to help, regardless of the consequences. But that isn't the problem. No. The problem is the very place she sought for the remedy. Now," he picked up the vial, studying the glinting blue liquid. "I want to know what this is, that is helping me. She says it's an extract from a herb. But I don't believe it. I feel it's something else. It's something out of this world, after all."

Martanja chided him. "And why don't you ask your sister?"

Kali couldn't. He felt embarrassed about doubting her and showing his suspicion. She would hate him for that. Ever since the beginning, their love had been unconditional and nothing had come in between it. It was just her and him, against the world.

"You are nervous around her, my lord. I wonder why, she's just a woman. What makes you so nervous around a woman?"

"She's my sister."

"Don't really matter in our culture," Martanja shrugged. "Wives, sisters, prostitutes; all are same for us."

Rakshas had an open relationship with their women, for their ancestors were incestuous in nature.

"It's the men that carry the burden of this world, my lord," he grinned.

"I'm sure they do quite well with that sense of burden, just like you."

Martanja stopped grinning and watched Kali in contempt. "You want to know what this is. It is indeed out of this world and from what my men say, it's from the Gods. This is a nectar of magical proportions. Incorrect dosages can make you go mad. Why didn't you get affected?"

"How do you know all of this?"

"A man who helps someone should know everything about who he's helping and what he's helping in," Martanja explained.

"And you didn't think of ever taking it?"

Martanja smiled. "I don't know. I never thought I was allowed."

"When has it ever stopped you?"

He laughed. "My lord, you understand me truly well."

"You didn't use it because Durukti made sure to never let it be found by anyone else. She has hidden it somewhere in the city and you don't know about it. You have tried searching for the elixir and the futile attempts have led you here, where you imagine the suras are the elixir and you drink it up," Kali explained. "What if I tell you I found the warehouse where she has kept it?"

"How did you?"

"My informants are better than your men." Kali signalled again at his twin generals.

Martanja looked at them with delight. "You know, I would really love to know how you all met each other. I'm sure it is a great story."

"We are all a part of the story's narrative, chief." Kali smiled.

Standing in the reservoir, which smelled of ore and fossils, Kali made sure to station the guards around the entrance to the warehouse. The Somas, as they were called, were right here, under his fist, unknown to Durukti. Each stone had a rough exterior, with a blue gel inside it, shining and casting brilliant kaleidoscopic images on the walls around him.

Martanja walked, touching the rocks. Kali stood there, at his one place, his hands at the back, letting Martanja enjoying the pleasures of this discovery.

"I'm glad to be here."

"I'm glad that you are glad," Kali responded.

Martanja turned around at that statement, blinking his eye. "Why are you doing this, my lord?"

Kali had a straight face. "These rocks, they have helped me to regain my strength. I thought it would help you with your eyes."

"Oh, they are gone, pulled out forever."

"Nothing a little magic can't solve."

"You believe in magic now?"

Kali came forward. "I believe in a lot of things now. It's like this has opened my mind to the universe. Now the existence of Gods and Goddesses, they appeal to me rather than repelling me."

"All of this is charming, my lord, but I seek honesty in your words and I find none. It's hard to believe, that out of sheer goodwill, you are helping me to bring my sight back."

"Goodwill is so rare that when one intends to do it, you think it's some sort of chicanery."

"Well said," Martanja nodded. "So tell me, what is it that you really want from me?"

Kali and Martanja stood ten meters away, their faces on opposite sides of each other as they continued to watch each other unblinkingly. Martanja waited for an answer. Kali didn't seem to be in a hurry. Martanja knew he didn't do it out of goodwill. He wasn't running a charity of course. But he couldn't quite state it in a manner so blasé.

"All right, Raktapa is not here and I need support. I have enemies in the office and I need someone I can trust. In return for your services, you'll be rewarded with the elixir, as well as gold from my treasury."

"Here we go," he laughed, coming forward. "Of course, you can trust me. I am on your side as long as I'm getting what I need."

"I just gave you what you need."

The Rakshas had a sly grin. "All right, I'm in."

Kali smiled, as they shook their hands to cement the deal.

"And for a person who you trust now, I should tell you. Beware of the prisoner your sister has brought in."

Prisoner? Arching his brows, Kali's mouth tightened.

"Oh dear, I suppose she hasn't told you that either." Martanja tapped Kali's shoulders. "I think it's time for a good, long conversation with her, for she fancies the village boy."

60

There was something about her face. It always glimmered under the shadows of the fire lamp. Her eyes had dark kohl, and an amber colour over her cheeks seemed to highlight her aristocratic cheekbones. Kali stood there at the door, hesitating for a moment to enter her bedroom, but then did so, fearing nothing. He had to stop the fear that was killing him. He felt he owed her too much, but he really didn't. She owed him. She loved him because he had protected her from the fire, sacrificing his other siblings for the sake of her.

She had worn a long night robe. In the shadow of the semi-dark room, her eyes lifted and saw him. Kali noticed her expression changed. She didn't turn. She smiled at the polished brass plate, letting Kali know she was glad he was here.

Kali walked to her and his fingers slowly massaged her shoulders, tightening around them as he began, "How are you doing today?"

"Interesting," she said.

They both shared glances on a reflective surface, as if they were afraid to look at each other directly. They were afraid of facing each other with their true countenances.

"Did I tell you that at the time we were homeless and we were hungry, you said to me that you had prayed for us?"

There was a hint of surprise that crossed her face. "Really? Me? Out of all the people?"

Kali smiled. "Yes, of course." He paused. "You were a believer once. I feel we all are believers when we are young. It's when we grow that we realise faith is overrated."

"What did I pray about?" She applied some cream over her arms. Kali knew it was an expensive cream, found in the bazaar he was attacked in. A shame, for he was not able to find out who that card reader was. She had possessed an eerie capability of frightening Kali to his bones. But she did tell him one thing. There would be power and he was not to be corrupted by it. Perhaps, the power from the so-called Somas is what the old lady told him about. And perhaps, the part that worried him the most was about someone close to him who'd betray him. Would it be her?

No. It couldn't be. She was too loyal. But then, everyone was fickle.

Beware of the prisoner.

She fancies the village boy.

He didn't know who this boy was, but the very thought of him brought a vitriolic emotion within him. He felt his lungs burning. He was feeling something he never felt.

Jealousy.

And so, to dissipate the feeling, he took the cream from her, almost snatching it. To her astonishment, he began to apply it on her. There was a flicker of confusion that crossed her face, followed by discomfort.

"What is wrong?"

Kali didn't listen. His eyes had widened, as he applied the cream, his fingers circling tenderly over her skin. "You prayed about us, about our well-being. You said to the Gods that we should get what we deserve, and that is a good life. And when I told you that prayers were worthless, and that the only one you should listen to was the one you love, you said that the person was me."

Durukti's brow arched. "I think that's enough cream."

Kali grabbed her by the shoulder as she stood up and made her sit down forcibly. Her jaw clenched, and her eyes widened as he began to massage her head, his eyes meeting hers, his teeth gritting. He slowly rounded his fingers down her neck, almost in a choking manner; running it through her long hair and gliding them across her temples.

"Stop it." He grabbed her by the face, while his other arm wrapped around her waist, slowly reaching for her bosom. "What..." His fingers entered her mouth, but she didn't bite them. Perhaps she liked it. Perhaps she was uncomfortable. He knew what he was doing was wrong, but he had to do it. It was like performing a brother's duty.

He let go of her face and his two hands grabbed her neck. "You went behind my back and you brought my cure. I love you for that, sister. But then you bring a villager and you destroy an entire village in the process without telling me. Then you hide the very cure that's helping me. What sort of a double game is this? You think you can repeatedly lie to my face..." he was sweating in cold rage, "and I would ignore it because you are my sister?"

She tried to resist him by flailing her limbs. She was trying to grasp for something, but she couldn't. Her face had gone red. Kali came forward; his head slowly touching her shoulders as he kissed them lightly and looked at her in the mirrored surface. "You mistook my love for you as submission to your actions. But never underestimate my silence for my kindness, because I'm back and not even you can hide things from me. If you ever dare to conceal facts about anything." She was choking and her eyes were frantic, but he didn't care. "I will forget that you are my sister."

He let go of her neck.

She collapsed on the floor, coughing and wheezing, as Kali walked back to her bed and straightened himself out casually, while she took time to catch her breath. When she was done, with veins protruding from her temples, she shot a look of contempt towards him, trying her best not to let him feel her wrathful gaze.

"You…don't…trust me?" She massaged her neck.

Kali shrugged. "To be fair, I don't trust anyone right now. So nothing personal against you."

"I'm trying to use the boy for our…"

Kali lifted his fingers. "You don't turn him against us. I never asked you to have an ally."

"I just thought with our friends turning to enemies, we would need a strong soldier on our side."

"What's worse than concealment? The fact that you think you need someone's help when you should know your brother is more than capable of it," Kali said, leaving the room.

But he knew where he was going.

He was going to meet the village boy.

He walked across the corridor of the prison. Many inmates came out to see who it was, past midnight, and when they saw it was Kali, they whimpered and fell back. One of them didn't. He used the choicest of words to abuse Kali.

Kali walked to the inmate. He had a strange locket. The inmate lolled his tongue around. "I don't get scared by you, outsider! You repel me!" He stuck his tongue out as a gesture of indecency.

And Kali did what any person would do in his position.

He pulled out the tongue, ripping it with ease. Kali tossed it onto the floor, while the man fell back, wailing in pain.

Kali could hear Koko gulping and Vikoko elbowing him.

"Should we, uh, my lord, send him to the infirmary?"

Kali looked at the weeping imbecile. "Nah, I like him that way," he grinned as he walked further.

The prison guards, shrivelled back almost, as they led Kali to the dungeon. The prison was more confusing and zigzagged than the ordinary lanes of Indragarh. It was surprising how Vedanta had crafted it. But then, Vedanta didn't believe in capital punishment, but in reformation; until Kali had come and changed it. He had seen too many men, too corrupted. He knew a punishment like imprisonment wouldn't do anything to an individual. Just because a criminal had been punished once didn't mean he wouldn't commit the crime again. He would. It was the way they were. They all were.

He reached the confinement where the so-called village boy was held up. What was so great about the boy that Durukti fancied him? There was no one in the entire world that Durukti looked up to romantically. What was so spectacular about him? A pang of jealousy and insecurity rose inside him. Was he too handsome or too noble or just too naïve? But worse, was the jealousy Kali faced, even healthy? As a brother, he should be protective. Not jealous. It was an odd choice of feeling. But he quelled it.

The cage opened. And he saw there was a lad sitting in a bucket of water, shivering, naked. The Nagas came forward and he was pulled up from the bucket, his hands and legs tied to an iron chain, multiple ones, as if he wouldn't be restrained by just one. Why would that be? That was odd for a villager. He was brought to the front and he had a brown loin cloth wrapped around his privates. He was too much in pain, such that he didn't even manage to look up for a while and when he did, Kali noticed nothing. He didn't look special. Sure, he had a muscular body and was tall, towering well over him. But what was so special about him?

"You are the prisoner everyone talks about." Kali walked, circling him as multiple Nagas held the boy by the chains, one holding him by the neck.

The boy didn't say anything.

"Your name, what is it?"

The boy didn't answer.

"Doesn't matter, though, I'll know of it soon enough," Kali

sniggered. "My sister, she's fond of you and thinks you can help us."

At that moment, the boy's head lifted. He looked through the wet hair that fell over his face. "You are Kali?"

Kali came forward, hands on his hips, raising his eyebrows, or at least what was left of them. "Ah, you know my name." He paused, laughing to himself. "It's funny how my sister thinks, after destroying your village, that you will help us. That is ridiculous, but that is exactly what a person who is meddling with things beyond her station thinks. She's young. Hormones, you know. She just wants to find a way to save you from the trial."

He impassively watched the boy. "But nothing can save you from the hanging. In fact, I think I have decided to not just let your execution be a public punishment for my sister to really understand her mistake and realise she doesn't have the right to like anyone she wishes to, but also to hook up a false trial. I'll let you have a trial. If you succeed in telling me why you did what you did, which is killing the officials of the state, you are free to go and do whatever you want to. I see prison is really affecting your…"

The boy instantly moved his hand, toppling the Naga that held him. The ground shook, the water in the bucket spilled as the boy came forward, his muscles tightening, the veins on his face appearing more prominently.

"You are special, indeed." Kali stood inches away from the boy. They were close, really close, but the boy couldn't come closer to Kali. He was tied down. "Very much so. I like that. And how do you do this?"

"I am coming for you, Kali. I am," the boy spat. "You can't have a trial about me because mortals like you don't have the power to conduct a trial. It's only Lord Vishnu who judges us and forgives us."

Kali scoffed. "A religious fanatic as well? What have I done to deserve such hatred from you? I'm excited though. Please, please, do so. Let the God of all Gods have a trial for you, perhaps when you'll go up or down. But till the time you are here," Kali's smile vanished, "I am your God and your Lord Vishnu." He spat in disgust. "And I'll show you how."

He snapped his fingers at the Nagas. "Kneel."

The boy was pushed down. He tried really hard not to, but he was continually lashed until he was left with no choice but to do so.

"See?" Kali patted the head of the boy who growled at him like a dog. Kali grinned. He liked troubling the innocent. The boy was misguided, perhaps fed wrong things about Kali, about how he was and what he is like. Thus, the hatred.

"Put him back in the prison. If he stays like this, he won't survive till the trial and I want him to be out there, in the open, for Durukti to see; how her choices have led to this poor boy's death. I want her to see and regret; realize that you don't go behind your brother's back," he spoke to himself more than to others, lost in his thoughts, before shaking himself up.

As he made his way to the door, he heard the rattling of the chains. Kali looked back and he saw the boy had his hair whipped back, his forehead visible and his eyes smoky and dark.

"I…will…see…you…there," he said.

But instead of fear in the boy's eyes, there was something else. There was hope. And then, the boy did the unthinkable.

He smiled.

61

Vedanta had been waiting yet again. But he didn't wait in a disgusting lane like last time. It was far better now, but outside the inn where Vedanta's men had been slain. Though everything had been cleared up, he told the innkeeper to not touch the blood. He wanted to show it around. He wanted to show Kuvera what his planning had done to his men. And he wanted to make sure Kuvera was adequately sorry for it.

It had been days since the event, but his mind hadn't recovered from it. He was petrified as well as angry. He was afraid; he dreamed of a girl with silver hair, ripping his throat apart. He had two guards in his room, wearing large bells on their feet and they were ordered not to rest one bit. When they got tired and moved, the bell rang and Vedanta woke up and scolded them. The bells were supposed to be an alarm for when someone had entered his room, someone unwanted. He had Urvashi's room blocked by five men.

"I'm not really comfortable with large men in my room watching over me," she had said, but she wouldn't understand the gravity of the situation.

Indragarh was officially a war zone now. He didn't like it since he would have to protect Urvashi more than himself. A thought about sending her to the South, to the Dakshinis, came to his mind. He had a few friends down there. Vibhisana was a great man when it came to helping out those in need, and Vedanta could trust him. But then, a thought crossed his mind. Vedanta had other enemies down south. It was worse in those kingdoms because Vedanta had fought with them over trade and territory issues. He had to be careful.

Now he stood in front of the inn he had systematically destroyed by sending all the women and men to prison. The innkeeper, the new one hired by Vedanta, had been working to make this establishment respectable. But the rooms where the murder had happened, needed to remain untouched.

In the wee hours of the night, while Vedanta waited for the Yaksha king, he was met by the innkeeper, who said, "There was a guest here, my lord. He has taken a room for himself even though I was very insistent we weren't…"

"You didn't give him *those* rooms?"

"No, no, kingship," the innkeeper whimpered, perhaps the sight of blood had disgusted the poor man. "Not at all."

"All right, let him stay. Just make sure to send the guards on that floor so if he moves, we know," Vedanta ordered.

He was respectful of private establishments, but not illegal ones. He was given the religious city of Indragarh by his father and he had made sure to worship the God of all Gods, Lord Vishnu, and the head of the Trimurti. He was someone who Vedanta would kneel before and pray to every week, along with Urvashi as well. He had built a large golden statue of him, in the midst of the city. Everyone would go and worship it. Though of course now, with the inclusion of the Tribals, many second guessed that Vedanta, who worshipped the Gods, had fallen prey to atheism—which was false.

Vedanta knew better now. He knew they had their own cultures, rituals and traditions just like Manav. They were all in the same circle of faith, just disbanded and castrated from the society, because of battles they had lost ages ago.

He had to focus on the objective, though.

Revenge. That was it. Whoever was behind it, be it Kuvera, Vasuki or Kali, he would be coming for them. But, as of now, he trusted Kuvera. He couldn't have done it. It would be potentially harming his relationship with Vedanta.

The wait was over. The rich smell of flowers came around when the Yaksha king entered the street, wrapped in gaudy robes and ostentatious jewels. He looked tired than the last time and his wistful energy had been lost.

"What am I summoned for?" he asked, agitated.

Vedanta wondered why. But he prodded him with further questions. He led him to the rooms, opening them one by one. "As you can see, all the sheets are red."

"Well, I know I seem to be a fashionable man, your kingship, but I just don't think it's necessary to show me random designs, since we are facing a political struggle at the moment."

"These are not designs." Vedanta signalled him to go closer.

Kuvera did so and he gasped, as he touched the fabric, touching the dry blood. He turned back, pale as ever, trying to take a deep breath. "You do realise I don't have the stomach for blood."

"You didn't mind Takshaka's blood."

"Well that was Naga blood; it smells different."

Vedanta didn't know if there was anything unique about a Naga's blood. He had seen it. It was the same colour, though he didn't manage to smell it like Kuvera.

"This clearly is Manav blood," he blurted. "Why are you showing me blood, man?"

"This is my men's blood," he said by way of explanation. "My ministers and my Senapati."

"I didn't do anything, your kingship. Whatever we did, we took a mature and a wise decision."

"Now it is backfiring, clearly."

"Did you manage to find out who it was?"

Vedanta nodded, taking Kuvera to the last room where the silver-hair murderer had been seen. "It was someone with a different kind of hair. Silver."

"I'll send my informants across the city, get the word out," he paused. "It won't be difficult to ask around, since the colour is indeed quite unique and I am sure someone has seen it."

Vedanta had a disdainful face, but Kuvera had a good army of informants. They relied heavily on the spying and disguises.

"Three rooms. That's like someone really had a grudge against you," Kuvera said, before Vedanta could even open the door.

"What do you mean? It's an assassin."

"Sure, but the assassin would never make such a mess, he or she would hit the target and leave," Kuvera explained, "by arrows, dagger or poison. But this one didn't go on that route. She probably drugged your men and then killed them, leaving all the women. So, yes, our enemy, whoever it is, has found someone who hates you. You must search for people who have a beef with you. Anyone in particular you remember?"

Vedanta didn't. All he ever did was help others. "A Dakshini perhaps?"

"Oh no. A Dakshini here would make too much noise." Kuvera narrowed his eyes. "And why now? He wouldn't want to cripple you like this; he'd rather go on a war against you and humiliate you."

"I see," Vedanta hummed, his thoughts running with the same idea of who it could be who did this. Was it the time he had killed the imposters or the robbers? He had hunted a few men in the jungles of Keekatpur, but they were Mlecchas. So who could have had a grudge against him? He opened the door and instead of finding an empty room, he saw a slender, lanky man standing, his back against them. He was wearing a tight vest, was armed with two daggers and wearing bejeweled slippers. His hair was all patchy, and his skin seemed diseased. He was watching the blood-stained pillows.

He turned. His face was a grotesque mixture of cherubic features and festering, scaly skin.

"I'm sorry to break up this party," Kali said, grinning. "I'm glad you have been served the wine as well." He walked to Kuvera and Vedanta, both of them now instantly petrified and backing off. "Don't be afraid of me. I seek peace just as you do."

"How did you find us?" Vedanta said, trying to keep a straight face.

"I've increased the strength of my generals to spy on my loyal friends." His hands slowly rounded around Kuvera and Vedanta's shoulders. "To see what they are up to. I didn't know I would need this service until you two began to behave differently towards me, especially you, Vedanta, who abjectly hates the company of the Tribals. The irony is killing me."

Kuvera asked, trying to get rid of Kali's hand over his shoulder, "What do you want?"

"What you two want," Kali said, "which is that we should work together, all of us. After all, we have one enemy now."

"Was it really him?" Vedanta asked.

Kali looked at Vedanta as if trying to gauge whether it mattered to him. "It has to be him," Kali said. "If not, well, it's an honest mistake on our part."

Vedanta could not help, but see the images of his dead wife and daughter. Kali had infiltrated their meeting and now Vedanta had no choice but to take help from him.

62

While Kripa and Bala decided to use loud speeches, drum beating and pinning posters up to distract people, Arjan had a different path. The spread of propaganda was only to appease Ratri as they couldn't say they were going to break into a prison. With an apple in his hand, he would walk casually around the prison's exterior, studying the intricacies of its architecture. Then with the use of what he had seen, he would sit and make rough sketches.

He had even met Shuko, while walking down the marketplace one day. He had almost forgotten about the bird. Shuko asked about Kalki and Arjan couldn't help but answer him honestly. He told Shuko to stay with him rather than flying away.

With Kripa and Bala on his side and Shuko busy eating curd, he explained. "The prison is the only architectural marvel in the city that is round in shape," he began to create a circle. "A little bit of curvature on the edges, if you notice."

"What is it made of?" Bala asked, his arms crisscrossing across his body.

"Iron, I suppose. I was not able to touch it."

"All right, move on, mate." Kripa touched the paper.

"Yes, so…" Arjan began to make some symbols in front of the main gate of the prison.

"What is that?", Bala asked mortified.

Kripa squeezed his eyes shut and tried to understand it himself. "Looks like bacteria to me. Why are you drawing bacteria, mate?"

"That's a bazaar shack, you idiot."

"That doesn't look like a shack. That looks horrible."

Arjan frowned. "I'm not an artist, so please, forgive me, you two." He ticked off the shacks. There are five bazaars in the city and this one is the biggest. And very strangely enough, facing the prison."

"To, make life difficult for infiltrators like us," Kripa explained. "All right, what else?"

"There is a pigeon post system that operates nearby," Arjan said. "And there is this one person, very trustworthy, who comes with some food in a cart and enters every day."

"Food for the prisoners," Kripa nodded. "And that's how we will enter," Kripa said.

"But he's the same man and if anyone sees it…"

Kripa snapped. "We need to be creative obviously. What is on the other side of the prison?" he paused. "That'll be the alternative."

"The Mining Street, as they call it, where the armoury is made."

"And what is that?" asked Kripa, pointing to the outer circle Arjan had made around the prison.

"Wires. The entire prison has barbed and serrated wires, which makes it difficult to get through," Arjan replied.

Kripa showed it to Bala. "I need something to break through there. Get it from the Mining Street itself, and we need three masks to hide our identities."

"And how do you plan to enter the prison through the back? There's no door."

Kripa smiled. "Mate, we need to make the door."

Arjan didn't really understand that day what Kripa had said, but he had been planning to go inside the prison, to know the basic structure of the prison. That's what Kripa told him to do. And he also told him not to get killed in the process, which would be immensely problematic as they would be short of one member.

And here Arjan had thought Kripa cared.

Apparently, the mysterious plan of the redoubtable Acharya was simple and yet complex. He wanted to know the insides of the prison and use the back door entry even though there was none. Arjan didn't realise why the plan would be genius until Kripa explained to them in detail. He said they would have to go and rob the reservoirs of Soma.

"We can't just rob it."

"I know. I'm working on finding some way to get it."

Arjan was displeased, but he had no alternative plan to work on. "And what do you plan to do with the Somas, which has wrecked our lives?"

"Make bombs out of it." Kripa had grinned.

Bala and Arjan glanced at each other.

"Do you know how to make it?" Arjan asked.

"I've taught my nephew to do it and it didn't go as planned," Kripa reminisced. "But I know, yes. We need a very little amount to help us get going. During the Mahayudh, many used Soma mixed bombs, which were commonly called Astras. We will use it at the back door, blast it open, enter the prison, free Kalki and escape instantly after that," he said that and for a moment, silence ensued, until Arjan began.

"What if it doesn't work?"

"There's always a probability of not working," Kripa said, "so yes, if it doesn't work, we will die and we would end up killing other inmates as well."

Arjan grabbed tufts of his hair in frustration. "And how do you plan to not kill others?"

"By placing it right where it's supposed to be, and for that, you need to enter the prison and see where we can plant it."

And here he was, standing outside the prison, with another apple to occupy him. The plan was absurd and unhinged and depended on a lot of variables. Kripa was the definitive version of craziness, coming up with absurd plans like these. Astras were considered to be given by Gods to a few warriors, but Kripa said it was nothing like that. They would need one more person in the team, Arjan knew. And he had seen the candidate who worked for Ratri. She was a cherub-faced; silver-haired girl. But he had seen her in action, agile and fast when she trained on the porch of Ratri's house.

"Her name is Padma," Ratri had said when she caught Arjan staring at her. "She was an orphan when I took her in; all her siblings were murdered in front of her."

It was odd, listening to Ratri being so melancholic when she would be the most unemotional person otherwise. "Who did it?"

"She wouldn't say. I've asked her many times."

Arjan was very intrigued. He hadn't liked her in any other way since he was not interested in girls. But she was different. She had a look of a warrior, hidden inside her. And later, he had seen Ratri yelling at Padma for having disappeared for hours and not telling her why.

"I don't like this. I don't like how you are not telling me what you are up to. But if I find out and I don't like it, I will kick you out of the house."

Padma had been quiet until she calmly said, "You already have, in a way, since you have taken those men in our mission."

"They are helping us."

"They are nothing but fools."

She was being derogatory, but she was right.

But for now, Arjan didn't have to care about a girl. His eyes calmly set on the man who was going towards the city with his wagon. He had all sorts of food items with him. Arjan whistled at Shuko, who was sitting on his shoulder. Shuko nodded and zapped towards the man, and with his short beak, grabbed a loaf of bread. The man, horrified, began to follow as Shuko teased him.

That was his chance.

Arjan, with quick strides, grabbed on to the wagon, with a shawl wrapped around his face to cover it, making his way inside the market. From a look over his shoulder, he saw the man was frantically trying to find his wagon.

Arjan couldn't help but smile. He reached the prison gates, passing through the market that was bustling with the smells of flowers and food, the sound of yells and raised voices; it was buzzing with sellers and buyers, haggling over the produce and wares on display.

The prison gate was blocked by two Nagas, who stood with their swords. At the sight of Arjan, they began to open the gates, before they stopped. Arjan had felt an elated sense of joy for a moment until he realized they had caught on to something. Arjan stopped, acting as if he was coughing, while the Naga appeared in front of him. Arjan had his entire face hidden with the shawl.

"Who are you?"

Arjan coughed. "It's me, man." He coughed again. "I'm ill, man. I'm just very ill today." His heart was thumping hard and his fingers had grown old. He was trying to bring his gruff voice out, trying to allay the guard's suspicion.

"You didn't need to come then."

"Duty, man."

"Why are you talking like that?"

Arjan sneezed and rubbed his nose on the Naga's breastplate. He got scared. "Oh! Dare you not! Let him go inside. Disgusting." The Naga frowned, wiping the snot off of the armour.

With a concealed smile inside his shawl, he made way slowly. Arjan was glad that his height was similar to the man who took the food inside the prison. As he entered, he noticed he was met by inmates. They were walking around, while Nagas stood calmly, guarding the inner prison complex. Arjan had to act his way through.

At the courtyard, inmates took their desired food; some choose fruits for themselves, others opted for glasses of milk. Arjan made his way forward then, inside the corridors, his eyes taking mental notes of the architecture, but he couldn't find anything that would lead towards the back of the prison. Everything seemed to be in the front.

Amidst the inmates who were ranting and yelling from the darkness, Arjan came round to find multiple windows, but each window merely opened out inside the prison courtyard.

The fortress was confusing. Arjan passed down many dark corridors, dodging the Nagas, until he was able to find the final window which would lead him out. When he looked out of the window, he could see the back of the prison, where it overlooked the Mining Street. He tried counting its location, but he had forgotten.

Arjan got an idea. He had been carrying a weapon to defend himself in the eventuality of an attack. He used it, by keeping it over the sill so when he would look at this window from outside the prison, he would be able to see. That is where the explosives needed to be placed.

Arjan went back to his wagon and began distributing food to each cage so they wouldn't presume something was wrong with him. He had to continue acting until he was out. The Nagas were less in number here, next to the cages. But soon he found the Nagas were walking up and down a particular cage. When he came forward, the Naga took some apples and bananas for themselves, grinning.

"No heat here, old man. Why do you wear such clothes?" the Naga asked.

Arjan just sniggered with his hoarse voice. He knocked on the cage, which the Nagas protected.

"He doesn't eat food."

Arjan noticed who it was and he wasn't surprised. It was none other than Kalki. He had been lying on his back, a thick beard covering his face, and his hair had grown longer than before. He looked weaker and sicker than the last time Arjan had seen him. Arjan's stomach convulsed in fear and relief.

Arjan tried to sound deep and gravelly. "The-there is someone out there calling ya two, saying something about a party or something amongst the guards."

"Party?" the Naga looked at the other guard. "They can't party without us."

"They are, surely."

"You keep an eye on him, old man. We will come back in an instant."

Arjan slowly nodded. "Yeah, sure, sure. I'm right here, you go on ahead."

The second Naga was reluctant and asked the first one, "We are given orders not to move from here."

"Orders? Pfft," Arjan growled and so did the other Naga. "Have some fun, snake."

"Yeah, have fun," said the first Naga, frowning. "We are tired of standing here in the dark."

Arjan couldn't agree more.

The second Naga managed to grin, though he was still uncertain. But he nodded and was taken by the first guard for the fictitious party. Arjan now knew how the foolish abounded every single tribe and race. He came forward, his hands clutching the rails as he looked at Kalki. For a moment, he pitied him, but he knew he had no time.

"Psst!"

"What?" Kalki groaned. He was sleepy, perhaps.

"Leave!" His voice was hoarse.

"It's me, Arjan," Arjan whispered.

There was a moment of silence as Kalki opened his eyes. He stood up, eyebrows arching, hands shaking as he came forward, wide-eyed as if he was seeing a dream.

"Arjan?" He pushed his hand out and they each other by the shoulders and hugged through the rails.

"It's going to be fine."

"I thought you had escaped somewhere else or perhaps perished." Kalki had tears in his eyes, which he swiped away. He looked so exhausted and almost dead.

"Kripa brought me here," Arjan said. "We are going to get you out."

"Did you get my message and come here?"

"Yes," Arjan paused. "You realise our lives have changed. We have to leave for the mountains as soon as we can get you out."

"He came to me yesterday."

"Who?"

Kalki looked sideways; his eyes were glittering with disgust. "Kali."

"What happened?"

"He thinks his sister likes me."

Arjan shrugged. "Why does every girl like you? What's wrong with me?" Kalki beamed at that and one could see vestiges of his former charm. "He's either being protective or jealous. He thinks I have stolen her heart and to prove he's the king of all kings, he's going to execute me in front of her and everyone."

"Without a trial?" Arjan was surprised. He had read about the city judicial system. Death was the last resort; and that too this was a recent phenomenon. The jury would sit, deciding his fate. Kalki's defence would be that whatever he did was out of self-defense. But Arjan knew that Kali would twist it into something else.

"A trial for him is just a formality. He's going to end it the way he wants it to end," Kalki spat. He was clearly angry, but then he was angry with everything that was around him.

"What are you planning to do for an escape?"

"You won't like the plan." Arjan pursed his lips and then he explained the entire explosives idea to him. Kalki just frowned.

"Have you found the location to trigger it off?"

"Seems like I have," Arjan nodded.

"Just remember to improvise." Kalki grabbed his shoulders. "And be careful, most of all. I would rather die than to risk your life."

Arjan shook his head. "I feel the same way. I am not the hero of the Dark Age; you are. You have to go there and protect and if you die, or if Kali finds out you are the one who will vanquish him, he will kill you, right at this moment. For now, he thinks of you as a sport."

Kalki hummed thoughtfully. "I just don't think of him as the Adharm anymore."

"Why?'

"Call it a gut feeling."

"But I thought…"

"I know I told you it was him, but when I met him, it just didn't seem that way."

Arjan nodded. It changed everything for him. But he couldn't say anything else because there was a bell tolling.

"It's an alarm." Kalki tapped Arjan's shoulder. "I think they know you are here. Run."

There were the sounds of heavy footsteps, calling out to the intruder. With one last embrace, Arjan tried making his way out, but there was no way out. The windows were grilled, and the corridors were perplexing. He threw away the shawl and reached the end of the corridor where he found he was in the courtyard area. He saw all the inmates gazing at him, as Nagas began to follow him.

Arjan knew he had to do something. With one swift movement of his sickle against the wall, he climbed it. Nagas were on the ground, yelling and milling all around him. Arjan continued climbing up, hoping the sickle would make a purchase on the stone walls and help him get away. He was so close to death, he could feel it. With one more stab, he saw the sickle was losing its grip. It wasn't going to hold his weight anymore. His fingers grabbed the stone edges, when an arrow came in his direction. It missed its intended target, but hit the stone slab. He grabbed the arrow and used it as leverage to climb even higher. One arrow had missed him, but the second didn't. It hit him right in the ankle. He moved suddenly and almost fell, but the sickle helped him.

"Come on." He was sweating. He didn't look down, for he knew he would be afraid and lose his grip on the wall. He finally reached the top of the wall, when the Nagas began to yell. He came up on top and laughed, but the stinging pain in his ankle made him lose control and topple. He realized he was going down, his hair whipping at the sudden motion; as he manoeuvered his body. Down he went, before landing on something soft. He realized he was saved by a farmer's cart. The farmer was yelling in shock, but Arjan just spat some hay out of his mouth. He realized the cart was placed right next to the prison walls.

This is a miracle indeed.

With a deep breath, he came out the hay cart and bowed to the farmer gratefully, before leaving for Ratri's house. He knew he had to do something. Kalki was right. They had to improvise and they had to get the Soma before his trial began, so that they could help him to escape. Though among all the matters that ran in his mind right now, there was one thing that struck out to him. Why did Kalki think Kali was not the Adharm?

63

Padma had realized that she was done with Ratri. She was a self-absorbed woman, whom she didn't trust anymore and Padma thought of leaving her. She wanted to leave Manasa's keep too. And settle in some faraway village.

Why such sudden burning hatred towards Ratri?

Because putting men in the house without knowing much about them was absolutely foolhardy and against every shred of common sense, according to her. For many years, she had strived for her trust and here were three imbeciles, who had no idea about propaganda, rumours or the administration, who had gained it in a snap of a second. They were there for the sake of being there. Ratri said that they were her niece's friends and as much as Padma had liked Lakshmi while she had been here, she couldn't stand the fact that Lakshmi's death had allowed these men to come into their lives.

Death was so simple for Padma now, because her brothers were crucified and burnt by the very king whom everyone wanted back on the throne on a de jure basis. Everyone except Padma.

When Ratri had announced Lakshmi's disappearance and the news about her eventual death, Padma hadn't been stunned. Death was alright for Padma. She was callous in these matters. Everyone died, she knew. In fact, she lived on the edge in a world that was on the precipice of chaos. That was a sad thought, she knew, but that was what she had grown up to be.

Even Aakash's disappearance had been a non-event for her until she realized there was a wild clamour to see the grand display at Lord Kali's fort. Padma had sneaked in, and laid her eyes on her ex-comrade—Aakash. He was impaled, killed by a senseless act of violence. Kali, she had thought, was the most suited and progressive ruler over Keekatpur. But now he was also doing crazy things. She was thoroughly unsettled by his twin generals too, who didn't have an ounce of expression on their faces.

Her hair tied in a bun and with a cloth wrapped around it, she entered the chambers where the play was being performed. While puppetry and mimicry shows were organized in the open bazaar area, the theatre was another beast altogether. Majestically proportioned, it seated the who's who of the city. It happened in the covered stadium, built over a stone platform.

Padma wouldn't have been allowed in, if it wasn't for Vasuki's summons. As she made her way to his little keep, where he was sitting alone, chewing on betel leaves, Padma saw the play. It featured animal-skin wearing men and women, with face masks. The atmosphere was redolent with the clanging sounds from the musical instruments.

Padma made her way on the top, by the stairs, while the lesser nobles sat at the bottom. She reached the top, where she found purple curtains partially obscuring the sight of the higher nobles and dignitaries. Two Naga guards were standing and they checked her, before letting her enter, even though she had a dagger on her. Perhaps Vasuki had told them that Padma was no threat to him.

Vasuki's back was facing her, as she entered. Padma didn't have to announce her entry for he already began speaking. "Good work with what you did at the brothel." Padma couldn't see his face, but she knew he was smiling. "You could have made it discrete and you didn't."

That was for a reason. Manasa had given her the destination and the orders, but she had given her the liberty to complete her assignment in any manner possible. And Padma chose the most violent one.

"Sit." Vasuki directed her to a small pedestal.

She obeyed. She was summoned here by Vasuki for something important or at least that was what the note said to her.

"You have done your one job well," he turned, his lips coloured red by the betel leaves, "but that doesn't mean, it's the end of it. It's Kali's turn now."

It was a surprise since she had been thinking about him just a while back.

"You want me to kill him?"

"Oh no, no," he waved it off. "Manasa said he can be useful if he's weak again. Easy to dangle a puppet, right?"

"What do you want me to do?"

"My sister…" he gave a note to Padma, "has a few boys running in the city, who note down every movement of the council. Apparently, they found that Kali's health that has been deteriorating drastically, before he rapidly recovered. Surprising, isn't it? Well he had help, from a strange herb or something and he goes to this place…" he pointed at the note, "often, to retrieve it for his health. I don't know how much is kept inside."

Padma unfurled the note, realizing it was a diagrammed map, clumsily made, but enough to give her an idea about where it exactly was. "And what do you want to do with it when I enter?"

"Burn all of it," he grinned, his teeth red. "Burn until the last of it is left and get that for me. I want to try it myself, to be honest." He chuckled.

"What about Vedanta?"

"We will come to him."

"I want him as well. When are you going to help me enter his fort and..."

Vasuki lifted his hand to halt her. "Manasa said to be patient about this. She gave you his men, right? You crippled him worse that way. Manasa said killing him won't do. If you want revenge from him, you kill the one he loves the most."

"Who is it?" Her ears were alert.

"Don't worry about that. Manasa will soon learn and tell you," with a simple shake of his head, Vasuki said, without any emotion running over his face.

The idea seemed fine, at least from what she had heard so far. Padma nodded. "I'll see what I can do." And before she drifted off, she saw the colours and the actors of the play again, with a great degree of interest and a great smile on her face.

"You have never seen the theatre, girl?" Vasuki asked, as his voice grew soft.

Padma shook her head.

"It's beautiful, isn't it?"

Padma smiled. It was many years since she had smiled properly. "It is." She saw the boy trying to take away the girl, who was wearing a mule's skin. "What's the story? Why do they keep dancing?"

"Dancing is the most elegant form of visual communication," Vasuki said. "Look closely and the story will form itself in front of you."

Padma glanced back at the stage. "How do you know all of this?"

"My father was a great man; a practitioner of such arts, and he made sure we were well-versed in our traditions of art and culture. He taught me a lot about it." His voice wasn't malevolent like before. It had deepened.

"What happened to him?"

"Killed. I was just sixteen when it happened," he said. "Quite young to lead a tribe, you might think. A civil war had ensued over this very question. It was just me and Manasa against a group of people who had defiled my father's throne and mine." He sighed, taking a deep breath, perhaps seeing the images of his chaotic past in front of him. "I apologize for speaking more than was required. I often delve into my life."

Padma was sitting right next to him, her back to the curtains that hid them, watching the play. "Can I sit here to watch some more? I would like to know more about the artistic aesthetics that goes in it."

"Sure, girl. I actually encourage more people to go for such pursuits," he replied, but she didn't look at him anymore.

For some reason, the death of his father resonated with her, reminding her of her relationship with her brothers. She had learnt so much from them, be it archery or sword fighting. They had taught her to be a soldier because they were ones themselves. Her three elder brothers were guardsmen to Vedanta and the fourth one, who had been younger, was aiming to be one. Like them, Padma had wanted to join the movement and become the first woman Senapati, until the tragedy had struck them.

"Was this something your father taught you?"

"Yes. Eating this garbage," he signalled at the betel leaves he was crunching. "I had begun..." he trailed off.

Padma turned, as she realized he didn't complete his sentence, when she found his throat had been slit and he was choking on his own blood, his mouth opening and closing mechanically. His eyes were lifelessly staring at her, with a faint look of surprise etched on his face.

Her eyes shot up; realizing it was done by none other than one of Kali's twin generals. It was the woman, with the golden hair, holding the bloody dagger over Vasuki's dead body. And the smile clearly showed that she was coming next for Padma.

64

Padma deflected the attack just in time.

With her daggers crossing each other, Vikoko tried to hit her repeatedly until Padma felt and grabbed her own dagger. With a sharp roll, Padma reached for her legs, and tried to trip her. It didn't work, and with a swift shove, Padma was tossed against the wall.

Vikoko came lurching at her, the dagger reaching for Padma's skull, when she deflected again. She was quick. They both had their weapons drawn against each other, their heads coming close, their eyes meeting. And then Padma, using the force of her bent knees, leapt up, leaving Vikoko dumbstruck. She came over Vikoko's back and with the hilt of her dagger, hit her on the head. With that, Vikoko fell down, but it wasn't the end of it. As Padma tried to stab her, Vikoko just pushed her away. Padma lost her balance and fell back, but she knew fighting with this large lady would be impossible after a certain amount of time.

Staggering, she made her way out, while Vikoko was struggling to come up. Padma realized that outside, Naga bodies were lined up against the chamber. Dead corpses just stacked one over the other. Padma raced forward, while Vikoko continued to chase her through the crowded theatre. Her bun knocked against the wall, and her silver hair was unfurled. She realized she had to do something soon. Her feet were quick and she came out of the recessed steps, dodging the guards while Vikoko calmly watched her leave.

Padma tried to find a transport for her while she saw Vikoko grab for her horse. Padma hated herself for not bringing a horse for herself. Padma sprinted forward, even as her chest ached with the exertion. She reached a circle a little way off, glad that Vikoko was not chasing her with an entire retinue of soldiers.

Leaving the circle and making way for the narrow lanes, Padma tried to find a place where she could catch her breath. But the sound of hooves would not let her rest in peace. Padma had never felt so frightened. She knew she would die one day, but only after killing Vedanta. Now, without completing the objective, she would have to die. And this death honestly scared her, even though she was otherwise sangfroid about the idea of death.

The horse appeared right behind her, almost reaching her; and Vikoko's sword was now trained mere inches from Padma's fleeing figure. With a sudden swipe, she slashed the air, cutting pieces of her hair. There was a tug at the back of her head as Padma sprinted forward. She knew if she didn't do something, she would be murdered in this empty street.

And then she hit on a plan.

Padma sprinted as fast as she could, leading Vikoko to ride her horse faster. And then Padma stopped. The horse continued to gallop further, until Vikoko realized what Padma had done. Padma struggled to take a breath, her chest heaving, looking up at Vikoko who was grappling with the horse and turning towards Padma. Getting her breath right again, Padma pulled out the daggers.

It was a face-off now.

The horse rode towards her, and Padma began sprinting towards it. Padma used the force of her feet to make a huge leap, somersaulting in the air, as she kicked Vikoko off the horse. But Vikoko did manage to slice Padma's skin with her sword. Vikoko collapsed on the ground, while the horse continued to run. Padma was standing over the horse, a smile on her face, as she proceeded for Ratri's house, while she saw Vikoko standing calmly, her horse being taken from her. She didn't chase it. Her sword was still in her hand and there was a look of naked aggression on her face.

Padma realized the gash over her torso was deep, as by the time she reached Ratri's house, she had lost enough blood. She didn't stop her horse, afraid Vikoko would follow her even though she knew she was out of harm's way. In front of Ratri's house, Padma tried to get off of the horse, which only hurt her, since it wasn't an ordinary sized horse. Padma took few steps further tentatively, her legs weakening, as she collapsed on the ground. She blinked for a moment and in the last moments before shutting her eyes, she saw a bird in front of her, perhaps a parrot, which began to squawk loudly. Dreamily, she tried to shoo the bird off, but it wouldn't budge.

And then everything turned dark.

Padma woke up to find she was bandaged and her buttoned tunic was off. Standing in front of her was the big man known as Bala, with a bowl of soup in his hand. Standing close to the library was the boy named Arjan, who reminded her of her youngest brother; and then there was the old man who gave her the nightmares.

"You took my clothes off?"

"Only the top, lass, in all fairness," the old man said. "You seemed in a pretty bad shape, come to think of it."

Padma recalled why. It was because of Vikoko. She admired the woman's skill and determination of not leaving her alive. Padma knew she didn't definitively win over Vikoko. It was her acrobatic skills that helped her.

"Thank you," Padma quietly said. "I could have died. Does…" she looked up at Arjan now. "Does Ratri know?"

Arjan shook his head. “We thought she wouldn’t want to know you were sneaking off to meet a Tribal king.” He walked in front of her and handed her the note that was given to her by Vasuki and which had a snake symbol on the top of the page. “Now, we know you were in trouble tonight but we will respect your privacy.”

Bala silenced everyone before Padma could speak. “Have soup, little one. You will feel better after this.” Padma nodded, trying to find a good excuse about why she had a note from Vasuki. She had to find a reason somehow. She took the soup and sipped on it from the edge of the bowl. “I can explain.”

“Please, lass, you can give us all the excuses you want to, but they won’t work on us now,” Kripa said. “Because like you, we are liars as well. We aren’t here to stop the Tribals and whatever politics you are in the middle of.”

“Then why did you lie to Ratri?”

“To hide, of course,” Kripa responded. “Like you do, while you help a Tribal.

Padma shook her head. “You don’t understand. It’s more complex than that. I have a mission I have to complete.”

“So do we,” Arjan said.

Padma sipped on. “And let me guess, you want my help with that?”

“Not really help,” Arjan said, taking the note that he had tossed at her. “What is this place? I have compared it to the overall city map and I know I have seen this place somewhere. What is this place? It is written here as well, ‘Kali’s lair’.”

Padma sighed. She didn’t want to help them, but she did not serve any master anymore; at least until Manasa would get to know that her brother has been assassinated. “It’s where he keeps his herb that makes him all right.”

“Herbs you say, eh?” Kripa grinned delightfully as if Padma had just told him the secrets of this world. “Thank you. That will be all then, thank you so much.”

Padma knew something was up. "Why are you really here?"

"None of your business, lass. It's like the time we didn't care about your business."

"You do realise," Padma began, "I was about to leave Ratri; so you ratting me out wouldn't bother me. But I will make sure to tell her everything about your antics before I leave."

Arjan shot Kripa a look, as if he was being an idiot. Then he looked back at Padma, tenderly.

"We are here to free my brother."

"Shut up, boy!" Kripa scolded.

"No, we can use her help," Arjan snapped. "She knows everything about the city and its keeps. More than us. She can guide us."

"Yes, she finishes her soup early as well, old man," Bala said, taking the bowl away from her, "Impressive, little one."

Kripa groaned in surrender.

"Brother? Who?"

"Kalki."

She hadn't heard the name, Arjan figured.

"That's why we are here and this place," he signalled at the note, "can be our gateway to get him."

"What is so special about this place?" Padma asked.

Kripa interfered. "It holds an ingredient which can be used to make a bomb to blow up a part of the prison where Kalki is locked—Happy?"

Padma didn't even know explosives existed. Fire balls, sure. Explosives were tricky and needed a lot of knowledge and expertise, which Padma see in any of them. But then she got an idea. "Who will make the explosives?"

"Guilty," Kripa raised his hands, as he briskly walked on the floor, impatient perhaps that so much had been revealed.

"Can he even make it?"

"He's an Acharya," Arjan said.

"But aren't Acharyas supposed to be at a Gurukul?"

"I am not! Happy?" Kripa grunted.

Arjan came closer to Padma, looking straight in her eyes. "I'm not lying. He's good. I trust him."

"All right, I will help you enter the keep, get whatever you need and leave," Padma said, since she knew she would hit the bulls' eye by playing on both sides.

"But I want something in return."

Kripa stopped pacing. "Let's hear it, lass!"

"I want a pair of explosives for myself."

"What would you use it for?" Kripa arched his brows. "You do realise, they aren't child's play, lass. They can destroy an entire place if you use it in the right quantity."

Padma raised her eyebrows, smirking but tight-lipped. "That's the reason I want to use it."

65

Standing next to his loyal twin guards, Koko and Vikoko, Kali watched the funeral procession of Vasuki. A smile, undeniably concealed behind the mask of grief, shadowed his face. He had worn a black dhoti, even on this day, with a long cloth wrapped around his chiselled body. He had trimmed his hair off with a knife, standing in front of the mirror. Feeling the traces of growth on his bald head, Kali realized he was ugly, even though Koko said he looked handsome. He didn't think so. He wanted to hide his face, disgusted with the scabby and sagging skin. He loved his hair, but with the illness, he had to let go of that vanity.

The funeral was over and all the council heads had been there. Vedanta was still petrified by Kali, which was nice since Kali liked fear in the Manav's eyes. Kuvera was glad, almost too glad, a gleaming smile over his face. Kali still remembered what had taken place the day he had stepped into their so-called secret meeting.

"What do you want?" Vedanta had asked.

"The same thing as you, I want to end all those who have gone behind me, starting with Vasuki," Kali had responded, though they didn't notice the subtle menace in his words.

For others, Kali knew, he was going mad. Vedanta and Kuvera were surprised he didn't even blink twice before finishing off Vasuki, who was integral for handling the police department in Indragarh. Because of Vasuki, the entire law and order of the city was functioning like a dream. But just like that, Kali killed him off.

Kali had a dream, a dream to hold all the Tribals together and constitute a powerful force against the Manavs. It was the war between the two that had caused his village to burn, and his siblings to be killed. After his parents' death, he was the one to take care of all his family members. But they all died gruesomely. A pity, Kali would always think about. He thought he would redeem himself if he didn't let other families get destroyed by the two warring factions. So he got them the truce.

Now, the truce didn't work. It was far more complicated than he had imagined. He had to do something else. Violence had been cementing only in the short run. He thought about Durukti and how he had mistreated her. Maybe, he was wrong, but it was the right thing to do. He had to put her straight, and he had his own reasons behind it. His parents had died because they were betrayed and he didn't want to go down the same path again. Asuras were an extinct race in the land of Illavarti.

Find your heritage.

He had to. He needed to reach the farthest recesses of the Asura lands, learn about their true language, a culture that was largely forgotten. He was a product of migration, as that's what his parents did when they were debarred from their own lands. Kali knew little of it for he was small, but many stories were narrated to him by his father.

When Kali would think about why he was destroying the life of the village boy from Shambala, it was not just because of Durukti, but because he had to make an example. Capital punishment was rare, but the village boy would be the first such exhibition. It could be done, by a snap of his fingers. Fear had to grip the city, suffocate it and submit itself in front of Kali. That was how he would be able to stop all the political killings and factionalism. Hypocrisy was fatalistic. And Kali was going down that path. But he knew that in order to end political murders, he needed to set stern examples. And killing Vasuki had been a step taken towards self-preservation, an almost adjunct aspect to Kali's personality.

The funeral was over. Vasuki's body was not burnt like others, but rested underground with coins, jewellery and a snake statue. He had learnt about the Naga rituals. They believed in after-life.

Kali didn't believe in this horseshit. For him, it was this life and he had to make the most of it.

Manasa looked at all of them, tears streaming down from her eyes. Her limp hand shook, as if it wasn't able to take the grief of losing her brother. And then she left.

Not a word was spoken. But then words were controllable, actions weren't.

Kali saw her leave and when she was out of sight, Kuvera was the first one to jump. "She's going to be a problem, commander. She's angry and she will take a drastic action. You need to make her sleep or else we will do."

Kali watched Kuvera. He was always a problem to him. "I'll talk to her," Kali said.

"Would talking help?" Vedanta asked, a little puzzled. "We should do what Kuvera said."

"Killing her would only lead to rebellion by the Nagas, and they hold an important position in the entire city. Don't let foolishness take hold of your brain. It has a habit of infecting weak minds," Kali grimaced, leaving behind the dumbstruck men.

He knew he had to do something.

But for everything, he must wait.

In his study, he had been going through the books of his ancestors, looking over for information about the Asuras. He had got several history books from the library as well, trying to understand the society, but none featured Asuras at any great depth. Most of the accounts were either secondary or even tertiary. He was disappointed. Asuras were termed malevolent spirits by some, while some said they were demons from hell. But none of it was an honest account.

He grabbed for the vial of Soma and swallowed a huge amount of it. Initially, it tasted of nothing, but slowly he felt the warmth affecting his skin from his insides, making him feel better.

And then the volume of book that he was holding began to change, and he realized the pages were turning faster, hitting him hard over the face. He watched as the pages of the books stopped and started to create its own shape that he was unable to comprehend for a moment. It eventually dawned on him that the page had contours of a human face.

"Search your heritage," it called out to Kali. *"Do not forsake them; they will lead you to your salvation."*

He flung the book against the floor. This was getting out of hand. Sweat beads had formed over his face, and he felt he had no other choice but to listen to those voices. What was going on with him? Why was he growing delusional? He had to stop acting crazy.

Salvation? What kind of salvation are the voices talking about?

Kali walked to the book and picked it up again. And he saw it was ordinary now. No face was coming out of it, talking to him. It was fine. Kali sighed, closing the book back, wiping his sweat.

Just then, there was a knock on the door. Kali bade the person to enter and Koko let the familiar figure through.

It was none other than Manasa.

With her showy robes, and identifiable limp hand, Manasa stood there silently for a while. Kali walked to the other end of the table and sat on the straw chair. His fingers danced over his temples thoughtfully.

"You called for me." Manasa's voice was razor sharp and cold.

"I did, indeed," Kali said, "please sit down."

Manasa did so, but it felt as if she was forcing herself to do it. Reluctance was stamped over all her actions.

"I hope you are not planning to leave the city."

Manasa didn't respond straightaway. She remained silent, until she eventually nodded, smiling. But the smile had an angry edge to it. "You know, my brother was murdered the same way my father was. Betrayed. And slit at the throat. The same modus operandi."

Kali nodded, showing sympathy through his expressions, to let Manasa know that he was deeply apologetic. "I have heard about your father. He was a great man."

"I don't plan to leave the city, darling." She beamed through cold and yet sad eyes. "I'm going to stay right here where I'm needed the most. I know that's what Vasuki wanted."

There was almost a hidden agenda building inside her, and Kali could feel it. She was calculative. "I just don't know who could do this to Vasuki."

"Oh I know who all did it." She looked at him sharply and Kali noticed there was a hint of bemusement on her face. "How's your health? You have been awfully alright; some might say it is a miracle since your health had been degrading rapidly."

"Durukti helped me." At the thought of Durukti, Kali pursed his lips. He had forgotten to apologize to her and she must be fiercely angry at him. He would leave instantly for her, after this blasted meeting. "Vasuki had come to visit me."

"I know he threatened you, Kali." She didn't even have the courtesy to call him by his title. She was blunt and straight. A part of it made Kali glad. At least, there was one honest person. "And you were attacked later by a Naga. But it wasn't us. If I find out, by any chance, that you had any involvement in Vasuki's death, I will skin and peel you alive because you have proved to be such a sore disappointment."

Kali nodded. "I'm sure you'll find the culprit. In fact, you can use my investigators, Koko and Vikoko. They will look into it as well."

"I already have my boys at service, looking to find whoever it was, my dear. You don't have to worry about my well-being." And she meant it as if she was aiming at Kali's well-being instead, which would be under duress and threat in the near future.

"All right," Kali coughed, feeling something was stuck in his throat. Perhaps it was Soma's after effects. Not only would it bring a warm taste to his mouth, but he felt like coughing his guts out. But then, he would be all right after that, just as suddenly.

"I had summoned you here for the latest trials that we will be taking up in the city. Vasuki used to be part of the council of judges, but now since his passing, I would like to pass you the title."

Manasa watched him, as if Kali was trying to get something out of her. But Kali showed no emotion. He knew if he would end up doing it, it'd only create more suspicion and animosity from the snake's end. He needed Manasa for administrative stability, even though she would stab him in the back with her dagger with the first chance she got. Manasa had to be shown that she still mattered, even though Kali had no care in the world to appease her. She had to be shown respect, as if her voice still meant something in the government.

"You want me to help you in the decision making?"

"In all fairness, the jurors make the decisions, but yes, we can overrule or accept them."

"Any particular men we are holding on trial?"

Kali shrugged, trying to act as if there was none that mattered to him in the process. "Not really. Just the ordinary folks. Be it flogging or branding, we need to decide which punishment to go with. Many trials occur in one day. It'll be mundane and it is not a compulsion if you don't want to come."

Manasa nodded. "It's always a pleasure to be accepted in this city's daily affairs."

That surprised Kali, but he showed no hint of it. He had a cold face, drawn back, his eyes malevolently watching her.

"Also since Vasuki has passed on, I'm putting up a letter for authoritarian locus standi. I am appointing myself as not just your puny judge in a stupid, unimportant trial, but also as the head of Nagas in this city. I will personally increase the police protection so that there won't be any more cases like this, at least for my people."

Manasa stood up, whispering almost. "You poked the wrong bear, Kali. Now, darling, see the world burn around you." And with that, she left, flinging the door shut behind her. There was an absolute silence in the room after that.

Kali sat there, in the chair. Did he really poke the wrong one? But then, he would have competition. What was the fun in not having conflict out of his actions? She would come. She'd not go back though. Kali would hold her in his vice-like grasp. He had to find how he would be able to kill his opposition.

And by opposition, it meant the entire council. Leaving him out.

66

Arjan thought he had lost the ability to be surprised from anyone now. He thought he had seen enough and he just wanted to go home, curl into a ball in his cot and rest forevermore.

They were standing in one of the rooms in Ratri's house, concealing much from her, as the candles burnt and gave light to the dim room. Arjan stood there in the corner, his fingers over his hips, the sickle dangling from his leather belt. He knew it won't be easy but the idea of battling Rakshas again was daunting. He had seen what they were capable of doing. His very bones shivered as images of the gruelling, bloody soil of Shambala came to his mind.

"We need more help," Padma said. She had a way with words, in terms of not just what she spoke, but also the way she spoke. It was a dialect Arjan was not familiar with. It reminded him of the south, the way Rakshas spoke. But the Rakshas had a deeper cadence to their pronunciation.

"What about secretly getting it?" Bala asked.

"Secrecy won't help," Padma shook her head, showing the diagram she had made while scouting the entire mud-keep.

Arjan saw the rough design and to his surprise, it was well made. Padma had a way with her hands as well. But then Arjan merely shook his head, finding himself too easily impressed with anything the girl did or said lately.

The diagram showed the structure of the keep. It was closed from all sides, just like the prison. With no ceiling on the top, it was supported by arches and guarded by constantly stationed guards. Inside, Shuko had told Padma and Arjan, there was a dome like structure under which the Soma was probably kept.

"Most probably we think that's where it is, but we need to scout and we won't be able to scout if we don't have more people."

"We can ask Ratri," Bala said again.

Arjan glanced at him keenly for Bala had gone red mentioning Ratri. That was odd, since Arjan had seen Bala and Ratri talking often, although Bala hardly seemed the romantic sort. But then again Arjan was so caught up in his own contrivances that he had forgotten the trivialities that surrounded him.

Bala added. "We hide too much from her, everyone."

"Look who's feeling guilty now." Kripa rolled his eyes. "Anyone else who gives a darn or is it just him?"

Arjan did consider the possibility of telling it Ratri but it would heed no fruit. "What do you suggest?" Arjan asked, looking at how Padma pulled out a gold coin, seemingly old-fashioned, and began to rub the edges of it, playing around.

"We hire people," she announced.

"Who would that be, lass?" Kripa asked. "I'm sure we can't find anyone who's as strong as a Rakshas."

Padma nodded. "We can't. But we can find those who are not as afraid of them." She paused, taking a deep breath, as if summoning her energies to speak up, before finally uttering, "Mlecchas."

Arjan stood there, frozen for a moment, wondering whether she had said what he had heard. He looked at Kripa, who also stared agape, while Bala just shook his head, shrugged and sat down on the ground. Arjan couldn't believe the mention of Mlecchas would come, yet again, in his lifetime.

"Uh, no, anything else, but not this." Arjan was stern as he watched Kripa. "Don't you have any other plans than making astras out of Soma?"

"Nothing of consequence, mate." Kripa was still thoughtful.

"This is not going well." Arjan sat with Bala.

Padma looked at them incredulously. "What is your problem with the Mlecchas?"

"They attacked us, those pussies!" exclaimed Bala. "They killed Arjan's father even!"

There was not even a hint of sorrow in Padma's eyes. "Yeah, and my brothers were killed and I have been trying so hard ever since to avenge them. And look where I am, stuck with wimps who can't get over their prejudices and grief."

She eyed Arjan carefully and then she knelt down, reaching out for him. "I know you have apprehensions about the Mlecchas. Yes, agreed they aren't good as individuals, but we don't need good men on our side right now. We need evil to fight evil."

"Where do you hope to find these Mlecchas?"

"Taverns, where they are often drinking and loitering," she showed the coin she had been playing with, "we can sell this off to an antique store and get a good amount out of it to rent the Mlecchas."

Arjan thought for a moment. He didn't like the idea at all and for a moment he was thinking of all the other possibilities that could work. But then none of it really seemed as feasible to him. He knew if he would go for the direct entry to the prison, the Nagas would kill him instantly. They were quite brutal last time and his ankle was still bruised and tender.

The scar on Arjan's face burnt. It reminded him of the time Keshav Nand had sliced it, testing the very limits of his capacity to bear pain with equanimity. And he knew at that moment, he needed someone like that on his team. The Rakshas were similar to Mlecchas, remorseless.

"All right." Arjan nodded.

Arjan had just entered the tavern when he noticed the Mlecchas, even from afar. The tavern hadn't been the dingy place he had expected, like the Madira's Chalice. Arjan laid his eyes on the counter where all the drinks were made. But that wasn't the surprising part. It was surprising however that the one who made drinks was a gandharv. Gandharvs were almost white-skinned, with pale, lilac eyes. Their faces had straight, conical noses and they were very good when it came to appeasing the rulers. It was written in history that the original gandharvs were servants for Indra and worked with him.

Arjan also happened to see the absolutely mesmerizing apsaras, who were walking, enticing the different men and women in the tavern. They weren't distinguishable from their counterparts, the gandharvs, but they were attractive, all of them. He tried to look away, but they all came to Arjan, flocking around him while Arjan shrugged them off. They were the minute Tribals, as Arjan had learnt, who had no representative, thus they moved along with other Tribals, migrating annually.

"Aren't you interested in women?" Padma asked, with a smirk, while walking towards a bunch of men who sat with their mugs and were yelling at each other, playing a game of pachisi. The memory scarred him and chilled his bones; how he had escaped death by playing pachisi but lost.

"No, I'm not," Arjan said.

"Men then? That's rare."

Why was it rare? There were those who liked the same sex back in Shambala as well, but they didn't have the same courage to admit it to people. Arjan had known about his sexuality a while back, but he never intended to explore it, since he had been stuck in a continuous chain of horrific events.

Padma reached the Mlecchas while Arjan stood at the back, watching her. The Mlecchas saw her, but ignored her, but Padma coughed again to get their attention.

"What you want, gal?" said one of the men. He had a dark and thick beard, inky black in colour. "We are not interested."

Padma didn't say much, but tossed a bag of coins onto the table. Everyone gasped at the amount, some turning their heads, while the apsaras sat wide-eyed. The main man stood up. "Dattatreya." He shook hands with Padma.

"Padma, and this is my friend, Arjan."

Dattatreya came forward, and brought his hands forward. "Dattatreya," he said again. Arjan didn't shake it back, even though he knew it was a foolish thing to do. He had to be friends with them, but his gut said no.

"What is your problem, kid?"

"Leave him," Padma interrupted, "he has had a rough episode with the likes of you."

"Which village?" asked Dattatreya with a brutish grin, as if he didn't mind the indecency of his ilk. But then, the man was drunk as a fish.

"Shambala."

"Arghh," Dattatreya nodded to himself, walking back to the table where his friends were counting the coins Padma had given to them. "A man had come here," he said, "old and scruffy, came with a friend and said they wanted us to raid a village called Shambala. But we said no."

Arjan narrowed his eyes. An old man who wanted to take over Shambala?

"Did you do it?" Padma asked.

"Na, it too much work for too less money. We live on easy work and blood, but with the money you gave us, we have no issues even if you ask us to die, milady."

"Great, that's exactly what you have to do."

"Where is the work at?"

"Here, at Indragarh."

There was a shift of expression on Dattatreya's face. "Here, not really our business, but uh, we won't do it." Dattatreya yelled in his language to pack the gold up and leave, "too less money."

"Why not here? What's wrong?"

"Indragarh is hostile, and we will be homeless if we get caught. We need enough to sustain us while we escape."

Padma looked at Arjan and whispered, "I don't have enough anymore." Arjan knew she kept more of the antique gold coins for herself, but she was selfish and surely wouldn't part with more of them than she already had. Arjan didn't blame her. At the end of the day, she was doing them a favour and not the other way around.

But then all said and done, he didn't worry about more money because Arjan was still musing over what Dattatreya had said about someone coming for them. Must be some megalomaniac, for all Arjan knew. As he had been drifting in his thoughts about the culprit, he swivelled his face, facing a familiar figure who had been hiding behind a table. Arjan noticed and realized it was none other than Kumar.

Racing forward, Arjan didn't stop when Kumar realized he had been caught. Kumar tried to move past the people, his small body tossing aside the others in the process. Arjan dodged a sudden oncoming wagon, feeling the brunt of this exertion in his ankle, until he leapt onto Kumar, who was trying to make a run for it. Grabbing him by the feet, he tossed him against the wall and looked straight in his eyes.

"What are you doing here?"

"What are *you* doing here?" Kumar asked.

"You have been following me. Why?"

Kumar, Ratri's loyal servant, looked uncertain. "Because Ratri knows what you all are up to and she wants to keep you in check."

Ratri knew everything?

"How?"

"She's not stupid and ignorant when it comes to all the long meetings you have with your so-called friends. And your friend doesn't have the common sense to keep his mouth shut."

Bala.

Arjan struck his head, sitting on the gravelly path. "Tell her I'm sorry."

"She doesn't need your sorry. She needs a foolproof plan. Do you have one? The big man said it concerned explosives, and she got scared, even though he tried his best to allay her apprehensions."

Arjan couldn't believe Bala had gone behind their backs. And for what? A mere infatuation?

"What do you mean?"

"She can help." Kumar patted his shoulder, with a grin. "She wants to fund your siege, wherever you plan to go with these bandits!"

"And why would she do that?"

"She has no choice," Kumar said. "And also because of Lakshmi."

Of course!

Arjan saw Padma had rushed outside as well; perhaps she had seen Arjan storming from the tavern. Padma, when she witnessed Kumar in front of her, was instantly flustered. She didn't say anything, and Arjan saw Kumar was just grimacing at Padma.

"We can have all the long silences once we get our work done," Arjan announced.

"What's happening now?" Padma asked.

Arjan patted the young Yaksha. "He just got our banker."

67

Kalki was standing in the midst of a wasteland. Horror seized him as he realized the wasteland was similar to one that reminded him of Mahayudh: acres of deserted fields, sprawling with bloody corpses, crimson pools of semi-dried blood, dull smoky skies and shattered chariots. Horrible as it was, Kalki found sympathy and synchronicity with his grief. This was a place of sadness, he thought.

"Most wars are fought out of overindulgence of desires," a smooth voice spoke from his behind him.

Kalki turned to see a strange man, with a flute and a yellow head-cover. It had a peacock feather jauntily sticking out on one end. He walked casually, with no marks and bruises on his body.

"What is this?" Kalki asked Lord Govind, one of his Avatars, the last of the Ancients.

"What it exactly represents." Govind did not smile, even though there was a hint of sardonic humour on his face. "Nothing. It's nothing."

Kalki didn't realise why he was seeing Govind when he concentrated to go back and practice subconsciously with Lord Raghav. But Kalki didn't mean to ask Lord Govind.

"Why have I been brought here?"

"For this outcome is to come again." Govind swivelled his head towards the carnage, and there was a flash of irritation in his eyes, before it died away. "And you will be there."

Kalki paused. "What am I supposed to do?"

Govind walked over to the other side, without answering Kalki's question. Kalki realized that Govind was kneeling down next to a corpse, which turned out was alive and in need of water. Out of thin air, Govind manifested water and Kalki saw how exactly he did it. The blood that was spilt, coiled in mid-air, as Govind closed his eyes, chanted till the ball of blood turned to a ball of water. With a swirling mass of mud from the ground, he created a jug and poured the water inside. He then tilted the man's head and made him drink it. And then the man turned into a corpse as well, his feet and arms growing cold and numb.

Govind closed the man's eyes and turned to face Kalki. "What we don't realise is that that ego can make us feel better, but helping can make us inspire others."

He stood up, looking at Kalki. "What should you do when the time comes? You should wait and you should learn. Never hasten your actions on a course, otherwise you will stumble. Whatever happens, happens for the best. For now, it may sound ludicrous, but years later, you will agree it was time well spent, each and every moment."

"What if they kill me before I reach my destination?"

Govind walked to Kalki, squaring up to him as he faced him. "You need to be quick, remember that." And with a sharp flick of his hand, Govind punched him. Kalki was astonished for a moment before he realized what Govind had just done.

"Also, you need to be smart. Words are mightier than swords, remember that. Use them wisely and you'll be a better warrior than you already are."

Kalki nodded. It was odd, standing in the empty wasteland with a man who was just a projection of his mind. He was saying what Kalki wanted him to say. It was how it worked. Sure, the images had a sense of coherence associated with the actual history, but they were elevated and enhanced by Kalki.

And then, just like that, he was sucked into a void, jerked hard, his back straining as he realized he had hit the granite floor, staring at the pit hole of Indragarh's prison. Kalki was glad the person in the next cell had been able to escape, although it made him jealous. Where were Arjan, Kripa and Bala? He was depending on them, but nothing had happened till now.

Days had passed.

And while he began to trail his long nails over the ground, trying to get rid of the boredom, he heard the sound of the sandals that had caused him so much worry. He saw, in front of the iron grills, none other than Durukti, looking at him wildly, but without any guards with her. The one who stood at the gates was dismissed by Durukti.

"My lady, we have been instructed by Lord Kali to not move regardless of anything," one of them said.

Durukti said, "Do you know me?"

"Uh, yes, my lady."

"Then you know I can cut your head off for speaking before me. Leave right now, for I must speak to the prisoner alone."

The Naga shrivelled with fear and with a slight nod, he made way outside. Durukti sat at the opposite side of his cell, her lips looking full, her eyes wide and blossoming and her face much paler than usual. Durukti was afraid. Kalki could see she was trying to hide her anger and fear.

Kalki, regardless of the history between them till now, slowly staggered over to her side, trying to catch her gaze, which she refused to meet.

"I apologize for everything," she began, afraid to even move her lips properly.

"It's all right." Kalki couldn't hold a grudge against her any more than he could hold it against his brother. Everyone had a path and everyone made choices and it wasn't her fault that her choice had led to such consequences. We all are heroes and we all are evil, in one way or the other. Durukti had tried so hard to avoid the war, but with every step, Kalki had tampered with and humiliated her and yet here she was, apologizing to him.

"I should have listened. Kali has gone mad. He had never hit me, even though I have not been the perfect sister most of the times, and yet a few days back, he managed to do the same. He has never taken a rash decision, such as harming a village boy like you for no purpose, and yet he's doing it. He has got a twisted sense of reasoning behind it and there is no method to his madness."

Kalki, as far as he could fathom from whatever had happened between him and Kali, felt Kali was threatened by Kalki. And by threat, it seemed it was emotional and physical in nature. Someone must have warned him about Kalki. And on the basis of insane threats, Kali was taking the desperate actions of repelling Kalki. Soma was taking its toll over his head perhaps, or perhaps he was taking too much and being subject to all sorts of delusions.

"Don't worry." He tried to pat her arm, but it clanged against the bars and caused a small spark of noise. He pulled his hands back, regrettably. "He's taking me to the trial."

"I know," she said, disapprovingly, nodding her head. "I suppose we need to do something about it." She paused. "I apologize for everything. I apologize for coming to your village, hurting you, breaking all your homes. I shouldn't have done that. I can't forgive myself, much as I want to. I hate myself for doing that. I was thinking of protecting my brother, that was my goal. And I didn't care. I can't believe I let my love for my brother, overpower me. It was all wrong. I know. I apologize for thinking that I was… uh…I would exhibit you for entertainment. I wouldn't have. I was mocking you. Why? There are times when people do horrible things to someone, but they don't mean it. They just want a reaction perhaps, and that's what I wanted from you. I shouldn't have done that. I should have left you there." She paused, sniffling. "He thinks I like you. And that's true. I liked you, but not in a romantic sense. I liked your passion, your integrity, your caring nature towards your people. It reminded me of all the things I want to see in a person, but something it is hard to see, since no such person truly exists. Everyone is selfish. You weren't. You cared. You actually did. I thought what if this boy was on my side? How many wonders could we have achieved? Even in the realm of searching for selflessness, I was being selfish. What a hypocrite I am!"

Kalki didn't say anything for a while.

"Speak, Kalki."

Kalki swallowed a lump, trying to choose the right words. "It's all right; whatever happened, it happened. But I need to escape, Durukti."

"I know. I know you do." Durukti turned, wiping her tears and facing him.

"Do you have any ideas?"

For a moment, Durukti hesitated, but then nodded. "Yes." She stood up, before proceeding to unlock the door that held him inside the cage. As it was opened, Kalki realized he had to have his chains opened as well, but Durukti had bought a mini axe with her, with which she began to break off the chains. She struggled with it; her feeble hands were not up for the task.

"Let me do it," Kalki said. Time was of the essence and Durukti was delaying.

She shot him a look of faux contempt. "Never condescend the one who frees you: they have the power of keeping you inside, as well."

Kalki grinned as she finally broke the chains. Once it was loosened, Kalki himself tore the other parts of the chain and then grabbed the manacle around his neck, pulling it apart. Kalki turned to face Durukti. Her pale cheeks had dried tears, her kohl was smeared, but she was impressed by Kalki's strength.

It was over, and for the first time in the longest time, Kalki felt his ankles and his wrists were truly free. He began to massage them, as a grin swiped over his face.

"We must leave now, before something happens," Durukti said.

As she was about to move for the door, Kalki grabbed her hands and pulled her to himself, embracing her tightly. For a moment, her body froze by what Kalki had just done, but then it warmed up, and careless hands ran across his topless back. Kalki liked her touch, but he knew it was the same touch that had murdered his Lakshmi. Kalki pulled himself back, struggling to pull up a smile as she looked flustered herself.

"Thank you." There was a sense of acute and heartfelt acknowledgement on his part.

Durukti nodded in return and began to move from the cage. Inmates began to rattle their cages, yelling and scowling at Kalki, who has been freed before even undergoing a trial. It was fun walking on his legs rather than being forced and dragged across the ground.

Shoving the grill gates aside, Durukti took Kalki to the field where the Nagas were standing as guards. Dodging them, Durukti had managed to take him out in the open, right next to the door, when she froze in horror.

Kalki realise why, when he peered down the alley. In front of them, fitted with torches, battle armour, axes and spears, Kalki saw Martanja. He didn't look the same like the last time. His eye defect had been healed miraculously, and he seemed to radiate vitality. He saw Martanja take a sip from a vial, which Kalki realized, held Soma.

It's happening all over again.

A malevolent grin played across Martanja's face as he whistled, and the army of Rakshas separated on both sides, leading a figure to enter the scene and confront Durukti.

It was her brother.

"Hello," he rasped.

He had gone completely bald since the last time Kalki had seen him and his skin had turned blacker than the sky, with his crimson-tinted eyes contrasting it horrifically.

"Grab them. And don't kill the boy." Kali's red eyes stared at him. "He has a trial tomorrow morning to look out for."

And Kalki realized that his futile attempt at escape had just led him to his death.

68

In the morning when the sparrows sung and the owls slept, Arjan learnt his brother was about to be hung, drawn and quartered.

And he had no idea how to respond to it. The numbness was surely what overwhelmed him, but it was also the fact that nothing could be done to help Kalki. With a heavy heart, he stood far from the mud keep where the Somas were kept, circled around it aimlessly. He knew he had to do something. Kripa was at his side with Padma and Bala. On the other end, the Mlecchas guided by Dattatreya stood, calmly. They had their weapons sheathed, waiting for the signal. There was only one door and that had to be attacked.

Arjan had his sickle, wrapped with coconut husk ropes. He held it like a scimitar.

He saw the Rakshas on the top of the keep, training their arrows towards them, perhaps waiting for someone to attack. And they would.

"The trial starts at sundown," Arjan said to them. "We need to do this fast and be successful at it."

"We will." Kripa sounded stern. "And if we don't, we can all have a hoorah about it…um…" He looked at Arjan's puzzled face as well as Padma's. "Let's hope it doesn't come to that, eh?"

Arjan began to move closer to the keep, while the Mlecchas followed him. Arjan acted as if nothing was wrong, looking at the apple cart, when he saw a bell-toller situated at the edge of the keep. He had to be executed first, so no backup would be called by others.

Sighing hard, Arjan was met by Dattatreya before he could even do something.

"This is a bad plan, aye? You said later at night, not morning."

"I know. But my brother is about to die if we do it later. And I can't have that," Arjan's blazing eyes made Dattatreya step back. He had a prejudiced anger towards Dattatreya already, even though Dattatreya was right. There was no plan, no method to this attack. This was going in, killing and getting out, hopefully not losing their lives in the bargain. This was a suicide mission with no coordination.

"Will you come with me or not?" Arjan asked.

Dattatreya hesitated, his eyes and mouth contorting into thoughtfulness. Arjan shrugged and turned to Kripa and Padma. He came forward, this time, drawing his spear. The gatekeepers, two Rakshas with long swords, came forward.

"What are you doing, boy? Leave before you regret it."

Arjan firmly sank his feet to the ground. He didn't move. In fact, for a moment, he couldn't move. He mentally goaded himself to advance.

One Rakshas came forward and from what Arjan had learnt from Kripa, Arjan swung his spear and stabbed the Rakshas, destroying his mouth with his weapon. At that motion, everyone was alarmed. Instantly the second one had appeared in front of Arjan. He lurched at Arjan and tried to dissuade him by attacking him continuously until Arjan had to use his spear and strike at his head, ripping his skin off.

Arrows were rained towards Arjan, and he kept blocking it with the corpse of the Rakshas, letting the arrows hit the back of it. Arjan realized the arrows had stopped and there was the sound of heavy footsteps, chanting and hooting. Arjan saw the entire army of Mlecchas was arriving at the gates, some knocking off the Rakshas that appeared at the gate while others shot up arrows at the keep, knocking the guards over. The bell-toller was the first one to be killed, shot in the head.

Arjan was helped in the front and pulled up by Dattatreya who nodded, before going inside the gates. Arjan saw he was accompanied by Padma and Kripa.

"Good going," Padma remarked, almost with a smirk.

Bala took the initiative of breaking the doors to the dome. But they were attacked by the gatekeepers, who pounced on them in a surprise attack. Bala grabbed one Rakshas, of the same height as him, while with his other hand he grabbed the other one. Bala showed no anguish as he choked them with his bare hands. In that moment, Arjan forgave Bala for revealing their plans to Ratri and causing them to be in trouble. But then, Bala did it out of goodness and for Ratri. Eventually she was brought round to agreeing to the plan, and she even agreed to finance the Mlecchas.

Bala came to the door and using his mace, he struck at it repeatedly. The wooden door creaked and finally splintered, leading to a flight of stairs that led downwards. With a quick check around them, Arjan saw the Mlecchas were clearly losing, less in number and not nearly enough to fend off the Rakshas. They had to just hold them off till Arjan could put enough Soma in the sack and leave.

Bala was first, ready to descend into darkness, aided by the faint light from the fire lamps. Padma took one for herself, pulling it from its iron handles. The stairway smelled of dead rats and sewage. Horrible as it was, the silence came off as worse, nearly unsettling all of them after the loud clamour of fighting from a while ago. For a moment, he was blind until he realized the staircase led to a passage, wider in size, the ceiling quite low. Bala had to bend his thick knees and crouch while he walked.

Arjan realized the passage leaked oil and water. Five Rakshas stood ahead of them, waiting to attack them. While Padma somersaulted and came in between the Rakshas' legs, climbing on their backs and attacking them, it was Kripa used the sword to attack them, wielding it superbly, with an elegant flick of his wrist. He deflected and spun webs of attack, swinging so fast that the Rakshas got confused. Arjan used his prowess at that moment, sweeping down, as he dragged the scimitar across the Rakshas' loins and ripping their privates apart. It was horrible and Arjan looked away in disgust. One more came on to him, pushed him against the wall, but he was pummeled by Bala's mace.

Sweat had drenched their clothes, as they all made their way deep into the passage, after killing the Rakshas. Now, since the Rakshas had attacked them once, they knew their weak points. They knew that they could not be attacked in a straight-forward manner, but could be taken down with an element of surprise. It wasn't like Shambala, where there were no trained men and women. Here, all five were used to their weapons, even Arjan, who couldn't believe his own proficiency at wielding the sickle, which he had transformed into a makeshift scimitar.

The candles across the end of the passage dimmed as there was another door, more like a rock-slab, that hid something behind it. Bala was the first one to go forward, to try to move it with a jerk. But it didn't work. Arjan helped as well while Kripa and Padma stood in front of it. As the slab moved, another Rakshas pounced towards Padma, grabbing her by the shoulder and throwing her on the ground, his blade next to her neck.

"Do not move!" the Rakshas growled. "Your woman shall die."

"To be fair," panted Kripa, perhaps of the exhaustion, "we don't really like the lass, mate. You can take her along with you if you want."

There was a hint of defiance in the Rakshas' face. But then he grinned. "You lie, old man. You are afraid. It is evident."

"What do you want?" Arjan stepped forward.

"I want to leave," the Rakshas whimpered, when Padma,

instantly sensing weakness, kneed him. He groaned and was about to hit her when Bala swung his mace and struck him hard. He was flung across the passage, his back hitting the floor. He must have become unconscious, for he didn't even stir.

"I was about to save you," Arjan said, defensively.

"Yeah, yeah," Padma shrugged, leading inside where the Soma awaited.

Arjan entered and his eyes beheld a small room, but packed till the door's edges with carved stone slabs, of different sizes, with blue coloured liquid brimming over. For a moment, Kripa stayed there next to him, dumbstruck. "Dear me, we meet again," he whispered and Arjan didn't understand what he meant. But then he instantly walked further and began to break the moulds of the rock.

"So this is the eternal gift of..." Arjan elbowed Bala, who was speaking without thinking in front of Padma, who was still in awe.

"These are not really herbs," she said, perhaps referencing to a conversation she had with someone else. "What are these?"

"Ingredients, I told you, lass," Kripa said, bending down.

"Why are they so wellg-uarded?" Padma asked, her hands holding the fire lamp.

"Because they can lead to a lot of destruction, if handled carelessly," Kripa sighed, shaking his head as he carefully touched the rocks, easily able to pull it off from the slabs and resting it on the floor. He tied the sack and nodded at Arjan. "We are done."

By this time, Arjan had knelt down and tasted the water that had surfaced underneath the rocks. It was oil.

"I don't get it. Why is it leaking oil?"

"Because, mate, these rocks aren't ordinary," Kripa said, "they are made of fumes and oil. I am not really certain why they leach oil, but they do and it makes it horribly flammable."

"And leave all this power to Kali right here?" Arjan said. "That's unacceptable." Bala had his arms crossed, his mace dangling from his belt. "Brother is right, old man. We should do something about this."

"We can worry about that later, mate. For now, let us just care about what we have to do," Kripa grunted, moving for the door. "You all don't plan to leave? The Mlecchas won't stay up there defending us forever. So let's get on with it."

None of them moved.

Arjan chided, "We need to do something."

"Like what?" Kripa scowled.

And then, Padma did the unexpected. She dropped the lamp down, letting the oil and fire mix together until the soma stones began to be engulfed in bright orange flames.

"Like this," Padma said, a sort of calm menace taking over her facial features.

Kripa's eyes widened while Arjan staggered to the front, leaving the room as a fireball exploded across it. Arjan shouted, "We need to close the room down, otherwise it's going to hurt us and spread to the upper levels."

Bala scurried in the corner and began to move the rock slab that he had moved aside earlier. Arjan helped him, but the hot burning rocks just flew out of the room. One of it even managed to hit Kripa's arm, who was standing in front of the room. "I've never seen a sight like this."

"Well you can stop caring about the sight and help us." Arjan pushed the rock as Padma joined him, but Kripa remained stuck to the spot.

"I could have done this years ago, but I didn't," he whispered to himself, the sound of his voice appearing muffled. "Why didn't I? Perhaps I was afraid because I just didn't want it to be destroyed. Perhaps I wanted it to be right here in Illavarti," he was having a fit, with a voice that was barely human, "for I just wanted them to be used by the people again, when the Dark Age would be over. Perhaps I saw too much hope," he paused, "but is there any left?"

And the slab was put back in place finally. Arjan sighed, the heat suffocating him, but he panted hard. He couldn't see or think for a moment, the smoke obfuscating his mind. He nodded and stood up, reaching out to Kripa and shaking him up. "What was that about?" Arjan said, looking deep in his eyes. The old man had secrets Arjan was not aware of and he didn't like that. Now Arjan felt what Ratri had been feeling earlier.

Kripa looked at him, his eyes glassy with confusion. "I don't know. A justification of my actions, perhaps."

Leaving the hole they were in, Arjan found himself in the cesspool of corpses and blood that surrounded him in the dome. He walked over the spilt blood, his gut wrenching tightly at the sight, his nose covered to stave off the stench. He reached outside and found Dattatreya with limbs cut off and his eyes gouged out. He hadn't survive and Arjan couldn't help but feel awful for him.

Death allowed you to feel anger and sadness at the same time. He never thought he would feel bad for a Mleccha and yet this siege had made him feel just that.

"We have work to do, brother," Bala said, patting his shoulders.

Arjan nodded, walking alongside his friends, leaving the keep, while the few straggling onlookers watched the survivors of the bloodbath. And then he witnessed the sun going down and most of the citizens rushing for the trial which was happening on the other side of the city. They were late and Arjan couldn't understand how, since they were down there for just a while. But then, time doesn't wait for anyone. The authorities of Kali would know what had happened to his precious Soma, but only perhaps after the trial.

"We are late," Arjan said, watching the sundown. Kripa and Bala exchanged glances, while Padma didn't care.

"I know mate." Kripa glanced at Padma. "I need your help and your help," he looked at Bala. "I need your help too, Arjan. For all I know, I need every bit of help I can get to make what I have to make so we can go there…"

"Hold on. We?" Padma was confused. "I was with you all only till here."

Kripa looked up, gritting his teeth. "Lass, whatever intentions run in your blood, let me tell you something important, very, very important. Your misery is a lot smaller compared to what we have undertaken. We are saving the saviour of our world."

It sounded ridiculously pompous, especially to someone who was not aware of their background or their circumstances.

"What kind of a saviour needs saving? I probably don't want to be saved by him," Padma protested.

"He's just not ready," Kripa explained, bringing the sack to the corner, for he was unable to hold it for too long. Arjan put his hand over Padma's shoulder, beseeching her to understand. Padma frowned and then nodded in agreement, after looking at Bala, who had saved her when the Rakshas had attacked her.

"What do I have to do?"

"Yeah what should we do?" Arjan asked.

Kripa grinned. "What we always do. We *improvise*."

69

The trials involved a hefty amount of bloodshed. They didn't wait for you. They didn't hunt you down. They had already hunted you and you were their exhibits of enjoyment. But there was tension, Kalki could see, as the judges were called during the trial. There was the jury on the east side, on a pedestal, all of them sitting together in a huddle. The citizens, the people of the city, were a little far off from the podium, which was the main arena for the accused to stand on and speak in his defence. The jury would then decide and the judge would execute.

Kalki was the only one who had four Nagas around him, swords pointed at his neck. Other prisoners watched him in callous enjoyment, grinning with their half-rotten teeth. He was standing amongst the scum of the earth and he hated it. There was a line of prisoners ready for their trial and at every moment, some would be flogged, while others would be stoned. The ones who had raped, pillaged or murdered, were given death. Which made his predetermined death sentence awkward, and without any logic guiding it.

He saw a strange woman with blue eyes, sitting on a snake-motif embedded throne, along with a fat man with a bald head and a mongoose wrapped around his neck. There was Vedanta, whom he could recognize from the sculptures, the so-called puppet king.

Then there was Martanja, sitting with Durukti, forcing her to watch the proceedings.

The man before him appeared in the middle and begged for mercy, kneeling down, hands clasped together. "I did not know she was a child. I did not know of it. I apologize, oh great lords, for I have sinned against the state and against the Lords like of you," he cried with passion.

Kalki didn't know what his crime was nor was it revealed in his words.

The jury nodded at Kali who said, "I have seen a lot of evil in my day but never has evil been defined clearly or understood. What is evil? I do not believe we live in a land of evil. We live in a land of ability. We believe greed is evil, but then isn't greed what we strive for, to make money? We believe lust is evil, but then isn't the entire world lustful, since we constantly seek to entertain our deepest desires? We are hypocrites. But I believe that evil is nothing, that all of us are the same. And that we need to be just to individuals like this man. You are free, man. Leave, but with five years of duty in King Vedanta's army, for he could use a forgiven man like you. Brand him!"

At that, the man was happy and rejoiced, as he was taken away by the Nagas.

Behind Kalki, another man said to him, "Can't believe he was given an out. Lord seems in a fine mood today, you are lucky."

"What did he do?" Kalki couldn't see who was at the back, but he asked about the prisoner who had just stood for the trial.

"Raped a child," said the prisoner. "There's no heaven or hell for people like him. But I think this is where he's supposed to be."

Kalki clenched his teeth. "Why aren't they letting their crimes be known?"

"Don't know much, man."

And then Kalki's name was called out and Kali, who sat in the middle, comfortably leaned forward and grinned.

Kalki stood on the ground while the judges, the apparent custodians of justice in this kingdom, watched over him. The sky was dull, the evening had come forth, and the stars were concealed under a thick layer of smoky clouds.

"Before you begin your defence, prisoner, I would like to tell the jurors that they should not be merciful with this man. He is a slaughterer of many of Lord Raktapa's men, in a siege my sister had undertaken for the protection of our people, since he was leading a rebellion against the state and the empire of King Vedanta."

The king had no reaction. He was simply bored and looked like he would rather be some place else.

"And the rebel deserves the highest punishment; for the state is the only true source of goodwill," Kali said.

And that was when the blue-eyed woman snapped in between, as if she was waiting for Kali to finish and when he didn't, she got irritated. "I would like to know on what grounds the accusation has been made." That was Lady Manasa, the brother of Lord Vasuki. The flag bearer introduced each judge in the council. Each member had their own insignia on a flag, which held some relation with their tribe, except for Kali, who had a strange flag of an owl on a tree with a blazing, blood-red sun at the back. Kalki didn't understand what it meant.

"Grounds?" Kali narrowed his eyes. "Grounds, you say? I have a witness to prove my words right. Call my dear sister on the stand."

Kalki saw Martanja pushing Durukti softly with a needle-like weapon. She came forward, her face weary, after spending the entire night sleepless. Kalki recalled how they had been caught and how Kali had ridiculed that Durukti was an absolute disappointment to him. Durukti should be dead for treason, but he forgave her, locked her in the room and threw Kalki back even though he tried fighting them. Ten Rakshas had come forward to stop Kalki and he was again left inside the cell. Martanja had played a big part in controlling Kalki, for he had enormous strength, more than Kalki now. And he had punched him so hard; that Kalki had almost spewed his guts out.

"Speak," Kali ordered.

Manasa began, with a motherly voice. "Don't let fear trammel your words, darling. Say what you feel," She paused and Kalki felt Manasa was on her side for a moment. But why? Did she have her own issue with Kali?

Kali scoffed.

Durukti gazed at Kalki and for a moment, they shared a moment of understanding. Kalki knew Durukti would do the right thing, perhaps, she would say something that would manoeuvre his situation against Kali.

"Yes. Kalki Hari is a murderer," she said, taking deep breaths as a heavy weight crushed Kalki's heart. "He had rebelled against a royal army and he was caught. He had been planning treason for a long time and was a bad influence on every villager in Shambala."

Everyone hooted. They began to throw rocks and rotten apples at Kalki. He closed his eyes and shook his head. There was no way out of this.

"Are you sure, my dear?" asked Manasa, softly, trying her best to seperate the lies.

"Yes," each word came out, clearly enunciated. "I'm sure."

Kali clapped. "There you have it! We have a reliable witness, the keeper of villages in the province of Keekatpur who has testified against the rebel. What do you decide, jury? What should we do?"

Kalki wanted to speak, but his chained hands and his horrible situation didn't let him. He realized it wasn't just death Kali wanted. He could have done that in the prison itself. Martanja could have stabbed him. No one would have known.

No.

He wanted humiliation for Kalki. He wanted Durukti to betray Kalki. He wanted all of it happening in public, so that he could relish it. This was not just about power. Kalki was wrong. Kali didn't think he was threatened. He wanted to show *he* was the threat and what better way than to do it in public? Sadism didn't have limits and even he broke all of them.

"Let the boy plead for his defence, as the rules suggest," Manasa intervened again.

Kuvera and Vedanta were awkwardly sitting down, when Kuvera said, "I think the charges are all correct, and we don't really have to hear…"

Kali raised his hand. "It's all right. Let the filth speak." There was a huge cacophony of sounds, coming from the people.

"Silence!" he yelled and his voice stopped all the people from even fidgeting. "Good. Speak now."

Kalki looked at Manasa, whose limp hand was wrapped with a strange purple cloth. She was waiting for him to say something, anything that would help his case. "My father died a few months back." Kalki began. "He was attacked and kidnapped by the Mlecchas. I rescued him, but it was to no avail, since my triumph over the Mlecchas had led to his death. That's what you call fate. It was written by the Gods that was supposed to die; and whether I saved him or not, he would die. That's what happened here. No matter what I plead or what I say, nothing will affect the final decision for the jurors," he signalled with his hand at the people, who sat together in a huddle, "for they are bribed or threatened by the great lord Kali," he mocked and spat, while his muscles rippled and strained, and his scars glinted under the remnants of the dim fire lamps. "I don't know if I've lived a full live but I've seen enough evil in this world to know that we need a change."

"Boring speech," Kali muttered. "Kill him!" he ordered the guards.

With the chains that were wrapped around his skin, he was pulled down by the Nagas. In front of him, Durukti grew restless and tried to move away from Martanja, but he didn't let her go. Kalki knelt down, and the very skies seemed bitter. He prayed to

Lord Vishnu, as he heard the thundering sounds of the axe wielder's footsteps; the man who was coming with the weapon of his death.

"You don't simply mean to kill him here?" Manasa protested. "This is outrageous. Why aren't the other council members speaking against the biases held by Kali?" But no one spoke. Kalki could almost see their tails tucked in between their legs.

Kalki's head was put on an anvil-like structure, with his neck craned forward so that the axe could make a clean sweep. The axe was placed gently a few times over his skin, in preparation for the final swing. He could see his life flash in front of him.

And then, the axe came from above, going furiously towards his neck…

Before it stopped.

Kalki opened his eyes, heart beating, as he looked up and saw the axe man was watching the skies, and even Durukti had stopped fighting and was looking up.

In the middle of the skies, almost covered by dark clouds, Kalki could see a swerving bird making its way towards them. The entire public watched in awe, and as Kalki's eyes focused, he realized it was larger than any bird he had ever seen.

It was a chariot. And it was coming this way.

But that wasn't the most surprising part about the entire scene. It was that the chariot was held not by horses, but rather two long wings on its side. Usually these rotating, wing-like structures were used to attack a large number of enemies on the ground. Instead, here it was being used to fly the chariot.

And then he saw his friends: none other than Arjan at the front, with Bala and Kripa at the back, holding a bow and arrow and spear respectively.

70

And the arrow was not for him. It was directed towards the Naga that was holding Kalki by the chains. It hit the skull of the Naga, as he fell back, dying on the spot. The chariot manoeuvred in the air as another arrow was shot from it to another Naga. The chains that bound Kalki were loosened and he felt stronger, so he pulled the third Naga and punched him hard. With no one to hold him anymore, he began to break the chains, but was unsuccessful.

His eyes went across to the suspended chariot that had been propelled by Soma, the tell-tale blue fumes coming out from the back, crackling with energy. A ladder was thrown down, which Kalki grabbed onto. And that was the time Kalki realized that Martanja was running towards him at full speed.

"KILL HIM!" Kali stood up from his seat. "And bring that beauty to me."

Arrows were shot at the chariot. But it was not affected. One was able to break its front, but it didn't crash. Though now, as Kalki was holding the edge of the ladder, he realized Martanja was close.

"Come up fast! The Soma won't let it last in the air forever," yelled Arjan from the inside of the chariot.

"How did you even do it?" Kalki shouted back. "And also, for the love of Gods, move forward!"

"Kripa calls it a Vimana, fuelled by Soma. We just had to burn the stones inside the chariot, leaving a small opening for them to release their power. We just had to find a chariot that had no horse. And also, yes, we intend to move," Arjan grinned. "But we aren't able to."

Kalki couldn't help but grin. The chains were pulling the chariot down perhaps. He realized he had to get rid of the heavy metal that was still attached to his body.

"I have to go back down. The chariot won't move otherwise. Wait here for a moment." Kalki fell back on the ground and began to look for a weapon on the Naga. And as he came forward towards the dead Naga, grabbing its axe, Martanja appeared.

"VILLAGE BOY!" scowled the Rakshas chief. "What kind of magic is this?"

Kalki didn't know how to explain it to him. But then there was no room for explanation as Martanja came forward with a twisted blade that had many conical edges to it. He began to thump it across Kalki's axe repeatedly.

Kalki somersaulted at the back. The chains were killing him and his energy. The large blade came forward against Kalki's face as he turned around. With a swift movement, he hit the axe against Martanja's knees. Martanja fell on his feet, but he stood up again, wiping the blood of it. It was so quick that Kalki couldn't wrap his head around it.

I need to use my weakness as my strength.

With the use of the chains, he began to move it so rapidly that the chain gathered a tremendous amount of momentum. And then he directed those chains across Martanja's face. With a quick sweep, they smacked him in his face. He fell back and collapsed on the floor.

Kalki then used the axe and began to smash it against the iron chains.

And he heard Kali's scream. "Don't let him leave!" Kalki turned to see that all the council judges, and the jury had stood up; even the citizens were hooting, surprised and elated by such commotion and entertainment. Kalki broke the first part of his chain and then another, before stepping out of his ankle manacles. But he could see Martanja was struggling to get up now.

"Take me." Kalki's gaze swept down and he realized it was Durukti who had reached out to him. "Please, take me."

Kalki, for a moment, thought about the tyranny of Kali, and how he would be protecting her from his wrath by taking her away. But then, she was the reason Lakshmi had died, along with all the village folks from Shambala. She was the reason he was here.

But he had to stop blaming her.

Kalki shook his head. "If there's one person who can help Kali right now, it is you. Save him. And change him if you can."

"You can't leave me here. Please," she begged, her hands folded together. "He'll kill me or do something worse. I don't know. I don't know what he will do."

Kalki grabbed her face and looked directly at her. "I will be back. Thank you for everything." He kissed her on the cheek and then sprinted towards the ladder, grabbing for it. He didn't have the time to see Durukti's face. And when he turned around, he saw Martanja was reaching out for the ladder.

The chariot manoeuvred forward, leaving the area over the podium. With a quick, fleeting jump, Martanja lurched from the podium towards the ladder. His jump was so high that he was able to grab the edge of the ladder. This led the chariot to tilt violently, but it still moved. And it escaped the zone where the trial had been taking place, making for the north.

Kalki was climbing on top, but Martanja was faster. With one hand over the rope, he grabbed Kalki's feet and tried to dislodge him. Kalki decided to kick him, but it didn't work. He clutched his feet and sunk his serrated nails into Kalki's already bruised ankle.

Kalki moaned in pain and with his remaining strength, he pushed him down. Luckily, the flying chariot had been going over a tall building and Martanja fell on that, rolling over.

Kalki and Martanja shared a glance of contempt, while he stayed there with his weapon.

"Come up," Arjan called.

Kalki gritted his teeth. *I have to end this.* "Throw me a weapon."

"Why?"

"Just throw it."

Kalki looked up and saw Arjan was tossing a sword.

Kalki grabbed it. It was sheathed so the blade didn't slice throw his hand.

"Hold it properly."

"Let the chariot stay here; rein it somewhere."

"Rein it?" Arjan's voice squeaked. "In what world does this look like something that can be reined? Where do you plan to go?"

Kalki pursed his lips. "I plan to end this."

Arjan shook his head in defiance, but Kalki jumped from the ladder, and he dived to the top surface of the mud building, where Martanja was standing. Kalki rolled over the ground and unsheathed his sword, his eyes down, hair dangling over his temples. He tossed the sheath away, as he came forward, with Martanja charging at him as well.

"What made you return, coward?" Martanja grinned. His teeth had grown dark, and his eyes had a certain dark energy, unlike the last time, when he would get nervous even at the sight of Durukti.

"You killed my people."

"I did. That wench told me too."

"She said to stop, but you didn't."

Martanja shrugged. "Eh, I was doing my duty, boy. Wouldn't you have? My men have their own minds as well. You can't blame them for it." He instantly attacked Kalki. Kalki deflected it with his sword. Martanja stepped back, his feet moving adroitly. "And also, if I could go back now, I would rape and murder everyone in that bloody village to get what was in there."

Soma!

"I can see it's infecting your mind." Kalki came forward and hit the blade against his blade, but it didn't help. He was quick.

"It isn't. It makes me stronger," Martanja said, as he finally leaped forward, attacking Kalki.

But Kalki knew where to stop and he did. He deflected it again. The sound of clashing metal roared in the sweeping wind, as Martanja tried to overpower Kalki with his sword, until Kalki kneed him. Martanja fell back, toppling over at the back. Kalki came forward and again tried to plunge his sword inside Martanja, but it didn't stop him, and he grabbed the sword by his hand.

"As you can see, I'm not ordinary anymore."

"Clearly." Kalki pulled back the sword while Martanja licked the blood on his hand. "My ancestors believed that blood held a vital component of nutrients that is supposed to egg on a warrior."

"Is that why they look so grotesque themselves?" Kalki grinned.

"Trying to be funny won't help you to escape this reality; you are stuck with me here."

Kalki swung his sword, with his feet parted. "You are wrong. You are stuck with me." And then Kalki came forward, advancing towards Martanja. He was able to stab him deep inside his skin and at that moment, Martanja grabbed him from the back, his nails digging into him, as they both fell from the edge of the building.

Kalki could feel the fast wind whipping against his hair as he finally realized he had fallen over a shack. He watched Martanja, who was already standing up by then and was moving away from Kalki, staggering over the ground, dragging his half-dead feet, scowling and mumbling to himself.

Kalki came onto his feet, each joint of his body hurting. He couldn't believe how bad it hurt. Kalki rounded off and realized, his blurry vision returning back to focus, that Martanja had his sword embedded in his body.

He was unable to walk properly and was grabbing attention of the citizens, who were watching him with disgust and contempt. Martanja was perhaps making his way back to his fort, to be healed.

But not again.

Kalki looked at the weapon merchant, whose shop he had destroyed. "I apologize, friend," he said to the man who frowned at him.

And then Kalki's eyes fell on the bow and arrow, made of simple bamboo, but blood tainted. It was not similar to the one he had used in his dreams with Lord Raghav, but it was quite similar to the ones that were made during the Battle of Shambala.

"Can I use it?"

The merchant guffawed at that.

Kalki didn't really care since he went for the bow and strung the arrow to it. He perched on the side of the road, his feet firmly planted. His arm was straight and his one eye was closed. He took a deep breath, calming his senses.

And with a slow chant to Lord Vishnu, Kalki let the arrow loose. It went straight, hitting Martanja on the skull, breaking through his scalp and finally making him collapse.

Kalki tried to walk as fast as his wounds would permit him, to see Martanja, who was lying near the gutter, his blood flowing over his mouth, eyes lifeless. The weak moonlight shone over the cesspool that had been created by the events of the night.

Taking a deep breath, Kalki realized he had won for the first time.

71

Manasa hadn't cried the day her brother died. They had promised, no matter what happened to each other, they wouldn't shed tears. They'd be strong and they'd fight back. And Manasa had been doing that ever since Vasuki's assassination. It was a clear plot by Kali, in which he had been assisted by Kuvera and Vedanta. But now, after what she had witnessed yesterday, not the suspended machine, but the submissive nature of the Yaksha and Manav king, she was certain of one thing. They were afraid of speaking out against Kali, as if they knew what he was capable of. They didn't want to speak against him in front of him, but Manasa knew they might be plotting to kill him the first chance they got.

Manasa was callous about apprehending the prisoner, that village boy. It was her way of showing she wouldn't take domination from Kali lying down meekly. She didn't care who the prisoner was. Clearly, though, he was important to Kali and that intrigued Manasa more than the mundane court proceedings.

She knew she had to do something about Kali. But perhaps, she has to take Kuvera and Vedanta on her side. The problem was, Kuvera no matter what, wouldn't even talk to Manasa properly, let alone side with her. The battle between the Yakshas and the Nagas was ancient, going back several hundred years. There was no start to why they hated each other, but Kuvera had done a spiteful thing to Manasa's tribe by stealing their Mani, which the tribe valued the most.

Manasa was sitting on the pedestal, her robes pooling over the ground while shadows formed over the walls. Manasa knew that Vasuki's death would mean most of the nobles in Naagpuri would be fighting over the Chief status. She had to return and fight for Vasuki's honor.

Should she fight or should she take revenge? It was most confusing. Manasa rested her functioning hand over her temples, thoughtfully musing, when she heard a sound. It was of falling dust and bricks. Her eyes darted, hand whipping towards the dagger that she had sheathed from her belt, pointing it towards the enemy, who had appeared from the window.

Lanky and slender in posture, the figure was familiar by the shawl that concealed the face, and her telltale silver hair. It was none other than her spy and assassin, Padma. The silver hair was knotted on top and a pouch sagged from her girdle where she kept all her antique currencies. She had sharp daggers sheathed and hanging from her waist and thighs.

"You could have sent me a note to inform me that you were coming. You didn't have to hide and enter, darling." Manasa smiled weakly at Padma.

"I'm practicing."

For what, is the question. Padma was a determined girl, reminding Manasa about herself when she was young and keen to be a warrior. Unlike the Rakshas, who tamed their women, the Nagas had their equality priorities straight. They believed women should learn warfare as much as men. But Manasa, regardless of her zesty attitude, was left behind because of her handicap.

Manasa sighed, realizing Padma was in angst. "What is wrong?"

"I was there yesterday. At the trial," Padma said.

"I didn't see you. You shouldn't be seen with that hair of yours anywhere," said Manasa, pointing to her eccentric hair.

"I was the one steering the chariot," she said.

The chariot was a deft presentation of science and magic. She still could not understand how it was possible. But Padma, by the looks of it, had no intention of speaking about it.

"I know it was all very shocking and nice, but that's not my concern. I want you to know that I have done what you asked of me," Padma said.

"What?"

"I burnt down Kali's lair, the one where he holds the herbs."

Manasa stood up, elated by Padma's words. She wanted the hug the urchin, but then she was too dirty for it.

"Dear me! Well done, darling."

She had heard that after the trial and the mishap, Kali's anger had grown worse when he realized something had gone amiss in the other side of the city, which he held dear. It wasn't clear, but his steps were brisk and he escaped rather than discussing much about the turbulence. Vedanta and Kuvera talked to each other and while Manasa eyed them, Kuvera turned back and he didn't have his annoying, triumphant smirk anymore. He was frowning. And he was afraid.

No matter how much she despised Kali, who had become sullen and ugly, she would congratulate him for taming Kuvera properly.

"But they were not herbs. They were stones," she said, arching her brows, now walking thoughtfully. "Blue in colour, just like a mani or a sapphire."

"Naagmani?"

"What is that?"

"Powerful gifted stones by Lord Shesha," Manasa said. "They were hardly ever found by our people and the one we did find is kept safely in our temple."

Padma shook her head as if her thoughts had muddled. "I don't know about all of that. I just thought of telling you I did my duty."

"For more gold coins? I brought them…" Manasa reached for a pouch when Padma's voice interjected her.

"No. I don't want any fancy coins anymore. I want something else."

Manasa swivelled her head. "Yes, dear?"

"I want to know what Vedanta holds most dear."

Manasa stayed still, contemplating. Padma did all of this for a reason. She was after Vedanta. She didn't reveal it then and even now her implication was far from direct.

"And what do you intend to do with it then?" Manasa gently prodded.

"That's my concern." She remained impassive.

Manasa knew she could send off Padma and if successful, she could cripple Vedanta, just like she had done earlier.

"All right," Manasa nodded. "Her name is Urvashi, his only daughter."

Padma smiled back at Manasa, before leaving by the window. The smile was of acknowledgment. She didn't care to listen about the plans. And by the Gods, if she succeeded, Manasa would have one less headache. If she didn't, Manasa would have to find another spy for herself.

Manasa had been summoned for the council meeting late at night. It was odd that her sleeping hours were replaced by working hours. But with two Naga soldiers on her side, she proceeded to the chambers where the meetings usually took place, in the government building. Manasa realized as the doors were opened; that the entire place, though lit by fire torches, had not a soul. Surprised, she walked further ahead, where the slab of rock used as a table was placed.

It was empty. Completely isolated!

What was going on here?

And that was when she turned over to find her two guards with swords were plunged into their hearts and their throats ripped out. It was so sudden that Manasa didn't have the time reconcile herself with the sight of horror, slipping over her robes and staggering over the floor, as she realised that the killers of her men were none other than the two humans, who had been forgiven at the trial and asked to serve in King Vedanta's army.

This was another ploy.

And then one of the Manavs shot a dagger across the room, towards Manasa. Realizing she had nowhere to go and nowhere safe to hide, she let put her hand in front of her, trying to block the eventual annihilation.

But nothing happened. The soldiers were puzzled. As Manasa opened her eye, watching them, she realized the dagger had stuck into her limp hand, the one without any nerves in it.

Instantly, Manasa pulled out the dagger from her hand and threw it back, this time sliding it into the Manav's head with ease. The other one came charging at her, yelling as loud as he could, but Manasa rolled over, confusing the soldier. She pulled out her snake-hilt dagger and sliced the soldier's knee. He fell on his knees and then Manasa stabbed the soldier in his back, twisting hard.

Manasa stood up, letting her heartbeat calm down as she casually made her way outside the gates. She stood in the ornate corridor, watching the other end of the corridor; where Koko, Vikoko and a few other Manav soldiers stood, trying their best to ensure she did not escape this encounter alive.

Kali was trying his best to kill her.

Perhaps it was about the trial, and how Manasa had defied him at every stance. He wanted her to act like Kuvera and Vedanta.

Servile and submissive.

But she wouldn't budge. Slowly, in the shadows, she glided

away from the corridor, moving to the exit. While Koko and Vikoko would have realized by now that she had defeated her assassins, they wouldn't realise she knew the alternate ways out of this building as well. But as she came to the path that led to the different exit for the building, she saw it was locked.

Just then, she heard the rapid footsteps of the soldiers on the floor above, probably spreading out to look for her. She knew she had to do something. She reached for the window, concealed by thick, purple curtains. She touched the edges and looked down. It was a beautiful sight of Indragarh, heavily guarded and patrolled by her own men. She looked down and could see the undulating waves on a waterbody's surface.

"She's here!" a soldier called out.

Oh by the heavens and hells!

Manasa shoved herself down the window. She splashed down into the water, like a heavy sack of grains. For a moment her body felt helpless, her view blocked by weeds and fishes, her eyes burning in the filthy water until she pulled her head out of the water, gasping for breath.

She began to swim; realizing Koko and Vikoko hadn't stopped there. They shot arrows wrapped with oiled cloth that they lit and shot into the water. One of them fell close to Manasa, but she avoided it and swam awasy as quite as possible, reaching for the shore. She rested against the shore, her hair weighed down by the greasy and dirty water.

She knew she couldn't stay here. The best option was to run and run where she would be safe. Manasa knew that threatening Kali, and defying him, would have logically led to this. But she never knew he would have the guts to do it in the open. He was a changed man and for the worse.

Back at her city, Naagpuri, she didn't even know how things were; she had been away for a while now. She had left her trusted cousin Kadru back there to look over things. *I hope everything is still all right.* There were many out there that hated her, but many loved her too.

She knew what she had to do now, as she panted for breath, a frown contorting her face. She would return again to Indragarh. And this time, she wouldn't come back alone.

72

Padma had thought of leaving for Vedanta's fort, but she left for Ratri's house instead, hoping to catch her so-called accomplices. She still wanted time to think over the actions she would be executing. The sad part was that she knew Urvashi, at least by face. She had seen her roam in the bazaar, flanked by her coterie of friends and guards. And this little knowledge made the action of trying to hurt her, a little more personal.

When she had entered, she saw Ratri with Kumar discussing something, while Bala walked up to her, patting her and perhaps asking for her forgiveness.

Padma retreated to the far end of the corridor, where she met Kripa, who was savouring a mug of sura, grinning at Padma.

"You look quite glad," Padma couldn't help but smile. The man was ridiculous but had the tendency of making her chuckle.

"Just enjoying the little things in life, lass," Kripa said. "And drinks are something you get so little of, but you enjoy them so much." He looked sneakily at Padma. "Aren't you packing? We leave in a while, at midnight or after that, perhaps."

Leaving? She had never thought of it. She had work here. She had to remain here for now. But then after taking her revenge, she had no idea what she'd do.

"I'll be staying here in the city."

Kripa narrowed his eyes. "You mad, lass? You are the best thing that has happened to us, mind you. I mean, you were the one who found us that chariot and dug two holes in it to put the stones in it to ignite. You knew all of it."

Padma grinned bashfully. "You all need to survive without me. I know it'll be hard, but I think it is necessary. And also, speaking of packing, you don't seem to worry about that yourself."

"I don't believe in materialism, girl," he grinned, sipping his drink.

Padma laughed, leaving him there, as she made way to her room to pack up for her one last duty, only to be interrupted by another familiar face—Arjan. Tall and muscular, though not as much as Kalki. His scar had almost healed, now just looking like an angry red welt across his face. But every time he smiled, one could gauge his innocence from the lost, bygone days.

"Where do you plan to go?" he asked quietly.

"Does it matter? I helped you. You should worry about that."

Arjan had a smile dancing over his lips. He was glad to be able to save Kalki, the so-called saviour. But she didn't care to know much about that. She didn't believe in the horseshit.

"I heard you talking to Kripa. You don't want to leave with us."

"Ratri isn't as well. Why are you so worried about me? Why aren't you asking her to leave as well?"

"Because," he paused. "If Ratri leaves, it'll be a problem and eyes will turn towards her. And also, you are a valuable member. Come with us."

"And what do I get in return?"

Arjan had no answer. He pursed his lips and lowered his eyes. "Not everything in life can be bartered in value terms, Padma."

Padma almost felt ridiculous for asking something in return, as she packed her sack with the zinc explosives Kripa had managed to make from the remaining Soma. He had asked her to use them only when absolutely necessary. She knew what she had to do with them.

"I don't know what you will do with the explosives and I have no right to ask you, but I just want you to know we can wait till you do your job or whatever it is. We can wait till then."

"Kali might find you till then."

"He doesn't care two hoots about Ratri. She's just a librarian to him, at the end of the day."

Padma paused. "My name is Padmavati." She didn't know why she told him her full name. It was something she hadn't even shared with Ratri. Perhaps it was his soft, delicate eyes, and the way he spoke with respect and intellect. She had some affinity towards him, unlike others whom she couldn't stand being with.

Arjan arched his brows. "That's a Dakshini name."

She nodded. "I'm from the South, yes."

"Do you know much about your heritage?"

The thought crossed her mind, of telling him, but she remained quiet. "We migrated, me and my brothers, during the Pact between North and South against the Tribals." Those were the dark times as well, when her brothers had been forced to stem Vedanta's madness.

"I ask you to come because he needs someone like you to keep him in check. You are a smart mouth sometimes, but generally a clever woman."

Padma sighed. "Where do you all intend to go?"

"North, towards Dandhaka, and from there to Mahendragiri."

"That's the snowy region."

"Yes."

She hated the snow. Grimacing, she nodded. "I'll see to it. Why but?"

"We weren't joking about Kalki being the saviour. He really is. You saw him."

Padma had, seeing how Kalki was able to adroitly manage the

iron chains around him, aside from the nerve-wracking fight against Martanja. But still, there must be some logical explanation, and she sought it.

"I'll see to it, Arjan."

Arjan patted her back and made his way outside, before turning back to look at her one last time. "What you have, the explosives, I know you must have a mission. But from what little I've seen, it's a horrible thing. And by the Gods, it shouldn't be used often. I know that you'll be using it for some purpose that you find right. My father was murdered by a Mleccha and I hated them until I met Dattatreya. I never thought I would have pitied a man like him, but I did. I even pitied the woman, Durukti, who had invaded our land."

He smiled to himself. "It's easy to hate, but difficult to forgive. If more folks did the latter, I'm sure we would live in a more peaceful world." And he left the room after that. With a heavy heart, Padma took the bag and slung it on her shoulders. She didn't know what to feel right now. She contemplated settling down. She had to think and react. Think and react. Think and…

73

Arjan drank a little bit of wine for the first time, calming his senses, watching the shadows from the fire torches over the ceiling. Arjan blinked twice, realizing that the pedestal he sat on, in the room, shook a little. He turned comfortably only to find Kalki had woken up from his slumber, slowly getting up. Setting his wine on the side, Arjan came to help him as Kalki held onto his ribs. He had grown so mature, so fast. Kalki had a thick beard, growing like wild weed over his face, eyes that were tired and hair that had grown scraggly. He had scars all across his body; lashes and red welts from the flogging.

It felt like yesterday that they were sitting at the farm, looking at the dipping sun, joking and elbowing each other, telling stories. They were brothers, separated by blood but joined by love. Shambala was a farfetched dream and he wished he could return, but Arjan knew it was over, for now at least. His mother was at the temple, and Arjan had written a note to her, telling her they were fine. But he didn't let her know where they were, otherwise she would be worried. Arjan was the last person to lie to his parents, but he had to. Circumstances were forcing his hand in this matter.

It's always what you never expect. It's always the innocent who has to take the fall in front of evil; the innocent who is spurred on to try and wage a war against the evil. A man born in riches can be corrupted easily. Humility is what makes a hero.

"I'm all right," said Kalki.

"You don't look quite right."

"Is that wine I smell?" he asked gruffly.

Arjan flustered, moving back. "I…uh…"

"Can I have some as well?"

Arjan laughed and poured some for him. Kalki took it in his hand, shivering, gulped it one go and returned the goblet to Arjan.

"Lakshmi always tended to…uh… me," Kalki said, not looking up, but down at his palms that had roughened through time. "I can't forget accept that she's dead." He paused. "But then, Ma had said, just because they are dead doesn't mean they are not around." He smiled at the thought.

Arjan patted his older brother's head, as he sat on the opposite side, staring at the fine man he had become. "I have to admit you have grown. In more ways than one."

"Says who?" Kalki smirked. "You out of all people shouldn't say this. Carrying a flying chariot over a trial."

"That was Kripacharya's idea."

"He's a…mysterious man."Kalki turned his head and watched Kripa, who was snoring at the doorstep, close to the corridor.

Arjan bit his lips before he continued, "I should say this, but I fear. I am perhaps getting a bit too paranoid."

"First instincts never lie," Kalki said.

"All right," Arjan nodded. "I met a Mleccha." There was a shift in Kalki's eyes, so he continued. "He told me that an old man was trying to goad them to attack Shambala."

"Old man? You think Kripa hired a bunch of men to kill my father?"

"Perhaps. Or just kidnap. Killing happened out of necessity perhaps." Arjan couldn't believe he was accusing a man who had helped in saving his brother.

Kalki remained impassive. "It's uncertain. There is no proof. Can the man identify Kripa?"

"He's dead, trying to save us."

Kalki laughed at the irony. Arjan did too. It was a pathetic scoffing sound, ringing in the room. The world was full of irony and insecurities. "We can only trust each other, perhaps."

"Yes. And Bala and the new girl."

"New girl?" Kalki was thinking, his eyebrows raised. "Yes, yes."

Arjan sighed. "Her name is Padma. She has a tough exterior, but a heart of gold somewhere inside. I know it."

"I'm sure. I trust your judgment. I'll look out for Kripa. We can't trust the old man."

"You are right. But he's correct about one thing. You need to leave for the hills, to learn the ways of the Avatar," Arjan said. "You can't sit here. You need to defeat Kali. He is growing crazy and his craziness has no limits."

Arjan could see Kalki was contemplating. A young boy from Shambala didn't want to fight the evil incarnate. He wanted the simpler pleasures in life instead.

"How is Shambala?"

"Shattered," Arjan shook his head. "We left in order to save you."

"Will we ever return?"

"I hope we do. When everything is all right, we will."

Kalki was avoiding the question, and it was evident. Arjan leaned forward. "Listen," he added. "I know it will sound harsh, but I need you to promise me something."

"What?"

"I need you to promise me that you understand we are on a dangerous path, and that you will undertake well-thought out plans and try and remain safe. We are leaving our zone of comfort. We are out there. And we need to be prepared, most of all."

"For?"

Arjan blinked. "If anything happens to me, anything at all, I want you to promise me that you will move on. To learn. To go and become what you are destined to become. Embrace it. Don't hold yourself back like you did in Shambala. You will continue to lose. It's all right to lose one person and protect the world in return."

"What if that person means the world to you?"

Arjan had no answer for that. Kalki was right in his own way. "I want you to promise me, nevertheless. Don't stop, otherwise you'll regret it forever. Return when you are ready and fight the Adharm."

"I can't believe it, hearing you talk about supernatural things."

"I've seen enough to believe."

Kalki chuckled. "All right, I promise. But I won't let anything happen to you."

Arjan went over and hugged his brother. They stayed locked in an embrace until Arjan walked over to the window with the refilled goblet. "I saw that you kissed the woman who destroyed our place. What was that about?"

"It was a peck, brother." Kalki was flustered. "And she's a misunderstood woman trapped by a megalomaniac man. I wanted to save her, but I couldn't."

"Because she hurt you?"

Kalki shot him a look of confusion. He was himself conflicted, and it was evident. "Or perhaps I knew she was the only one who can humanize Kali."

"In the process of doing good, brother, I hope you didn't ruin her life." Arjan didn't feel any sympathy for Kali's sister, but Kalki had known her, and Arjan knew better than to judge someone before hearing her side of the story.

While Kalki had gone in deep thoughts, Arjan's eyes flew towards the city, where he could make out the dark shadow of a lurking figure, covered in a shawl. Arjan knew who it was—Padma.

She had left, even though he had subtly warned her not to do.

"I will be back." Arjan thrust the wine glass toat Kalki. "Enjoy this, and stick to your promises."

Kalki smiled. Arjan did too, before leaving him in the room.

Arjan had a sickle dangling from a girdle at his hips. And he was proceeding down the dark streets. In the wan light, with the hooting owls, and the bats in the air, crept Arjan, unnerved by the scenery around him. He saw Padma, away from him, but still walking at a brisk pace. When would that girl learn that there were things bigger than her? But then, he didn't know her story. And it was wrong again to judge her.

Perhaps it was a necessity, for all Arjan could guess. He soon realized that she had begun to dodge the night patrollers, who surprisingly weren't the usual Nagas. Most of the patrolling police were either Manavs or Yakshas.

Arjan let out a deep breath, as he turned into another alley, away from the main road, realizing that she was leading towards the royal fort.

It was Vedanta's fort. He saw her, with acrobatic finesse, climbing over the wall and going on the other side.

Arjan, quickly paced up to the wall, and tried to vault across the brick wall, though his ankle didn't allow him to. He used his sickle, clawing it deep in the wall, and then with that, he forced himself up, catching the edge and finally reaching over the top and falling onto the other side. Pushing aside the shrubbery near the top, he saw the large bell-tower inside the fort, with armed soldiers walking about. Catching his breath once again, Arjan followed her. He had no idea why he was doing what he was doing, but he wanted to save her and also see what she was up to.

If she got caught, she'd have a better chance of escaping with him. She was useful and from what he had learnt, one mustn't let useful people leave in a hurry. If Kalki found out, he wouldn't agree. To be fair, Arjan had a lot of reasons to be here and many didn't make sense to him. Kripa always gave him the creeps, but Padma didn't. She was brutal and honest. Something Arjan hadn't seen in this world much.

And then she saw her climbing one of the main towers, reaching over and hiding from the lights. Arjan stayed down as she had lurched inside the window. He wanted to leave, but then concealed in the shrubs, he saw a guard approaching the path in front of him. He remained still.

And hoped to Gods that he wouldn't be caught.

74

Bala wasn't impressive. In fact, he was not impressive in any way. And yet, she found him to be a kind-hearted man. Ratri knew he was almost a decade younger than her and she had no amorous feelings towards him. In fact, they were friendly just like she was with Kumar. But many in the house thought of them as a couple, which was absurd. Then again, it was Bala's fault as well, since he blushed around her. Maybe he liked her, and she found it cute, but it would never be reciprocated. She had better and more important things to do, especially with the things now happening in the city.

She had been furious when found out that they were planning things behind her back. She had grand plans of taking down the new order, but none of it made sense to them. They just wanted to free their comrade. It was a futile attempt that ended up being not so futile since the escapee, a fugitive, was inside her house. And if anyone had seen him entering the house, she would be dead.

But she decided to help them.

Why?

It was because they reminded her a lot of Lakshmi. She had been a kind, adventurous soul who didn't listen to anyone but herself. And that's exactly how they were. They weren't bad people. They had different ways of doing things. And she shouldn't judge them for that. Except for the old Acharya—he was slimy, unintelligible, dirty, clumsy and horrible in every sense. She hated the kind, the Acharyas, for having little knowledge and then using that knowledge to entice poor villagers into sending their children to them and earning a few coins. Education shouldn't be imparted around a tree.

Ratri, while writing a few letters to the officials for the inauguration of the library, had sent out plenty of invites, even to the likes of the Tribals. She had to act nice, portraying herself as a liberal. In the pool of light cast by the candle, she scribbled names and signed on papers, when she heard the footsteps. She looked up and it wasn't Kumar. It was Bala. His tall, thick frame was covering most of the space in the room. It was a surprise to Ratri how big a Manav could be, in equivalence to a Rakshas. She continued to work, ignoring him, as he stood there, hands in the front, his mace making a sound as its edges rattled over the floor.

"Uh, thank you for everything."

Ratri nodded. "It's all right. Anything for Lakshmi's friends." She would have thrown them out if it was otherwise.

"I hope we meet again."

Ratri had been told by Kumar that the guests would be leaving for their next destination, wherever that was. Ratri didn't care to ask. It was not her business.

"Me too. I hope that." She pulled up a smile. "I'm glad you were honest with me." But why was he? He could have lied like the rest.

"Yes. I apologize," his voice was hoarse but had a gentle edge to it. "For the others. They were afraid of telling you."

Ratri stopped her quill at that. "And you weren't?"

"Many don't know, uh, but I recognize a person in the first instance. And you seemed like a person who would help us, going to great lengths, and not minding it."

Her face had no expression, but she liked the fact that he had truly understood her.

"I won't, yes. But I have limits as well."

"Of course and before we cross them, we plan to leave."

"I'm glad," she said, as she signed more letters.

"And about the…uh…"

"You don't need to speak about it." Ratri's cheeks were turning red. Damn!

"You sure?" his voice squeaked. He was nervous.

"I'm sure. Believe me."

Ratri shook her head, recalling all the days that had led up to this. The time she spent with Bala, it came like a fever rush. She had been a careless fool. She had been drinking a lot lately. Perhaps it was the way she mourned for Lakshmi, for not having a family, for living with a Yaksha. She had no lover. It was her choice, of course, but there days when the stars would speak back to her and she would know she was going delusional. On one of those nights, Bala had caught on to her. She was standing on the roof, at the edge. And before she could fall and break her limbs, he had grabbed her and pulled her towards him. She had mistakenly kissed his chest even, leaving the mark of her red lips on his skin. She had foolishly hiccupped and giggled. Bala had grabbed her and taken her back to her room and tended to her. Burly a man though he was, he didn't allow Ratri to kiss him.

"You are drunk. You are not thinking straight," he had argued reasonably.

And in the morning, he had presented a bowl of soup to her, claiming it was a tried and tested cure for hangovers.

"What did I do?" She was massaging her head, acting as if she didn't remember, but she did. It was awful and embarrassing. A woman of her age shouldn't do any of it.

"You were shaken up. You are fine now," he gently smiled. And from then on, whenever there was any spare time, Bala would come and talk with her. And it wouldn't just be about trivialities. He would talk about his deepest insecurities. And Ratri would do so as well. Ratri had no problem sharing them with him. It was as if that night, they had bonded over her drunken stupor.

"How did you reach the position you are in, Lady Ratri?" He had asked.

She had bad memories about it. "I wasn't always so taciturn and serious. I had a sister back in Shambala, Lakshmi's mother, but in order to learn, I had dressed up as a boy and left to study in a Gurukul. Back then, girls weren't allowed education. In fact, even now also, girls aren't given the same treatment. I didn't care. I cut my hair, strapped my breasts and left for it. And that was where I learnt the most."

"I'm surprised no one wondered how there could be such a beautiful boy amongst them," Bala had joked.

"It became worse though," she sighed, looking down. "The Gurukul, it had bad days, especially towards the end. When during a bath, the Acharya caught me, saying I didn't have the body of a boy but of a girl, he forced me to leave. I begged him. He told me I could stay. But I had to…uh…" she shook her head. "I had to pleasure him." She was tearing up now, even as Bala tried to dispel her bad memories by hugging her tightly. "I was confused and broken. He forced himself on me, and I stayed there. The nights were painful. And I wanted to go home. But I knew if I went go back, I wouldn't be able to complete what I had started. I wanted go to the city, and learn from a scholar."

Bala had his eyebrows arched now, worried and a little angry. "I'm sorry. What did you do then?"

"So I went inside his hut on one night, and I cut off his privates when he lecherously beckoned me towards him," she pulled up a smile at the gory memory.

"That is impressive," he laughed, slapping his knee.

"That was. But now that I think about it, it was kind of bloody."

"I've learnt, Lady Ratri…"

"Call me just Ratri."

With tender eyes, Bala continued. "I've learnt that we live in a violent world, surrounded by violent men and women, doing violent things. It's dark, bloody and I am used to it."

"That's why you are with them?" she signalled at his gang, who were talking to each other in the other room.

"No," he shook his head. "The world might be bloody, but there's still hope and they give me that. They promise me a better tomorrow. And it feels good, to have hope in a hopeless world."

And then he had leaned forward, "I wanted to ask you to not get furious, but know things and try and understand them. We didn't mean to hide, but now it is important that we should tell you..."

From then on, he had revealed the plan, because he trusted her. And it was nice to be trusted, even by a tavern guardsman. She had sent Kumar to spy on them, to know their moves so they wouldn't make a stupid mistake. She wanted no damage to come to her, but at the same time, she didn't want Bala to get in trouble either.

It was nice talking to someone, but he wouldn't be around anymore for that.

"Might I get an embrace?"

"Aren't you asking for too much?"

"Wasn't it you who kissed me first?"

"That was me drunk," she blushed.

He laughed. "You remember then. You are such a bad actress."

Ratri shook her head as she came forward and embraced him, her nails digging into his skin, the scent of soap from his hair permeating her nostrils. She felt so small around his wrapped arms. "It was nice having a friend like you," she said, pulling back.

He had gone red, like always. "It is the same for me. I hope I return and we talk more than we usually did."

"I'll show you the theatre here."

"Is it boring? Will I understand?"

Ratri held on to his hands. "With me, you'll understand everything."

And then there was a knock on the door. Ratri let go his hand as she saw Kumar coming out of his hole, reaching for the door. Ratri whistled at Kumar to not open it right away. Ratri nodded at Bala silently, and he swiftly walked to the back, waking up Kalki from his room, Kripa from the corridor, as they went downstairs.

Ratri walked to the door, opening it, only to find a familiar figure, staring at her. Bald head, sunken eyes and dark skin, a black dhoti wrapped around his waist, and a black robe wrapped across his chiselled, lanky frame. It was none other than the Commander of the city.

"Hello there," Kali rasped, showing the letter in his hand, while he stood in front of his twin guards.

"I got your invite. Might I come in to talk for a while?"

75

Astras, explosives made out of Soma ores, were wrapped in a cloth. Kripa had said that she needed to burn the leaves sticking out of it, let it reach the ore and then it'd burst. It would give her enough time to throw it across at her target and run away while it caused a huge explosion.

But igniting it to kill a little girl was the burden she would carry herself. But she couldn't find the chambers of Vedanta where she could detonate the bomb; perhaps he wasn't even here at the fort. Though she found Urvashi's room, clutching the balcony parapet outside her room. She could hear her faint voice.

"You can leave," she said to someone.

"But princess, kingship has told me not to."

"I don't care." The voice was childish. "You stay out there. I don't like anyone watching me sleep."

"Kingship will cut my head off," the soldier pleaded.

"I will do the same if you don't leave."

There was a scuffle. "Can I at least close the windows?"

"I like the breeze. Do you want me to die in this heat?"

"No, no, of course not, princess," he whimpered.

"Good, leave then."

The door was shut off. Padma waited, still clinging to the edge, her fingers wanting some rest, but getting none. She could feel the sting as she waited. It had been close to an hour when she could finally hear the faint snoring from Urvashi's room. She came up and jumped inside, making sure her feet made no sound. She saw that in the midst of the candles that burnt in her room, books were piled up, with a cot high above a pedestal. Padma walked towards Urvashi, counting her breaths, not making any noise. Urvashi. She was beautiful, with curly hair, looking angelic while she slept. She was unharmed by this world, unlike Padma. She had been gifted her childhood, unlike Padma.

Jealousy poisoned her thoughts like a wasp's sting, as her hands reached for the astras. Should she light them up and leave them like that? That was what she had come for. Destroying the one thing Vedanta valued most, leaving him dead from the inside. That would be a worse punishment than death itself. He would weep and hurt himself, finally resorting to suicide. These thoughts amused Padma, especially since she had lost her only family because of him, burnt and hung like traitors. Anger had made her promise herself that she would bring him to ruin, just like her brothers had gone down.

Things had changed since then. She had met and she had lost people. She still remembered the day she was being taught hunting by her youngest brother, Surya, the one who was set to join the army. They were in the forest, in one of the woods that surrounded Indragarh, and they were hunting a jackal. Padma, without the use of an arrow, tried spearheading the animal, but it hadn't worked. It dodged and chased for his life, even as Padma shot multiple arrows at it, finally resulting in a win.

The jackal had lain there, while Padma and Surya walked to it. It was still breathing, for the arrow had struck his paws.

"Well, this is something," the honeyed voice of Surya echoed. "You didn't kill him."

Padma pulled out the dagger and knelt, ready to strike, when Surya grabbed her wrist.

"Nah, leave it," he said.

"You crazy?" chuckled Padma. "We could have a nice fur pelt for ourselves, with winter approaching."

"I know. But you see, clothes and food are not as important as teaching your little sister something." Surya said. "Your anger let this animal fall on the ground. But you didn't win."

"I didn't win? I have laid it to the ground. Bah!" she retorted.

"I know. But just because it's down, you haven't won. The world has taught us that to move forward, one must defeat the others. But I don't see it that way." He pulled out the arrow, the jackal still breathing hard, panting, as Surya pulled out a cloth and poured some antiseptic cream on it, applying it to the wound. "Kindness and love is what this world needs the most."

The jackal slowly stood up and instead of attacking Surya or Padma, who had instantly pulled back, the jackal licked Surya, like a dog on a leash. Surya gave him some food, which the jackal ate from his hand. "Because kindness, my dear, always reciprocates."

Padma, now standing in the centre of the room, set down the astras. She went for the candles and knelt down to light the them up, even as thoughts somersaulted and collided inside her. Her hands were shivering. And as she was about to reach out for the astras, the flames almost touching them, the girl turned over in his sleep. She backed off, silently, of course, worried, with sweat beads trickling down her face. She came forward to see Urvashi had shifted her position, and right under the cushion of her arm, was a wooden figure. It was carved perfectly, had a conical nose and defined head. It was clear to Padma from a cursory survey of the room that Urvashi was fascinated by wooden figurines, just as Padma loved collecting antique coins.

It's easy to hate but difficult to forgive.

She turned around and her eyes met Arjan's. She almost shrieked at the sight of him, but he instantly put his palms over her lips.

What was he doing here?

"Who's there?" Urvashi's voice echoed in the room, as her eyes slowly opened and saw Padma and Arjan in the room. "Who are you?" She backed off against the corner of the bed, her night gown crumpling in the process. Using her toy as a weapon, she put up a brave front and asked, "What do you want?"

Padma had no real idea what to tell her. Arjan was confused himself.

"You are assassins, aren't you? Father told me all about your kind. But who are you?"

Padma grimaced at Arjan, who mouthed at her, "We need to leave."

"GUARDS!" Urvashi yelled.

Padma's heartbeat increased, as she grabbed the astras from the ground, reaching forward and jumping from the window with Arjan, uncaring that they were jumping to their deaths. She realized this mid-air, while Arjan used his sickle to claw at the fort walls, until their feet hit the ground and they started dashing away.

"Why did you follow me?"

"To make sure you didn't do anything foolish." Arjan was running beside her.

"But you shouldn't...have...uh...done anything foolish in trying to stop me from doing anything foolish." She was confused and she was panting, the exertion from her getaway muddling up her words.

They were making their way towards the wall that led to the back side of the fort. But now, the bells were being rung, and soldiers were following them. They could hear the horses following them from across the stables. Padma reached for the wall, her limbs acrobatically leaping up, till she reached the edge, one leg hanging over the other side, while she leaned down to grab Arjan. He tried to jump, but he couldn't. He used the sickle to make a leap and as he grabbed her hand, his face contorted into a painful expression.

He fell back, unable to stand up. He turned around and Padma saw an arrow had pierced him. Multiple fire arrows were being shot at Padma, but she was dodging most of them.

"Come on!"

Arjan was still making his way up, his feet struggling, as another arrow struck one of his feet. "I-I can't." He looked up, his face pale as the moon, tears around his eyes. "Leave now."

"I can't. Not without you."

"If you stay…" the barks of the hounds were really close now. "They will kill you and me. One of us needs to be there with Kalki."

"I don't care about Kalki! I care about you."

Arjan smiled. "If you do, if you really do care about me, go and protect him. Please. Stay with him and take him where he's supposed to go. Please, promise me." He held out his hand.

Padma nodded, grasping his hand, when the soldiers finally came up close. The hound leaped at Arjan, but with a swift flick of his hand, Arjan clawed its face and flung it away.

"Leave now! I'll try to stop them!" And then another arrow hurt him and he was pushed against the rocky wall, blood trickling from his mouth, pooling over his tunic.

Padma looked at Arjan once, perhaps for the last time. A broken boy who had seen the world for its truth, just like Padma, and who was about to meet his death, unlike Padma. He didn't deserve it. She did. And she manoeuvred and lurched down from the wall, running as quickly as possible, as a volley of fire arrows were rained down on her.

For the first time in a long while, Padma couldn't help but shed tears for another person.

76

Ratri led Kali inside her house, but Kali chose to walk around. He scanned his surroundings, Ratri noticed, like a hawk, smelling and letting his ears move back and forth, as if he was trying to get a sense of the place. Ratri led him to her study, but Kali sent Koko and Vikoko out in the back, to check the other rooms.

"I apologize," he said, his voice cold and calculating. "I have grown to such a stature that many want to kill me. It's customary to do a formal checking and recce. Please, lead me."

Ratri did, sitting on the opposite side of her study, while Kali came forward and sat in front of her. "You have a fine Yaksha servant at your disposal." He patted the Yaksha's head. "Thank you for the water, but I won't take it." Kumar went back, mumbling to himself.

Kali studied the room, while Ratri continued to watch him. The silence was killing her and thanks to the Gods, she had a basement ready, where there was a passage leading out of the house and out in the open. It was for emergencies just like this, since she was heavily mired in propaganda and knew one day she had to escape when her house was cornered by swordsman and archers. They must have left, since Koko and Vikoko returned, shaking their heads, and Kali nodded back at them. Koko and Vikoko were popular by now, the twins that had taken the city under their fist. They were everywhere and most people were scared of their towering, brute personalities.

"I never thought I'd be meeting you."

"Why is that? I mean, Vedanta had told me so much about you. It was a shame he took away your seat in the government and put you in-charge as a librarian with a fancy title to it. But we both know it was to get rid of you."

Ratri smiled forcefully. *What was this man getting at?* At a closer look, Ratri could see how his veins were popping out of his skin. He used to look different, she recalled, with a rather handsome face, long hair and a charming, disarming smile. At least that was what she had seen when Vedanta was announcing the new leaders of the city and she was amongst the many nobles, forced to clap and applaud.

He had changed. But what had made him like this, only he knew.

"Vedanta had a poor sense of judgment in your case, so I've decided to replace him."

"With whom?"

Kali smiled as if it was obvious.

"Oh," smugly Ratri nodded, "you."

"Yes. I have decided to be the king now, since matters have forced my hand. I can't do anything but agree. Many in the government feel that way. We tallied and saw."

"Why wasn't I invited?"

"I asked Vedanta. He said it didn't matter."

For all she knew about Vedanta, he couldn't have said that. Perhaps the so-called absurd tally was bribed, forced or even fictitious.

"But I, an upstanding citizen now of this city, decided this would not be the case. So I came here to take your vote. What do you propose? Do you think I am capable of being a king?"

He was acting strangely. It did not seem likely that a person like

Kali would bother to travel to the house of a mere functionary, in order to get her vote to legitimize his rule.

"Your silence assures me of a positive response," he nodded. "I'm glad and, of course, thank you for this invite," he signalled at his guards who went outside, his voice raising high. "You have been gracious enough to do that. I always believe books are a way of to heaven. And we can all go on that path if more of us tend to be readers. You have built a healthy, literary heritage." He nodded to himself, as his guards came forward with huge terra cotta pots in their hands. "When I see what is happening in the city, I'm often reminded of a time back in the village I had been temporarily staying at. It had a small tailor's shop I worked at, just as a roller. You know what a roller is?"

Ratri shook her head.

"It's the least important and most boring job you can come up with," Kali said. "You need to take the clothes the tailor gives you, roll them and keep them packed. That was it. Anyway, we worked at a barn. We got a customer one day, asking us to refund the money we took. And mind you, we took nothing but meager coins for the work we did. We asked why. He showed us his garment, which was torn. It was odd. When he left after receiving his coins, we began to look around, and you know what we found?"

Ratri remained quiet.

"Rats. All inside the hay, hiding. Whenever we tried to catch them, we couldn't, because they were able to escape, those little creatures. We tried to ignore them, but they managed to tear our clothes and we were losing business. People said we didn't do our jobs well. We were on the brink of unemployment when my master, the tailor, got an idea. You know what he did?"

"No. What did he do?"

"He burnt down the barn."

"What about his employment?"

"He could build the barn again, but he couldn't kill the rats.

So he burnt down the barn. It was a lovely sight." He paused. "I realized that day in order to win some, you lose some."

Ratri pursed her lips, as she looked at the terracotta pots the guards were holding onto, finally realizing what it was about, the entire story.

"What is going on?"

Kali stood up, announcing, "A sign of my respect." He signalled to Koko and Vikoko, who began to spill water everywhere. "I am blessing you with the holy liquid," he smirked.

But the smell was a giveaway. Ratri stood up and pulled out the knife from underneath the table, where it had been glued.

"It's oil."

"Hence, it's holy. For fire is where I grew up in and it's fire where you will die."

"Why are you doing this?" She plunged her blade in the air, but it didn't reach Kali for he was quick enough to grab her by the throat, pushing her against the wall.

Koko and Vikoko used the fire lamps in the house, letting them race across the spilled oil. As she was held captive against the wall, she could see her house burning down around her, the smell of charred wood and paper engulfing her nose.

"I have ravens in the city that speak to me, whisper in my ears about the infidels that have corrupted my city. And guess who they whispered of recently?" he whispered in her ears, his voice raspy.

"*You.*"

Ravens?

Of course. Spies. Informants.

But who? Padma. Was it her? No. Was it Kalki? Oh no. Did Kali follow them here when they were returning? It could be possible.

"We should leave, my lord," Vikoko said, hearing a sudden noise.

And that is when Kumar entered with a sword, trying to attack and succeeding in doing so, as he sliced Vikoko's armoured leg.

Koko came forward near Vikoko and slashed the head of the Yaksha. Ratri yelled in shock, her lungs burning with the smoke, as she coughed and cried. Vikoko groaned, touching the bloody stump on her body, as she kicked the head of Kumar across the room.

"They are always such little idiots," Kali sighed, pushing her against the wall, as she felt pain blurring her vision. Ratri flung the dagger that had fallen to the ground, piercing deep into Kali's neck.

Kali stopped. His hand reached out for the blade. He calmly pulled it out, looked at his blood, and touched the back of his neck. It didn't even affect him.

"Nice try, my lady. Perhaps in the after life, you can learn not to hit a God with a mere blade," he winked, leaving her in the fire. She staggered on the floor.

She tried to save herself from the fire that had begun to engulf the entire room. Ratri could feel the burn in her lungs, because; the room was slowly running out of clean air to breathe. Her last coherent thought before she passed out, was noticing a pair of feet near her head. But wasn't Kumar already dead?

No. The feet belonged to none other than Bala, who had come to rescue her. "What happened?" he cried to her, but words wouldn't make their way out of her mouth.

"You returned," Ratri smiled weakly, as Bala broke through the burning wreckage around them, trying to get them both to a safe place.

"I had to. I couldn't leave the most amazing person I met to die," he stopped. "Ugh, the basement door is closed." When the ceiling suddenly caved in, she realized, dimly, that she could see stars in the sky. She swivelled her head, focusing her vision, when she realized her entire house was on fire. It was over. Everything she owned or she would ever own, her partner, Kumar…

And then she felt a sudden change in her position, as Bala's arms weakened and she fell to the ground. She looked up. There were two arrows in Bala's chest. Ratri turned and saw Kali with Vikoko and Koko, who were using bows and arrows. Bala took out his mace, breaking the arrows, even as blood spilled from his chest.

"You must run."

Kali yawned, as he came forward, letting Koko and Vikoko rest their weapons, his eyes blinking as he turned to Ratri, who was still on the ground. "I told you. Rats just come out when there is fire. And then they die." He was close to her, with a sword in his hand, when Bala blocked her.

Ratri yelled, trying to make Bala understand that Kali was somehow immune to blades and other weapons, when everything happened all at once. Bala smashed the mace, but before it could hit Kali, his hands stopped him and he twisted Bala's thick, burly arm with ease. Ripping his shoulder joint and bones out, Kali pierced his sword into Bala's neck at the same time, skewering him, and his eyes went lifeless. He then twisted the sword upwards, shattering his skull. Bala's body, lifeless, lay on the ground, as tears stung Ratri's eyes. She reached out for him, seeing his face, destroyed by Kali's ravage.

It can't be.

And she turned, rasping, her eyes venomous, as she reached for the mace that Bala held. Kali brought a sword down on her back, neatly piercing and tossing her to on the ground. She retched then lay still, her eyes seeing nothing.

77

Kalki thought he had seen everything until the fire blazed inside the house they had just escaped from. The tunnel had led them quite far from it, and he was glad he was away from the wretched man, Kali. But then, the house was aflame and Kalki tried and failed to stop Bala from leaving.

"I have to go, brother," he had said.

Kalki, his energy dead and his joints hurting, shook his head. "No, he'll kill you."

"I won't let Ratri die."

And Kalki understood what Bala was feeling. That's how he had felt as he raced across the plains of Shambala, only to find Lakshmi dead. He understood it, but he knew Bala would be in grave trouble if he went.

"Stay safe."

Bala nodded, and with a smile, said, "I believe in you, brother. I believe in the cause. Bring back order again." And he left, sprinting across the field.

Kalki remained there. The fire had caused most of the house to crumble. Where was Arjan? Where was the new girl Padma? Why was everything so dire?

It had been an hour and the house he had lived in, was now ash. People had gathered around it, but Kalki didn't understand why. Kalki began to trudge forward with Shuko over his shoulder, when he was toppled over to the ground by Kripa.

"You shouldn't leave. Let's go, Bhargav waits for us."

"I don't care about some man in the hills. This is my family," Kalki began to walk away, gritting his teeth. He had reached and exited the plains, when he saw the heartrending sight before him. A group of people looked at him, some even recognizing him as the prisoner who had escaped on the flying chariot. Kalki found in front of him, two corpses, hideously massacred.

It was Bala, his face destroyed and Ratri, a sword sticking out of her spine.

Kripa had managed to catch up to him as Kalki fell to the ground, tears welling up in his eyes, his fists clenching with hatred. Kripa gasped, as he tugged on to Kalki, pulling him away.

"You can't see this."

"I have to kill him," he said, his mind had wandered to the time he had the racing contest with Bala. Lakshmi would have hated Kalki, now that he had let her aunt die as well. All the deaths were now weighing him down.

"You will. But everyone recognizes you, mate. Come with me," he pushed him, away from the crowd.

Kalki pushed the old man away. "You don't get it. I have to kill him now."

Kripa remained there, not even moving. "And then what? Get caught again like last time, when you went all heroically in front of Durukti? Do you want to get trapped again, stuck in that vicious cycle and keep having us free you?"

"There's no 'we' anymore," a voice came from behind.

"Oh for the love of the Gods," Kripa grunted.

Kalki turned to face a tall, agile girl, with shrewd eyes and silvery hair. She had a pale and drawn face. As she came forward, Kalki realized she had been crying. "It shouldn't have happened…I told him it was a bad idea, but he didn't listen," Padma said.

"What do you mean?" Kalki was panting now.

"Arjan followed me to Vedanta's palace," her voice was quiet.

"No," gasped Kalki, his nightmares were coming true.

"Did he die as well?"

"I-I don't know…" she began to cry again.

Kalki grabbed her by the shoulders, squeezing them tightly, making her wince.

"How do you not know if he died or not?"

"I couldn't see…" she choked.

"Leave her!" yelled Kripa, grabbing Kalki's hand, and who felt a force come over him.

He left Padma. She lay there mutely, on the ground. Kalki looked up. From afar he could see hooves throwing up dust in the air. It was the Manav soldiers.

"We need to leave now. Fast!" Kripa urged.

"I can't. I have to check if he's okay…"

"He's dead!" yelled Kripa. "All right? Arjan is dead, Bala is dead and Ratri is dead and if you stay here longer, we will all die as well. Now I know you don't like either of us, but we need to leave. All of us, mate. I know you want to kill Kali. He did all of this and I agree with you." He clasped Kalki's face, and for a moment, Kalki felt he was looking at him like a son. "But you can't let Durukti's episode happen again. You can't go there and get caught, getting imprisoned. You will return after learning the Ways of the Worthy and you'll be able to defeat the Adharm. But for that, we need to leave."

You need to move on if something happens to me, Arjan had said to him.

No. Kalki chose to believe that Arjan was alive and well, and he would be out there, surviving somehow. Shuko had been flapping his wings, confused, until Kalki realized that he had let his anger control him and he had to calm down. Shuko sat back on his shoulder again.

"Will you come with us?" Kripa asked Padma.

Kalki looked at Padma and both of them shared a look of guilt and embarrassment, before she agreed. She wiped her tears. Kalki felt guilty for hurting her, but only for a split second.

"I'll go with you," she said.

Kalki suspiciously eyed her, but chose not to speak just then. He was overwhelmed by grief and anger.

The people of the city were watching as the Manav soldiers got closer.

"Let's go." Kripa offered him his hand.

"How do we…" he tried to find words. "How do we escape?"

"I have got some horses lined up, from a friend in the city; he'll get us the transport."

Kalki nodded, taking the old man's hand, and looked at his broken, new team of people. He looked at the man he couldn't trust and the woman who had left his brother to die. And he wasn't sure if he was ready for a journey with them.

But he had no choice.

78

For weaklings and traitors, death was the only path.

When it came to Kali, he didn't care about them. They were worse than the scum of this land, thrown and pitted against each other. They suffered the most. They should. He hated them. What he did to Kalki's accomplices was exactly what they deserved, and perhaps even more, if he had the time. But he had to leave. People were gathering and it was not a nice image to see their new king be a killer in the streets. They had to respect him after all.

Durukti deserved the same fate, but she was his sister. The blood between them stopped him from doing anything. But he knew what he had to do with her. He would keep her in control with Symrin, her handmaiden, who be his spy. He had given her gold to speak to him whenever Durukti was a nuisance or try to do something.

But softness and tenderness crushed him whenever he saw her face. Now, as he stood there, in her room, he asked her, "Would you come for the coronation?"

He didn't have to try so hard in getting the crown from Vedanta. The Naga leaders were dead, except Manasa, about whose death he and lied about it. She wouldn't be returning for sure. Vedanta was afraid and Kali intended to feed on this fear.

Durukti was sitting on the window sill, looking at the stars. "Why is your chest bloody?"

Kali was so muddled up in his thoughts, he had forgotten about his dishevelled frame. "I was handling some business."

"Did you kill him?" she asked.

Surely, she spoke of him. Kalki. The mysterious villager from Shambala. Just because of that, Kali wanted to burn down the village, but then he hadn't lost all sense of reasoning.

"Yes," he lied.

She turned. There was no sympathy in her eyes. "Good."

Good?

"What happened to you?"

"I just thought he was a different person. But he's not."

Kali walked over to her, close, as he clasped her hands. She looked at him, sternly, brows arched high. "I apologize for my actions recently," Kali sighed. "I was hurt and angry. Martanja had a way of influencing people. He convinced me that you were lovers with him."

"You should care more about the city than my life."

"But your life is important to me." Kali wanted to hug her, but he held back. No matter how distanced they had grown, he still loved her and he knew she loved him back, despite the hatred.

"What had gotten into you?"

"Some people bring out the worst in you," he spoke, regarding Kalki. He was too strong for his own sake, just like how Kali was. Perhaps he had been subjected to the Soma as well. "Each one of us has a dark side and it comes out eventually. It's not planned." He tightened his hand around her. "But some people also bring the best out in you. I don't want to lose you because of our recent squabbles. You had your own right to do what you wanted."

Durukti clenched her teeth and slapped him as hard as she could. Kali took it, calmly, sighing. "I think I deserved that."

"You don't own me, brother. You're damn well right you deserved it."

"Does that mean you forgive me?"

She looked at him for a moment. Kali came forward, embracing her, and for a while she didn't reciprocate, until she hugged him back in relief. He pulled back, looking at her with wistful eyes.

"Would you come for my coronation?"

"Do I have a choice?"

Kali knew exactly what to say to appease her. "Yes, you do. You don't have to if you don't want to."

A smirk pulled up her cheek. "I will."

He wasn't sure she meant it or if things were back to normal, but at least the façade of it was. He couldn't revel in it for long since a voice came from behind him.

"My lord, the men from the keep have returned from the infirmary and are waiting for you," Koko's familiar voice spoke.

The word 'keep' alarmed Durukti. "What have you done with the medicine I brought for you?"

"My dear," he dexterously ran his fingers over her collarbone, "they were not just mere medicines. They were an elixir. And sadly, they have been destroyed."

She raised her brows. "What do you plan to do? Search for more?"

Kali hadn't thought of that. Each part of his body felt more than better. He hadn't felt fitter in his life and it had crossed his mind, to travel in search for more. But then did he need it? He had kept a pouch of it, just in case his illness returned. But for now, he was content.

"I'm a king, sister. I have better things to worry about." He slowly kissed her on the cheek. "Thank you for everything. Without you, there is no me," he whispered and he meant it.

Kali left the grand room, glancing at Symrin, who was making her way in. They shared a look before Kali left with Koko and

Vikoko towards the main chambers, near the fort's garden, where he had impaled the propagandist. He reached and found five men, bandaged and standing calmly, with their arms at the back. More guards from his fort were standing guard behind them. They all looked worried.

Kali saw they all were Rakshas, Martanja's men, who were supposed to keep the Somas safe.

"Do you remember…" he began, walking calmly back and fro, as he saw their huge, injured bodies, "who those culprits were?"

All of them shook their head to say no.

"Can you recognize any one of them if they return?" He played with his fingers, looking at his nails, paring them against each other.

One of them nodded his head.

"Stand in front."

The Rakshas did.

"What is your name, son?"

"Pradm."

"Pradm," Kali nodded. The man had a huge gash in his chest, which was festering. "Would you manage to recognize them if they are back? Did you have a good look at their faces?"

"Yes, my lord," Pradm said.

"Good," Kali turned to the others. "Koko, Vikoko, kill them all."

Pradm gasped. Koko and Vikoko, quick on their feet, slashed their heads. Some protested, but Kali's other guards stabbed and severed their torsos. Pradm watched in horror, while Kali shifted his gaze away from him. "Don't worry. They were useless. Raktapa, your chief, would have mutilated them already if you returned to him like that. I did you all a favour."

Pradm shivered, in spite being a big man himself. Something about Kali made even him afraid.

"But you won't go anywhere, don't worry, Pradm. You are going to stay right here, with me. Won't you?"

Pradm weakly nodded.

"Great. You are the new commander for the Rakshas force in the city. I'll send a note to Raktapa telling him about your post and the circumstances surrounding it."

"But I'm just a soldier." He had a weak voice.

That's just what I need.

"You are more than that, son." He patted his chest, leaving Pradm in the midst of decimated Rakshas. "And also," he said without looking at Pradm's face, "tomorrow is my coronation. Please make yourself available."

Kali stood as Vedanta, the last king, came forward. He had a forced smile as he put down the crown over Kali's head. But it wasn't just the crown. He put several other pieces of jewellery over Kali, including rings, bracelets and necklaces. Kali had a smirk. He had worn a robe, made of silk and fur. Vedanta turned away, clapping, while a row of people, nobles, and aristocrats lined up to congratulate him.

Kali turned to his right and watched Vedanta slowly clap with his daughter, who seemed like a problem at first sight. She didn't have the courtesy to clap, but rather had a frown on her face. Kali didn't mind the indecency. She was just a child, after all. He even saw Kuvera, giving his plastic grin, fake as ever. He was pleased however that Kali was able to defeat his arch enemies: the Nagas. On the other end, he saw Durukti, who looked pleasant today, with Symrin on her side. Behind Kali, Koko and Vikoko stood on opposite sides, standing still like devoted soldiers. Pradm was in the front with his Rakshas guards, kneeling down to their new king.

Kali stood up to speak. "I have been bestowed with this great duty by the people's man, the last King Vedanta. He was gracious enough to give me this opportunity, on seeing I had better and more progressive ideas to work with." And more so because he had threatened him for Urvashi's safety.

"I have thrown out the Naga tribe from our city." Many uproariously cheered that, and Kali had to calm them down. "I sent them back to their home city." Though it was a lie. He had put them in one place under the impression that Manasa had summoned them. And then, he had killed each one of the Nagas, with archers stationed nearby. "Thus more Manav soldiers have been inducted, and we can restore status quo as best as we can."

Everyone clapped. He had just waged a war with the other Nagas. But for now, he didn't care. He had broken his own pact, but that was the only way to stop all the feuds.

"Enjoy the feast and the drinks and the women, of course."

And here, the apsaras entered, dancing in highly revealing clothes. Kali could see from the corner of his eyes that Durukti was feeling ashamed, while Vedanta grabbed Urvashi's hand and left from the place. It was a sight to behold.

Kali sat on his throne, his hands dangling from the arms of his throne, as he casually positioned himself. He had great plans for the city, but he wouldn't stop here. He'd go for the other ones now. He was strong and he was back.

Koko leaned forward, while Kali saw the nobles enjoying the sight of the prostitutes. "My lord?"

"Yes?"

"Lord Vedanta has left."

"I know." Kali was dismissive.

"As you had placed your guards in his fort, they were quick to notice a familiar prisoner they had earlier seen."

"Familiar, you say?" Kali raised his brows. "Call him here."

"All right, my lord."

And within moments, the prisoner was brought in, with his head covered in a sack, and hands tied by a tight rope. Kali drank his wine, as he signalled the sack to be lifted.

When the sack was removed, it revealed a familiar figure. With wounds across his body, the boy was the same one he had been seen during the trial, assisting Kalki's flight.

Pradm, who was standing right there, ran instantly towards Kali and nodded. "It's him, my lord. One of them."

Kali sighed, walking clumsily and spilling his wine in the process, as he came close to the prisoner. "So you thought destroying my property would be a good idea?"

Pradm interjected. "My lord, should I cut him open?"

"No, that'll be too easy." He looked at the boy, patting him on the shoulder. "We'll have some fun with him. Death is too quick and too easy a punishment. What is your name, boy?"

The boy, instead of responding, spat on Kali. Kali wiped it off, watching the huge scar that ran across the boy's face.

"The name is Arjan," the boy began, "and if you want to survive any longer, you should kill me right now."

Kali liked him. Oh, he liked the boy already. He was feisty.

We'll see, boy. We'll see.

79

He wasn't dead.

Durukti knew that a boy like Kalki, splendidly powerful in his own right, couldn't die so easily. Kali wanted to make her believe this premise, perhaps trying to take away her hopes that there was a hero coming to save her. But Durukti didn't need a hero. She had to be careful. Regardless of Kalki leaving her with a stark raving madman, whom she once knew as her brother, she didn't hate Kalki. She had to show she hated him so that she could evade Kali's suspicions.

He wasn't the same man anymore. He acted differently these days. He felt different too. And worst of all, he looked different. The once golden-eyed boy with wavy hair was replaced with a bald man, with skin that matched the colour of coals. Was it the effect of the Somas?

Sure, she wished Kalki could have taken her away. And there was still a certain part within her that wanted to slap him. But he had a different path to go on and she had a different path to travel. She couldn't force it on him.

'If there is one person who can help Kali right now, it is you. Save him. And change him if you can," Kalki had said to her.

Ah. Change was futile now. Chaos had engulfed Kali's mind. He had forced Vedanta down from the throne by threatening to kill Urvashi if he did not abdicate peacefully. Power had corrupted him to the core. Once he had wanted nothing but peace, but now Kali didn't care. He would crush and topple anyone who blocked his way. He had betrayed the very men he had entered into the agreement with, turning acrimonious towards his own sister. Durukti didn't feel guilty. There was nothing she had done wrong or at least she felt she hadn't. She wanted to run away, but escaping wasn't the answer. Docile manipulators live long, and she planned to do that. And yes, she would try to change him while she stayed silent. Oh yes, she would. It hurt her to see him this way. It killed her every day. She wanted to go back and be with Kali, in the way he used to be, away from the civilization, in a happy ending that now seemed far-fetched.

The skies offered nothing but darkness. The stars didn't glimmer. The winds were easy and light, just softly coursing over her skin. The almost burnt out candle made her realise that she had given her dress to Symrin for washing, as she intended to wear it the next day. She left her chamber, looking for Symrin. She had been her trusted aide and friend for a while now, and even though Kali's transformation had begun after imbibing the Somas, as suggested by her, she could have hardly known the effects it would have on Kali.

She walked casually along the dark corridors. She hadn't seen Symrin since the coronation.

Oh how awful it was, the coronation! Some were glad, while most had openly hated Kali. He had made a lot of enemies today.

She saw some soldiers, Manavs, who were standing and discussing with each other about the current king and how everything was disrupted in the current political milieu. On seeing Durukti, they shut up immediately.

Durukti didn't pay heed to their nonsensical gossip. She came to the point. "Have you seen my handmaiden?"

"Uh, my lady, we last saw her in her room," one of them coughed up the answer.

Durukti nodded as she left the men, walking to Symrin's quarter, which was away from the main building and inside the smaller one in Kali's fort. Durukti reached the corridor, which was curiously lacking guards. The walls were made of roughly hewn stone, while the floor was covered with the lingering shadows that appeared from the fire lamps that lit the pathway on both sides. She finally reached Symrin's room, when she heard something. There were voices. Surely one of them was Symrin, but the other…it was strange sounding. It was of a man.

So late at night?

Symrin hadn't told Durukti about any man in her life and yet…

She didn't wait. She slowly pushed the door open, and peered inside the room. It was dark, with only two small candles throwing weak light over the room. The windows were curtained, and not much was visible, except Symrin, who was kneeling down, her hands clasped together. Durukti couldn't open the door further, for if she did, Symrin would get to know of her presence. Light illuminated Symrin, with long fingers of shadow dancing on her pale skin.

The energy or the power, coming off from the man or whatever it was, had a certain aura. Durukti wanted to see who it was, and it was her every right, but she wanted to hear what they were talking about first.

"Good work, my child," the voice spoke, sounding like it belonged to an old man and yet there was a tangible youthful inflection and cadence to it.

"Thank you, Master." Symrin lowered her head. "Everything worked out as per the plan. The White Horse is on his way to the North, with your uncle."

"Indeed," the voice rasped. "It's like dominos. You hit one and everything falls in place."

"Just like how you told me to tell Durukti about that story of my so-called father and the man who was looking for his wife's cure."

"Yes. It worked, didn't it?" he paused. "It wasn't a story, however."

"It surely worked," she grinned. "Who was that man, Master?"

"Who else? Kalki's father."

"You met him?" Her voice quipped.

"Of course." The shadows flickered. "It was me who forced him to take the Somas from the cave."

Symrin swallowed. Durukti could see that she was about to say something she would regret. "I'm afraid, Master," Symrin began, "I hope Kali didn't see me when I read the cards in the bazaar."

"Don't worry, you were disguised well," he said, "but choose your assassins carefully next time. We were fortunate the Naga was killed before he could reveal who had hired him."

"But it worked in our favor. Vasuki was the casualty of the entire misunderstanding."

The voice rasped, "Do not be excited about deaths, Symrin. What we do, is for a bigger cause."

"Why don't you just help your uncle, Master? After all, you both want the same thing."

"No." Sadness corroded his tone. "He didn't want this Age to have a battle like last time. But I did. I have no choice and now that I have triggered this, he has no choice but to do what he didn't want to do."

Symrin meekly nodded. "You have been working really hard, Master, from the time you poisoned Kali to get him ill, so that Durukti wouldn't have any choice, but to get the Somas for him."

"Much before that," he paused, his voice wheezing. "You can say I had molded both of them without them even knowing about it."

"But how did you know it was Kali who would be Adharm?"

"I had used the Eye of Brahma. I can see the past, the present and the future, and I saw what kind of chaos was to be brought on. Only an Adharm can do so," he said. "I apologize, child, for I did not explain all of this to you before, since we did not have enough time and also because I was uncertain whether you would give these details away."

"No, please. Do not apologize, Master, I beg of you. Though the Eye…" Symrin's eyes widened with delight, "where is it, Master?"

"Not with me, as I am now waiting for the White Horse. I had used it a long time back during the Breaking to see if everything was in place and I had seen glimmers of who would be Dharm and who would be Adharm in the future."

"Be careful, my lord," she pleaded.

"Do not worry."

And Durukti couldn't hold back any longer. She had to see the person who was manipulating everyone in the scene, causing everyone harm. She slowly opened the door further, carefully positioning her face and craning her neck forward, so she saw the light which emanated from the man. But little could be seen of the man himself. He surely was a reflection. But how was he able to communicate then? What sorcery is this?

And that's when she saw it. Regardless of the lack of clarity, there was one clear thing that struck out to Durukti, causing chills to run down her spine.

He had a scar across his forehead.

TO BE CONTINUED…

SATYA YODDHA

KALKI

THE EYE OF BRAHMA

Read two exclusive chapters…

PART THREE

THE COUP AT INDRAGARH

1

He fell.

He couldn't see much. Though he could *feel* a lot. Heavy rocks brushed against his arm, tearing his skin. And thorns pricked his ankles and knuckles. He heard water somewhere; the steady noise of flowing water. Gashes, bruises and wounds marked his body, his dhoti was scorched.

Flexing his biceps against the ground, he tried to get up.

"KALKI!" Someone called out his name. It was a girl. Damn, wretched girl. He didn't even talk to her, yet she called for him. But then, it wasn't her fault, he had fallen ll off his horse from a mountain slope.

Kalki leaned against the rock, watching the skies that were overcast. The voices echoed from behind, but he didn't care. He remained silent. He wanted to be away from them and hence he welcomed his fall, albeit a result of his clumsiness. He watched the dank forest, with its verdant foliage and canopies. But he was trying to get rid of evil, away from Indragarh, and from Shambala, where the entire chain of events had started.

"KALKI!" It was the man's voice now. Kripa. What a bloody mess! At least he didn't drink anymore.

"MAN!" Another voice appeared and this was not familiar. In fact, it came from near him.

His ears strained, head cocked forward, as he saw there was a small cave that led downwards from the slope of the mountains. And from there, a head was peering at him.

"Man?"

Kalki narrowed his eyes. "Uh," he looked back. He could see Kripa and Padma were descending from the mountains on their horses. The uneven paths were their problems and Kalki hoped they would come fast since the creature that stood in front of him looked anything but tame.

"Man?"

Kalki was frozen at his place. "Man, yes," he responded.

"Man," he nodded.

He showed himself and Kalki realized he was wearing a lion-skin over his head. He had a strange furry neck and a hairy chest as well. He had a convoluted frame, with a humped back and slightly misshapen limbs. He looked hungry, and ready to attack Kalki. He walked on four legs like an animal, but when he stood straight, he was taller than Kalki.

"Me, Simha."

"Simha?" Kalki had heard that name somewhere.

"Darooda Simha," he clapped, with a manic smirk over his face. "You, man," he poked Kalki. His nails were so sharp that he drew blood.

"Darooda, eh?" Strange name, but then the man had whiskers emanating from his mouth. Kalki was surely in the wrong lands.

"Darooda." He began to jump lightly over his legs, beating his chest and hooting.

"You don't need to be so excited, friend." Kalki mustered a grin. He didn't like the Tribals, never did. They destroyed his village, killed the love of his life and left his friends to die. The Manavs irked him enough as well, but not as much as a Tribals. And yet, here he was, standing in front of one, trying to be friends with him.

"Food?" Darooda asked. "Hungry?"

"Uh." Kalki was indeed hungry. By the Gods, he had forgotten when he ate last. Apples perhaps, a few hours back, but they didn't sustain you for long.

"Mutton, inside."

"I don't eat meat, friend," Kalki said.

Darooda slumped his shoulder in disappointment. "Meat good."

"I know."

"Come," he signalled towards the cave, "food."

"I wait, for my friends," he told Darooda, pointing at Padma and Kripa, who managed to appear with their horses at the right time. They had brought Kalki's horse as well.

"What in the heavens were you thinking about that you fell from the horse, eh, mate? You are an Avatar, but even you should consider yourself lucky that you didn't die," Kripa scolded.

Darooda instantly squealed and rushed back, scampering for safety near the cave's entrance. Kripa got down, grabbing the rein of his horse. He patted Kalki. "What's with him?"

"Darooda Simha."

"I asked what's with him, not who is he, mate," grunted Kripa.

"Must be your shouting that he got afraid of."

Kripa scowled.

"I know he is a Simha," he added.

Simha. The name sounded so familiar that it made his ears stand with curiosity. "Where have I heard this?" Then he recalled. It was at the Gurukul, with Guru Vashishta, where he had read about the ancient tribes.

By this time, Padma had reached down as well, gazing at the creature. She was a short woman, ugly and horrible. But then it was Kalki's anger that made him see her in that way. In reality, she was tall and slim, had a straight face with kohl-lined eyes and short, cropped silver hair.

"Looks like a Tribal," she said.

Kalki ignored with a grimace. Padma noticed that, but didn't say anything. He didn't like her, and he had every right to hate her since, because of her, Arjan had been kidnapped, and was perhaps dead. Kalki didn't know what had happened to him and the very thought of it unleashed a maelstrom of hateful and vitriolic emotions within him.

"He is one, indeed. Simha," Kripa added jovially, "once a grand tribe like the Suparns. Simhas were the unknowns, the proud beings, the heroes. Narasimha, as the legends say, had defeated an Asura, whom no one could defeat. But Simhas are generally devotees of lions, and wear their skin as protection and grow their hair on their face like a lion. Most went missing after a while, and it was presumed they were extinct."

"What led to their extinction?" Kalki asked.

"It was the battle with the Manavs, where the Tribals lost. But this was during the Mahayudh."

"Simhas are that old?" Padma asked.

"Simhas existed far before these present times. Back then, the Ancients fought with each other, and a plague had ravaged the land, known as Breaking, which was an aftermath to the Mahayudh."

All of it was clear for Kalki, but it only made him wonder how old Kripa was, since he had claimed to be a hundred years old. But then the Mahayudh happened earlier than that, But this was Kripa's chronology, and he didn't trust him a lot. History was convoluted and confusing and he had better not dwell on that; otherwise he'd end up with a headache.

"Very," he nodded. "They were warriors, worshippers of sun, and now look at them, gone mad. He must be a descendant," he signalled at Darooda, "who has forgotten his heritage. Poor fellow."

Kalki asked, "How did they go mad?"

"During the Mahayudh, there were radiations used…"

"Radiations?"

"Bombs," he snapped at Padma, glaring at her, "the one you took for your personal cause."

Kalki saw her looking at her pouch, which she perhaps still carried.

"They were used in heavy quantities, while the ones I gave you, lass, are ordinary. The ones used during the Mahayudh were horrible, causing many to go crazy. The Kings came after that, but none survived. Even the participants of the war left for the mountains and died horribly after starving for days on end."

It would have sounded too dark and grim to Kalki earlier. Now he was used to it. "What should we do then?" Kalki asked, concerned about Darooda. The man must have seen enough wrongfulness in the world.

"Do? We go for the north, as we were supposed to." Kripa reached for the horses, trying to manoeuvre them on the opposite side, to go back from where they came.

"What about him?"

"It's raining," Padma intervened.

Kalki ignored her.

"We go back," Kripa said. "Mate, we aren't helping every crazy we meet on the road, just so you know."

"Do you plan to help anyone at all, or will you just let everyone die in the process of making me a warrior?" Kalki blurted.

"It's going to rain hard," Padma intervened again, and Kalki could hear the rolling sounds of thunder.

Kripa flared his nostrils. "What do you mean by that?"

"You know what I mean by that." Kalki came forward. "Arjan told me, before leaving, about something he had heard."

"What did he hear?"

It was raining torrentially by now. But none of it mattered to Kalki, as he had squared up to Kripa and was glaring at him.

"YOU TWO!" yelled Padma. "It's raining, we need shelter."

"We go in the rain," Kripa announced solemnly. Kripa was an old chap, with nerves pushing out from his fragile skin. He had a stinking mouth and dark hair that was greasy and matted.

Kalki shook his head. "No, we stay and we stay with Darooda."

"I'm not staying with a madman."

"Food," cawed Darooda, quietly from the corner.

Padma pushed both the men forward towards the cave. "While you two imbeciles quarrel, I'll rest in the shelter. Hello, Darooda," she grinned, while inching the three horses inside the cave, away from the rain.

Kalki stayed there for a moment until he shrugged. "We both know you are more than what you show. I don't expect answers, Acharya. But I seek to know the limits you will cross in order to make a warrior out of me." And with that, he left the old man in the rain. He'd surely not die of cold or rainwater, since he was an immortal, blessed by the last Avatar himself.

Kalki had the power to make someone immortal as well, but he didn't want to face the moral conundrum of doing the same. Endowing someone with immortality could be a gift or a curse, and in this case, Kripa surely had a curse. He had gone mad like Darooda, but at least the Simha seemed to be nice.

Shuko, his parrot, sat down over his shoulder and began to chirp, "Pisach! Pisach!" which Kalki didn't understand. He had sent his bird to see if any danger was lurking around and the foolish bird was just uttering gibberish. Kalki entered the cave to find Padma standing at the entrance, frozen at her place. He looked at her dark, dilated pupils when he realized, there was something he was missing. He looked up at the cave, which was like any cave up in the mountain. Empty, desolate and filled with dirt and mud.

And yet, unlike the other caves, this one had real people, tied up, with their mouths gagged by ropes and cloth. They were whimpering, tears lining their faces. They had bruises all over their knees and torso. Two of them were woman, and the third was a bald man, with a strange tattoo over his left eye, in the shape of an arrow. Perhaps a Manav, but Kalki couldn't make out clearly.

"Food," Darooda Simha began to jump, clapping his hands, beating his chest.

"Them?" Kalki swallowed a lump.

"No," he shook his head, as if Kalki had misunderstood him all this time.

"*You.*"

2

Out of all the things in the world, Arjan had never believed himself to be a wrestler. And here he was, stationed to be an exhibit for the entertainment of the nobles, the aristocrats who dined with the best of mutton and wines, laughing with their women who sat on their laps, as they watched two hulking bodies fighting each other.

Arjan realized he was to do that. With bonds over his hands, he watched the wrestlers with the rest of the prisoners, as they grabbed each other's shoulders, feet trying to maintain balance, trying to topple each other. One finally did and broke the other wrestler's neck. This was a game where no one cared who would live or die. Arjan breathed a sigh of relief since he didn't have to go now and fight. He had to wait and learn first.

The entire arena was full and in the forefront, sitting with his guards, was Kali. He was enjoying himself, as an Apsara sat over his lap, as he laughed and cheered. The nobles put bets on the outcomes. They all looked hedonistically dishevelled.

Arjan felt like retching in such an environment, which was supposed to be the city of Indra, and which had a huge Vishnu statue as a symbol of purity. But none of this concerned Kali. Gambling over life and death was the new fashion now.

"Shhh," a voice came from the back.

Arjan stood in the middle of a huddle of sad, petrified faces. The ragtag group was barefoot, with bloody bruises on their backs. They were led by Master Ranga, their trainer and jailor. Arjan hadn't learnt a lot from him since he wasn't taken seriously due to his size.

Arjan turned to see a boy, perhaps a little older, but wide-eyed. He had hair that fell over his temples and he was a little plump, unlike the others. Arjan was a bit surprised, since the prison meals were barely adequate, and the milk smelled like the sweat of a hag's breast.

"My name is Vikram," he said, "how do you do, fella?"

Seriously?

"I had seen you out there, on the flying thingy, while I was waiting for my trial." He was bright-eyed, grinning, and perhaps too shocked to be here. "It was a wonderful sight. How do you operate that, fella? Need to know, you know. I'll get out and find myself a nice barn where I'm going to work on the latest inventions."

"I hate to be blunt, but we are looking at our deaths here and you worry about the flying thing?"

"Oh, they just put us on show to scare us." Vikram waved his hand off, that was chained by metal manacles. "Only the best fight, while rest of us just train and don't get anywhere, as no one wants to see a boring, non-competitive match, you know?"

"I'm sure things will change soon." Arjan gritted his teeth. He could feel it. Ever since Kali had become a king, he had replaced the Nagas, who had mysteriously vanished overnight, with Manavs as jailers and officers in the prison. He even took over the last king's fort. If it was up to Vedanta, Arjan would have died, for trespassing with a silver-haired girl as Vedanta said. But he was brought in front of Kali, as Kali had ordered all of them to be judged in front of him.

The fight had ended and Kali had come forward, declaring the winner, with applause and hooting from one side, which had bet on him. The wrestler had a stern and straight face, with broad, dark features. He had angry and stubborn eyes, and skin as dark as charcoal. He was handsome, and something churned inside Arjan's stomach, which he dismissed. The last thing he wanted was to sexualize a fighter, especially one that he would end up fighting soon. But he knew if he did fight with this one, Arjan would be smashed into a pulp.

He went by the name of Rudra, one of the names for Lord Shiva.

"Our best fighter," sleekly Kali spoke, "none can beat him, and none will." He held up Rudra's arm. "You feast with me today, boy." He slapped Rudra's back, who nodded with a grunt, before moving towards the horde of amateur wrestlers, where Arjan stood.

Praying to some higher God, Arjan didn't want Kali's slithering golden eyes to find him. But then, Kali walked up, as he said, "You all are going to be trained to fight and continue the legacy of the great Lord Jarasandha." He talked about the megalomaniac emperor of Aryavarta who was an Ancient, ruling before the Breaking. He had died horribly, courtesy of Lord Govind, who along with Vrikodara, had set up a wrestling match. Jarasandha couldn't die; as he was an Asura, a race now extinct. He couldn't die, because he was drunk on Soma, or that's what Kripa had said about him while they were travelling towards Indragarh. Kripa talked about these incidents as if he had lived through them. Jarasandha was finally killed when his body was sliced into two parts and thrown on opposite sides. Confused, he couldn't form himself again, thereby dying.

None of these things happened anymore. But then he had seen Kalki.

Kali stopped at Arjan's side. He glared at him, his eyes first narrowing and then widening. Arjan could feel his breath, but he showed no fear or anger for that was exactly what Kali wanted—for Arjan to react. But he controlled himself.

"You," he grabbed Arjan's shoulder, pulling him from the crowd.

Arjan was forcibly taken away, gritting his teeth, as he was put in the midst of the gamblers, who sized him up. Arjan frowned, his hands still bound. He didn't understand why he was pushed into the arena when he wasn't even trained. He was just another prisoner. Rudra stood still, watching Arjan, and wordlessly ridiculing him with a look of scathing contempt. Up close, Rudra wasn't even that good looking!

"You are weak!"

"Why are we sending off an amateur? Train him first!"

"He doesn't even have the muscles!"

All the voices came from the crowd and Arjan had a hard time guessing who was who.

Kali came in between the two fighters, as he grabbed Arjan by the shoulder, locking him in his grasp. For a king who didn't wage too many battles, Kali was strong, his biceps thicker than Arjan's, and a body that looked like it was carved out from granite.

"Why don't we have a little fun, eh?" Kali grinned. "Why don't we let Rudra, our star fighter, fight with someone who is yet to be trained?"

Arjan's heartbeat rose.

No.

Master Ranga came forward, trudging carefully and meekly speaking out. "My lord, the boy has no idea how to defend himself. It won't be a fair fight."

Kali looked at him as if he had made an offensive statement. "Does it look like I care? We need competition. We don't care if it's fair or not."

Everyone began to clap and hoot.

"But my lord, I have others Rudra can compete with. There are others, fit and fine, for him to fight with," he paused, frightened he had spoken unbidden. "Let me train him first and you can then do what you want to do with him."

Kali came to Master Ranga, who backed off. "Leave," he coldly rasped and the jailor slowly scurried to the back.

People clapped loudly, laughing. Arjan failed to notice Vedanta or Kuvera amongst the crowd.

"Let's have a bet," yelled Kali. "Who do you think will win?"

Everyone called out Rudra's name. In fact, Rudra sniggered at the question, glaring at Arjan, who chose to remain silent and impassive. Thoughtful, he began to think of other ways to defeat. Rudra, trying to recollect all the instances where Rudra had bared any chinks in his armour, while fighting with the other wrestlers. Rudra locked the enemy, grabbed their neck and twist it. Sometimes, he would force the body to plummet down on the ground, and then break its bones.

Arjan slowly swivelled his head towards Vikram, who was gulping in tension. The very plump man had told Arjan that only the best went to fight. Ah, but Arjan knew damn well that Kali would take his revenge for spitting on him, stealing his Soma, burning it and then helping in the convict escape. If one would think about it, Kali was actually being generous in not just feeding Arjan to the lions. But glancing back at Rudra, Arjan did feel unwarranted shivers run down his spine.

The Manav guards came forward, opening Arjan's chains and then tossing him on the ground. Arjan, feeling the mud on the ground, looked at the open sky. The entire place was small, but the ring of seats around the arena were arranged in hierarchic height, to accommodate a greater volume of audience.

Arjan stood up, cracking his knuckles. Rudra was in front of him, grunting, a playful smile dancing over his lips. Arjan glanced at Kali, who had sat back. Kali rubbed the top of his nose and then with a sweep of his arm signalled the fight to start. The trumpet blew from somewhere. Everything went blank for Arjan and by the time his visual senses came in the foray, he was pushed against the ground and pummeled by the hulk of a man. His back brushed harshly against the ground, the wounds from the arrow still stinging, his eyes tearing up as he felt the hurt.

Horror seized him as Rudra grabbed for his neck, but Arjan dodged him, deflecting his bulky arms with his sinewy hands. Whenever Rudra would come forward, Arjan would sweep his hand and knock him. Rudra finally wrapped his legs around Arjan's, coiling tightly, and turned his upper body to the other side, slamming Arjan's front torso against the ground. Rudra leaned forward casually, as he began to bite his skin, while he whispered, "Liking it much?"

Arjan arched his brows, confused by the man's words, but with the might he had, he pushed himself from thc ground and Rudra fell back. The crowd stopped jeering for a second as Rudra began to stand up, twitching one side of his shoulder as if he had an itch.

"You are good," Rudra grinned, "but sorry. In order to survive, I have to kill you."

Arjan's feet remained frozen as Rudra chased towards him, his hand clenching into a fist as Arjan raised his arms in defense. It was no more wrestling. It was a show of brawns and punches and kicks.

"Sorry friend, no more escape for you."

And there was no escape. As Arjan tried to fidget, Rudra punched him, breaking his nose. Blood streamed down his face and into his mouth. The pain was ringing in his head, obscuring the field of his vision. His heart was thunderously racing.

Rudra finally began to choke him. Arjan, gasping for his breath, tried to get him off, but it didn't work. He was beginning to see darks spots, as he slowly choked from the lack of air, his eyes shutting on its own accord, welcoming the darkness.

TRIBES

RAKSHAS – Intelligent humanoids, born in the South on the island of Eelam, are strong in combat and have tougher skin compared to other Tribals. Their average height goes above six feet. They have a patriarchal system and their culture, regardless of their furiousness, is quite backward. Most of them worship Lord Shiva, but are often considered by others as atheists. They have black skin and oiled hair.

NAGAS – Royalty and aristocrats living in the city of Naagpuri which floats on a lake. Nagas worship Lord Shesh Naag and Lord Vishnu. Nagas are diplomats more than warriors, but have grown their military system over a period of time. Women are respected in their culture. They are said to have blue eyes and fair skin.

YAKSHAS – Short in height and mischievous. They are considered the least threatening, but are very good in finances. They worship only their king and not any god. They lack military and political skills. Yakshinis, the female counterpart of the Yakshas, are rare. They live in Alakpur which is in the midst of a desert. Their Tribe is considered the richest of all.

ASURAS – Extinct race. Not much is known about this Tribe. They were considered to be the reason behind all the evil in this world. There was a great hunt of this Tribe where many Asura children, women, and men were slaughtered and hanged due to the superstitions about them. Some survived and have been wandering. They are atheists.

DANAVS – Brothers of Asuras, they are supposedly as tall as trees and as huge as mountains. They were the arch-enemies of the gods and had been put to sleep for their walks could create tremors. They are grandly fantasized during bedtime stories and many have not seen them since the Breaking.

PISACHAS – Cannibals. Live over swamps in Daldal Lands. They worship the 'the fittest'. They believe in karma and they ink their bodies with each crime they have committed. They are considered to be mentally unstable and only a fool would cross their lands.

VANAR – They live in Dandak Hills. They are considered to be vastly knowledgeable. They have hairy bodies which are sometimes ridiculed as being defected. They have gone underground and they choose not to be friendly towards visitors. They worship their protector Lord Bajrang who is considered an immortal and their king.

NOTE: There are other tribes that are not in the list. They are yet to be researched and documented.

– Ved Vyas.

ACKNOWLEDGMENTS

A book is comprised of not just the writer's hard work, but many others' as well. And I would like to list all those who have supported me in this venture to bring out the first book in a fantasy series that is without doubt my magnum opus.

I would begin with my parents. My father who with his everlasting support and love is the reason you find this book in your hand. We had disputes in every creative decision we took towards this project and because of those quarrels it has come forth beautifully. My mother who being a staunch Christian had accepted the idea that her son is writing on a Hindu god, putting her beliefs on the secondary. Her acceptance and her support was enough to make me realize one must be a human first and religious, second.

I would like to thank my editor who tirelessly sat through eight hours every day editing, rewriting, and finessing it. She molded it and I am ever green grateful to her.

I would like to thank Anuj Kumar for helping it launch through Kalamos Literary Services and being eager to create and launch the first myth-fantasy of our publication. I am also grateful to Artthat Studio who made this beautiful cover, Ajitabha Bose who filled this cover with amazing fonts and styles. My PR help Dimple Singh and Seema Saxena (Jashna Events) who supported me and were enthusiastic about it.

I would also like to thank Gagan Kabra for his amazing contribution to the trailer and posters. He has worked harder than me and made this project successful.

And in last, I would like to thank you, my reader. You are amazing and I hope you enjoy this book.

Kevin Missal is a twenty-one-year-old graduate of St. Stephen's College. He has recently released the first book of the Kalki Trilogy, *DHARMAYODDHA KALKI: AVATAR OF VISHNU*, which has received praise from newspapers such as *Millennium Post* and *Sunday Guardian* who have termed it as "2017's mythological phenomenon".

Kevin loves reading, watching films, and building stories in his mind. He lives in New Delhi and can be contacted at: kevin.s.missal@gmail.com.